Quantum Void

Book Two in the Quantum Series

By Douglas Phillips

Table of Contents

1   Ripples

Friday, May 20

Nala Pasquier slid the bangle bracelet off her wrist and placed it on the security table. The metal detector at the entrance to Wilson Hall was a new addition, a sign of changing times. Fermi National Accelerator Laboratory was once a place known only to the locals of Chicago, but its relative anonymity had disappeared eight months ago. First contact. Life beyond Earth. These days everyone knew about Fermilab and the secrets of the universe uncovered there.

Nala waved to the security guard. "What's my new word today, Angel?" She correctly pronounced his Spanish name, *An-hel*.

"*Descubrir*," the guard answered with a tight smile.

A particle physicist is not easily stumped, but Nala was forced to pause as she gathered her belongings. "Use it in a sentence."

"*Él descubrió una mosca en la sopa.*" Angel crossed his arms, challenging her capacity to learn the language one word at a time. With dark brown skin and a last name that was often confused as Hispanic, most people were surprised when Nala told them she was half Haitian and that French was the language of Haiti, not Spanish.

"Discover?" she asked tentatively. "He discovered a fly in the soup?"

The guard nodded with approval. "*Está bien*. You got it."

Nala laughed. "*Descubrir*. Discover. That's a good word to know in my business. Thanks Angel. *Yo quiero descubrir algo nuevo hoy.*"

"You want to discover something new today," Angel echoed in English. "Your Spanish is getting better, Nala." His pride was obvious.

"I have a good teacher." She waved once more and continued into the building's interior atrium, an open space that soared to skylights

1

far above, mirroring the expansive ambitions of the scientists who worked here.

Perhaps she would discover something today. Her work in the new science of quantum space had advanced by leaps and bounds thanks to a few tips from an alien source. It was an exciting time in particle physics, in part because there was still much more to learn. At their heart, all scientists are lifelong students of nature.

Nala took the elevator to basement level three and then descended two flights of stairs even deeper into the Earth. She walked a long concrete hallway and rounded a corner. The sign on the door hadn't changed—*Diastasi Lab, Authorized Personnel Only*—but it no longer took a top-secret security clearance to become one of the authorized few.

Their work with extra dimensions of space was now public knowledge. Government classification had finally been lifted, and Nala was back in touch with colleagues at other labs, former friends who'd thought she'd disappeared off the face of the earth. Her stunned friends, even her mother, had been kept in the dark for years. *Um, yeah, Mom, we figured out how to reach into a fourth dimension and compress distances by a factor of a billion.*

Spatial compression had already made unmanned spaceflight obsolete. The stars were now within easy reach for any probe, camera or radio link. Interstellar travel for humans was not yet possible, but one step at a time. Earth was now connected into a vast web of alien civilizations. The future was wide open.

Nala tapped her badge on the security pad and pushed open the door. "Morning, Thomas. Sorry I'm late," she said to the stout red-haired young man at the lab's workbench. Thomas, her lab assistant, was hunched over a signal generator, one of a hundred electronic components that covered the bench and filled every available shelf and niche in the overcrowded lab.

Thomas looked up with a grin on his bearded face. "Och, you're a wee scunner, you are." The accent was fake, but it was also pretty good.

She pulled a chair close to the workbench and turned on a computer. "That's a new one. Are we Scottish today?"

"For a wee spell, lassie. Perhaps 'til midday lunch," Thomas replied.

"Or as long as you can keep the Sean Connery accent going?"

"Possibly 'til then, aye."

Thomas wasn't Scottish. Or Irish. Or German. He was Russian on most Wednesdays. And every Monday, he became a strange cross between Ricardo Montalbán and the swashbuckling Spanish cat from *Shrek*. A bit wacky, most definitely an oddball, but mostly Thomas was fun. Anyone with a rebellious streak and a touch of drama was okay in Nala's book.

"We'll amp it up a wee bit today, my friend." She settled into her normal position in front of a set of three large computer displays at one end of the workbench. She tapped the keyboard, a panel with gauges appeared on one display and she moved a slider labeled tau to her chosen value. It was a simple command, but potent, backed by the largest particle accelerator in the United States.

Four floors above in the Fermilab main control room, colleagues who operated the accelerator would be at this very moment awakening the giant machine, inserting protons into its heart, and initializing the powerful magnets that formed the two-mile ring of the Main Injector loop. Soon, those protons would be screaming down a curved pipe at close to the speed of light—eighty thousand laps every second. Most people had a hard time wrapping their head around that kind of speed, so someone had installed a digital counter on the Main Injector tunnel wall, a sort of odometer that ticked once for every thousand laps. As the protons reached full speed, the counter's digits became a blur.

One hundred twenty-five gigaelectron volts. A beam of protons with that kind of power could burn a hole through your head. It had happened once before in Russia—to a visitor who'd accidentally peered into an opening with a live beam. The results were not pretty.

Nala and Thomas ran down an operational checklist together, validating system status and checking their lab equipment. Thomas adjusted the alignment of a pink pipe that pointed straight into a clear plexiglass box above the workbench. The box was ground zero for the neutrino beam that would shoot through their lab at near light speed. Thomas placed a compact webcam inside the box and inserted a rubber tube through a hole, the other end of the tube connected to a large tank of nitrogen.

Finishing her checklist, Nala looked up. "Shall we?"

"All systems are go for launch," Thomas said, temporarily lapsing into his NASA ground controller's voice.

Nala picked up a handheld radio from its cradle. "Is Cody working today?"

Thomas nodded. "Aye. That he is."

She keyed the transmit button. "Cody, Nala. Got anything flying around the loop yet?" The question was purely a courtesy. She could feel a slight vibration in the floor, which meant the accelerator was already spinning particles around its racetrack.

The radio hissed, followed by a man's voice. "Where've you been, Nala? Hell, we've been on standby pretty much forever."

Five minutes late to the lab today. Taunts were just part of the game with these guys. "Okay, that's enough, smart-ass. We're ready down here when you are."

"Stand by." A few seconds later, a high-pitched hum reverberated from the overhead pipes—the sound of protons, ramping up to obscene energy levels. "One-twenty-five gig," Cody said. "We're

4

up to full speed. You've got targeting control, but I'll manage the neutrino oscillation."

"Gotcha." She clicked a few times on her computer. "Let 'em fly."

"Protons away."

Somewhere behind a thick concrete wall, a magnetic gate opened and a stream of fast-moving protons blasted through. The particles smashed into their target—a disc of graphite no bigger than a coin. A stream of pions ripped out the other side, decaying in picoseconds to neutrinos and headed straight into Nala's lab.

The background hum increased dramatically to a loud buzz that filled the room. Thomas put on sunglasses and focused on the webcam inside the plexiglass box. As the pitch of the buzzing reached an irritating level, a brilliant blue flash blasted from the box, accompanied by a loud pop. Thomas didn't flinch.

When the flash dissipated, the box was empty, and the nitrogen tube had been cleanly sliced where it entered the box. Even after hundreds of launches, the disappearing act never failed to impress.

"Tau is perfect," Nala said, her eyes glued not to the plexiglass box but to her computer screen. A window popped up showing a live image returned by the webcam, now positioned in another dimension of space.

As it had done a hundred times before, the magic of expanding a quantum-sized dimension forced a corresponding compression of ordinary space. From the perspective of the camera, five hundred million kilometers had just compressed to almost nothing and the planet Jupiter was suddenly within camera distance. The giant planet appeared on cue, beautiful in its color but oddly flat in shape. More like a disc than a sphere, but any three-dimensional object looked that way from quantum space. Compressed, flattened.

"'Tis near enough to spit upon," Thomas said, his Scottish accent returning. He checked another computer screen. "The 4-D volume looks right. Nitrogen density is 1.24 kilograms per cubic meter—plus the camera. About 10 percent higher than yesterday." A silly grin appeared on his face. "No sign of any *Pasquier* waves."

"Fuck off," she said with a glare. "You know my opinion on that arrogant bullshit." Using her last name was another part of the game. They were monitoring for gravitational waves, but Thomas was intent on renaming everything. Last week he'd threatened to submit the *Nala boson* to a certification board. The week before, the whole Standard Model would be renamed to the *Donut Box*, with each type of quark and lepton changing to Glazed, Sprinkles, Choco, and so on. Actually, she had kind of liked that one.

Her fake-glare morphed into a smile and she turned to her computer. "Be ready to monitor, my friend. Initiating collapse."

She pressed a key, and within seconds the surrounding air wavered like heat waves coming from an oven. Her computer screen wavered too, even the surface of the workbench.

That's not right, she thought. The gravitational waves they sought were so weak as to be nearly undetectable. A slight tremor. A wiggle. This was a sloshing bucket of water.

Ripples propagated through the air and within seconds had permeated the room. The walls, floor and ceiling pulsated in a slow oscillation. Waves penetrated her body, making her own bones feel as pliable as everything else. On an intellectual level the unnatural panorama was eye opening but there was no denying a far more primitive reaction—the feeling of slipping off the edge of a cliff. Both her mind and her heart raced.

"Anomaly!" Nala's voice sounded like she was at the bottom of a well. She grabbed the handheld radio from its recharger and pressed the transmit button. "Cody, shut it down!"

The edge of the workbench pushed into her hip in rhythmic surges as if it were trying to get her attention. The computer monitors hanging on the wall above the workbench deformed like they were sheets of rubber. Then, as quickly as they had started, the waves dampened.

The air calmed, the floor and the workbench resuming their previously solid existence. On the other side of the lab wall, the enormous particle accelerator spun down until the loudest thing left in the room was Nala's heart, pounding inside her once-again-solid chest. She leaned against the workbench and took a deep breath.

"Whoa. What the hell?" Any particle physicist routinely dwells in the realm of the bizarre; quantum physics is not for lightweights. But over weeks of experiments, she'd seen no precedent for today's gymnastics.

Thomas stepped toward her keeping both hands on the workbench. "You okay?" he asked.

"Sure, you?"

"A bit queasy."

"Yeah, me too."

They stood in silence for a time. Anomalies are expected in groundbreaking science, even welcomed as opportunities for discovery. But lack of control was always disturbing.

Nala plopped into her chair and turned to the computer display. It showed a line graph that looked like it had just been through an earthquake. "Wow. Tau went crazy there for a minute, even sinusoidal."

Thomas peered over her shoulder. "And here I thought you smarty-pants physicists had this four-dimensional stuff all figured out."

Nala took another deep breath, her heart calming. She glanced back at her lab partner. "Yeah... I thought we did too."

A loud cracking sound caused them both to jump. It came from the plexiglass test box at the other end of the workbench. A tiny light hovered in the center of the box. The light hadn't been there at the beginning of the test.

It was a pinprick, nothing more, but far more brilliant than any dot ought to be. Nala shielded her eyes and drew closer. A fine mist slowly circled the point of light, forming a disc shape that spiraled inward. It gave the appearance of a miniature galaxy only a few inches across.

"Fascinating," she said.

As they watched, there was another crack, and a bit of the plexiglass case broke away. The chip joined the mist to be drawn into the point of light. Yet another crack followed, splitting the far side of the box.

"Holy shit," Nala said, stepping back. "Whatever it is, for such a little thing it's got some punch."

And then, as quickly as it appeared, the light silently faded away. The mist twisted delicately for another turn and then evaporated, leaving the box empty once more.

Thomas stood behind, watching the last wisp of the gracefully pirouetting mist. "Kind of pretty," Thomas said. "But unexpected."

Nala concentrated her stare into the test box, searching for answers. Both the waves and the pinprick of light were anomalies, no question, unseen in any previous test. Were they related? Could they be re-created? The effect would need more study. They could be on the brink of a landmark discovery. A breakthrough.

Of course, it could be dangerous too.

2 PVC

One month before...

Davis Garrity ran a hand through his wavy gray hair and checked that his tie was straight. There wasn't enough time to stop by the men's room before the meeting, but his reflection in the polished metal of the elevator doors was sufficient. There was no point in achieving grooming perfection anyway—salesmen did that, and he was certainly no salesman. Davis made deals. Nobody was better.

The elevator doors opened at the twenty-fourth floor of the office building, one of many gleaming glass towers of the downtown core of Austin, Texas. Davis strode down the hallway, briefcase in hand, and pushed open one of the double glass doors etched with a stylized logo featuring a lightbulb and the company name, ElecTrek.

"Davis Garrity for Stan Wasserman," he told the receptionist.

"Welcome to ElecTrek, Mr. Garrity. Mr. Wasserman would like you to join his team in the east conference room." Davis signed in and the receptionist pointed the way.

The conference room was directly across from reception, a space designed to be more public than the interior hallways and offices behind secured doors. It was also designed with visitors in mind. Photographs straight out of a shareholders' annual report adorned the walls. One provided a view of scenic rolling hills with an occasional wind turbine dotting the idyllic scene, almost like an industrial decoration. Another showed a sea of solar panels glinting in the sun. A third displayed a modern power plant with a young family strategically positioned in the foreground, apparently ready for a tour from a smiling guide wearing a hard hat.

Davis set his briefcase on the table, took a seat and waited. He knew it wouldn't be long. The client was aware he'd already signed one of their competitors. Naturally, their interest was piqued.

A few minutes later, two men and a woman walked in. The taller man reached out with a hand. "Davis, glad you could make it. Stan Wasserman, nice to meet you in person." Wasserman introduced the others, Teri Barker, chief environmental engineer, and Jake Schroeder, ElecTrek's vice president for Texas Power Operations.

"Thanks for your time today," Davis said with an elegant bow of the head. "I can assure you, it's going to be the best meeting you'll have all week." Lesser dealmakers might set expectations low to give the appearance of delivering high, but Davis could afford to start high and stay there. Final delivery would be stratospheric.

Wasserman responded with his own play. "Let's hope so. Things are getting tight around here, and we'll need to find cost savings in every process. You said on the phone you could give us more than just nickels and dimes."

Davis was impressed with the I'm-just-a-poor-man counterplay, but of course, it was all an act. With electricity rates fixed by friendly Texas commissioners and with oil, gas and coal prices still depressed, ElecTrek's financial position was rosy for the foreseeable future. Still, a good dealmaker doesn't embarrass his client with facts. If Wasserman said things were tight, they were tight. The meeting would require the full pitch, and Davis was prepared.

"Ladies and gentlemen, I'm going to save you a billion dollars, maybe more... right now, right here in this meeting."

He waited a few seconds for the words to sink in and then pointed to the pictures on the wall. "As a side benefit, by next week, I'll hand over a new crowd-pleasing photograph you can hang on this wall that will change your company's image forever."

Their skeptical looks were standard and expected. Davis had no PowerPoint slides and no glossy brochures to hand out; those were bits and pieces that amateurs used. Much better to go straight for gold. He opened his briefcase, withdrew a small white plastic pipe and set it on the table. Eyes around the room squinted.

The pipe was open at one end and closed on the other by a rounded top, painted blue and orange. It looked like a short piece of irrigation pipe commonly found at any home improvement store.

"I give you the Garrity Cap," Davis said with a flourish of his hand.

Wasserman picked up the plastic tube and held it close to his face, turning it in his hand. The others looked on with interest. It was the critical turning point of the meeting, where he'd either walk out with a contract or be thrown out as a con man.

Davis continued, cranking his pitch a notch higher. "This simple device—backed up by Garrity nanotechnology—will literally save the world. I kid you not. Once its larger cousin is installed at your power plants, operating costs will plummet, and profits will soar."

Wasserman handed the plastic pipe to Teri Barker, who peered inside, looking for working parts. "You said on the phone you had a carbon-capture device. This is PVC pipe."

"Funny, isn't it?" Davis asked. "That sometimes the most innovative technology comes in such a simple package." He pointed to the pipe. "With the Garrity Cap installed on each of your stacks, you can turn off your billion-dollar carbon-capture system; you won't need it. And forget about building any more of these money-sucking showpieces. Let's be real. A 6 percent reduction isn't a realistic carbon-capture program—it's just a very expensive public relations campaign. Are we in agreement on that?"

Their shrugs gave him the answer he had expected. Carbon capture at any coal-fired power plant had never made it past the demonstration phase, even with heavy government subsidies. Power plants across the US, even those that had converted to natural gas, continued to discharge large quantities of carbon dioxide daily.

Davis knew the industry well, including how their bottom line was calculated. "With the Garrity Cap on every stack, you'll capture exactly 100 percent of the carbon and everything else you currently send into the air. By the way, you can turn off your sulfur dioxide scrubbers. You won't need them either. Go ahead and burn local Texas coal instead of importing that expensive stuff from Wyoming. Hell, burn garbage, burn old tires, burn whatever you like—it won't matter in the slightest. Your emissions will still be precisely zero."

He pointed to Jake Schroeder. "By next week, you'll be running the greenest electric power facility on the planet. Your EPA permit? Tear it up. Global warming? Climate change? Gone. Mr. Schroeder, you're going to be a hero."

Wasserman was shaking his head, but in a good way, more puzzled than negative. "Nice pitch. But empty claims aren't worth much. Tell me again how all this magic is supposed to work?"

Davis reached out, and Teri handed him the plastic pipe. "I lied," he said. "What I hold in my hand is a bit more than just your ordinary PVC pipe." He held it out for their inspection, pointing the open side toward them and then turning it over to show the closed top. "This closed end is not closed at all." He pulled a pen from his pocket and pushed it inside the tube. He tapped the pen on the cap's top like a magician would knock inside a trick box. "We hear the pen tapping. Our eyes see this as a sealed end… but it's not. This tube twists into another dimension, a place we can't see, a place not even in this world."

Davis's grin broadened to a smile. "Yes, we're using dimensional technology, the same technology you've heard on the news when they told us about all this crazy business with aliens."

Schroeder contorted one side of his face. "That pipe is an alien device?"

Davis shook his head. "Nope. Not alien. Built right here in America. So is the dimensional technology. But instead of using this technology to find aliens, we're taking the same idea to save money… and save the planet."

Davis held the pipe in one hand, his other hand a few inches away. "This pipe is really twice as long as it looks. We can't see the rest of it because it makes a right-angled turn into a fourth dimension. My company created both the pipe and the space that it's plugged into." He waved his arms in the air. "That new space is right here, right in this room."

"We've all heard the news stories," Schroeder said. "Talking to cyborgs a million miles away? Pretty fantastic stuff, and I'm not sure I believe it all. But you're saying the technology is real? How do we know this isn't just a PVC pipe you bought at the hardware store?"

Schroeder was turning out to be a good straight man. Davis pulled out a pack of cigarettes from his coat pocket. "Mind if I light up?" he asked with a smile. Of course, the answer was predetermined.

"Sorry, Davis, we're a no-smoking workplace," Wasserman said. "Maybe you could just answer Jake's question."

Davis pulled out a lighter. "I intend to. With visual proof, if you'll allow a one-time exception to your smoking policy." Davis lifted his eyebrows and waited for the next response.

"You're going to show us how this works, but you need a lit cigarette?"

"Yes, I do. It's quite an intriguing demonstration."

"Okay, whatever," Wasserman answered. "Do what you need to do."

Davis nodded, lit the cigarette and took a long drag. He blew smoke into the air, away from where the others sat. "My apologies for the smoke, but you did want proof."

Wasserman pulled his chair closer and the others leaned forward with elbows on the table. "Okay, same draw, same amount of smoke." He took another long drag on the cigarette, its tip burning bright red. He picked up the plastic tube and held its opening to his lips.

13

His audience drew in closer still. He puckered his lips and gently blew. The sound of his exhale was the same as before, but nothing came out of the pipe, not even traces of smoke around its edges.

Schroeder reached out with an incredulous look on his face. "Wait a second, that's got to be a trick. You didn't really take a draw the second time." He took the cap from Davis's hand and examined it once more.

Davis held out the cigarette. "Try it yourself."

Schroeder looked at him and then Wasserman. He took the cigarette, sucked on it and immediately expelled the smoke in a fit of coughing. "Okay, the smoke is real," he said when he'd regained his composure.

Schroeder took a second draw and blew directly into the short pipe, his lips not quite touching. Smoke came out of his puckered lips, but it quickly disappeared into the pipe and didn't come out.

Schroeder held the pipe up to the light and peered inside. "There's got to be something absorptive in there."

Davis tilted back in his chair and looked up at the ceiling. "Do you see anything except the inside of an empty plastic pipe?"

"No," Schroeder admitted. "I don't. What the hell are you doing here?" He tapped on the very solid-looking rounded cap at the closed end. "Where'd the smoke go?"

Davis laughed. "Gone. No longer in our plane of existence, my friend. Permanently eliminated, just like your power plant emissions will be."

Schroeder looked at the pipe in one hand and back to the cigarette in the other. He started laughing. "Well, I'll be damned."

The ElecTrek lawyers would be next, waving a memorandum of understanding and a joint nondisclosure agreement. The documents would clear the way for a full-scale demonstration at their Bastrop plant, which would then lead to a signed contract, renewed annually... and, of course, many millions of dollars flowing into Davis's bank account.

The amazing thing about it all was this deal was just one power company in one state. Many more would follow, and Davis was quite sure he would soon become very rich.

3 Briefing

Daniel Rice sat in the *hot seat* in a stuffy committee room deep in the bowels of the US Capitol building. A row of stern-faced representatives faced him. Daniel had been here before. It wasn't testimony. He wasn't under oath; there were no cameras and only one microphone. A congressional briefing, conducted behind closed doors to maximize candor. He enjoyed this newest part of his job about as much as a visit to the dentist.

The weathered man at the center of the dais was the chairman of the House Committee on Science, Space and Technology. He had asked questions that were vaguely science-oriented, but the follow-on conversation made it abundantly clear that his scientific knowledge was modest. Still, he was an improvement on the previous committee chairman. The years of prominent politicians openly hostile to science were thankfully over.

"Dr. Rice, let's shift the conversation to Core," the chairman croaked.

Core was, of course, the extraterrestrial cybernetic organism occupying an alien megastructure in four-dimensional space near the star VY Canis Majoris. Everyone on Earth knew that much. Core self-described as part biology, part quantum computer, and served as a central communications hub to a collection of alien civilizations. A gatekeeper.

Over the past eight months, Core had revealed bits and pieces of the alien civilizations that it represented: a web of interconnected planets previously unknown and invisible to curious human eyes spread across several thousand light-years of space in one corner of the Milky Way galaxy. Each planet connected to the central hub through the newly discovered technology that compressed space.

The chairman continued. "You and others have met with this entity Core eight times now. Beyond the revelation of this new *boson* it doesn't appear that we've gathered much in the way of new science. Would you agree?"

The hyperbolic paraboloid boson was the newest addition to the Standard Model of physics, responsible for the shape of space itself. Once Core had revealed the fingerprint of the new particle, ecstatic physicists around the world had quickly confirmed its existence and spun off multiple studies to examine its properties.

"I'm not sure I would agree, Mr. Chairman. While it may be true that Core reveals only what it wants us to know—and by the way, I completely agree that this perceived caginess can be frustrating to scientists—"

"Not to mention the military," the chairman added.

"Yes, our military and security organizations are fully justified in their cautious approach toward Core. But that said, I would argue that Core has at least hinted at additional science that will be disclosed at future dates. For example, it has alluded to an entirely new branch of physics that describes the quantum nature of time. We are only in the beginning stages of this exploration but the yin-yang device that was left in the Russian Soyuz capsule is a prime example of technology that uses this new science."

The chairman looked up from a paper on his desk. "I understand this device was turned over to the Russians along with their capsule."

Daniel shrugged. "Yes sir, an obligation of the international space treaty. But we had a good look at it before it was passed along to the Russians. I believe the device itself is not as important as the science behind it."

"Which Core continues to withhold."

"Technically true." Daniel seemed to be constantly defending Core though he felt the frustration as much as anyone. *Too soon*, Core often said. *You will learn.* Daniel had become the de facto representative, the scientist who had made first contact with an alien intelligence and often the central figure in subsequent conversations.

Each session was much like the first, a radio link via compressed space that allowed for voice and data transmission. A live video link showed the exterior of Core's structure—the *hand grenade,* they had joked. Although its surface never changed, a mesmerizing parade of alien devices orbited, each apparently functioning as a communication link back to a home planet. A joint effort among Earth's space agencies was working to build a similar communications relay that would eventually replace the flimsy duct-tape-and-baling-wire electronics package cobbled together at Fermilab.

"I believe some topics are left for future conversations," Daniel continued. "The current focus is on the newly announced mission to the Dancer's planet, Ixtlub, and on the portal technology that will take us there. In this area, Core has demonstrated a level of openness that has elevated the fledgling science of exobiology to a major branch of study. We have received a detailed map of the self-replicating molecule that powers all life on their planet, similar to our DNA. Needless to say, biologists are having a field day comparing the two molecules. This information will certainly be of use when we make physical contact with the species of this planet and dramatically advances our understanding of what it means to be alive."

Several members of the committee nodded their heads. Biology was one of the sciences that seemed to be poised for explosive growth and the politicians were eager to capitalize on funding for studies in their home states.

"We've also received considerable information on the two intelligent species who inhabit the planet. I've read some of the documentation myself and I envy those who will be selected for the mission. Assuming we get a video feed, it's going to be quite the show."

One of the minority party members perked up at this comment. "Dr. Rice, you've been on television and at other public appearances so

I'm sure you're aware than many people don't trust these aliens and have grave concerns about the announced mission. What assurances do we have that it will be a friendly meeting and what safeguards are we establishing in case it is not?"

It was an age-old question, and eight months without any aggression hadn't dimmed raging fears in the slightest. That the aliens hadn't "shown themselves" was a common rallying cry among critics even though Daniel had pointed out that the viral video of the beautiful and delicate creatures they'd called the *Dancers* had more than five billion views on social media platforms.

"I am aware of public concerns," Daniel answered. He could have pointed the congressman to one of several children's science programs in which Daniel had appeared, including a fun *Sesame Street* bit designed to provide comfort to preschoolers about alien life. He decided against it.

"As you know, Congressman, NASA has joined with ESA to plan the mission in tight alliance with our national security agencies. I'm confident they will produce a plan that will both be diplomatic and ensure global security. In addition, Core revealed in our last session that it will provide an emissary to Earth, an android in humanoid form who will prepare us for our first encounter with another civilization and act as our guide on the mission. I believe this is a positive indicator that demonstrates Core is primarily focused on diplomacy, not security.

And lastly, the new transfer portal that is under construction at Kennedy Space Center will give us physical access to any other location in the galaxy with a corresponding portal. It's important to note that this technology, like any network protocol, requires a handshake from both sides. That is, our portal is open only when we permit it to be open and the same is true for the destination portal."

The congressman grunted. "We may have built this portal, but the design was alien. Who's to say what it will do when they turn it on?"

It was true that none of the engineers involved in the portal assembly understood exactly how it would work. Most expected it would be one of the first actions taken by the android, who was due to arrive on Earth within days.

4   Katanauts

Marie Kendrick could almost sense the ghosts of the past walking the halls of this historic place. The Neil Armstrong Operations and Checkout Building at Kennedy Space Center in Florida went all the way back to the 1960s Mercury program. Interior spaces had been upgraded over the years to support the changing needs of each spaceflight era, but the exterior of the building was still vintage 1960s. She could easily imagine Ford Falcons and Chevrolet Impalas, tail fins and all, scattered across the parking lot.

She stood alone at the center of the O&C clean room, as they called it, a cavernous space long enough to hold two Airbus 380s end to end. The Apollo Lunar Excursion Module had been assembled here in the 1960s, as well as most of the sections of the International Space Station in the 1990s. The overhead cranes used for these historic projects still hung from the high ceiling, but now idle.

The O&C clean room was no longer used to assemble spacecraft and no longer quite as clean. It had been repurposed as a gateway to other worlds. Alien worlds.

Marie brushed back a strand of hair and stared up at the large banner that spanned one wall, imprinted with NASA and ESA logos and the words *Mission to the Stars*. She marveled at the circumstances that had brought her here. It had been a roller coaster of emotions over the past several weeks.

It had started with the announcement of the first mission to an inhabited alien world and the selection process for the lucky few who would go. They would visit a watery planet more than three hundred light-years from Earth, inhabited by creatures that appeared as delicate wisps swaying in ocean currents—intelligent creatures known as the Dancers.

I was so close, she thought.

The right education, the right background. Years of NASA experience, including eighteen months working directly for Augustin Ibarra, the administrator of human spaceflight. She'd been a key player in the mysterious disappearance, and recovery, of the Soyuz capsule and its three astronauts, and a partner to Daniel Rice, a science guy straight out of the White House. She even had a presidential commendation.

In the end, her sparkling CV hadn't been enough to grab one of only two slots allocated to NASA. Two others had been selected, both with spaceflight experience, a skillset missing from Marie's resume.

As she stood in the O&C clean room, that particular job qualification now seemed entirely unjustified. A large white oval doorway dominated the center of the room. For this mission, no one would be flying. They'd simply pass through a portal.

It had been erected on a raised platform—literally a doorway about eight feet tall made of polished white metal, looking not much different from an airport metal detector. For now, it was a portal to nowhere. Step through it and you'd still be standing on the platform inside the clean room. But that would all change once four-dimensional docking technology was initiated. The big event was less than a week away.

Administrative coordinator. That was the response to her application. It wasn't a rejection, of course. She would still be involved in the details of the mission. She'd even be managing much of the training and preparation process. But she wouldn't be going anywhere, at least not now. There would be future missions to the Dancers' planet, assuming this one went well.

The Dancers. Just a funny name that someone had made up— was it Daniel? Possibly, but that was eight months ago, and a lot had happened since then. The lone video of the aquatic species from the planet Ixtlub, a name few could properly pronounce, had gone viral worldwide. A new NatGeo series featured jellyfish-like creatures, and a summer blockbuster movie was in the works, already cross-marketing a

22

line of toys featuring squishy sponge creatures. Of course, no one had yet met them in person. But four intrepid explorers soon would.

The lucky team members formed a tight group on the raised platform, standing alongside racks of electronics equipment and computer displays—the Transfer Command Station. Two men and two women dressed in blue jumpsuits listened to a NASA engineer who provided a briefing of the systems that would assist in their upcoming journey. Marie checked the training task off from a long list on her tablet computer.

They'd been labeled *katanauts*. In the days of extra dimensions and compressed space, explorers to new planets now traveled by way of the *ana* or *kata* directions, the fourth-dimensional equivalents of *up* and *down*. The days of rockets flying through outer space were over, a mental image now as quaint as a 1950s sci-fi movie.

The key player in the construction and operation of this new technology was not even from Earth. The alien android called himself Aastazin, but nearly everyone shortened it to Zin, a change he didn't seem to mind. He stood behind the katanauts on two shiny metallic legs. Officially, Zin was Core's emissary to Earth and would guide the team once they passed through the gateway. Rumor had it that Core's brain was a quantum computer and that Zin's intelligence was derived from a quantum entanglement with his maker.

He was mostly copper in color, though his exterior was said to be a mix of high-performance metals and carbon fibers. He had a head and two arms ending in hands, which he often rested on metal hips, giving him a very humanlike stance. Most people agreed there was nothing coincidental about the human form or his apparent male gender. The robot's internal intelligence had occupied bodies of many types. His current incarnation was merely this month's shell. When on Earth, assume a human form so as not to scare the locals, or something like that.

Their systems briefing complete, the group moved to a set of four reclined seats, each supported by a pedestal that disappeared into a slot in the raised floor. They looked like a row of dentist chairs, but they were far more than that. The mission documentation described the chairs as critical safety equipment that would keep humans alive during the dimensional transfer.

As the engineer pointed out the various features of the chairs, Zin stepped off the platform and sauntered over to where Marie stood as if he recognized her at a cocktail party. His smooth motion and amiable demeanor were remarkably human.

Marie removed her glasses. "Hi, Zin, um, what's up?" she stuttered. The android had never been threatening or even aggressive, but it still took some adjustment to think of him as a colleague.

Like his body, Zin's face was humanoid too. His flat eyes, spaced wider than most, were able to pivot slightly out of their sockets in a quick snap to glance left or right. The move was mesmerizing and probably gave him excellent peripheral vision. He had no ears and not much of a nose either. It was hard to find an audio input site anywhere on his head, but he seemed to hear everything that anyone said.

His mouth worked very much like any human's, including a flexible tongue and lips. Marie figured the combination was probably required equipment if you wanted to speak a human language. The head itself stood on a narrower mount than a human neck, and he could turn it three hundred and sixty degrees. He'd stopped performing this feat once someone had told him it looked like a bit from a horror movie.

"What do you think so far, Marie?" Zin said in flawless English. "Is the training going as you expected?" Strangely, he had an American accent when speaking to the Americans but sounded British when speaking to the Europeans. His mannerisms and hand motions changed as well to match each person. He spoke French from time to time with the sole katanaut from France, but English had been selected as the mission language, and he stuck to it for all but the most informal communications.

"We're right on schedule," Marie told him. "And everyone seems to be clear on procedures so far."

Zin had no eyebrows, but a thick ridge above his flat eyes was adjustable. He pushed it down, remarkably mimicking a look of concern. "That's good to hear, but not exactly what I wanted to talk about. Do you mind if I ask a more personal question?"

"Um, sure." It would be interesting to learn what Zin considered personal.

His forehead ridge moderated. "Learning your languages and mannerisms has been relatively easy, but a true understanding of human nature is more difficult. My job as your guide and liaison, is complex, and first contact between any two civilizations is significant. If, for whatever reason, I was *not* meeting your expectations, would you tell me?"

An interesting question. Very deep.

"I'll answer, but first a question back to you." Marie smiled. "How would you react if we were dissatisfied?" Thoughts of crazed robots attacking helpless citizens weren't easy to sweep from her mind.

"It depends entirely on the person," Zin said with a flick of one of his flat eyes. "Criticism from some members of this team could be dismissed as inconsequential. But if the criticism came from you, I would be deeply humbled and highly motivated to improve."

What a gentleman. Better than most guys I've dated.

Marie put a hand on his cold metal arm. Could he feel her touch? "Zin, you're doing just fine. No complaints. If you get the feeling we're not completely on board, just remember, we're new to this. We thought we were still fifty years away from having conversations with androids."

Zin's mouth turned up at the ends—more than needed for a smile, but if she castigated him, it would ruin all the fun. Zin might be a bit quirky, but so were some of Marie's best friends.

One of his eyes performed a gymnastic maneuver that would have won a gold medal, apparently picking up activity almost behind him. "It looks like they're almost done. Join us for the next session? I think you'll find it interesting." He motioned to the platform, and she followed.

Tim Tannenbaum, a top American astronaut with beefy arms and buzz-cut hair, sat in one of the reclining dentist chairs, strapped in with a seat harness that looked like it had been borrowed from a high-performance military jet. The NASA engineer pointed at several buttons on the armrest. "If anything goes wrong, just hit Reset," he said.

Tim casually looked up from his reclined position like he might ask someone to bring him a beer. "What, no control stick for manual override?"

"No need to fly at all," the engineer replied. "The Reset button automatically recycles to baseline, returning you home."

"Pretty simple," Tim replied. He unlatched his seat harness, swiveled off the chair and stood up. He patted the engineer on the shoulder. "Good job, man. Works for me."

Zin motioned to the engineer. "Finished?"

The engineer nodded. "Yeah, I think so. Any questions about transfer preparation?" He looked around at the silent group. "Okay, back to you, Zin."

Zin positioned himself to the center of the group. "Thank you. I'm sure everyone is fully enlightened on both suit-up and pretransfer procedures." Zin scanned the faces, his average height allowing for easy eye contact with the team. "Next, I want to explain exactly what will happen to you during the transfer. I'll also touch on why it works just this way, but I promise I won't bore you with the details."

26

As far as Marie knew, *the details* had never been shared for most of the new technologies Zin and Core had brought to Earth. Any of the NASA engineers would jump at the chance to be bored by those details if Zin ever decided to share them.

Zin waved to the row of dentist chairs. "As soon as you are comfortably seated in your transfer stations, the retracted hood will extend, covering your face. A yellow light will flash, but you may not even notice it. The flash initiates a spatial transformation that will reposition your transfer station—and you, of course—both dimensionally and temporally. That is to say, you will shift slightly out of normal 3-D space, but you will also shift slightly away from the normal direction of time."

"Shifted in time?" asked Wesley Woods, an English sociology researcher. Wesley was one of two team members selected by the European Space Agency. With sandy hair and freckles, he seemed to match his Yorkshire home. "Forward or backward?"

"Actually... neither," Zin said, his English accent exactly matching Wesley's. "I won't go into it just now, but suffice it to say that forward and backward are not the only directions of time. There are others."

"And this yellow light can really control time?" Jessica Boyce asked. Jessica was the only professor in the group. Marie had never had the opportunity to work with her, but Jessica was the star of several NASA videos beamed down from the International Space Station as part of a science program for high school students.

"Unquestionably so," Zin responded. "Time is no different from space. Both are quantized dimensions of our universe. Both are managed by means of coherent neutrinos, as your scientists have already learned for quantum space."

Time control? Marie thought. *Hoo, boy. It might be best if they don't give us the details.*

Eight months prior, the missing Soyuz astronauts had somehow been frozen in time by the same alien technology before being returned to Earth. It was hard to believe that Zin, or anyone, could wield such power in a flash of yellow light.

Zin walked over to the portal, and the group followed him. He pointed to the oval doorway. "The portal is nothing more than a four-dimensional path from Earth to Ixtlub, with the three-dimensional distance between these two planets highly compressed. It's a common method of transfer used widely around the galaxy. But for humans or any biological organism, it requires a temporal offset to avoid death."

Tim crossed his arms, a smirk on his face. "Thanks for not killing us, Zinny old boy."

Zin swiveled his head rapidly. "I hope you don't think—" He stopped, and his metal eyes made a clicking sound as they turned upward. "Ah, yes. Sarcasm, I believe? A uniquely human style of speech, utterly unknown elsewhere in the galaxy."

Tim shifted on his feet and said nothing.

"Continuing," Zin said. "Once the portal is activated, I will step through to the anchor point at Ixtlub and verify that it is positioned correctly. Each of you will enter the portal seated in your transfer stations, which will slide along this track." A single slot in the flooring led from the four chairs directly through the portal.

Stephanie Perrin raised a hand. The second woman on the katanaut team, Stephanie was a French television reporter. Her position at a twenty-four-hour French news channel, along with her popularity across most of Europe, had made her selection almost inevitable. Like most of the others, she'd been to the ISS and had provided a remarkably poetic and very personal description of spaceflight to viewers back home. With her glossy black hair, a heart-shaped face and dark eyes, the average Frenchman—in fact, most European men—put her at the top of their list of beautiful women. She flashed her gorgeous smile regularly, both on TV and in person.

"So, as an artificial life form—" she started. "I'm sorry, Zin, I hope that's not offensive." Zin shook his head no, but Stephanie seemed to adjust anyway. "As a *nonbiological person*, you don't need the time offset like we do to survive the trip?"

Zin shook his head again, turning it farther left and right than any human would. The move was vaguely creepy, but at least he wasn't spinning his head in full circles. "No, Stephanie." His English words took on a slight French accent that matched Stephanie's. "I have personally completed more than seventy dimensional transfers with no ill effects. The danger is only to cellular biology, not to any electric brain function."

Stephanie pursued her line of questioning. "The astronauts from last year's Soyuz incident reported that they did not remember returning to Earth from their 4-D orbit. Will we remember the transfer?"

"No again, Stephanie," Zin said. "But never fear, the time you lose will be short, just a minute or two." He lifted his flexible lips into a smile that looked forced but was probably the best he could do. "You'll see the light flash, and then... Ixtlub. Honestly, I think you'll enjoy the experience."

Stephanie didn't look too sure. "I read that we're each going to wear an audio-video headset. Will it be a live feed? I'm sure viewers around the world will want to see what happens during the transfer."

"Live streaming is not supported by this particular portal technology," Zin said. "But never fear, you will each wear a recording device that is switched on by your command. By all means, turn your camera on during the transfer. Viewers will see the same thing that I do when stepping through a portal. Except, of course, that they'll miss the ultraviolet experience, always where the real action is."

Tim and Wesley chuckled. Zin acted like he didn't understand what was funny.

"Sorry, Zin, it's not you," said Wesley. "It's just that sometimes you say things just like we would... a little too much like us."

"Should I back off?" Zin asked.

Tim laughed again.

Zin's mechanical eyes flitted to the left side of his head, where Tim stood. "English expressions and human mannerisms are designed into my language module, but I can alter my style, if it would make our conversation more natural."

"No, no. Don't change a thing," Tim said. "All the wacky robot stuff is the most entertainment I've had in years."

Zin held his angled eyes on Tim and provided no further facial expression, at least none that humans might notice. But Marie imagined an irritation from his silence. She had worked with Tim before, and the English expression *jerk* came to mind.

5   Murphy's Law

Monday, May 23

Marie sipped from a cup of tea, her shoes off and her feet propped up on another chair. The break room was a good refuge from the activity of the O&C clean room and gave her a quiet place to catch up on personal affairs.

She perused an email written in Russian. It was good language practice, but it didn't hurt that the email was from Sergei Koslov, the commander of the lost Soyuz mission and her part-time love interest. Intercontinental romances didn't work very well, particularly when lovers were from adversary nations, but they had tried. Sergei would always be special.

Another message caught her attention, a recording from last night's *Nicole Valentino Show*. The guest on the popular late-night show was Daniel Rice.

"This I've got to see," Marie said, starting the video.

Nicole sat at her desk, chatting with the band leader. "My next guest has been here before, but I didn't get to meet him... I think I was sick that night? Yeah, Ricky, is that your recollection? No? Booze?" The audience laughed.

"Yeah, that was probably it—too much booze that night. Well, I've fully recovered, and tonight we get to talk about aliens, cyborgs and travel through the fourth dimension. He's the scientist who changed the world. Please welcome Dr. Daniel Rice."

The audience applauded, and Daniel walked across the stage. He looked a little out of place. He'd been a regular on morning and the late-night shows, but a scientist never seemed to fit among the stars of Hollywood.

Nicole greeted Daniel with a hug, took her seat behind the desk and waited for the applause to die down. "So, how are things between you and Core? That's the cyborg's name, right?"

"Uh, right," Daniel answered, rather uncomfortably. Marie couldn't imagine what it must be like to be in front of the cameras and all those people. If put in the same situation, she'd melt into a puddle on the floor. "Core has turned out to be an enigma. Quite helpful, full of new information, but strict in following a galactic procedure, if you will—a set of rules that it doesn't talk about."

"I see," Nicole said. "So, at this point, *it* is not your new best friend?" The audience laughed, perhaps at the genderless pronoun or perhaps just the way she said it. Core made it clear that it had no gender, compelling humans to drop their initial use of *he* and *him*. The topic seemed a never-ending source of amusement for some.

Daniel laughed too but then resumed a more serious tone. "Here's what I would say about Core and whatever policy-making body it represents. They are brilliant, highly advanced, benevolent, as far as we can tell, but... wary."

"What, they don't trust us? Can't imagine why." More laughter.

"Well, I get a sense that they have undisclosed procedures for how they would react to anything we might do. For example, let's imagine that we got a bit too aggressive with our newly discovered capability to compress space and we started sending spy satellites to monitor their communications or take close-up pictures of their planets."

"Sounds reasonable to me. You're saying they can snoop on us but we can't snoop on them? I want to know who these people are."

"Yeah, I do too. But we need to be careful, listen and learn, without being brash. We shouldn't expect that our Earth-centric concepts of alliances and enemies will hold up in this new arena. There are some entirely new rules of civilization that we're just beginning to learn."

Nicole's eyebrows lowered, her face contorting into a look of scorn. "Don't you watch the SyFy Channel? We already know how this goes. When do they invade Earth to steal our water and mutilate our cows?"

The audience roared, and Marie laughed along. Nicole knew exactly what she was doing. Regardless of the information governments released, social media posts from around the world made it abundantly clear that fear was widespread, even when expressed in slightly comedic form. The attack would begin with mountainous warships floating in the sky. An interdimensional doorway would open in every city, through which giant insects or lizards with slime dripping from sharp fangs would appear. There were as many variations as there were imaginations in the world. Many thought the aliens were already here, hiding beneath a layer of human skin in a devious disguise.

When the noise from the audience died down, Daniel spoke. "Alien invasion? We're conditioned to think this way. After all, our history is mostly a story of one group of people invading another group's country. We're used to it. So naturally, we think that's what will happen this time. But try to step outside our limited experience and thoughtfully examine the situation. What do we see? A collection of alien civilizations, scattered across thousands of light-years, that shows every indication of being at peace with each other. Why would they invade Earth? What do we have that they want? Water? Sorry—it's one of the most common molecules in the galaxy, we find it practically everywhere. How about cows, or even people, as a food source? Every one of these civilizations has a biology fundamentally different from ours. To them, I doubt we'd taste very good."

"What if they just want our planet? 'So long, humans,'" Nicole mimicked in a bloodthirsty alien voice, "and they just zap us out of existence."

Daniel was beginning to get that look of the self-assured scientist that Marie remembered so well from their time together. "We've already discovered several thousand planets within a few hundred light-years of Earth. There are probably millions more out there, and many of them may be like Mars, devoid of life but potentially habitable. With a galaxy as big and diverse as the Milky Way, finding good real estate is not a problem. Again, they have no reason to take Earth from us."

"So, your bottom line is they really don't care about us?"

"That's my feeling. They're inviting us to join their group— granted, in some limited way. But if we decline, we can just go our own way. I'm not sure it even matters to them which choice we make."

A head poked into the break room, and Marie paused the video. It was Stephanie Perrin. "I thought I might find you in here," she said. "They're looking for you. Ibarra wants you ASAP."

Marie put her phone away and slipped into her shoes. "That doesn't sound good. Was it Carol?" Ibarra was the administrator for human spaceflight operations at NASA, and Carol was his assistant.

"A woman," Stephanie said. "I didn't recognize her, but she looked a little... um, how do you Americans say? Bent out of shape."

Probably Carol. Marie thanked Stephanie and hurried down the long corridor.

Ibarra's corner office was at the far end, and Carol's desk was positioned just outside. "Glad to see they found you," Carol said as she approached. She nodded to the office. "Go on in, he wants you."

"What did I do?" Marie asked.

"You'll have to talk to him."

"Oh, come on, Carol. At least give me a hint. Am I in the firing line or just an innocent bystander?"

"No can do." Carol shook her head. "You're on your own. Get in there."

Marie took a deep breath, straightened her glasses and brushed her hair back. "Okay, but send in the paramedics if you hear any screams."

Carol grinned. She knew something.

Marie knocked and opened the door to Ibarra's office. A slender Hispanic man with a full head of gray hair looked up. "Oh, good. Marie, please come in. Have a seat."

She scooted a chair from the side of the room to the center and sat. Her heart beat just a little faster now that she was in the crosshairs of the man who had ruthlessly transformed NASA from a government agency to a government-corporation consortium. There had been casualties along the way, with several top-level players leaving altogether.

"Something going on?" In Marie's experience, direct but polite had always worked with Ibarra. "Anything I can help with?"

Ibarra smiled. "Help? You're center stage, depending on your eating habits."

Marie rolled her eyes. "Okay, what's going on? Carol was just as obscure."

His lips tightened and the lines in his face seemed to deepen. "It's been a rough couple of days, tougher still that the launch is tomorrow. That's why you're here, Marie. Let's have a little talk."

Marie physically gulped.

"But first, a question. Do you eat peanuts?"

"Augustin, really... what's this about?"

"Do you eat peanuts?" he repeated.

"Yes, occasionally."

35

"So, no allergy?"

"No. What are you—"

"That's it, then," Ibarra interrupted. "Jessica is out. You're in."

His words hit her like a hammer. A flush rose quickly into her face, followed by a tingle in her neck. "I'm… in? You mean, on the team?"

"That's exactly what I mean. You're on the Ixtlub team."

She wasn't sure she was hearing him correctly or that her brain was even functioning. "But Jessica—"

"She's been told. There's nothing she could have done differently. Unfortunately, she's allergic… to peanuts. She disclosed it on her application, but when we selected her, we didn't know much about the planetary environment. Now we do."

"They have peanuts on Ixtlub?" This was starting to sound like an elaborate joke. If it was, she couldn't bear to hear the punchline that might be coming.

"No, of course not," Ibarra said seriously. "There's not a single plant we share in common. But a peanut allergy is not related to the nut itself. People are allergic to a rare protein that, on Earth, appears only in peanuts and a few other roots. On Ixtlub, things are different. The same protein is rather common, in the soil, even in the atmosphere. There's no way we could have shielded her from it. If I send Jessica there, she'll die."

He was still talking nonsense. "I'm not even an alternate. I'm the administrative coordinator. I don't understand."

Ibarra walked around to the front of his desk and leaned against it. "This is where it gets a little strange," he said quietly, almost like he was talking with no one but himself. "He specifically asked for you."

"Who?"

"Aastazin."

It was flattering and confusing at the same time. "Zin wants me on the team? That's very kind, but doesn't he understand we have procedures? There are designated backups."

"He says you increase the probability of success." Ibarra looked very serious, and tired too. Maybe he'd already been down this path of explaining to Zin how NASA worked. "He says if you don't go, he'll need to cancel the mission, or at least postpone to a later date."

Marie pondered the sudden change of events. Zin was caring, thoughtful and extremely polite. It seemed he also kept some secrets.

"Augustin, you know I want to be on the team. It's a dream come true. But I don't know what I've done to deserve Zin as my benefactor." As much as she wanted to jump for joy at the news, the circumstances were odd. "How do you feel about this?"

His voice was gentle but firm. "I think you'll make a great team member. I always did, but I could fill only two positions. I figured you'd be on a future mission."

"But Zin forced your hand."

Ibarra nodded. "He did. And he won't explain why, either, which rubs me the wrong way. It's all about probabilities, he said. Like he's computing something in his head."

"Is it Core?" Marie just blurted it out. She wasn't sure she should be repeating rumors.

"Yeah, I've heard the same stories. Core and Zin are connected somehow. We had a long conversation. He doesn't deny it, but he says it's irrelevant to his recommendation that you be on the team."

Marie lowered her head in thought. "Wow. This is so sudden."

Could she really do this? They were only a day away from launch and she hadn't read nearly as much of the mission documentation as the other team members. Twenty-four hours. Not much time before four people would take their position on the transfer stations and slide through the portal. Could she be one of them?

A smile crept across her lips. She envisioned herself standing on the surface of another planet, a dim red sun in the sky and exotic plants around her. Would it be like that? She didn't know, but there was still time—she'd cram. She'd be ready for the most incredible opportunity of her life.

Ibarra seemed to be reading her mind. His normally hard look softened, almost fatherly. "Marie, we're behind the curve."

"Don't worry, I've got this," she lied. "I'm totally ready to go."

He seemed unconvinced. She had always been a terrible liar. "Make sure you are. You'll need to be sharp when you get there. Hell, even before. We're bypassing the alternates. Adding you to the team is bound to cause some hard feelings."

"Jessica or Tim?" Tim was the only team member she'd had some experience with, and not in a good way.

"Jessica won't be an issue, she gets it," Ibarra answered. "Marie, it's your job to merge into a team that wasn't expecting you. It might not be easy, but everyone on this team is a professional, and they damned well better act like it. Tim or anyone else. The stakes for this mission are high, so if there's a problem, you tell me."

Marie nodded, even though she knew right away she'd never do as he suggested. She'd prepare and be ready for whatever came.

~~~~~~~~~~~~~~~~~~~~

Marie walked briskly, her head down, reading prelaunch mission notes on her tablet. It had been four hours of much of the same: reading, skimming where possible, rereading for items that probably should have been memorized at this point in the training program. Safety procedures, life support systems, transfer procedures, customs and protocols. It went on and on. The documents were dense in places, too technical in others. She'd never manage to get through it all in time. Launch—or more precisely, the portal connection—was tomorrow afternoon.

A blur in front. She bumped into someone and looked up. "Sorry!"

It was Jessica Boyce, and Marie immediately thought of peanuts. "Oh, Jessica. Sorry, I was…"

"Reading?" Jessica asked. "You've probably got a lot to catch up on, I expect." Jessica's eyes were tired, her hair out of place, her expression disenchanted. "They told me last night. Congratulations."

"Oh, Jessica, I'm really sorry." There were a few things she could have said. *If it had been up to me… They should have…* But the words wouldn't have been truthful. Jessica was no dummy, and Marie's disappointment at being initially excluded had been obvious to anyone.

Jessica waved one hand like she was swatting a fly. "Eh, whatever. It's done now. They did what they had to do."

"You're not mad?" Marie asked.

"At you? No, not your fault." Jessica pointed down the hallway. "Hey, are you heading to the role-playing exercise?"

"Uh, yeah," Marie answered.

"Walk with me, I'm going there too." Jessica held out an elbow. "Let's make a united entrance, shall we? You and me." Marie hesitantly put her hand in Jessica's arm.

Jessica's attitude was surprisingly magnanimous, given the situation. The two women continued down the hallway together, arm in arm. "Very kind of you," Marie offered. "I don't think I understand. Why are you—"

"Still attending training?" Jessica glanced toward Marie and kept walking. "I have a job to do. I'm now CAPCOM. Earth-based team support. Communications to you guys in the field."

39

"And you're okay with that?"

"Maybe not okay. It hurts, but I can live with it."

They walked silently down the hallway and turned a corner. Marie brought them to an abrupt stop at the entrance to the training room. Inside, the rest of the team stood in a circle of conversation.

Once they walked into the room, all eyes would turn. She couldn't imagine what Jessica must be feeling. *If it were me, I'd be hiding in the darkest closet I could find.* She turned to face Jessica.

"What?" Jessica asked.

Marie spoke from the heart, clearly and forcefully. "You're the bravest person I've ever met."

Jessica provided a weak smile and shrugged one shoulder. "Eh, I have my moments." She put a hand on Marie's shoulder. "It's all yours now. You make us proud, okay?"

Marie nodded and held tightly to Jessica's arm, and they walked through the doorway together.

6 Bosons

The average person doesn't ponder the role of bosons in the universe while floating naked in a sensory-deprivation tank, but no one had ever called Nala Pasquier average. She floated in salt water, making no movements in the dark, coffinlike chamber. While her body relaxed, her mind raced.

The waves. The point of light. What were they? Come on, scientist, this stuff is not that hard. A fucking chimp could do it.

Sensory deprivation calmed the senses, allowing the mind to focus and develop deep insight. Apparently, not this time.

Focus on bosons, the framework of the universe.

She was close to an answer, but it would need to be drawn from the deep recesses of her mind. Every physics student knows there are five bosons: gluon, photon, W, Z, and Higgs. Yet now, there was a sixth: a particle that shaped space itself. At least, that's how Core had explained it.

Our friendly neighborhood cyborg. Provides the clues but neglects to mention the details. Some friend.

Core spoke in vague generalities. The new HP boson was the glue that held space together—or more like an elastic strap, because space could not only warp into gravity wells, as Einstein had postulated more than a century before, it could also stretch and compress.

Learning how to compress space had taken humans to the distant star VY Canis Majoris, where advanced alien technology—and Core—had been waiting. That had been months ago, and they had made significant progress since. Her lab was ground zero. At the flip of a switch, she could expand an infinitesimal dimension that only a quark would notice into something room-sized, or larger. And when she did, normal space responded by compressing. It had no choice; the HP boson enforced it.

The HP, or hyperbolic paraboloid boson, was named because of its tendency to bend space into a saddle shape, or as some call it, a Pringles potato chip. Geometrically speaking, a hyperbolic paraboloid is the opposite of a sphere. It's a curved surface that is open in every direction and never intersects itself.

Now that physicists had learned of the existence of the HP boson, they had quickly determined one of its intrinsic properties: HP bosons are naturally attracted to quarks, the fundamental particle that makes up protons, neutrons, atoms and molecules. Pair an HP boson with a quark, and they warp space a little. Pair a few trillion bosons with a few trillion quarks, and they warp space a lot. We call it gravity.

But the real discovery was when HP bosons were allowed to roam *free* without any quark pairings. Then, the boson worked its magic, expanding quantum space into an open structure—a Pringles kind of structure.

Nala knew all of this. She'd proposed half of it, her name now commonly circulated in physics publications. Free HP bosons could be tamed, managed, put to useful purposes. She could already create 4-D space; maybe there were other applications, too. Artificial gravity? That would be pretty cool.

But before they could install artificial gravity plates at the International Space Station, there were problems to overcome. The HP boson was probably responsible for the waves she'd seen in her lab. The pinprick of light, too. There really was nothing else to blame.

Or was there? Could it be the baryon-to-boson ratio?

That was what Jan thought. Nala's partner in physics was a Dutchman with a name pronounced *Yawn*, as she routinely teased. Jan was the theorist, Nala the experimentalist, and Jan's latest theory was that the density of mass played a role in the stability of space. Nala had been measuring density for weeks to find out.

And where was Core on all this brand-new science? Silent. They had submitted questions, but the answers that came back were either vague or the classic cyborg bullshit line: *You'll learn, in time.* Core might represent the combined intelligence of a hundred civilizations. Its moon-sized cyborg innards might be more advanced than any computer on Earth. But as a science colleague, it was coming up short on details.

As her frustration built, her thoughts turned audible. "Fuck this, I'm getting nowhere." The sound of her voice automatically engaged the lights inside her float pod, and she opened her eyes. The smooth fiberglass surface a few inches above her face was lit in a violet color that pulsed in intensity. Near the center of the curving top was a single LED, glowing pink.

The tiny LED over her face reminded her of the pinprick of light in the lab, and it stirred thoughts residing deep in her subconscious.

Wait a second.

She lay perfectly still, her naked body floating effortlessly in the warm salt water. Deep thoughts bubbled toward consciousness.

She had collapsed space. But what if it hadn't returned to quantum size? What if it had vanished altogether? A singularity, a zero-dimensional point. Could such a thing exist? Black holes were singularities, but a black hole derives from quarks, not bosons.

Maybe the pinprick was a different kind of singularity, triggered by free HP bosons. They warped space just as much whether free or paired with quarks.

A Type 2 singularity. That's what Jan would call it.

It was an interesting possibility. A wave of relief spread across her body. Insight. It was why she used the float pod. It allowed her mind to focus. Nala pushed upward on the violet surface, and the pod opened like a clamshell. She stepped out of the pool, rivulets of water sliding down her brown skin and onto the tile floor.

She'd need time to flesh out this new idea. Further experiments would certainly be needed. She'd talk to Jan. Bounce the idea around and see if it made sense.

Free of the confines of the float pod, Nala found the ordinary world invading once more, and trivial pursuits like getting ready for work took the place of deep thinking.

Nala pulled a towel from the shelf and wrapped it around her body. Deciding on a hairstyle for the day, she studied her image in the mirror. The tangles of long brown hair over bare shoulders, the not-quite-straight nose, and too-porous skin. People called her beautiful—Daniel had. An African beauty, he'd said, more than once. But those compliments had been in the heat of passion. She didn't see the beauty today.

Nala stuck her tongue out at the mirror and scrunched her nose. She recognized the symptoms. A momentary lack of confidence triggered by insecurities in her love life. Daniel was in the past. Done. Over.

An image of Daniel popped into her head. The last time he had been in her house, standing bare-chested beside the float pod with the very same towel wrapped around his waist. His embrace was strong enough to lift her into the air and drop his towel to the floor. Her heart rate picked up a bit at the memory.

Over? Well... maybe. Funny how thoughts of sex always followed physics. Did other people do that too?

She shook it off and forced herself to transition to the mundane tasks of readying for work. A touch of makeup, hair pulled back, and brushed white teeth. She selected a feminine but professional outfit: magenta trousers, white blouse paired with a camel blazer. The sharp, clean lines projected an aura of her professional life—a story of a confident intellectual, a scientist ready to explore the edges of the universe. The image was not only what she wanted others to see, it was also meant to be absorbed by her psyche.

Less than an hour later, Nala Pasquier stepped into the control room at Fermilab. She walked up behind the long-haired skinny guy, seated at the curved desk.

"Hey, Cody," she said. Dozens of large screens covered the wall in front of him, and he was engaged in the details on one of them.

Cody turned around. "Oh, hi, Nala. Look at this." He pointed to the screen, where a trend line threaded through a graph of several hundred data points. "The instability we saw last time started just after we hit maximum expansion. But no indications prior to then."

Nala leaned over his shoulder and examined the screen. "Came out of nowhere, didn't it?" she answered. "One minute, normal expansion into a fourth dimension. The next, all this wavering shit."

"Definitely a local effect," he said. "I didn't see anything here in the control room." He returned his attention to the graph. "But the data tells the story."

"Let's go with a larger expansion today," Nala said. "Assuming the wavering returns, I'll have Thomas measure its radius away from the neutrino target box, and we'll get multiple data points to plot this thing out."

Cody swiveled to face her. "Uh... Nala... I'm thinking the Department of Energy guy might have an issue with that."

"He's here?" Nala asked. The safety inspector had the power to shut down the whole lab if he found infractions. He'd gotten a whiff of the bizarre side effects they'd encountered and had found some cracks in the concrete near the Diastasi lab. But luckily, he was an engineer, not a physicist. That gave her plenty of room to work around any objections he might have.

"Leave the DOE guy to me," Nala said. "I'll explain things to him. Just be ready to go."

Cody grinned. "Explain things? Will that include any ass kicking?"

She waved a hand. "Would I do that? Cody, I'm five-two, a hundred and twelve pounds. I don't kick anybody's ass."

"Physically? No. Verbally?" Cody shrugged.

She waved him off. "Don't worry, he's an inspector. I'll give him the final say."

"Hah! This guy is doomed." Cody was generally agreeable, but it helped that Nala outranked him. "You want me to control neutrino amplitude, or Thomas?"

"You. It'll free up Thomas for data collection."

"Okay," Cody said. "But these waves are kind of freaking me out. Keep that radio handy."

"I always do." She patted Cody's shoulder and headed out of the control room and down to the lower levels of the sprawling facility. The safety guy would no doubt be down in the operations support office—there was always hot coffee, and the support team usually brought in pastries.

The anomalies they'd witnessed were definitely freaky, but manageable. Yeah, the lab had wavered a bit, but that was no reason for the Spanish Inquisition. Not that she couldn't handle these government inspector types—after all, he had no real understanding of the work she was doing.

Scientific discovery is not without personal risk, she rehearsed in her mind. *Galileo was found guilty of heresy and imprisoned. Jenner, Pasteur, Salk and others who developed vaccines were constantly exposed to pathogens. Curie died of radiation poisoning. But without these pioneers, where would we be today?*

It was an argument that might resonate with another scientist, but it wasn't a pitch you gave to a DOE safety guy. Instead, when she walked into the support office and found him munching on a chocolate-frosted doughnut, she calmly spoke of hyperbolic paraboloids and baryon-to-boson ratios. She agreed to limit the accelerator to 125 GeV and asked Joanne, their support tech, to attach a new first-aid kit to the lab wall. She also flashed her best radioactive smile—the kind that made men melt.

In the end, she prevailed, and the inspector signed off on continued research. These people always underestimated her.

7 Caps

Davis Garrity waited impatiently inside a warehouse south of Austin, Texas. On the other side of a glass enclosure, the shipping manager consulted a real-time tracking map and assured Davis the truck would arrive any minute. It would be carrying two full-sized Garrity Caps, ready to install on the stacks at ElecTrek's Brazos power facility. Another truck with two more wouldn't be far behind.

He wasn't kept waiting long. The huge warehouse door rolled up to the ceiling, revealing a loaded flatbed truck that slowly backed into the unloading area. The caps were bigger than he had envisioned, even though he'd personally provided the specifications to the company in New Jersey that had constructed them. Each cap was partially enclosed in a wooden shipping frame, about fifteen feet on each side and ten feet tall. Just two caps filled the available space on the truck.

"You taking the delivery?" the truck driver yelled to Davis.

"Yeah, drop them here," Davis answered. He'd have the second truck take one directly to the Brazos plant for a full-scale test. It would take a special crane to position it at the top of a five-hundred-foot smokestack, but installation costs were a pittance compared with the billion-dollar carbon-capture system it would replace. The other three caps would be held in reserve upon completion of the test. Davis had no doubt it would be successful.

A warehouse employee drove up in a forklift and unloaded the framed caps. Davis signed the paperwork, and the truck left.

Now alone in the warehouse, Davis approached one of the industrial caps, as big as a backyard swimming pool and painted in bold blue and orange on the outside. With the cap lying on its side, Davis stepped between the boards of the shipping frame to the cap's interior. Inside, clean white PVC surrounded him, a giant version of the sample PVC pipe he'd used in his demonstration. Davis pulled a piece of paper from his jacket pocket and compared the design layout with the real thing.

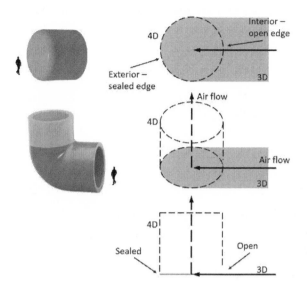

Just like the first image at the top left, the real cap also looked closed, but Davis knew it wasn't. The image beneath was closer to its actual shape, an elbow joint. The upper portion of the elbow was simply invisible to the human eye.

Not sure I'll ever understand this 4-D stuff, Davis thought. *But I sure do like it.*

The effluents from the smokestack would make a ninety-degree turn at the top of the cap in a direction Davis couldn't see or point to. He rapped the knuckles of his hand at the top of the cap—solid. The drawing identified the cap's crown as the *exterior sealed edge*. It wasn't really the top, it was simply the beginning of the elbow. The place where the pipe twisted into a fourth dimension of space. The upper portion of the pipe was just as real, just as solid, but unseen.

Under pressure, momentum would carry the stream of gases around the corner, through a hole in three-dimensional space and out into *nowhere*. A thousand tons a day of soot and toxic gases would simply disappear. It made Davis smile.

49

8 Gateway

Arm in arm, Marie and Jessica entered the training room. Conversation stopped and every eye focused on the two women. The others had definitely heard the news.

Zin approached first and held out his three-fingered hand. "We were waiting for you both to begin our final training session." He gently touched the arms of both women and ushered them into the center of the team.

Stephanie shut off her camera and threw her arms around Marie and Jessica in a group hug. She said nothing but gave a purposeful nod to Jessica and a supportive glance to Marie.

Handshakes and a light hug from Tim and Wesley were a bit awkward, but Jessica's idea that they should walk in together had been pure genius. Marie would never be able to thank her enough.

There was less drama than Marie had expected, but she was still relieved when Zin asked, "Shall we start?" The group gathered in a circle, and Zin stood in the center, smoothly pivoting his head to make eye contact with each person.

"We've covered everything at this point—systems, communications, safety and so on," he began. "So, this afternoon I want to combine all that you've learned and do some role-playing, specifically to focus attention on interspecies etiquette and protocol."

Zin explained that he would play the roles of both intelligent species found on Ixtlub—the Dancers and the Workers—providing realistic responses to questions. They would focus first on the Dancers, the dominant of the two species. "You won't have to worry about your words, as I will take care of all translation, but please be aware of body language, as you've previously learned. We will be guests in a place that will feel strange to you, and any initial meeting between very different species can be a bit tricky. Thus our practice today."

Zin dimmed the lights in the room and took a position in front of the group. "Welcome to Ixtlub," he said in an altered voice, with gurgles coming from the back of the throat for each hard-consonant sound.

Marie smiled. This was going to be fun.

Tim started, asking how much the Dancers knew about humans. Wesley followed with a question about social structure. Zin was completely in character with his responses, though he returned to being the instructor on occasion, cautioning Tim to lower the volume of his voice and Stephanie to avoid looking up at the ceiling when she spoke.

"They're not going to be hovering in the clouds, Stephanie. Look at them as you speak, and they will appreciate the physical connection. It's one of the behavioral traits both humans and Dancers share—eye contact. Even if you find it difficult to locate their relatively transparent eyes, they will notice yours easily."

The back-and-forth continued until everyone had asked more than one question except Marie; it was clearly her turn. She took a deep breath, pressed her hands together and remembered to look straight ahead. "Do you have communications satellites orbiting your world?"

Zin frowned. "Let's stop for a minute." He walked over to Marie and pushed her hands down to her sides. "Please, never put your hands together—not in a praying gesture, not in grasping, not in clapping. Did you recall reading this in the etiquette guide?"

"Um, I might have missed that," she said.

"It's a sex thing, Kendrick," Tim said, his voice remaining louder than it needed to be. "They do it to each other. You know, tentacle to tentacle."

"Thank you, Tim," Zin said. "Just remember, Marie, your hands, particularly your fingers, will seem very odd to them. They grasp objects by wrapping a stretched tentacle around them, which is why so many of their tools are cylindrical in shape. As Tim points out, only in intimate contact do the proboscis extensions at the tips of their tentacles stretch out, very much like your fingers."

"Sorry," Marie responded sheepishly. "I can see this might be a sensitive topic. I'll study up on it."

"Thank you." Zin backed away and addressed the group. "Everyone, hands and feet are your most disturbing physical features. Hands, because the fingers are always extended and are so manipulative. Feet, because they look like deformed versions of your hands. To avoid frightening anyone, please, always keep your feet covered."

It was an embarrassing start as a new team member. For the remainder of the training, Marie stood ramrod straight, kept her fingers curled and made no hand motions at all. Probably overkill, but until she had time to read what everyone else had already learned, it would avoid further correction from Zin. She began to wonder what he had seen in her. Maybe he was having second thoughts about his choice.

When the session was finally over, Marie headed straight to the break room, a good place to read. She made herself a cup of tea and pulled out her iPad. *Document 4a, Etiquette When Addressing Dancers.*

"Kendrick," said a voice.

She looked up to see Tim standing in the doorway. "Hi, Tim. You know, it's okay to call me Marie."

"I guess you were never military, were you, Kendrick?" he answered.

"NASA Operations. Instructor for ISS systems. No, never military."

"Yeah, I remember taking a class from you," he said. "On ISS heating and cooling systems, I think."

"I remember you as a student, Tim. Very well." There were some students that stood out no matter how much you tried to forget them.

Tim stepped into the room and waved an arm in the air. "What the hell are you doing here, Kendrick?"

"What do you mean? Ibarra assigned me. I was moved to active status to replace Jessica."

Tim came closer, looming over her. "Yeah, yeah, I know. Ibarra passed over the alternates to pick you because he's got to have a second woman on the team. Hell, I don't care how many women we have on the team. But why are *you* on this team? You're a teacher, not a rocket man."

Marie didn't move from her chair. There was no point in trying to correct Tim's assumption. She sipped her tea. "You won't be a rocket man either, Tim. We're going to sit in a chair and glide through a portal."

Tim closed within inches. "Is that what you think, Kendrick? That's it? You're going to step out of your comfy chair into a room that looks just like home except maybe it's got a few odd-looking flowers growing at the windowsill?"

"I don't really know what to expect, Tim. Do you?"

"Bet your ass I do. I've been there. Flight controls that freeze up, spacewalks that take too long, hatches that won't close, onboard fires. I've dealt with those emergencies and kept my head straight. You know anything about that?"

Marie didn't respond.

Tim stepped back into the doorway, as if intentionally blocking the only exit. "Kendrick, I don't know what we'll encounter on the other side of that portal, but I can guarantee you that it will take more than just rote procedures or a pretty smile—it'll take intestinal fortitude and a whole lot of courage. You got that on your resume?"

Marie tensed, pushed both hands together under her chin and then, hearing Zin in her head, set her hands down. "There might be more on my resume than you know about, Tim. But thanks for the pep talk. If I need any more encouragement, I'll be sure to let you know."

Tim shook his head and looked briefly at the floor. "Look, I don't have anything against you, Kendrick. But you're in way over your head and you haven't figured that out yet. Once you're on the other side of that portal... well..." He narrowed his eyes, did an about-face and left.

Marie sat alone, shaking.

Nothing like a good cup of tea to help reduce anxiety. She sipped, the warm tea sliding down her throat, but the anxiety remained.

She closed her eyes and pictured herself on the exotic planet once more. Standing alone at the top of a hill overlooking a pink ocean with glints from the dim red sun. Wispy clouds drifted across the sky and thin grasslike plants grew at her feet, bending gracefully under the gentle wind.

Tim might be right. The other side of the portal would probably be nothing like that.

~~~~~~~~~~~~~~~~~~~~~

The O&C clean room had been transformed overnight. Marie knew it would. Had her job remained administrative coordinator, she would have been responsible for making it happen.

The white oval portal still stood alone in the center of the room, with four transfer stations—the dentist chairs—positioned on its platform. But to one side, a low barrier separated the transfer station from bleachers that were now mostly filled with people. The place looked like a basketball arena.

Zin led, followed by the four katanauts dressed in blue jumpsuits, a NASA or ESA patch on one arm and a *Mission to the Stars* patch on the other. As they started across the wide floor and made their way to the center, applause rippled through the stands of spectators. Reporters lined the barrier, cameras rolling.

"I had no idea it was going to be this public," Wesley said to Marie, walking at her side.

Marie nodded. "Once we decided against the clean-room concept, NASA figured this should be like any launch. Observers, spouses, politicians... and the press."

"Except they're a lot closer than they would be to Pad 39C," Wesley noted. "Let's hope nothing blows up."

Marie inspected the former astronaut's eyes. He didn't seem to be kidding.

Several NASA engineers sat at the Transfer Command Station surrounded by computers and other equipment. Jessica, the "capsule communicator" for the launch, stood at one end wearing a headset. The terminology from the days of rockets would die hard. With an entirely new method of space travel, the roar of a rocket would be replaced by two 4-D bubbles. A large one generated from Ixtlub, a smaller one from this room by using technology Zin had orchestrated. The unseen bubbles would intersect at the portal doorway. Four chairs would simply slide along a rail and disappear through the portal, transported across three hundred and fifty light-years of space that had been compressed to almost nothing.

The team exchanged handshakes and hugs and waved to the crowd and the cameras. A few minutes later, Jessica called out in a loud voice that could be heard across the entire room. "We have 4-D detection! Countdown commencing at T-minus eight minutes."

They gathered closely around Zin. "Ixtlub has initiated on their side. You know what to do," he told them. Marie did. At least she hoped she did. The pages of documentation had become a blur, and her body was running on pure adrenaline.

The first step was the remainder of the suiting-up process. They each donned a lightweight headset with an earpiece, good for transmitting and receiving up to ten kilometers and a built-in video camera that could record for several hours. Tim strapped a belt around his waist, the signal repeater for the whole team that allowed for communications back to Earth via 4-D space.

Next was a small oxygen bottle that hung on Marie's hip, with a clear tube connected to a tiny cannula inserted into her nose. A little uncomfortable, but vastly better than a full pressure suit and helmet. The Ixtlub atmosphere, like Earth's, was mostly nitrogen, but the oxygen content was only half of Earth's 21 percent. Without the cannula, they would quickly become dizzy or disoriented. A water bottle was clipped to the other hip, with a small waterproof fanny pack in between. Zin carried a larger case containing spare oxygen bottles, additional water and food sufficient for their two-day trip.

Once she was fully suited, Marie sat in the third chair. It even had her name on it. A technician reclined the chair and fastened the hip and shoulder straps that connected in a center buckle. "Just push the center button to release," he told her. He did a quick communications check and she gave him a thumbs-up.

"T-minus two minutes and counting," Jessica declared. "All systems are green."

A launch control officer verified that each team member was seated and indicated his authorization to proceed. When the countdown reached one minute, the hoods on the backs of the chairs automatically positioned themselves over each person's face. It was Marie's first opportunity to see what might be under the mysterious device. Disappointingly, there was nothing more than a single LED, unlit.

Beneath the sides of the hood, she watched the technicians back away from the chairs. Wesley sat to her right and Stephanie to her left. Stephanie made eye contact. The mock silent scream on her face did nothing to disguise the broad smile.

"T-minus ten seconds, nine, eight, seven..."

It's finally happening. I'm leaving Earth.

Her heart pounded. She was thankful there were no biometrics included in their gear. Better to be nervous in private.

"...three, two, one. Launch initiated."

The LED flashed with a yellow light as brilliant as the midday sun. The world—and time itself—froze.

9   Dancers

The blast of yellow light was shockingly bright. Marie reflexively drew her hands over her eyes and waited for the afterimage to fade.

Sunglasses would have been a nice option.

Logically, the flash was not the first, but the second, bringing her back to consciousness. Time had passed, though how much was not clear. She had no memory of the gap, just a vague feeling that her existence had been altered in a way she'd never experienced before.

As the hood automatically lifted, she opened her eyes. An empty space surrounded her, with dim light glittering. She lifted her head from the chair. Stephanie to her left, conscious and looking around. Wesley to her right, detaching his harness. Marie pushed the button and the straps fell away. She sat up straight and stared in awe at the very alien scene.

Amazing.

The four transfer chairs were lined up across a flat green platform, inside a room-sized bubble of air, with a dome of clear water all around. They were on the floor of a shallow sea, with shafts of reddish light penetrating from a surface not far above. The platform was wide enough for the chairs, but not much more. Beyond its edge, a seafloor of white sand stretched out for several hundred yards and eventually rose to a hill in the distance, covered with dozens of white buildings with blue tops. It reminded Marie of the charming towns that graced the hillsides of many Greek islands, though it was entirely underwater.

To the left, just beyond the edge of the dome of air, a forest of giant kelp swayed gently in ocean currents. The dark green plants seemed to reach all the way to the surface. Marie pushed from her chair and stood upright. Tim and Wesley were also up and walking around the platform. Just beyond her teammates, but still inside the air bubble, stood a white oval portal. It looked identical to the portal at the O&C building, now very far away.

58

We made it. The other side.

She smiled at Wesley and he smiled back, remaining silent. No one dared interrupt the mesmerizing quiet and beauty of the place. Marie stepped forward, toward the wall of clear water at the front edge of the platform. There was no glass barrier; the water itself formed a smooth surface starting from the platform and arching over their heads.

Approaching within inches, she reached out a hand and touched it. Wet and soft, just like touching any water surface, even though this one was nearly vertical. She released her hand. The surface wobbled slightly but remained in place.

"Wow," she whispered. "Surface tension, but somehow controlled."

She extended an index finger, slid it through the water barrier and withdrew it. Her finger returned wet, but not a drop came out from where she'd poked.

Stephanie moved in close, a red light on her headset indicating her camera was recording Marie's interaction with the wall of water. "No sign of our hosts," she said as the recording's narrator. "But their planet is stunning."

Marie wasn't ready to think; it was enough to absorb the picturesque yet unfamiliar scene. She leaned back, looking straight overhead. The bubble was considerably higher than any room ceiling, perhaps fifteen feet overhead. Well above, through ocean currents and surface waves, she thought she could see blue sky and clouds, though the cloud edges were tinged with red, like sunset.

Blue sky is nitrogen, just like Earth.

Marie wondered how far it might be to the surface and whether they could swim—only in an emergency, of course. Her heart pounded with an instant adrenaline spike. She looked around, panicked. "Where's Zin?"

Stephanie switched off her headset cam. "Good question."

Tim checked his communication relay. "I've got nothing. Zin was supposed to walk through before us. He should have been here when we arrived."

Without Zin, this mission would deteriorate very quickly. She recalled what Tim had so bluntly explained the day before: things do go wrong.

"Don't panic," Wesley said. "We've got the comm link and the chair recall buttons. If for some reason Zin didn't make it through the portal, there's no reason we can't return to Earth and reorganize. Tim, let them know."

"I already did," Tim said. "No response yet."

Wesley was right, but the feeling of abandonment was still disconcerting.

"Somebody's coming." Stephanie pointed out to the sandy hill, where a vessel of some kind moved through the water. Cylindrical, and silver in color, like a small submarine. As it approached, its size became more apparent, as large as a bus. Its motion stirred the white sand on the ocean floor. The vessel had vertical and horizontal fins that pivoted, turning it as it neared the platform. It stopped and lowered to the seafloor, and a hatch opened at its stern.

A figure descended to the white sand, cocooned in what appeared to be a bubble of air like their own, but smaller. The diffraction at the bubble's surface distorted the view of the being inside. "This is it, gang," Tim said.

Stephanie switched on her headset cam and everyone else followed suit. With lanky arms and legs, it walked across the sand toward them. "Wait a second, that's not a Dancer," Wesley said. "It's Zin."

The wavering image sharpened as the familiar shape of the copper-colored android moved closer. The egg-shaped bubble of air surrounding him reached to the sandy bottom and moved with him as he walked.

He waved a hand in greeting and leaped up to the edge of the platform. As he entered, the wall of water magically parted and resealed behind him, leaving both Zin and the platform entirely dry.

"So sorry," he said, ignoring the aqueous miracle he'd just performed. "I intended to be back before you arrived, but discussions didn't go exactly as planned."

Marie heaved a sigh, relieved not only that Zin had been found but also that he seemed so at home in this strange world, as any experienced guide should be.

"We thought we'd lost you," Stephanie said.

"I do apologize," Zin replied. "It was only a slight detour. I believe we're back on track." Stephanie touched his arm, looking just as relieved.

"Nice trick with the bubble, Zin," Tim said.

"Fairly simple, really," Zin answered. He touched a small, almost hidden wire on his hip that extended two feet straight out to his side. "Enhanced electrostatics increase the natural tendency of water molecules to adhere to one another. You will each be doing this while we're here."

He addressed the whole team. "I've just spoken with my counterpart, and the change in plans is minor. Instead of using their meeting facility, the Dancers wish to greet you right here. This platform is normally just a transfer station, but there seems to be some nervousness on their part."

"They're worried about us?" Stephanie asked.

Zin tilted his head in a very humanlike way. "Mmm. Cautious, I would say. The Dancers can be quite bold, but I've noticed a reluctance too. You are only the second intelligent species that has visited Ixtlub."

"So, will they join us here on the platform?" Wesley asked.

"No," Zin answered. "But near enough that you will get a good sense of them. If this first step goes well, there will be more. Are you prepared?" He looked around, and each team member nodded.

Zin pulled a penlike device from a slot on his belt and spoke into it. The sounds he made were guttural, complex, muffled and weighted heavily toward sharp consonants like *x* and *k*. The words, if they were words, were unintelligible, but the variety could certainly pass for a spoken language. The device responded, emitting more of the same sounds.

"They're coming now," he said.

Everyone watched the vessel, floating less than a hundred feet away. A form descended from the open hatch. Metallic, with coloring similar to Zin, but an entirely different shape. The thing looked like a bell, complete with a clapper hanging below it. Its top sloped to a slender crown whose surface was marked by several circular shapes. The clapper gently rested on the sand and then pushed off toward the platform. They'd all seen photos of Dancers. This being was similar, but different.

"My Ixtlub counterpart," Zin explained. "Aainatonia. She speaks English, fluently in my opinion, though her style is oriented to a Dancer thought process."

The bell-shaped being bounded in long arcs over the sandy bottom to the platform's edge. She seemed not to have any mouth but formed perfectly audible words that passed easily through the several feet of water between them. "Welcome. You are as your images. Very fine. I am Aainatonia, an assistant."

No one spoke for a second as they absorbed the odd circumstance. Finally, Tim spoke. "Good to meet you, Aa... ina... sorry. Can you hear us?"

"Quite well," Aainatonia replied. "Your sound transmits by water and air. It is good. Aastazin is called by you, Zin. If helpful, you may call me Tonia."

"Easier," Tim said.

"Each of you is comfortable inside?" Tonia asked.

"She means inside the bubble," Zin added. "Any dizziness? Cannulas all working?"

They all nodded. Marie had completely forgotten the oxygen tube was even in her nose. Tonia pivoted, and the clapper, which was apparently flexible, twisted with her move. "I present to you, new friends." She issued some unintelligible sounds.

From the hatch a white form appeared, followed by another, and another. Four in all. Slender jellyfish, if there was a single description for the elegant creatures. White, but translucent. Each slender head smoothly transitioned to a body that ended abruptly in an outward flair, like a girl's skirt. Protruding from below the skirt was a thick vertical stalk and several tentacles swaying like ribbons around a maypole. Some of the creatures retracted their tentacles and stalk higher, almost completely hidden by the skirt. Others allowed them to dangle.

One of the creatures bent forward and shot straight ahead, instantly stopping next to Tonia and dropping its stalk to the sandy floor. Side by side, the similarity in shape between the soft white creature and the metallic Tonia was obvious, just as Zin approximated a human form. Another creature zipped to the front, moving twenty feet almost instantaneously. Their speed through the water was nothing less than remarkable. With all four gathered next to their guide, the line of humans faced the line of Dancers with only a few feet of water separating them.

"Jellyfish," Tim mumbled. "Just like the pictures."

"They're beautiful," Stephanie said. "Better than the pictures."

Wesley turned to Zin. "Protocol? I'm sure we can do more than stare at each other."

"I suggest you start with a question," Zin answered.

Wesley looked eager and gave a slight bow. "Thank you so much for inviting us. I'm curious if the water transmits your voices?"

Wesley had at least ten questions prepared in advance—they all did. But now that they were just steps away from obviously intelligent creatures, Marie imagined the conversation might become somewhat more impromptu. She hoped none of them would say or do something that might be taken wrong and remembered to keep her hands at her side.

One of the creatures dipped slightly and issued a guttural response oddly mixed with a few high squeaks. Tonia quickly translated. "She welcomes you and wonders if you can hear her."

"Perfectly," Wesley replied. "This is great."

Stephanie pointed to her camera headset and asked if she could record. Tonia left the response to the creature on the end. It promptly pivoted in a full circle and tipped its head to one side, almost comically.

"He's posing for you," Zin said. "I believe your video is authorized."

Stephanie switched the camera on. "We're already using the words *he* and *she* and our briefing documents explained that you are male and female but honestly, I can't tell the difference. Can you help?"

There was some conversation between Tonia and several of the Dancers. Finally, Tonia responded. "They ask you the same question."

Stephanie doubled over laughing. "Oh, my God, we're really at the basics!"

Tonia continued. "Yes, two forms. You may use the words male and female, but they do not have the same meaning. Males are darker with a straight central spine. Females are lighter and less straight."

The briefing documents used a similar description but also mentioned that unlike humans, there was no height difference between Dancers.

"Does anyone see that?" Stephanie asked under her breath. "I sure don't."

"Try to practice," Tonia said.

Stephanie blushed. Sound traveled well, and Tonia didn't miss a thing.

Zin spoke in the Dancer language and then in English that he had explained the differences between male and female humans. None of the katanauts asked for the precise anatomical translation or how Zin had gained this information.

Each person took a turn asking a question, mostly drawn from their predefined list though a few unrehearsed questions popped up and Zin didn't object. Some were about physical biology and eating habits, some about customs and social structure. The Dancers responded with many of their own questions and Zin translated as various team members responded.

You live on the surface? Yes, in homes not very different from yours on the hill.

Your science? Biology, chemistry and enough physics to get us here.

Do you have a second species? Not like you do, but dolphins and chimpanzees are pretty smart. Dogs, too, Wesley added.

Many of the questions from one side were reciprocated on the other. Marie watched carefully, especially when each Dancer spoke. There were differences between them. The shading, though subtle, was definitely lighter on some. One Dancer who seemed to match the female description had asked questions slightly different from the others, more involved and with deeper meaning.

"Can I ask a question specifically to the person at the right end of the line?" Marie asked. Zin translated, and the Dancer at the end dipped slightly in response. "Your homes on the hillside are quite beautiful. I'm curious what they look like inside. Does each house belong to a person or family? Do you sleep and eat there like humans do? How about... sorry, I guess I have a lot of questions." She could think of ten more she'd like to ask, but Zin had recommended they take it one step at a time.

Once the translation was provided, the Dancer dipped several times as she responded. Tonia translated. "She is very happy that you ask. Houses are shared, and eating is often communal. But spaces within each house are individual. She invites you to see her space."

"I'd love to see your house... your space. Yes, I'd like that very much," Marie answered. She turned to Zin. "Can I do that?"

"It might be a little complicated, but not impossible," Zin replied.

"Because of the water?"

"No, not at all. The water is no issue. You saw me walk across the sand. Once set up, you could do the same and walk right into her house. No, the complications might be with others who share the house. Particularly if they are Dancer youth."

"Oh, I didn't think about that."

Zin turned to Tonia. "What do you think?"

Tonia turned to the Dancer female on the end, and they had an extended conversation with considerable dipping.

"Why do they dip?" Marie whispered to Stephanie.

"I think they're laughing," she responded.

Tonia spoke in English. "Quite good. Very good. The youth in her home already know the human form. An artist in their city makes human dolls. The smallest youth play with them."

"Oh God, now I've heard everything," Tim said.

"Please visit," said Tonia. "But just one. You, please." She pivoted to Marie and spoke in the Dancers' language to Zin.

Zin acknowledged. "Tonia will set it up," he told Marie. "This will actually work out well. We'll split up. Marie, you will follow Tonia to this Dancer's home while the rest of us visit a science laboratory and a kleek shell processing facility."

"Really?" Marie said. "Wow, I'm honored. Tell her I'm really honored to be invited to her home."

Zin performed the required translation and the Dancer dipped several times.

"I don't think they're laughing," Marie whispered to Stephanie. "Maybe the dipping is more complicated than that."

"Or maybe it's just a nervous tic," Stephanie mused.

Without saying a word, Wesley broke ranks from the line of humans and stepped forward to the wall of water. He looked straight ahead to his counterpart in the middle of the line of Dancers. The Dancer twisted its central spine, the rod they'd earlier called a stalk, and pushed off the sand to move forward, close enough that Wesley could have reached out and touched it. Marie tensed.

Please, Wesley, no handshake, she thought, but she didn't say anything. Neither did Zin.

Wesley seemed to be thinking the same thing because instead of reaching out, he stood tall and then dipped slightly to his right. He waited, and the Dancer dipped too. Then he dipped left and his counterpart followed. That was all they needed and within a few seconds the two were doing a dance—synchronized or not, it was hard to tell.

A base drumbeat appeared from nowhere and coincided with their motion.

"Are they doing that?" Marie asked. "The drumming?"

"Yes, I believe they are," Zin answered. "I've never seen this before. It's really quite interesting."

There were certainly no drums around and no discernable motion from any of the Dancers, yet somehow, they were generating the sound.

Marvelous creatures, Marie thought. They seemed so simple, yet they had created a society of high technology, with advanced tools and education. Their history must have been just as complex as human history. You didn't become a civil society without some pain and strife along the way. Perhaps it still existed somewhere, just not here.

10 Beextu

Mykonos. Maybe Paros or Samos. One of the Greek islands. The Dancer's town was a spitting image. Small white and blue houses, curving cobblestone streets, even colorful flower boxes on the corners of each house. Beyond the lack of sidewalk cafes, the major difference was that this town was submerged under a hundred feet of seawater.

Marie followed closely behind Tonia and the Dancer, whose name she couldn't pronounce until Tonia graciously shortened it to *Beextu*. When Marie said the name, the Dancer dipped both left and right, clearly delighted to hear her name spoken by the human. The creature tried to say *Marie*, but it came out *Meezhie*. Close enough.

Their air bubble technology was wonderful. Zin had fitted a belt around Marie's waist, with a canister of nitrogen and a wire that reached out to one side and touched the wall of water. Somehow, the wire transferred an electrostatic charge to the water and created an egg shape that surrounded Marie and moved with her every step. No matter which way she turned, the ground was solid, if damp, and unless she extended her arm fully, she never got wet. It was like walking through a downpour with a transparent umbrella.

She allowed her fingers to extend for just a moment, long enough to skim the surface of the wall of water. Caribbean warm. She touched a finger to her tongue. Salty, even saltier than an ocean on Earth. They'd already talked about microbes and whether there were dangers to humans. The same argument that Zin had made for abandoning the clean room on Earth also applied to Ixtlub. Whatever microbes were in this water had followed a different evolutionary path from that of any microbe on Earth. Their ability to survive within a human body was unlikely. Of course, Marie had just put that theory to the test.

Somebody has to be brave, why not me? Deal with it, Tim.

She marveled at her surroundings. They walked—she walked, they flitted—up a narrow path that wound its way across the side of the main hill of the town. The buildings mostly looked like family houses, but a few were larger. All had windows, including shutters that could be opened or closed. Occasionally they passed a house with a Dancer inside, which usually resulted in a quick flit away from the open window, or the flash of a tentacle and a shutter quickly closed. She wasn't sure if they were naturally shy, or whether she represented something the regular townspeople weren't expecting to see.

She watched Beextu move. It wasn't quite swimming, but her body was definitely pushing water. Most of the motion was in the skirt that surrounded her body, with her tentacles merely dangling below. Sometimes, especially when going up a hill, she would touch her central stalk to the ground just between cobblestones, flex and then push off, giving added propulsion. It was a move both graceful and powerful. These creatures could move very quickly when they wished.

They crested a small hill and stopped at a door to one of the houses. The door itself was dark green and appeared to be made from the kelp trees, just like the platform where their transfer chairs waited. Beextu squeaked and the door opened.

This is going to be really interesting, Marie thought. She reached up to her headset and switched on the video camera. She followed them inside, ducking through the low doorway. Her air bubble easily kept up, and she found herself standing in a small room with several passages off in multiple directions. There was no furniture, but the walls were decorated with a color pattern that varied in intensity, shifting as if the pattern were projected.

Beextu and Tonia pivoted to face her. At this close distance, it was easier to see Beextu's eyes. Circular, and protruding only slightly from the top of her smooth crown, but translucent white like the rest of her body, which made them blend in. Zin's comment during training finally made sense—that human eyes would be easily noticed. She thought about her own dark eyes and how much they contrasted with her light skin. Human features taken for granted turned out to be unique. Whether they were beautiful or ugly depended on whom you asked.

Beextu said something, and Tonia translated. "She welcomes you."

Marie looked at Beextu, not Tonia. "Beextu, this is amazing. I can't tell you how happy I am to be here." Even if most translated words would have to come from Tonia, repeating Beextu's name might help to make a personal connection.

The Dancer swayed gently and was silent for a moment. There was no telling how the protocol for a social call worked on this planet. Tea and cookies? A tour of the house?

Conversation and connection. These were keys to bridging any gap between intelligent beings. It probably didn't matter that their backgrounds and biology were different. If they could find common ground, good things would follow.

I must appear strange to her. An alien creature in her house. She may be just as nervous as I am.

An idea popped into Marie's head. Her watch, wearable technology, had a few photos from home stored on it. She touched its screen and swiped a few times to find the right picture.

She looked up at Beextu and carefully moved her arm closer to the edge of the air bubble. She twisted so Beextu could see the image it displayed, a boy about five years old petting a rabbit. "My nephew, my sister's son. His name is Owen." Marie held her hand over her heart. "He's a sweetheart. Cutest little boy on Earth."

Beextu came closer, twisting the top of her body. Tonia translated, though there was no telling if the relationship with the boy would be clear. Did they have sisters or sons in their society? How did their children come into being—through birth, through hatching, in a petri dish? At least some of this information was probably in one of the NASA documents that Marie had never managed to read.

Beextu's translucent eyes came within inches of the edge of the bubble and she peered at Marie's arm and watch. Would she even understand what she was looking at? The ability to make sense of a three-dimensional object portrayed on a flat screen might not be universal. Even cats and dogs back home had a difficult time with it.

Beextu backed away and then, in a burst of water that made the air bubble bulge inward, she sped away and through one of the passageways.

Marie looked at Tonia. "Did I do something wrong?"

"I don't know. Please wait," Tonia answered.

A minute later, Beextu reappeared from the passageway, slowly, with small figures following, hiding behind her. As they approached, Marie leaned to the right to see around Beextu, and the tiny figure flitted, quickly disappearing again.

"I can't see them very well," Marie said. "But I think I know who they might be."

Beextu spoke and Tonia translated. "Youth. They are mine. I told them you are human, a real one."

Marie bent down slightly. "It's okay, I won't hurt you." Tonia translated.

One tiny head peeked from behind Beextu, followed by another. They moved farther away, miniature versions only a tenth the size of an adult, but complete with tiny skirts and skinny tentacles. Their heads bobbed up and down like a spring, and their skirts rolled with waves. Beextu looked positively stiff by comparison.

"Oh, my God, they're so adorable," Marie gushed. She adjusted her headset, hoping the video camera was capturing the scene. "Will they come closer?"

"Give them time," Tonia said without translating.

"They're so sweet, Beextu. Beautiful children, er youth."

Tonia translated everything in the back-and-forth between Marie and Beextu.

"Thank you, Meezhie," Beextu said. "They will grow, as plants do. As humans do."

"How old are they?"

"Four hundred days, very young." Marie had read that a day on Ixtlub was somewhat longer than on Earth. Their equivalent age must be a few Earth years. According to the same information, Dancer lifespans could be as long as one hundred and thirty Earth years. Beextu's children were just as she said, very young.

Marie bent lower and her voice rose naturally, childlike. "What are your names?"

"Not yet," Beextu said. "They will take names later."

"Can they speak?"

"Yes. Too much. They don't know when to stop."

There were some squeaks from the tiny Dancers and Beextu spoke directly to them. One of them squirted off to the right, faster than Marie had seen any of the adult Dancers move. Just as quickly, it returned to Beextu and circled her several times, squeaking repeatedly before finally settling down.

"He makes a show for you," Beextu said.

"Because I'm new?" Marie asked.

"He says you look like his doll."

Marie laughed, and the tiny Dancers zipped behind Beextu at the noise. "Oops, sorry, I didn't mean to scare them."

"Their doll makes no sound. You do."

"I'm not a doll, I'm real." Marie spoke to the children, hoping they too could understand Tonia's translation. "I'm from a place called Earth. Your mother and I are friends." Marie looked up at Beextu. "Or at least I hope we will be."

The ice broken, Marie and her new friend had many questions and much to say to each other. Tonia translated every word, though the delay in a longer conversation was somewhat irritating. The more they talked, the more Marie felt comfortable within the alien place. The difference between their outward appearance was impossible to ignore, yet intellectually they had more in common than Marie expected.

Beextu was well educated in science. Her primary expertise was in the biology of her species—and of the Workers, the land-dwelling species who were on the other end of a fascinating relationship of symbiosis. At first, Marie thought Beextu might be a physician, but her knowledge was broader than just biology. She easily spoke about their planetary system, understood the difference between their red dwarf star, Earth's yellow dwarf and the hypergiant where Core resided. She demonstrated a knowledge of orbital mechanics and even answered Marie's practice question on whether they had launched satellites. Yes, they had, with the help of the Workers.

Beextu held an official role of some kind within a government body. She had regularly engaged with Core and with other members of the galactic consortium. Beextu's experience with the consortium and her perception of future human involvement consumed the rest of their conversation.

Toward the end of the visit, Beextu's children ventured close enough to Marie that one poked its head through the air bubble and for a moment was within arm's reach. Marie wanted to touch the miniature Dancer, but a quick motion from both Beextu and Tonia made her think better of it. There were still some barriers that weren't to be crossed.

~~~~~~~~~~~~~~~~~~~~~~

The day was long, but eventually darkness fell across the shallow sea. Their overnight accommodations consisted of one room with several narrow passageways, each dead-ending in a cove where soft material had been placed for sleeping. The main room had walls on three sides but was open to the sea on the fourth, the water held back through the technique of enhanced surface tension that the Dancers managed so well. The room was located halfway up the hill and the view across the picturesque town was magnificent. Beyond the edge of the town, perhaps a mile away, the white-sand seafloor stretched undisturbed into the distance.

The room also had tables and chairs, sized appropriately for humans, and the team was happy to get off their feet for a short break. Zin had distributed a tortilla wrap to each person, a compact and simple meal and a welcome reminder of home.

Marie soaked in the view like she was enjoying a moment at a Caribbean restaurant. She had finished telling her story of Beextu's house and her children. Stephanie asked if she'd captured it all on video. "You can't imagine how well that's going to play on TV when we return home."

"Yes, it's wonderful that you were able to learn more about their families as well as Beextu's role as representative," Zin said to Marie. Zin still stood while everyone else sat. "But in your description, you implied there was some measure of disharmony? Tell us."

"Yeah, a very interesting conversation," Marie said, finishing her food. "Core came up a lot."

"So, they've met Core too?" Wesley asked. He sat at the table across from Marie.

"Yeah. Tonia is Core's emissary to the Dancers, just as Zin is ours. The Dancers' first contact with Core was about a hundred years ago. Since then they've had contact with several other civilizations... through Core. I guess he's kind of a clearinghouse for the developed planets. Maybe even the matchmaker." She looked up at Zin, who was standing close.

"Roughly, yes," Zin said. "It depends on the civilization, though. It's tricky business."

"That might be an understatement," Marie said.

"So, it sounds like you learned something?" Wesley probed.

Marie looked up again at Zin. "Well... it's a bit awkward. Sorry, Zin, I'm just not sure if I should repeat this with you here."

Zin turned his brow bulge down in the middle. Was he insulted? His facial expressions could be surprisingly human. "I can leave, if you wish."

"On second thought, maybe you should stay," Marie answered. "It might be good for you to give us a response."

"Sounds juicy," Wesley said. "Do tell."

Marie took a sip from a water bottle. "Well, Beextu and I were talking about their history, and how they met Core—and it's pretty similar to our history, except that the Dancers have a reliance on the Workers for their technology—but that's another story. Anyway, I told Beextu that Core seemed to be pretty good about teaching us what we need to know as the newbies to this galactic group, and then she talked over me before Tonia had finished the translation. I'd never seen her interrupt me before, she had been so polite. But she said that humans should be wary in our relationship with Core, that he might not be serving our best interests."

"Wow," Tim said. "That's kind of bold. And she said that with Tonia standing right there?"

"Tonia translated it."

They all looked up at Zin, who stood motionless, without comment. Stephanie raised a hand. "I wonder if the translation was

76

accurate. What words did she actually use? That we should be *wary* of Core?"

"Yeah, that's exactly the word that Tonia translated, *wary*. I asked Beextu if Core had misled the Dancers or done something wrong, and she just said that they had learned their lesson over time."

Wesley pushed his chair back from the table and crossed a leg over one knee. "Zin? Care to comment?"

Zin pulled out one of the empty chairs and sat down, facing the group. "You call me Core's emissary, but that's not accurate. I am your aide for the purposes of representing humans to the Dancers and the Workers of Ixtlub. Nothing more. When my mission is complete, I'll be assigned another task, probably in another sector of the galaxy and with an entirely different exterior body."

"Which doesn't answer the question," Wesley responded. "Should we be wary of Core?"

"The relationship between humans and Core is your business. As I said, it varies considerably by civilization, and much depends on your own actions."

"You make him sound like some power-hungry god," Tim said. "Do we have to worship him, or else?"

Zin's tone was flat. "Never underestimate Core's power; it's greater than you realize. But in equal measure, take confidence in the truth that it has no animosity toward humans." Zin looked around. "Does that answer your question?"

Wesley shrugged and no one else offered anything more.

"Good, then," said Zin. "We will rest at this location and, in the morning, transfer to the surface to make contact with the Workers."

If Zin wanted to move on, Marie wasn't concerned. The whole conversation with Beextu had been recorded anyway. The revelation that Core wasn't entirely benevolent or hadn't been completely honest probably wouldn't go over very well with the heads of NASA—or for that matter, the heads of government. But there would be time to sort through the implications when they returned home.

11 Decoherence

Jan Spiegel walked into Nala's lab, holding a single sheet of paper with a graph on it. He looked upset, but he usually did when experiments weren't going as planned.

"A singularity? Really, Nala. You're jumping to conclusions the data doesn't support."

The two physicists squared off routinely, but only on an intellectual basis. Nala had the greatest respect for Jan. "It's a quantum system, Jan. The superposition of multiple eigenstates must collapse to a single value upon observation. It doesn't matter if its size is a nanometer or a kilometer, it's still a quantum system."

"Yes, I agree," Jan answered, "but you're suggesting that a wave function collapse of a quantum system becomes a *literal* collapse of physical space."

"Decoherence is decoherence," she responded. "A wave collapses to a particle; four-dimensional space supported only by HP bosons collapses to a point."

Jan rubbed his chin. "A singularity? You think you created a point of zero dimensions?"

Nala flipped both hands to open palms. "Well, it's gone now. You're the theorist, I'm just the lab jockey. You tell me."

Jan stood up and softened his tone. "Look, Nala, I'm not denying what you saw." He studied the graph on the paper. "Yes, collapse of boson-supported space to a singularity is theoretically possible, but there's not enough data here to prove it. Repeat the experiment, but start with a larger volume and higher mass. Then let it collapse and measure the baryon-to-boson ratio as it drops. If you can get data all the way down to this spinning-singularity-light thing, then I've got something to work with."

Jan dropped the graph on her desk and left. Nala silently stewed for a while. Regimentation was required for good science, but it was a state of mind she didn't enjoy. Jan was right; he usually was. Experimentation provided data, data provided guidance toward reality, and the whole point of science was to expose reality.

Nala turned to Thomas, who sat at the other end of the workbench, inexplicably wearing a leather Viking helmet complete with horns. With his curly red beard sticking out below the hat, he could have just walked off the set of a Norwegian historic film. "Okay, Thomas, let's crank it up again."

"Ja. You vant bigger?" he said with a Scandinavian accent. Her colleague was originally from Minneapolis; maybe that explained it.

"Ja, Thomas. Set tau to, uh…" She studied a diagram posted on the wall. "Six point five, ten to the minus ten. Then we'll bring it to zero faster than last time. But be ready to measure the ratios. It'll collapse fast as fuck."

"Hmm. How fast does fuck collapse?" Thomas asked no one in particular.

"Fast." Nala smiled and patted Thomas on the shoulder. She reached for the handheld radio. "Cody, let's go again. Same oscillation."

The radio crackled to life. "You got it, Nala. Protons coming up." Nala and Thomas inserted earplugs, now standard procedure for the larger spatial compressions.

The room vibrated almost immediately, with a buzzing in the pipes above their heads. The pipes now carried a stream of light-speed neutrinos, their oscillations locked in phase. A tremendous burst of blue light blasted from the target box on the wall, followed by a bang louder than a gunshot. The camera inside the test box disappeared on cue.

Nala removed the earplugs and checked her computer monitor. "Expansion into 4-D looks good. Spatial compression of 3-D is right on target." An image of two brilliant blue-white stars appeared on the monitor, a view from the camera now light-years away. "Big-time compression, my friend. Where did you point to this time?"

"Mizar," the Viking replied. "The double star in Hellevagon."

"Hellevagon?"

"Norwegian constellation, otherwise known as the Big Dipper."

"Nice." Nala adjusted a few controls and checked her computer monitor one last time. She turned to Thomas. "Okay, ready for the collapse?"

"Ja, sure, you betcha."

She pressed a few keys, and the vibration immediately grew. The air in the lab started to waver like the heat above a fire. The vibration increased to a thunder.

The strange waves grew rapidly. The workbench beneath her hands rolled like an ocean breaker, deforming not just its surface but the keyboard, the computer display, and every other piece of electronic equipment stacked upon it. Above the bench, a thick pipe vacillated like a garden hose.

"They're back!" Thomas yelled.

Nala reached across the workbench and pulled the portable radio unit from its base. Before she could key the transmit button, there was a loud crunching sound.

That's not good.

The whole world buckled like a piece of paper that had been crushed into a ball. The workbench split in two, computer screens shattered and sparks flew in her face. Her chair jumped to the ceiling and then slammed back to the floor.

"Ooof," she spewed as she hit the floor spread-eagled. The radio flew from her hand.

The room twisted into an L-shape, then a U-shape, and continued into a circle. More glass shattered and sprayed across the deformed room amid the sounds of carpet tearing, of wood creaking, twisting and snapping, of metal scraping against metal.

She had no idea what was up and what was down. With equal parts confusion and terror, she felt her whole body might be tearing apart. She screamed, and she heard Thomas screaming too.

The twisting room turned upside down, and shelves threw electronics boxes that crashed against walls, ceiling and floor. She desperately reached out and managed to grab the only solid thing she could find, a support bar screwed into the wall. For a brief moment, her head stabilized.

Straight ahead, the wall with the plexiglass box was gone, replaced by a gaping hole, intensely dark in its center, but with streaks of bright light pouring in around its perimeter. A radio unit flew across the room and was swallowed by the massive hole, disappearing into nothing but blackness. A portion of the workbench broke off and was also sucked in.

"Thomas!" she screamed above the tornado-like uproar. "Grab something!" She ducked as a small refrigerator unit tipped over, slid across the tilted floor and fell through the threshold of the dark hole. The bar she gripped became the ceiling and her body dangled below. Wind-whipped flying glass shredded her pants and cut her legs. She winced at the sting but held on tight to the bar.

On the far side of what was left of the lab, she saw Thomas, his hands wrapped around the leg of a table that appeared to be bolted to the wall, or what was now the ceiling. Directly below both of them, the dark hole continued to swallow everything that fell into it.

Her hands were wet with sweat and the bar was slippery. The roar continued all around and she could find no refuge. A huge crack appeared in the wall above her, the wallboard shattered and the bar she held broke free.

Falling. Darkness. A hard surface and pain. Blowing wind carried bits of debris into her face. She covered her face with her hands.

The wind lessened, and the noise subsided. Lying on her stomach, she reached out and felt debris. She pricked her hand on a sharp piece of metal, drawing blood. Lifting her head, she saw a circular light in the distance, but the light grew dimmer with each second until it finally closed to a pinprick.

Some distance away, Thomas screamed.

12 Workers

Hawaii at sunset—the surface of Ixtlub was just as beautiful. The soft orange light from the dwarf star cast a golden glow on trees that resembled palms. The warm breeze brushed delightfully across bare skin. Marie took in a deep breath, almost forgetting she wore an oxygen cannula.

They stood on a grassy hill overlooking a long white-sand beach at the shore of a shallow sea that stretched to the horizon. Somewhere beneath the water were the Dancers' towns and cities, but the only evidence of their existence was a few small structures that broke the surface in places.

Four humans absorbed the tropical scene in silence and awe.

"I could move here," Stephanie finally said. "A little chalet over there, just by the stream." The breeze tousled her hair; she looked like a model in a beachwear shoot.

The Dancers' emissary, Tonia, was due to join them any minute, though how she'd move across dry ground was anyone's guess. Tonia would be bringing *the gift*, as she'd called it: an advanced communications device produced by the Dancers and normally worn by the Workers. As she had explained the night before, the device would need to be calibrated for human use—by matching its function to a specific person's brainwaves.

The device provided deeper insight into the physical world and living things. It could analyze, compile, translate and interpret complexities that no brain could possibly process alone. It extended intellect, and it was the primary communication path between Ixtlub species. To fully understand the relationship between Dancers and Workers, a headband was required.

A longtime technophile, Marie found the idea of enhanced brain function irresistible. But on a personal level, it might also provide a direct link to Beextu. Later, perhaps on some future trip, Marie might visit Beextu alone, just the two of them with no translator or guide. They would pour a glass of wine—or whatever Dancers consumed—and talk for hours, comparing notes about their lives, their customs, science and politics. When they parted, she'd hug Beextu as a sample of how humans interact with good friends. The alien communications device would be the catalyst to make it possible.

For this mission, Tonia could offer only one headband and asked for a single volunteer. Wesley and Marie raised their hands together.

As the team sociologist, Wesley was the natural choice, which Marie quickly acknowledged. "Sorry." She pulled her hand down. "It makes more sense for Wesley to take it."

But Zin had intervened. "I disagree. Wesley should observe the Workers unenhanced. A sociologist will produce a more accurate assessment by starting with an unbiased, equivalent view of both species. Marie, however, is quite the technologist among us. I believe the device should be calibrated for her."

It was a little awkward and surreptitious. Once again, Zin seemed to be Marie's benefactor, though his reasoning in this case was logical. In the end, Tonia and Wesley agreed. Tonia held an array of sensors against Marie's forehead, took some measurements and said she'd return the next morning with a calibrated headband.

That time had now come. Marie leaned against a car-sized volcanic rock as they waited for Tonia and the device. Beyond the trees and bushes of the lowland jungle, a cone-shaped peak towered in the distance. Probably the volcano that had blasted the rock into its current position. The volcano looked dormant now.

Tonia approached along a graded dirt pathway, moving far more rapidly on land than her underwater body would seem to allow. The stalk below her bell-shaped midsection pushed off the ground in rapid pulses. She literally vibrated her way across the surface.

She came straight to Marie and held out a rubbery tentacle that gripped a circular silver band. "Calibrated now. For you only."

Marie held out both hands and accepted the gift. "Thank you, Tonia. I'm honored to receive this technology. I... can't wait to try it out."

"Do so now, please." The others gathered around.

"How?" Marie asked.

"I believe you wear it," Zin said. He stood to one side of the group. Zin could be surprisingly quiet when he wanted to blend with the background.

Marie examined the metal ring. There were several components attached to it, but if there was a proper way to wear it, she couldn't tell. She placed it over her head, pushing it down until it stopped above her ears. "Like this?"

Tonia dipped. "To activate, tap twice on the side."

Marie did as instructed. "What's next?"

"You won't need my help," Tonia said.

And she was right. Marie looked up. The deep azure sky was still dotted with pink clouds, but it was now interwoven with a much more complex overlay of colors, lines and data, as if her own eyes had suddenly become computer displays.

A gradient of color represented temperature, with warm shades of orange near the surface cooling to green and blues higher up. The visual wasn't labeled in any way as temperature; Marie simply understood. Embedded within the colors were directional wind vectors, as if someone had thrown a handful of straw in the air and each shaft had aligned with the local swirls and eddies of moving air. The lines twisted in real time as the wind changed.

"Oh my God, it's magical," Marie said. "So rich. It's like I've never seen the sky before."

"You understand how to use the device?" Tonia asked.

Layers, she thought. Many of them, each depicting one facet of the wealth of information making up the physical world. Flip between them, visualize them separately, or together. "Yes, I see how it works." How she'd come to this realization was a mystery, but there it was. No training required.

Stephanie stood next to Marie and looked in the same direction. "What do you see that I don't?"

"It's really quite amazing." Marie described it as best she could, though her words didn't really do it justice. She started to take the headband off to let Stephanie try it out, but Tonia held out a tentacle.

"Do not. Marie only."

It was unfortunate the amazing device couldn't be shared. The colors were vibrant, and the information depicted was so detailed. She could have spent the rest of the day just absorbing the Newtonian physics available in every direction, but Tonia interrupted. "Use the visceral communication layer and we'll begin."

Without the headband, Marie wouldn't have had a clue how to choose this layer, or even what data it provided. With the headband, it was obvious. She flipped, and the visual demonstration of atmospheric motion disappeared.

"Today is different," Tonia stated to the group. "Unlike Dancers, you do not meet Workers. It is better if Aastazin explains." She motioned to Zin with a tentacle that looked almost like gold foil.

Zin stepped to the front. "What Aainatonia means is that we won't be meeting them, we'll be observing them. Please don't take it personally, but the invitation to come to Ixtlub was from the Dancers alone. Initially the Workers refused to participate on religious grounds. You are outsiders, and the Workers live by a principle they call *doubt*, which helps them distinguish good from evil. Doubt was cast upon you by their spiritual leader, which precluded any formal meetings." He looked around at each person on the team. Most seemed to take the slight in stride. "The Workers' initial stance was firm, but it was moderated by some influence from the Dancers. It was one of the topics that delayed my arrival yesterday."

"The Dancers twisted an arm, as humans say," Tonia added. "They offered more kleek shell."

"Yes," continued Zin. "The Workers grind a particular seashell to powder and smoke it. Kleek shell is found only in Dancer territory, and so it becomes a powerful currency between the species."

"They agree now to limited contact with humans," Tonia said. "You will be allowed in their community but will observe only."

"Is that alright?" Zin asked. There were nods all around.

"Marie will observe more," Tonia said.

Zin nodded. "Yes. Be aware, Marie, that you will visualize what the rest cannot. Feel free to let others know what you see."

The nearby trees parted and a large animal with multiple legs stepped through. Tonia swiveled. "Our escort arrives."

The Worker stood on four sturdy legs that angled like the hind legs of a horse. Each tapered to a padded foot. Two additional armlike appendages dangled in front ending in a flat hand, like a flipper. Its body was covered in a thick carpet of hair that glistened with oil of some kind. It had a long neck that lifted from the front and ended in a cone shape that was split into four sections that moved like lips over a central mouth. There was no head to speak of, but two slender stalks protruded from the conical end of the neck, about eight inches long, with glassy blue marbles perched at the ends.

The beast stopped before it reached the group and stood tall on its four hind legs. Stretched to its full height, the Worker towered over them. Marie's visualization provided details, though she had no idea how the information entered her mind: 3.4 meters in height, 1,240 kilos.

Giant sloths had roamed the Earth before humans. There were some similarities.

Tonia motioned to the slothlike creature. "This Worker will escort us. Do you have any questions?"

The creature's mouth moved, its four segments shifting as if it were chewing. It emitted a low groaning sound. *Follow me*, it seemed to be saying.

"Did you guys hear that?" Marie asked, looking around at her teammates.

"Yeah," Tim said. "The thing is a farm animal."

Marie had heard the same groaning sound but also its meaning. It had not used words per se, but the meaning was just as clear. This was definitely no farm animal.

"Only you will understand," Tonia said to Marie. "The others will hear only vibrations."

Beastlike, but intelligent. It was dressed, too... in a way. A dull-colored cloth hung over its back, with holes cut for each of its four hind legs. A patch of cloth hung over its rear end, covering sexual organs—at least, that was what the visualization indicated. Two sex organs; each individual was both male and female.

The Worker turned and started down a gravel path in a slow, plodding step. Tonia and Zin followed behind, and the group of humans fell in line after them. From behind, the Worker smelled. Not like a farm animal and not entirely bad, but a foody smell, like cheese, or maybe warm milk.

One planet, two intelligent species, Marie thought. *But they couldn't be more different. Something similar could have happened on Earth if dolphins had developed further.*

~~~~~~~~~~~~~~~~~~~~~~

The Worker village was less developed than anything they'd seen in the realm of the Dancers. Buildings were made of wood frames with rusting metal roofs and sides open to the air. The tropical trees and dense vegetation gave it a South Pacific island look. They walked along a curving main road of dirt. At one point a vehicle passed by, rolling on multiple wheels that could easily have been made of hard rubber.

They turned down a smaller dirt path, which brought them to a clearing in the trees and the largest building in the village. The noise of machinery could be heard, with much activity visible through its open sides. A mechanical view of a factory seemed to appear on its own inside Marie's head. She visualized a repetitive process, an assembly line with the clamor coming primarily from the machines, not the dozens of Workers who took positions along the line.

"We will pass through the factory just once," Tonia said. "Observe, but please do not stop. We will talk once we arrive in their quiet room."

It was a sweatshop, literally. Metal machines were everywhere, turning axles, spinning drills and generating an overwhelming heat. Steam-powered, as Marie's mechanical visualization told her, though there was also overhead lighting that looked similar to electric lights on Earth.

Long tables with Workers on each side held parts of some kind that were being passed from one individual to the next, each Worker fitting a new component into the device and checking its function. Their flat flipperlike hands were split down the middle, and the creatures were surprisingly adept at manipulating cylindrical tools that helped in their work.

Unfortunately, the place stunk—a combination of an oil smell and the stink of rotting food. Most of the smell seemed to be coming from tall open-top cylinders positioned next to each table. They looked like garbage cans.

Every Worker wore a headband almost identical to the one on Marie's head. In their case, it rested near the end of their necks, looking almost like a dog collar. Marie flipped to a communications layer and visualized a deep blue radio link between her headband and the nearest Worker, but the same link cascaded from one Worker to the next. None of the beasts spoke; their headbands provided full communication as they assembled the parts of whatever machine they were building.

They worked with an intensity and maintained undistracted focus. Marie could feel it, sense it. Remarkably, a group of humans was walking through their factory only a few feet away from their activity, yet none of the Workers seemed to notice.

She could have picked up one of the metal bars leaning against a post and struck one of the Workers across its back, but there was little doubt that its focus would have remained fixed on its purpose. Bred to work? Or controlled by the headband? The answer wasn't clear.

One Worker turned to the cylindrical garbage can, lowered its neck and spewed a stream of greenish-yellowish liquid from its mouth, some of which splattered across the cylinder's side. Another Worker next to it did the same. The disgusting moves were repeated as a wave of Workers spat into the cans and then returned to their work. It appeared to be a group bodily function of some kind, like a communal bathroom break. The stink in the factory increased noticeably.

They exited the factory, and Marie and Stephanie exchanged glances of disgust. The group was ushered into a separate building, the only one they'd seen with walls. The noise of the factory disappeared when a door closed behind them.

"Well, that was revolting," Stephanie said.

"Their work disturbs you?" Tonia asked.

"Not their work, their lack of personal hygiene. Sorry, I don't mean to be critical. I guess they're just different from us or the Dancers."

"The variety of life is notable," Tonia answered. "Even on your own world."

"My apologies to all of you," Zin said quite sympathetically. "I neglected to warn about the spitting. Their digestive systems are similar to your own, except that the bile you generate in your liver occurs in their throats. They must excrete it back through their mouth on occasion. I should have mentioned this, but my olfactory sensor was turned off."

Stephanie spoke quietly to Marie. "I'm withdrawing my earlier statement. I don't think I could live here."

"Not even on a temporary ambassador status?" Marie asked with a grin. "We can tag-team. I'll be the ambassador for the Dancers, and you can take the Workers."

"Very funny," Stephanie answered. "I think I'll stick to reporting."

~~~~~~~~~~~~~~~~~~~~~~~

Their guide brought them to two more buildings. The first was another factory, this one enclosed. The headband provided precise measurements of the components being manufactured, giving Marie a clear indication of high technology. At one point, the images projected into Marie's brain became distorted and fuzzy. It gave her a queasy feeling, and she pulled the band off for a few minutes.

Like virtual reality motion sickness? The queasiness soon passed, and she replaced the band on her head as they entered the second building.

It was described as a ceremonial hall, though as Tim suggested, church seemed to be a more apt description. Several Workers sat in a circle, drawing smoke from a communal pipe and chanting. Kleek shell, Zin identified. Their words honored their ancestors. It was all very interesting until one of the Workers pulled a small rodentlike animal from a box and popped the wriggling creature live into its mouth.

92

After the ceremony, they moved to an empty building next to the church for a lunch break, but no one was very hungry. Stephanie and Wesley engaged Zin and Tonia in a deep conversation about the relationship between the Dancers and the Workers. Tim sat on a porch step, sending a video message back to NASA through his hip-mounted relay. Marie wandered outside through the open doorway.

Still wearing the headband, Marie flipped through several fascinating layers of visualization. She scanned the palmlike trees and noticed the transpiration of water through their leaves and the process of photosynthesis discharging oxygen. Even if plant DNA was entirely different, plant chemistry was the same as on Earth.

A new layer popped up—something to do with communication alerts, though Marie had no idea how it had been selected. She tapped on the side of her head. "That's funny. I'm not sure I'm in control of this thing."

Tim looked up from his message. "Well, Kendrick, if you aren't, then nobody is."

From behind the church, the sky lit up in red.

Help me!

Marie swiveled, looking for the source. "Did you hear that?"

"Hear what?" asked Tim.

"A cry for help."

"You might want put that thing in airplane mode," Tim said. The red color behind the church intensified.

I am lost. Please help me!

It groaned. The cry was from a Worker, Marie was certain.

"Someone's in trouble." Marie ran a dozen steps to get a better view around the church. The visualization showed a red glow hovering over a clearing in the trees. An open platform stood alone in the clearing

93

with a figure standing in its center. "I'll be right back," Marie said to Tim and started toward the platform.

"Kendrick, just stay put," Tim griped. "You're imagining things."

Marie heard him, but the information within the communications alert visualization advised her otherwise. The deepening red color signified suffering and fear. A Worker was in agonizing pain. Marie ran toward the platform.

I have sinned. Doubt has been cast upon me. Save me!

The platform was a low wooden frame with another large plank of wood standing straight up from its surface. Heavy wood, very solid. The crying Worker was tied to the vertical plank, unable to move. Marie stopped at its edge and surveyed the scene. Except for the bound Worker, no one else was around. She stepped onto the platform.

Help me, Highest One. Please help me.

The Worker writhed in agony. A bloody slice had been taken from its hide in a loop around its body about two inches wide. A yellowy pus oozed from the terrible wound and fouled the platform. Bloody straps tied each leg to the plank.

Finally realizing the full extent of the horror, her stomach churned. "Oh my God, they've scalped it and tied it up with its own skin."

Tim came running up behind her. "Kendrick. What the hell are you doing?"

Marie spun around, her blood boiling with anger. "Monsters! They're crucifying their own!"

"Kendrick, it's none of our business." Tim grabbed her elbow.

"The hell it isn't." Marie felt the blood pressure in her head ready to burst the band. "Torture is everyone's business."

Marie suddenly felt dizziness sweeping over her. Overhead, the red sky turned black and her vision distorted. The Worker, still twisting against its bindings, transformed into a figure composed of thousands of dots. So did the platform. Vibrating dots, a bizarre scene of colored pixels all wiggling in place.

She lurched forward, trying to find something to steady herself. She touched flesh, bloody and oozing. She pulled her hand away and held it before her eyes.

It wasn't her hand at all. Thousands more of the vibrating dots covered what should have been fingers. The dots changed before her eyes, coming alive like a swarm of insects.

The buzzing, vibrating bugs crawled up her arm, advancing quickly. Her heart leaped and she shook her arm violently. Below, more insects covered the platform and began creeping up her legs beneath her jumpsuit. They pricked her skin with needlelike claws.

But it's not real. None of this is real.

The headband told her so. She fought to believe its lesson even as the sharp pain of a thousand insect stings invaded her nervous system.

She pivoted to run and fell off the platform. As she lay on the dirt, a wave of nausea overcame her. The last thing she saw was Tim's face, pixelated, vibrating, with hordes of crawling insects pouring from his eyes.

13 Brainwaves

The four katanauts walked briskly behind Jessica and past a line of reporters in the Kennedy Space Center O&C clean room. Zin followed at the rear, perhaps symbolically now that his job as guide was complete. All smiles, they waved to the cameras and acknowledged the applause from the small audience that rimmed the barrier. Tim high-fived his way down the line.

"Welcome home. How was it?" yelled a reporter as Marie walked past.

"Outstanding," she replied with what little enthusiasm she could muster. True enough for the first day of their mission. It would take some time to absorb and process the disturbing parts of the second day. Her mood was nearly as foul as the stench of Worker spit. Quite the opposite of how she had pictured their return.

She'd recovered from what was surely a hallucination. The crawling insects had eventually disappeared, and after waiting a few minutes for her pounding heart to calm, so did the fear. But the episode of the tortured Worker and Marie's subsequent collapse left her with a general unease—as if the mission had been compromised. Marie looked for someone to blame, but there was only herself. She shouldn't have tried to intervene in Worker justice. The emotional intensity had triggered something in the headband. Something inside her head too.

Jessica led them to another part of the building and paused just outside a kitchen, where the smell of coffee wafted into the hall. "Take some personal time, everyone," she told them. "Restrooms to your right; drinks and snacks are available in the break room. In a few minutes, we'll go into the debriefing room as a group. No press and no cameras, but there'll be plenty of big shots from NASA and ESA in there, so be ready."

Marie examined the alien device she held in one hand. Its highly polished silver surface and evenly spaced electronic components around the outside made it look a little like a crown that a princess might wear.

Yeah. The big shots will certainly want to hear about this thing.

She handed the ring to Jessica. "Hold this for a second." Without waiting for a response, Marie headed into the women's room. Stephanie was already there, checking her hair in the mirror.

Marie headed to the first sink and splashed cold water on her face repeatedly. She stared into the sink, watching the water circle the drain and droplets fall from her nose.

"You okay?" Stephanie asked.

"Yeah, fantastic," Marie said in a monotone.

"You don't look fantastic. You look beat."

"Yeah? Well, I'm doing cartwheels inside."

"It's that crown thing, isn't it? You hate it."

"There's no rule that says you have to like your job." Marie splashed more cold water on her face.

"Don't wear it anymore," Stephanie suggested. Her sympathy was welcome, but her solution was unrealistic. "Tell them you're not the right person to be handling such a burden."

"Yeah, *that* conversation would go well."

Stephanie swiveled. "Then *I'll* tell them."

Marie looked up, water dripping off her chin. She pointed a finger at Stephanie. "Don't you dare!" Her tone was sharp, her voice loud. "I volunteered, and I'm going to see this shitstorm through to the end, so just stay out of it." She immediately regretted her harsh words. Stephanie looked shocked and hurt. Marie hardly recognized herself.

She lowered her head and leaned both hands on the counter, water dripping from her nose. "Sorry, Steph... I... sorry."

The only women on the team had bonded, becoming more like friends than coworkers. How could they not? Together they'd visited another planet, and with all the drama of the second day, Stephanie had been nothing but kind. Marie felt like a different person had invaded her body. She'd never yelled at a colleague or a friend in her life.

Stephanie came closer and put a hand on her shoulder. "You've been through a lot. More than the rest of us. Be careful, will you?"

Marie smoothed the water off her face and reached for a paper towel. She looked Stephanie in the eyes, searching for the broader intuition provided by the alien device. An unnatural ability to see more than just reflected light in the visual spectrum … the ability to *visualize*.

Marie wasn't wearing the alien headband. Stephanie's eyes were eyes, nothing more. Marie dried her face with the towel and spoke quietly. "All my life, I've prepared for this opportunity. To step up. To make my family proud, make myself proud. To do what those macho guys out there couldn't do. It's here now, the opportunity. Maybe a little weirder than I'd imagined, but I'm not letting it go."

Stephanie nodded. "I get it. You're reaching for something bigger. Something important. I've been there myself. Sitting in that Soyuz rocket ready to launch, I figured I'd made the biggest blunder of my TV career. But I went ahead with it anyway."

Marie smiled and then chuckled. "Well, at T-minus ten, you probably didn't have many alternatives."

Stephanie laughed. "No, I guess you're right. So much for my grand words of inspiration for you."

"Steph, I've seen your broadcasts. You've got plenty of inspirational words in you. But maybe not this time."

Stephanie put a hand on each side of Marie's face, leaned close and kissed her once on each cheek. "*Mon amie.* As you Americans say, hang in there. Okay?"

The debriefing room was crowded with many faces that Marie didn't recognize. The NASA contingent sat along one side of a long table, Augustin Ibarra along with several other NASA administrators. The vice president of the United States sat at the far end of the table. She'd never seen the man in person before.

A NASA debrief specialist guided the conversation, and scientific people and administrators peppered the katanauts—and Zin, who chose to stand at the rear of the room—with questions. There was plenty of video from their mission, of course, but they all seemed to want to hear the story firsthand.

Stephanie provided commentary as they replayed the video from her headcam, both underwater and on land. Tim provided color as he recounted their visit to the Dancers' laboratory and described Beextu's warning about Core, even though he hadn't even been there to hear it. Marie added detail but otherwise let Tim's smug conceit slide since he was the de facto team leader.

Wesley, being the team sociologist, wrapped up one of the more heated discussions—the symbiotic relationship between the Dancers and Workers. The ESA director had asked the most questions, and he had one more. "The Dancers clearly characterize themselves as superior but benevolent. But all the evidence suggests a more sinister relationship. Perhaps master to slave?"

Wesley pondered the question before answering, as he had all the others. "Let me address your question obliquely first, then more directly. The Dancers are very open and quite forthcoming with what we might consider sensitive information. We were, for example, welcomed into one of their most advanced scientific laboratories. In fact, the lab was the whole reason why we were brought to this specific town. As we toured, we asked many questions, and none went unanswered. I explain this because each of us got the feeling that not only did they have nothing to hide but also that hiding information may not even be within their character."

"Oblique, but I understand your point," the ESA director said. "And it matches their unprompted revelation about Core. But more directly, what about the Workers?"

"Clearly the Dancers dominate the relationship," Wesley said. "The Workers would be nomadic scavengers without their guidance. But I found no hints of forced bondage, no subservience to the Dancers in either custom or law. They live with separate rules of law, separate policing and justice systems, separate religion. In fact, the Dancers have no religion, only the Workers. I can point only to one case of potential injustice, and that is the Dancers' willingness to withhold kleek shell—a kind of tobacco that the Workers consume. The substance is likely addictive, and the Dancers may use it as both incentive and punishment. But that's hardly master to slave; perhaps more like a dealer to an addict."

"How about the ring the Workers wear?" asked one of the engineering heads from NASA. "Could it also be a tool of enforcement or punishment?"

Katie, the debriefing specialist, stepped in. "That's the next topic we'll cover. The alien device, provided as a gift to Ms. Kendrick. Should we switch to that topic now?"

Several heads nodded, and Wesley acknowledged them. "I don't have anything else to add, and of course Marie is our expert on the communications device."

Katie resumed. "Fine. Just to set the stage, the device's purpose as interface between the Dancers and Workers was reasonably well understood prior to the mission, but none of us knew that it could be adapted for human use. Marie, could you tell us more about how you received this item and give us a sense of its capabilities?"

Marie cleared her throat. "Sure. It's right here." She held up the headband for everyone to see. "It's still a bit of an enigma, but at its simplest level I would say it provides a visualization of the physical world. Forces and motion, light from any portion of the EM spectrum. Things like that. Plus, it manages the complexity of the incoming data, providing mathematics and analysis on the fly. The engineers will have to tell you how it gathers and processes so much information, but what it presents to me is a very elegant view of a very complex world."

"The Dancers gave it to you?" Ibarra asked. "Why you?"

"It wasn't really the Dancers; it was their representative, Tonia. She visited our sleeping quarters at the end of day one and explained that each Worker wore one around its neck, or snout, or whatever you call that part of its anatomy. She said it provides the Workers with insight that they couldn't achieve on their own. Apparently, the Dancers think of it as their gift to the Workers because it boosts Worker intellect to something closer to the Dancers' level. Without it, the Workers would have never developed technologically."

Marie looked down at the alien headband lying on the table. "So, why me? Well... Tonia asked if we'd like to experience its capabilities for ourselves, and I volunteered."

"To be clear," Katie added, "we believe the device was initialized specifically for Marie. No one else can use it."

"That's right," Marie said. "Tuned to my brainwave pattern, or something like that."

"And they offered it to no one else?" Ibarra asked.

"Tonia said she could only make one."

Wesley raised a hand and added, "Zin suggested Marie would be the best candidate. As I recall, the rest of us agreed."

Zin stood silently at the back of the room. Now that she had experienced the full effect of the alien device, Marie wondered if Zin had known what it might do to her. Intentionally scrambling her brain didn't seem like it fit with Zin's character.

"Does the device still work?" asked a European man whom Marie didn't recognize. "Even now that you're back on Earth?"

"It should," Marie answered. "It was intended as a gift to take home. A benefit to humans in general, not just me."

"So, you can *visualize*, as you say, things that no one else can?" the man asked.

"Yes." Marie knew what the next question would be.

"Can you demonstrate this to us?"

Marie looked at Ibarra, her eyes asking him if she should do as requested.

"Is it safe?" Ibarra asked Marie.

"Oh, yes. Safe. It certainly doesn't affect anyone else, just me."

"It doesn't hurt, does it?" Ibarra asked.

"Oh, no. Doesn't hurt," she answered. "It's just... foreign." Her heart beat a bit faster. *Foreign* was the understatement of the day. With twenty people staring she wasn't ready to explain her personal problem. She'd talk to Ibarra alone. Later.

"So, what could you do with it in this room?" Ibarra asked.

"Probably a lot," Marie answered. She could only imagine the capability of the device within an ordinary office building on Earth. She'd already seen what it could do on Ixtlub.

Marie took a deep breath. Putting the headband on in front of all these people was like trying on a new bikini. You never knew what embarrassing part of your body it might expose.

I'm the messenger. Step up to the task. Be brave.

She lifted the ring from the table and placed it over her head. The headband fit snugly over her hair and rested just above her ears. Everyone in the room watched as she tapped twice on a component at her right temple and closed her eyes.

Her head swiveled as her eyes remained closed. Her mind envisioned pink. "Wow. Right away I see electricity. All around us."

She stood up and pointed straight overhead at a pink line glowing brightly in her mind. "There's an electrical wire above the ceiling. The wire runs to the wall and then down behind the wallboard to an electrical outlet." She pointed directly to the pink glow on the wall.

"You can see the electricity?" a woman asked.

"A pink glow. It tells me it's an electromagnetic field," Marie answered. "The wire stands out like a sore thumb, but there's a weaker field, slightly less pink than the wire, all around us. It's a north-south orientation, so it must be Earth's magnetic field."

"Hang on," Ibarra pulled out his phone and accessed a compass app. "Based on what you see, Marie, point north."

She stood and pointed, her eyes still closed.

Ibarra examined the phone and nodded. "Spot-on."

"But electromagnetic fields are just one layer," Marie said.

"Layers?" somebody said.

"Yeah, I can control them. Many layers of information, most of them color-coded. I'll flip to another one."

"Did they teach you how to do this?"

"No. I..." She wasn't sure they'd believe her. But this wasn't the place to obfuscate, so the unvarnished truth came out. "They didn't teach me any of this. My ability to control this, well... it feels like I've always known how to do it."

She could visualize their reaction; she didn't need to see their faces. Skepticism. The device told her everything she needed, mapped out in a pattern that was easily recognizable. Every observable event—visual, audible, vibrational or otherwise—was measured, matched, and displayed for her to absorb. Big Data, a computer scientist would call it.

Show. Don't tell. They'll come around.

"Mr. Vice President," she said. "Your heartbeat." She tapped rhythmically on the table with her fingernail. "Put a finger to your carotid artery and see if I'm right."

She didn't need to see that the vice president had done just that and confirmed to everyone that her taps exactly matched the rhythm he felt.

"You're just one, Mr. Vice President. I see every heartbeat. Every breath, too, and more." She flipped again, not even realizing how she did it. The space in the room warped, bending toward some point far below their feet. "I see gravity. I'm not just experiencing its pull, like we all do. I can see it."

"What does gravity look like?" asked an older man sitting next to Stephanie.

"Bent space. Bent everything. Nothing in this room is quite straight."

She flipped again to a scene of staggering complexity. Infinitesimals, everywhere, all around. Each tiny bit interacting with every other tiny bit. Trillions, quadrillions, vastly more. The sheer number was overwhelming, yet somehow her mind grasped them all simultaneously. Moreover, she could zoom in or out at will from a single speck to a collection of trillions.

"The molecules of air, nitrogen, oxygen, argon, carbon dioxide and water." She waved her hands over her head and tilted her head up, her eyes still closed. "They do a strange dance with each other down at the microscopic level, with varying levels of interaction above that, all

104

the way to the larger eddies at the macroscopic level." She pointed to the back of the room. "There's a lot of turbulent motion from a flow coming out of that air conditioning vent."

Complexity was by far the most difficult visualization. There were just too many bits of information. How could any single mind keep track of them all? She couldn't, yet somehow, she did. The complexity hurt, not with any pain, but with an intense anxiety, as if she was responsible for the trajectory of individual molecules in the air. It weighed upon her; it scared her.

It was time for the closing act, and she knew exactly which layer to choose. She flipped again, opened her eyes and looked around the room. She caught the eye of one of the ESA administrators near the back of the room. "No, sir, I'm not."

He looked puzzled. "Not what?"

"Making this up."

"You're suggesting you can read my mind?" he asked.

"Isn't that the statement you were about to make?"

He shifted uncomfortably in his seat. "Yes, I suppose, but not quite that bluntly."

"Wait a second." Ibarra held up a hand. "You can read minds?"

"No, sir," Marie said. "It's like... I can see you, or maybe it's an image of you that hasn't quite happened yet. But in my mind, you're already talking. I can't hear the words, but I can still make out what you're saying. It seems to be accessing tiny bits of time that exist at the subatomic level. I have no idea how I know that—it's kind of freaky."

Ibarra said nothing and kept his hand in the air for several seconds like he wanted her to read his mind.

Marie shrugged. "Sorry, nothing."

"True, I guess," Ibarra said. "I wasn't going to say anything, I just wanted to wait and see what you came up with... as a test."

Marie swiveled quickly to the ESA admin. "I agree."

"You agree with what?" he asked, his eyebrows furrowed.

"That Mr. Ibarra's test was unscientific. You were going to say that, am I right?"

He nodded without comment.

Marie closed her eyes again and tapped the side of the ring. She took it off and laid it on the table. She lowered her head and sat down. "I'm sorry, it's tiring."

The device was more than tiring. It produced an instant spike of anxiety and a mood swing far worse than any PMS. She would need to elaborate, including the hallucination she'd experienced on Ixtlub, an event that would certainly be in Tim's written report. But the mental collapse had felt so personal—like something wrong in her own brain, not the headband.

Maybe she'd ask Zin to join her in Ibarra's office. He might be able to shed some light on how the device was supposed to work. After all, he had seemed very supportive on Ixtlub just before their return to Earth.

No one else on the team could have done any better, Zin had told her.

14 Singularity

Within the Fermilab control room up on the surface, walls shook, lights flickered, and dust rained down from ceiling tiles. A deep rumble from far below screamed catastrophic structural failure. Cody's training in emergency procedures kicked in. Alarms sounded, emergency services were notified, and within five minutes Cody had the accelerator shut down. His next moves were purely personal.

The steps on the metal staircase were a blur as he raced downward. The smell of smoke was unmistakable, but there were no obvious signs of what had gone wrong. He held his portable radio transceiver in one hand. Multiple calls to Nala had gone unanswered.

At basement level three, a fire crew had just arrived and were connecting a hose into a water outlet. One of the crew yelled at him as he rushed by, but he didn't pause. The hallway was cloudy with smoke and dust, but still no sign of a fire. Nobody was going to hold him back from finding out what had happened.

He turned the corner and skidded to a stop. His mouth hung open.

The Diastasi lab was gone; most of the hallway too. He stared into a cavernous crater of shredded concrete. Dangling wires showered sparks, and severed pipes emptied their contents into a vast hollowed-out sphere, an empty space where the interior of the building had once stood. On the far side, at least forty meters away, the hallway continued as normal, though the overhead lights flashed on and off irregularly. The empty hole was as deep and high as it was wide—as if someone had taken a giant ice cream scoop and removed a ball-like chunk from the building.

"Jesus Christ," Cody whispered. He ran one hand through his hair. "What the hell happened?"

In the center of the hollow space floated a single point of light, intensely bright but concentrated. Smoke and dust slowly circled in a disc shape, spiraling inward toward the light.

Cody's heart pounded and his eyes watered. "Nala! Thomas!" he yelled into the emptiness.

There was no response. How could there be? There was nothing left of the lab or its occupants. His colleagues—his friends—were gone.

~~~~~~~~~~~~~~~~~~~~~~~

Jan Spiegel wore a dust mask over his nose and mouth with safety glasses covering his eyes. Jae-ho Park, Fermilab's director, was outfitted in the same way. Both men stood behind plastic ribbon with the words *Do Not Cross* repeated along its length. On the other side, the hallway flooring was badly broken before disappearing into the monstrous hole.

On the far side, a ladder leaned against what was left of the corridor floor, and the voices of several firemen could be heard from the depths of the hole.

"It's gone, the whole lab is gone," Jan said, shaking his head from side to side. "It's impossible to believe."

"What happened?" Park asked. "Any idea yet?"

"Instability of some kind," Jan answered. "Nala had found some anomalies, but we didn't have enough data to know what was going on."

"And the light? You think it's a singularity?"

Jan nodded. "Probably. Nala described something similar yesterday, but much smaller. She thought she had created a singularity from the 4-D collapse. She must have adjusted some parameters and made it worse."

"It wasn't Nala's fault," Park said solemnly. "We all did this."

Jan hung his head. "You're right. She explained the spatial instabilities to me. I threw it all back on her shoulders. I should have helped. Hell, I should have told them to stop."

Nala's explanation was the most likely answer. Four-dimensional space had violently collapsed, taking three-dimensional space with it. The light hanging in the center of the hole was all that was left—a singularity, a zero-dimensional point of energy, lacking any mass or volume. The phenomenon would require more study to determine if the theory was accurate. Unfortunately, the only lab in the western hemisphere that could do the job was now crushed into oblivion, along with the scientists who operated it.

Jan swallowed hard. They had made progress, but there was still so much they didn't fully understand. Like any discovery, they had unlocked a treasure of knowledge with enormous potential to benefit humanity. But dangers lurked, made clear in the cruelest of ways. Jan had underestimated those dangers, and Nala and Thomas had paid with their lives.

~~~~~~~~~~~~~~~~~~~~~~

Emergency responders had scoured the pit and the side corridors for any signs of survivors and checked the rest of the building for damage. Police were called in too, but they did little more than gather information from witnesses and file a missing persons reports. The first responders eventually gave way to the more technical people, those who better understood the function of one of the most advanced scientific facilities in the world.

The Chicago office of the Department of Energy sent the same safety inspector who had signed off on their adjusted operating plan only a few days before. He seemed upset that he'd been fooled by "that female physicist" until someone told him Nala had been killed in the accident. Then he quieted down.

DOE managers and engineers arrived, some from out of state. They set up monitoring equipment at the edge of the pit, sampled the air, and photographed the magically floating light in its center from every angle.

Later, hazard inspectors from the International Atomic Energy Agency arrived. None of the visitors could provide any insight into the accident, and their only recommendation was to suspend operations. Given the damage, restarting operations wasn't even an option.

Those who were already there, the team of physicists and engineers working at Fermilab, continued to be the best source of ideas as to what had gone wrong and what they might do differently. Most of the assessment fell to Jan Spiegel.

15 Electricity

The hot Texas sun and southern humidity were a powerful combination. Davis Garrity took off his suit coat and laid it across the seat of his rental car, hoping his neatly pressed shirt would hold up for another hour. Today's meeting was outdoors by design.

He took shelter under a lonely live oak tree, the power generating station's nod to landscaping. The sparse shade did little to relieve the steam bath of ranch country east of Austin.

The facility was one of the largest in the world. On one side was a railyard. Three times each day, a long train of more than a hundred cars pulled up and unloaded its contents. Forty-five thousand tons of coal a day, every day. In the center of the expansive complex were four enormous steel buildings, each one larger in bulk than any of the gleaming skyscrapers in downtown Austin. Coal entered each building via a covered conveyor belt. Electricity came out the other side, carried by high-voltage towers that disappeared across the rolling hills toward Austin and San Antonio.

Towering five hundred feet into the air above each of the four buildings stood a gray concrete smokestack. Two of the stacks poured a whitish cloud into the sky. A third stack did the same, but since it was venting through a carbon-capture system, the smoke density was somewhat lower.

The fourth stack, the one closest to Davis, was topped with the newest symbol of clean energy—a blue-and-orange Garrity Cap. Its bold colors and placement high above ground allowed it to be seen by anyone within twenty miles of the facility. Not a whiff of smoke came out.

Garrity pulled out an oversized sheet of paper and compared his client site sketch to the real thing. The sketch's simplicity made it more likely to be reprinted, posted online and presented on television news. Free publicity.

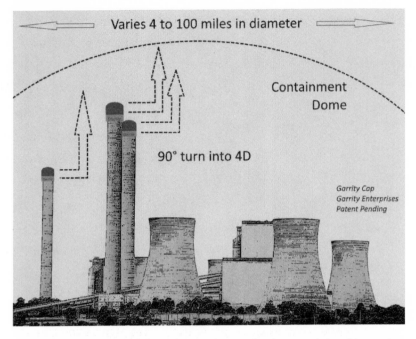

Varies 4 to 100 miles in diameter

Containment Dome

90° turn into 4D

Garrity Cap
Garrity Enterprises
Patent Pending

He had a second diagram in the works that explained how the containment dome was set up and managed. Davis didn't really understand that part of the equation, but his Romanian partners did. He'd been lucky to make the connection. A friend of a friend. A few phone calls, and he had been put in touch with a science lab in Romania of all places. What they did and how they did it was fancy footwork as far as Davis was concerned, but the Romanians claimed they could do the same thing that the US lab had done. Fermilab, the one that was in the news these days.

Best of all, the Romanians seemed anxious to get their foot in the door, and an industrial application in the United States was just the ticket. Davis had a good imagination. He didn't need to know exactly how this extradimensional space thing worked, only that it did work. Within two weeks, the Romanians had proven their ability to perform the space-science magic and a few days later Davis had a signed support contract.

Davis grinned like a kid who'd just discovered the hidden cookie jar. Manufacturing cost, a mere forty thousand dollars. Installation cost, not much more. Operating costs, relatively cheap thanks to low-cost Romanian scientists. For less than three hundred grand, he had just eliminated more than five million tons of carbon dioxide, sulfur dioxide, and other emissions. Conventional technology couldn't do half the job at a thousand times the price.

With the Garrity Cap, ElecTrek's operating costs would plummet, the citizens would get their electricity and nothing else but clean, sweet Texas air. And Davis... well, this gig was like printing money, with a hundred more customers lined up once he was done.

A black car with a state government license plate appeared from behind the nearest of the generating stations. It pulled up to the parking lot where Davis stood. Two men got out.

Davis reached out a hand. "Stan, how are you?"

Stan Wasserman introduced the heavyset man beside him as Ralph Lewis, head of the Texas Commission on Environmental Quality, the state agency that approved environmental permits and provided oversight for utilities.

"Commissioner, it's a great pleasure to meet you," Davis said, shaking the hand of the unexpected official. He knew Lewis by reputation; most citizens did too. An industry insider elevated to a government official, Lewis was well known for his colorful approach to regulations. In a TV interview that had gone viral, he had been quoted as saying that since scientists couldn't be trusted to tell the truth about climate change, they shouldn't be the ones setting limits on industrial emissions. When asked who should, he had famously replied, "Naturally, the people who know it best. Industry."

Davis didn't care what the rules were or who made the decisions, as long as those rules resulted in an expenditure by the power companies. The bigger the expense, the better. It just meant more savings once the Garrity Cap was installed.

Lewis's grip was strong and his voice gruff. "You put that colored cap on the stack?"

"Yes, sir," Davis answered. "The Garrity Cap. Zero emissions forevermore."

"So Stan told me. And it doesn't matter what they burn—the type of coal?"

"No, sir, they can choose whatever source of coal they want. Carbon emissions will still be zero. Sulfur too."

The commissioner turned toward the tall smokestack, seeming to judge for himself whether emissions were indeed zero. He waved at Wasserman. "You sure number four is still running?"

Stan Wasserman laughed. "Hard to believe, Ralph, but we've got unit four running at maximum turbine speed today. Doing the same for the other three units too... comparing apples to apples."

The commissioner nodded, his stubby fingers rubbed across his chin. "This could be good, real good. Will ya switch to Texas coal?"

Wasserman shrugged. "I don't see why not. Whether we're burning subbituminous from Wyoming or lignite from Texas, once you exclude emissions control, the cost per BTU is pretty similar. Clean coal, dirty coal. It doesn't matter."

"Don't call it dirty," Commissioner Lewis said. "Rename it. Call it *clean lignite*, the pride of Texas."

"Clean lignite," Wasserman repeated. "Now that's a word combination you don't hear every day."

"If y'all have some free cash floatin' around, you might think about investing in Texas lignite stock. After we get done rebranding, as they say, I'd be surprised if those stocks didn't take off for the heavens." The commissioner turned to Davis, who ignored the obvious insider trading remark. "How fast can you get caps on the other three stacks?"

Davis knew the question was coming, and he was ready. "Commissioner, you'll be happy to hear that I have three more caps sitting in a warehouse less than an hour away. As soon as Stan gives me the green light, we'll get them installed faster than you can get the TV news cameras out here."

"I tell you, son, you readin' my mind."

Having the air quality commissioner for the state of Texas standing right in front of him was an unexpected bonus. The timing was perfect. Davis reached into his pocket and pulled out a smaller version of the easily recognizable blue-and-orange cap. He held it up for both men to see.

"What the hell, Davis?" Stan said. "You always carry one of these around to do your magician's trick?"

"The trick's even better this time," Davis said. "With the commissioner here, it's a good time to unveil phase two of my plan."

Both men looked at the small PVC pipe, perplexed. It had none of the grand statement made by the huge cap on top of the smokestack. But once its purpose was understood, the little brother packed just as much punch.

"Phase two goes way beyond power generation, beyond every industrial emission. Let me show you." Davis opened the door to his rental car and pressed the start engine button. He closed the car door and, with the engine still running, walked to the rear bumper and bent down, coughing for effect. "Typical car exhaust. Plenty of carbon dioxide and carbon monoxide. Bad stuff, even with today's auto emissions standards."

He fitted the cap over the exhaust pipe and remained squatting, his head very near the exhaust pipe. He took a deep breath. "As fresh as a spring morning. Gentlemen, with the Garrity Exhaust Connector, that smog layer hovering over Houston that we're all so familiar with? We'll never see it again. I've already contracted with a company that can have a half million of these manufactured in a few weeks."

The commissioner seemed deep in thought. "Well, I'll be damned. Same thing? Zero emissions?"

"Yes, sir," Davis answered.

"No carbon at all?"

"None."

"Jesus," the commissioner said. He turned to Wasserman. "A two-for-one." He rubbed his chin again. "Yeah... we could do some mighty fine promotions on this one. This little gadget on the tail end of every car makes good ol' Texas gasoline a lot more attractive, plus it gets rid of the global warming thing all at the same time."

Wasserman laughed. "Damn, Ralph. Aren't you the guy who says global warming is all a hoax?"

"Hell, it's just politics, Stan. We say what we say. But now... we got a chance to act. The public loves action."

Wasserman shook his head, a good-natured smile on his face. "You know, Ralph, the wonders of this world will never cease to amaze me." He slapped the commissioner's back. "Ralph Lewis, the face of the climate change deniers everywhere, is now going to be the world's savior. The guy who solves global warming."

They were neglecting Davis's role in world salvation, but it didn't bother him in the least. Let the big dogs take credit—that was his motto. As long as their cash kept rolling in, it was all good.

16 Regulators

Daniel Rice drove up the busy boulevard through Austin, Texas, crossing over the Colorado River. Dozens of gleaming office towers lined the other side of the river, and the Texas state capitol building loomed at the far end of the street. Austin wasn't the modest city he remembered visiting as a child. Tourists still came to witness a million or more bats emerge each evening from crevices under the Congress Avenue bridge, and many of the older sections of downtown still had that 1970s look, but an entirely new business district had sprouted skyward over the years, giving Austin a big-city feel.

A few minutes later, he pulled into the parking lot next to the J.J. Pickle Federal Building, one of those dated "modern" buildings from the age of Led Zeppelin and ABBA that now looked terribly out of place among the skyscrapers. In the lobby, he searched for Environmental Protection Agency on the list of agencies. Fifth floor.

It felt good getting back to work. Real work. The kind that didn't involve alien cyborgs or guest appearances on late-night television shows. His current assignment was positively dull by comparison, and in Daniel's mind dull was just fine. The case was still related to the new dimensional technologies trail-blazed by Fermilab, but then maybe everything would be from here on out. The world had changed eight months prior. Science, culture, and business too.

It was an unusual circumstance. The EPA had issued an air quality permit to a power plant in Texas. Nothing strange there. But the director at the EPA was concerned about this case, primarily because four more permit applications just like it had come in. It wasn't every day that a major power plant proposed to redirect effluents into another dimension.

The EPA was stumped. The proposal satisfied every regulation. It certainly wasn't illegal dumping. Didn't produce any hazards to flight, or wildlife, or water quality. The caps at the top of smokestacks weren't even a visual eyesore. They had no reason to deny the permit—except that it didn't feel right.

The EPA administrator had called Spencer Bradley, the president's national science advisor and director of the Office of Science and Technology Policy, and Bradley had put Daniel on the case.

A scientific investigation. It was what Daniel did. Or at least, it was what he used to do before he'd become the primary representative of the human species to an alien civilization, before he'd conducted five Q&A sessions with Core, and before he had become the face of science to the general public. Even if the case was dull, it felt like coming home.

This type of meeting was always tricky. Ostensibly, it was a technology review between the EPA and representatives from the power company. But in this case, the power company, ElecTrek Inc., had asked a contractor to represent them—the guy who had come up with the plan, Davis Garrity.

The office of the EPA district manager, Jeffrey Finch, was small, with a dirty window overlooking an alley. Finch pushed an oversized paper across his desk to Daniel. It was a diagram of the power facility, showing an orange-and-blue cap at the top of each of three smokestacks. The cap made a right-angled turn with dashed lines indicating that it somehow disappeared into four-dimensional space.

Daniel brushed his hair back with one hand as he examined the diagram. "Impressive, if it really works. They've tested this?"

Finch, a younger man with curly hair and wire-rim glasses, sat back in his chair. "I've seen it myself. Amazing stuff. I really don't understand how the 4-D part works, but the cap reduces the emissions to zero. The ElecTrek Bastrop County generating station is easily meeting every EPA standard—heck, zero is zero. They're banking daily carbon offsets that are blowing every other utility out of the water."

Daniel looked up from the papers. "I know what the 4-D technology can do. It's astonishing, no question. And maybe this pipe invention could work." Daniel shook his head. "But damn, they got this system up and running fast. Have you reviewed the process they're using to create this containment dome?" He pointed to the curving dashed line enveloping the power facility.

"I haven't," Finch said. "Only the emissions control device, which in this case is the cap. It's dead-simple: a twelve-foot-wide cover made from PVC. No moving parts, and it doesn't affect the power plant's function in any way. There's really nothing else for us to review."

"There's the four-dimensional space they're using as a dumping ground."

Finch shook his head. "Our legal guy says that's beyond scope. The Clean Air Act speaks to emissions control devices and air quality standards—in three-dimensional space, mind you. ElecTrek has fulfilled their obligation to demonstrate control and meet the standards. I don't have the legal authority to ask them to do any more."

Daniel recognized the problem, an age-old dilemma of regulatory authority precisely constricted by the very legislation that had created the regulations in the first place. It would literally take another act of Congress to expand their authority to another dimension of space. Government oversight usually lagged well behind the pace of technology.

Finch glanced at a message flashing on his phone. "One minute, Mr. Garrity just arrived." He stepped away to an outer office and came back with two men in tow. He introduced Daniel to Davis Garrity and Ralph Lewis from the Texas CEQ. A Texas state official accompanying Garrity provided a big hint that the businessman had done his homework and established the right connections.

"Nice to meet you, Dr. Rice," Davis Garrity said. "I've seen you on TV talking about four-dimensional space, and in a very entertaining way, I might add. I do love your descriptions of this strange outer space fellow you've been talking to. Quite the story."

"It is, Mr. Garrity," Daniel answered. "Quite the story. But today I'm playing a different role, as a federal science investigator invited here by the EPA."

"Of course," Garrity said. "I understand you have some questions about the ElecTrek project?"

Before Daniel could respond, Lewis interjected. "We can save you and the feds a helluva lot of time. This whole thing's gonna be on the local news tonight. The nice folks over at TV4 were all over it. Davis and I just got back from the Bastrop plant. Still no emissions. Clean as a whistle."

Daniel sat down and waited for the others to take a chair. The meeting wasn't going to end until he had all the information he could gather, pleasantries notwithstanding.

"Glad to hear," Daniel said. "We all like clean power plants. Commissioner Lewis, I understand that your state agency had to sign off on the permit in addition to the EPA. Did anyone in your office conduct a review of the process that creates the containment dome over the ElecTrek facility?"

"Not directly, no," Lewis said. "Texas CEQ doesn't regulate airspace, but we did pass the permit application along to the FAA. They declined to comment."

Daniel nodded. He could just imagine what people who regulated aviation safety thought about receiving an air quality permit application. "I'm not surprised. Not within their domain either. Gentlemen, it seems that we have multiple agencies, none of whom are responsible for examining this new technology." He turned to Garrity. "Mr. Garrity, do you mind if I ask some questions about this process?"

"I'll do my best to answer," Garrity responded.

"Great. Let's talk about neutrinos. To create four-dimensional space, you have to start with a coherent beam of neutrinos, right?" It was a fairly basic question, one that Daniel had explained multiple times in science programs targeted at high school–aged kids.

Garrity looked slightly perplexed, like he'd been asked to name the capital of North Dakota. "Uh, right. Coherent neutrinos."

Daniel leaned forward in his chair. "Can you tell me what kind of positioning accuracy you have for a neutrino beam that is targeting Austin, Texas, all the way from Romania?" Neutrinos stopped for nothing, not even the bulk of the Earth, so there was no reason to doubt that the Romanians could send a beam through ten thousand kilometers of rock. Accuracy was the only question.

"Oh, the lab handles all of that," Garrity said, very sure of himself. "I couldn't tell you how many miles we are from Romania, but I do know the scientists over there are very accurate."

Daniel stepped up to the next level but still stuck to a question that anyone creating 4-D space would need to understand. "Okay. There are a couple of techniques for maintaining a permanent 4-D bubble. Are you locking the phase oscillation or using the newer harmonic resonance technique?"

Garrity's face went blank. "Uh… I know we have that covered, but I'd have to ask my colleagues in Romania to be sure."

The pattern was plain—a test was in order. "How about the chakra of the phlebotinum atoms?"

"Don't worry, Romania's got that covered too. They take care of it all."

Daniel nodded. "Mr. Garrity, how well would you say you understand the process of redirecting effluents into four-dimensional space?"

"I've got a patent pending on it. I invented it."

"Nicely done, it *is* a clever idea. But I'm a little concerned about the basis in science. Mr. Garrity, there's no such thing as phlebotinum and atoms don't have chakras. People don't either, by the way."

Garrity shrugged. "So what? Like I said, Romania handles it."

Daniel took a deep breath. He wasn't going to let this slide. They'd already seen a major blunder from the Chinese attempting to use this technology. "I understand your reliance on your partner in Romania. But it's clear that you personally don't have any knowledge of the process or even the basic facts of the science."

Ralph Lewis interrupted, holding up a hand in front of Garrity. "Dr. Rice, let's not talk about your facts or my facts—it doesn't get us anywhere. Let's talk about what *works*. Go out to the Bastrop facility and see for yourself. It works."

It was always astonishing how badly mangled the meaning of words had become in the modern world, especially those words related to science. There was a time when a fact had been an accepted truth. Not anymore. For some, the word *fact* had become synonymous with a claim or assertion. Any person offering an argument could simply stack up their own set of alternative facts and, in their mind, be entirely justified. It often left Daniel wondering if there was any hope for the evolution of the species.

Daniel glanced at Finch, who just shrugged. He probably dealt with this type of ungrounded argument all the time. It wasn't the time for confrontation; this was a mission to gather information.

"Okay," Daniel said. "I'll take you up on your offer to visit the plant."

"Stan Wasserman's your man," Lewis said. He nudged Garrity, who wrote a phone number on a business card and handed it to Daniel. "I'll let him know you're coming."

~~~~~~~~~~~~~~~~~~~~~~

Daniel sat alone at an Austin hotel bar, absorbing the events of the day. A late-afternoon tour of the Bastrop facility had provided an opportunity to witness firsthand the remarkable application of 4-D technology. The plant manager had walked him through the combustion building, where pulverized coal was blown into a firebox that boiled water to steam and spun huge electric turbines. Inside, the facility was hot and noisy, but outside, the towering smokestack looked unused, capped at its top without a trace of smoke coming out.

Clean energy from coal. It would certainly make a good brochure or television commercial, but it didn't sit right with Daniel's wider view of how things should work. Somewhere out there in the weird world of four-dimensional space was a cauldron of exhaust. Maybe it would remain safely tucked away in its own corner of the universe, but the number of unknowns was disturbing.

Daniel picked up his vibrating phone from the bar counter. A call from Spencer Bradley, probably to see how the initial meeting had gone.

"Hi, Spence," Daniel answered. "I've made contact, but I can't say I have any answers yet."

"It's not that," Bradley said. His voice was serious. "It's news. Very bad news, I'm afraid."

Daniel felt his body tense. "I'm here."

"There's been a terrible accident at Fermilab. An explosion of some kind. There were casualties."

A chill ran across the back of his neck. He felt he knew what Bradley might say next.

"One of them was Nala Pasquier. I know the two of you became close. I'm so sorry."

The phone slid down Daniel's cheek as his grip loosened. He stared straight ahead, absorbing the meaning of Bradley's words. Tears began to fill his eyes.

17 Fermilab

Missing and presumed dead.

Bradley's information was not likely to be wrong. Fermilab had reported a massive explosion that had produced a forty-meter hole in their underground facility. Expressions like *presumed dead* always left a door slightly ajar to allow for hope, no matter how slim the chance. But when crisis comes, rational people force their intellect to dominate emotion and reckon with reality. Daniel was not there yet.

She couldn't be dead, he thought. Daniel recognized the symptoms of denial. The psychiatrists would probably label him as a textbook case. Nala wasn't just a lost colleague, she was a lost lover. And not just any lover, a regret. A relationship full of mistakes. A woman he had wronged through neglect.

You're compensating, the therapists would tell him. *Your personal guilt is clouding your normally analytical mind.*

Beautiful, bright, talented Nala. A ballet dancer with an attitude. A brilliant physicist with a wicked tongue. Silenced. When had he seen her last? It was March... no, April, at a Fermilab communication session with Core. He had stayed in the office for only a few hours and given her no more than a light hug. Just a shadow of the burst of intensity their relationship had enjoyed a few months prior.

The guilt poured over him. He had abandoned the relationship, and he was still not sure why. Some of it had been the logistics of busy professionals living in two different cities. But it wasn't *just* that. Daniel couldn't put a finger on it, but it was hard to imagine how any psychoanalysis mattered now. Nala was dead.

But no... she isn't.

His analytical mind wouldn't permit the conclusion. There simply wasn't enough evidence. Yes, an explosion. Yes, missing people presumed dead. But this was Fermilab, where alternative explanations were entirely possible. When Soyuz astronauts had disappeared, everyone had jumped to the same conclusion. Missing and presumed dead. There was a lesson to be learned. In the insanity of the four-dimensional world, things disappeared routinely.

The hotel bar was nearly empty. Daniel took a sip from his glass of bourbon. He pushed the chunks of ice around with a finger. Nala used to do the same thing, an endearing quirk. She'd said she didn't even notice she was doing it, perhaps just a nervous thing.

He remembered the first time he'd met her—an interview at her office and a clandestine meeting at a bar later that night. She was nervous then. He was the investigator and she was the informant. He'd been tough on her.

Daniel's eyes teared up and his throat tightened.

How things had changed since that first night. Nala was the kind of person who held you at arm's length until she knew you. But once that barrier dropped, she didn't hold back. Laughs turned to playfulness. Sweet kisses escalated to aggressive sexuality. Any hesitation she displayed in public was quickly abandoned once things were private. Clothes and inhibitions disappeared quickly. Daniel had soaked it up. Every man wants to be wanted, and Nala seemed to have learned that lesson early in her adult life.

He wiped away a tear rolling down his cheek. *You don't know what you've got until it's gone.* True words. As life clicks by, the missed opportunities and the unspoken words are things that stick with you, often painfully.

His mistakes were obvious now, even if he still didn't understand why he'd made them in the first place. Text messages that he didn't take the time to answer. *Busy—will get back to you.* More than one phone call that he'd cut off to rush off to... what? Something more important? At least, it had seemed important at the time. He'd missed her birthday even though she'd told him twice.

125

And then there was Haiti, a missed opportunity if there ever was one. She'd invited him to join her on a trip ostensibly to visit her mother in Port-au-Prince. Contrary to most people's expectations, including Daniel's, Haiti wasn't a vast slum among the palm trees. Luxury resorts dotted a coastline of white-sand beaches and turquoise water. They would stay together in a beach cottage, she offered.

She described a tropical heaven, a winter getaway. But from Daniel's perspective it was much more. It was alone time with Nala. He imagined days walking barefoot on the sand and nights unwrapping the pleasures of this unpredictable woman.

He'd been ready to book the flight when all hell had broken loose at work. An email from a prominent scientist had accused the administration of covering up the real purpose of their sessions with Core. An alien weapon had been offered, the scientist had said. It was described as a miniature hydrogen bomb that could be embedded almost anywhere without detection and would render nuclear détente irrelevant to whichever country could grab the technology first. Many had believed the story.

It had taken Daniel several weeks to uncover the source of the misinformation and dispel the rumor. In the meantime, the personal opportunity had slipped by and Nala had gone to Haiti alone. Another time, they'd both said, but time has a way of pushing forward and leaving those opportunities behind.

Her texts had become less frequent and then stopped altogether. He would give anything to speak with her once more. To apologize. To start over, if he could.

Daniel picked up an extra napkin from the bar and dabbed his eyes. The analyzing in his head would no doubt go on for months. In the end, if acceptance of Nala's death was required, it would be the hardest thing he'd ever done.

But the next step was easy—and essential for his peace of mind. He picked up his phone and searched for the next available flight to Chicago.

~~~~~~~~~~~~~~~~~~~~~~

Fermilab was familiar ground, particularly Wilson Hall, the towering office building in the center of the accelerator complex. Daniel had lost track of the number of times he'd been here since their first contact with Core.

Except for the emissary robot, no alien lifeform had visited Earth in the eight months since that day. Most people saw this as a positive sign—at least the aliens weren't attacking. But it also meant that if humans had questions—and there were many—it required a trip to a star nearly four thousand light-years away, where Core was located. The only way to get there was through compressed space, and the only way to compress space was with a high-energy particle accelerator. For the first few months, Fermilab had had a monopoly on interstellar space travel.

But by January, the Large Hadron Collider in Geneva had duplicated the technology, and Europeans had hosted two of the scheduled sessions with Core. Later, the Chinese, having admitted their responsibility for the Soyuz mishap, had offered the world's newest and most powerful accelerator in Qinhuangdao. It had been used on one occasion, mostly a symbolic gesture of international cooperation.

Daniel knew things had changed the moment the taxi entered the Fermilab parking area, filled with police, fire and US government vehicles. Both the atrium and the top floor of Wilson Hall were busy with activity. Many of the new faces were people wearing uniforms that displayed arm patches from the Department of Energy or the International Atomic Energy Agency.

Daniel walked down the corridor of interior offices on the top floor of Wilson Hall. He slowed as he passed the one office that was empty and dark. The plaque by the door read *Nala Pasquier*. Several bouquets of flowers were stacked along the bottom of the office window, and someone had written *We love you, Nala* on the glass. A lump formed in Daniel's throat. This trip wasn't going to be easy.

He continued down the hall and stopped at Jan Spiegel's office. The slender man with light blond hair looked up from his work and waved through the window for Daniel to come in.

"Daniel," Jan said. "Good to see you again." He stood up and shook Daniel's hand with a solemn face. "I wish the circumstances were better."

"Good to see you too, Jan. I'm sure you're busy, but I wanted to come by and offer condolences to the staff."

"Thank you. We're all still in shock." Jan's eyes fixed on Daniel's. "Condolences to you too. I believe you have lost as much, maybe more." Jan motioned to a chair, and Daniel took it. Jan closed the door and leaned against the edge of his desk. "She loved you."

The words were unexpected. Nala had never said them, and even if she'd felt that way, how would Jan know? Daniel had never mentioned his relationship with Nala to Jan or anyone else at Fermilab. They'd been discreet, or so he'd thought.

"She told you this?" Daniel asked.

"Not in those exact words, but I could tell. You're surprised, Daniel. At her or me?"

"Both, I guess." They had never declared their relationship to be a secret, but it was hard to picture Nala divulging personal information to Jan.

Jan seemed to understand the issue. "Nala and I shared a connection deeper than you might know." He held up a hand. "Only as colleagues. But an intellectual connection to a person can be profound. The pain of her loss is very personal to me."

"Her *loss*, as you and everyone says," Daniel said. "I was told that no bodies were found. How sure are you?"

"Daniel Rice, the skeptic in all things." Jan thought for a minute and then stood up. "To be honest, no, I'm not certain. But come with me and judge for yourself. I believe this is why you came to Fermilab today, is it not?"

Jan walked out of the office, and Daniel followed him down the hall. There was only one possible destination, and Daniel realized that Jan was right—it was the reason he had come to Fermilab.

They called the elevator and dropped past the ground floor to level B3, deep underground. They exited to a concrete corridor that Daniel knew well, but the corridor was now blocked by a barrier and what looked like a hastily erected guard station. Jan signed a log and the guard waved them past the barrier.

As they turned a corner, the familiar pathway changed. The right side of the corridor was gone. Twisted rebar protruded from the smashed concrete wall, and the broken floor fell away into an enormous pit. Security tape hung from the intact wall on the left to the cracked remains on the right. Beyond the tape and destruction, a single bright light hovered in empty space.

"Jesus," Daniel whispered. A spotlight had been set up on one side and shined into the dark cavity. It illuminated a rotating disk of dust at least ten feet across.

"The blast shook the whole building," Jan said. "Pictures fell off the walls up on the fifteenth floor."

Daniel peered over the edge of the broken floor into a deep pit. He couldn't see the bottom.

"Thirty-five thousand cubic meters of reinforced concrete was pulverized to dust," Jan said. "The fire department sent some guys down there. They found a few scraps of materials that may have come from the lab, but no bodies."

Daniel continued staring into the scene of destruction, feeling numb. "I see your point. Thanks for showing me."

"If it helps, it was probably over quickly. Our systems operations guy was caught in it too. Thomas, I think you may have met him?"

It took Daniel a minute to register the name and to tear his thoughts away from what the blast must have been like. "Uh, yeah. Thomas. Funny guy."

"He was; a very funny guy. He'd worked here for more than ten years. Always happy, always ready to try something new." Jan's features tightened, looking angry. "But he's dead now, and so is Nala."

A strange mix of emotions filled Daniel. Grief, skepticism, denial, all tangling with one another. Perhaps it was simply his ability to logically analyze anything, including his own emotional struggle. He hoped so, but he recognized he'd need to set that struggle aside for now.

Daniel pointed to the strange light in the center of the pit. "What is it?"

"We don't really know," Jan said. "It's one of the things I'm working on." He pointed to a metal stand set up near the edge of the pit. Several electronics boxes were stacked on top and an array of antennae and sensors of unknown function connected to a pole that rose above. "We're monitoring everything we can to try to make sense of it. No doubt it's a byproduct of the collapse of quantum space, unintended. Before the accident, Nala told me she created a smaller version of this in her lab. She thought it was a new type of singularity."

"A singularity? But not a black hole?" Daniel asked.

"No, definitely not a black hole. That would involve enormous mass, and any particle accelerator works only with quantum-sized particles. But singularities may come in different forms. This might be a singularity formed by bosons alone and related to the collapse of four-dimensional space. It may share some properties with a black hole."

Jan pulled out his phone and picked an app that drew a large purple arrow on the screen. A label next to the arrow marked it as *Gravity*. "The app is using the accelerometers in the phone to point straight down." He tilted the phone and the arrow twisted, continuing to point down. "But watch this."

Jan stepped closer to the edge of the pit and reached out as far as his arm would allow. The arrow on the screen wobbled, pointing more toward the light hovering in the center, as if it were a compass needle drawn to a nearby magnet.

"Gravity is different here. We're gathering more data, but we still don't know exactly what's going on. Or why."

Jan pocketed his phone and backed away to a safe distance from the edge. He grabbed a piece of rebar sticking out from the shredded wall and pulled like he wanted to tear it out. "It's absurd that we're still struggling with this. For months, the whole world has shouted its praise for the great discoveries at Fermilab. Talk even of a Nobel Prize. But you see the reality." He waved toward the destruction. "I feel like an undergraduate student who has only barely scratched the surface of the subject. We were playing with fire, all of us. I shouldn't have allowed Nala to continue to test."

He picked up a loose pebble of concrete and tossed it into the open pit. The rock made an unusually elongated arc in the disturbed gravitational field before finally turning down to the bottom of the pit. "I've spent most of my time since the accident searching for someone to blame. This was not an accident. It was inevitable. Entirely predictable. Much of the blame falls on me. I left everything in Nala's hands, even after the instabilities started showing up. I'll be second-guessing myself for a long time to come."

Jan turned to Daniel, his anger showing. "But I also lay blame with this so-called friend of ours, Core. This *intelligence* out in space knew exactly what we were working on. This *thing* even pointed us toward HP bosons as the answer and expected us to study further. But where was the warning of the danger?"

"You're right, we need to ask," Daniel said.

"And we will," Jan said, determined. "Unfortunately..." He pointed to the destruction.

"There's CERN. You could go to Geneva. We could reach Core with their help."

"I've already asked. Unfortunately, the IAEA has asked government particle acceleration labs worldwide to suspend operations until the Fermilab investigation is complete. Several weeks, minimum. I'm in touch with several sympathetic colleagues at CERN—and they are considering my request—but the bureaucracy over there can be slow."

"How about the Chinese?"

"We're working that angle too, but so far they haven't responded to our request."

"I can help," Daniel said. "I'll make some calls."

"That might help, yes. If we can reestablish the communications with Core, I have a lot on my mind that I'd like to discuss."

"You're not the only one. I'm sure we can find another accelerator that can connect us to Core. Heck, they're even creating 4-D space out of Romania now."

"Romania?"

Daniel started back down the corridor, and they continued talking as they walked. "Yeah, that's the case I was working on before I came here. A guy in Texas has a contract with a private Romanian lab. Apparently, the Romanians have your coherent neutrino beam all figured out."

Jan rubbed a hand across his forehead. "It wouldn't be hard. The word is out. With the classification lifted, we shared our techniques in a series of published papers. Any decent physicist with a gigaelectron-volt accelerator could reproduce it."

They took an elevator to the lobby of Wilson Hall, its interior atrium soaring far above. "Based on what you know about the accident, should we shut this kind of business activity down?"

"Is your Texas guy a decent physicist?" Jan asked.

"He doesn't know a proton from a coconut."

"Better shut him down, then. I'm still dealing with a lot of unknowns. If we get some answers from Core, maybe we'll be in a better place. Otherwise, it could be weeks, even months, before we know how to prevent this from happening again."

"Getting the answer out of Core will be tough. Like squeezing juice from a rock."

"Now you're starting to sound like one of us," Jan said.

Daniel shook his head. "I can only imagine what Nala had to say about Core."

"A barrage of profanity that would singe your ears."

"Yeah," Daniel sighed. "She always was a delicate thing."

18 Isolation

Nala woke to a sizzling sound and the smell of something burning. A foul smell like oil or creosote. Her head throbbed.

She opened one eye. Darkness surrounded her, but a dim light came from somewhere off in the distance. She lay on her stomach, her chin and open mouth pressed against a hard floor. A large piece of broken wood rested just in front of her face. She pushed it away.

A groan, a man's voice, muted and far away, brought her back to reality. "Thomas!" she cried.

Nala could hear him, but pain and disorientation made it difficult to get up off the floor, much less find her colleague. He was alive; his moans verified that much. She was surprised to be alive herself.

She pushed up from the hard surface onto her knees. A wooziness in her head made the simple task a major effort. There was something about the air that didn't feel right, but at least there was air.

A pinprick of light hovered in one direction, dimly illuminating a sea of debris all around. Shattered wood, bent metal, piles of broken wallboard and glass shards were everywhere. She recognized a portion of the workbench and a metal frame filled with smashed electronics that at one point had been part of her lab.

She inched forward on hands and knees toward the light. Pain shot up one knee, and she lifted it from the floor. There was enough light to see a small piece of glass that had punctured her pants and buried in the skin. She pulled it out and a spot of blood appeared. She examined herself. Both pant legs had rips, and her bare arms were cut in several places, but the blood was already congealed. Nothing appeared to be broken, and except for a throbbing headache, she felt no other pain. Thomas moaned again.

He's hurt. I've got to find him.

She tried to stand; shoes would spare her hands and knees from the broken glass. The ground felt uneven, and her head spun. It was like trying to stand on a half-inflated beach ball. "Hang on, Thomas, I'm coming," she shouted. Her voice disappeared into nothingness.

She took faltering steps toward the light. The moans seemed to be coming from that direction. Several chairs were overturned, the mini-fridge sat on its side, and piles of books, broken pipes and many other obstacles made the going slow.

Now standing, she could see that the debris field ended abruptly on one side, with nothing beyond but jet-black darkness. At first, she thought it was a shadow cast by something large blocking the light, but as she came closer, a very definite edge became apparent. The surface that she walked on and the debris that covered it ended at a vertical wall of darkness. The wall was speckled with thousands of tiny sparks randomly distributed across its surface. The sparks popped and crackled like drops of water in hot grease.

She didn't dare touch the dark surface. Danger is obvious even when its form is entirely unknown. She searched along the sparkling wall toward the bright light in the distance and finally found him.

Thomas was on his back, arms splayed, and eyes closed. He lay among splintered boards in a pool of blood. She climbed over the debris and bent down by his side. His left leg protruded into and beyond the black vertical wall. A ring of sparks around the perimeter of his leg sizzled and popped where it touched the wall. It smelled like bacon frying.

"Holy shit. Thomas, this looks..." *Bad. Worse than bad.*

She grabbed him under both arms and dragged his heavy body a few feet until the sparks stopped. The lower portion of his leg was missing where it had touched the wall. His pants were soaked in blood.

She pushed aside more debris and kneeled next to his face. His breathing was shallow. She spoke gently in his ear. "I'm here, Thomas.

I've got you." She patted his arm and steeled herself to the task she knew would be gruesome. She carefully lifted the ripped pants to reveal a bloody leg cleanly sliced at midshin. Nausea was immediate, along with a dizziness that weakened her resolve. She took a deep breath.

You can do this. Thomas needs you. Stanch the bleeding. Your first-aid training, remember?

It seemed like ancient history, but portions of the training surfaced to her conscious thoughts. A tourniquet. She looked around and found a roll of masking tape. Not much strength in paper tape, but it might help. Her thoughts clarified. Use clothing strips instead.

Thomas was too heavy to turn over; she'd never get his pants off, so she removed her own. They were made of light material and already torn in places, making it easier to get a rip started. A minute later, she had produced several long strips of cloth from one leg. The tinny smell of blood was strong closer to his severed leg, but she held her breath as she wrapped the strips just above the slice and tied them off as tightly as she could manage. The pressure of the binding did seem to slow the bleeding.

She ripped off the other leg of her pants and wrapped it around the end of the stump, then tied her belt loosely around the whole package. A primitive bandage, but it would have to do. If the first-aid kit was buried somewhere under all the debris, she might find it and do a better job of nursing later.

Nala scanned his body for other wounds but found nothing obvious. Except for the leg, he looked uninjured. His face was pale from blood loss, but he had fewer scratches from flying glass than she did.

She leaned in close. "Thomas, can you hear me?"

He moaned slightly.

"You're alive. Alive is very good." She pushed her cheek up against his and spoke into his ear. "Thomas, I'm going to take care of you. You're going to be alright. Okay?"

He opened his lips slightly, but no words came out.

"Don't try to talk. It's okay. I'm going to try to find some medication and water for you." Blood loss meant fluid loss. He'd need water. She'd remembered that much from her training. He was also in shock. She couldn't remember the procedures for shock, but keeping him warm seemed like the right thing to do. She stood up and looked around for anything that might help. There were no blankets or towels, but she did find some shredded carpeting. She grabbed a large piece and laid it gently over his chest. She took another piece and placed it under his head.

Water. I had some in the fridge.

She made her way back into the darkness and located the mini-fridge. The dented door was jammed closed, but she managed to pry it halfway open. Inside were three water bottles, undamaged. The simple success made her smile. She carried the bottles back to Thomas, lifted his head and poured a small amount of water on his lips. Most of it dribbled onto the floor.

Should you give water to an unconscious person? I don't know. Probably not.

"Fuck!" she said under her breath and then screamed out, "I wish I had some help here."

Communicate. Find out what happened and where you are. Get some help. They must be looking for us. But where are we?

She recalled the circular hole that had shredded her lab and sucked everything into its darkness, unmistakably a dimensional aberration. It was certainly no closet they'd fallen into.

If this was 3-D space, her handheld radio would still work. Even if it was 4-D space, it still might work if she could successfully point it back to 3-D.

However the fuck you do that. She shook her head. *Girl, you're in a world of hurt. Find the fucking radio.*

She searched, pushing through the debris and examining each object in the low light. Most everything was broken, bent or shattered. The remains of a voltage meter, wires, neon light tubes, smashed. She found a sweater she kept in the lab to keep warm on cold winter days and placed it over Thomas's legs. After a few minutes without finding the radio, she stopped and stood straight up.

"What the hell am I even walking on?" she said aloud. She swiveled to the bright light. "And what the hell is that?"

The "floor" wasn't like any of the floors at Fermilab. Even in the dim light, she could make out stripes and other markings in it. The stripes weren't debris; they were part of the floor, but they were irregular, not like tile or carpeting. The markings were mostly gray and tan, but there were some other colors.

She did a quick three-sixty. The debris field had a teardrop shape, with its apex near the light and spreading out radially from there. It also looked like there might be two vertical edges, a sizzling wall of death on each side of the debris field. Only one direction was undefined—away from the light. It was just darkness out there; no debris, no sign of any vertical walls and no indication of any further lights.

Something on the floor wiggled, and her heart nearly jumped out of her chest. "Shit!" It wiggled again. A rat? She slowly reached down and picked up a large splinter of a two-by-four. She threw it at the wiggling thing. The wood bounced across the floor and stopped, but the wiggling continued.

Whatever it was, the thing wasn't running around, it was just wiggling in place. She stepped closer. It looked like a shred of cloth blowing in the wind. But the air around her was completely calm. In fact, the air felt no different from being indoors. She reached down to grab the cloth, but her fingers simply touched a hard surface. The cloth wasn't a cloth at all—it was an image, a video of a cloth blowing in the wind like an animated GIF that repeats indefinitely. She stepped on it and the cloth stopped wiggling.

"What the hell?"

She lifted her foot and it started waving again. "Okay, this is freaking me out."

She turned to the bright light hanging above Thomas and screamed as loud as she could. "I want out of here!" She hardened her lips and yelled again at the light. "And so does my friend."

She stepped purposefully over the debris, marching straight toward the light. As she walked, it seemed to recede. She walked past Thomas and past most of the debris, yet she was no closer to the light. Ahead was a smooth surface of the mottled gray and tan stripes with only a few bits of the debris, mostly smaller stuff. She took ten more paces and stood on a clean surface. The light was still no closer.

The proverbial distant light at the end of a dark tunnel. Am I dead?

Nala wasn't superstitious. This was not a passageway for spirits. No ghosts were floating by, heading to a mythical heaven around the next corner. Her mind had little room for baseless supernatural claims. But humans are hardwired for fear, particularly of the unknown. A shiver passed down her neck and legs.

Focus. You're smarter than this.

The light must be the same aberration she'd seen in the lab, and probably related to the hole they had passed through. Both were a byproduct of her manipulation of 4-D space. Her thoughts clarified.

We're on the other side.

They were in a space she'd created, or maybe some blast zone created during the explosion. Wherever it was, that light sure looked like the one she'd seen hovering in her lab. Brighter, maybe bigger. But just as unexpected.

Fucking HP bosons.

She'd been playing around the edges of spatial instability, testing, probing. She'd certainly prodded the beast awake. It was an implosion, not an explosion. A collapse of four-dimensional space that had taken a chunk of three-dimensional space with it.

But why now? What had she done differently? The collapse rate? Jan's concern about the density? She would need to study it further. Ratchet up the 4-D volume in smaller steps to see exactly when things became unstable.

Nala slapped her forehead. *Oh yeah, I blew up the lab.*

No more experiments, ever. If Jan was here, he'd have some insight. He might even have an idea on how to reverse the problem, assuming they had any useful equipment left.

The bright, shining light was the key. *I tried to tell you, Jan.* There was no doubt in her mind: the light was a singularity, though it was hard to see how that bit of information could help.

Nala dropped to her knees. Thomas was badly injured. Both of them were stuck in an unknown kind of spatial aberration with no exit and no way to get help. The outlook was bleak and emotionally draining.

Damn, I wish Jan was here. Or Daniel.

19 Thoughts

Daniel sat at the desk in his Chicago hotel room and wrote a brief note on a sympathy card. He stuffed the card in its envelope and addressed it to Mrs. Esterline Pasquier in Port-au-Prince, adding the address a Fermilab HR administrator had provided for Nala's mother. Wholly insufficient, but it would have to do.

It felt odd to perform the required steps of condolence and healing when he still had doubts about the conclusion. In the 4-D sense, Nala could be standing right next to him and he wouldn't know it.

There was much to process from the day's events, and he needed a mental shift. He started a shower and let steam fill the bathroom. Stripping down, he stepped in and allowed the water to pour over his head. Personal chaos doesn't mean your job can be ignored, and his current assignment had both technical and political challenges. With the accident at Fermilab, the stakes in Texas had just gone up.

Suspending the power plant operations, even if only temporarily, was the right thing to do, but the best approach would require some thought. The shower had always been the best place to do it.

EPA regulated air and water quality. NRC regulated the safe storage and use of nuclear materials. FEMA stepped in to protect and recover from natural disasters. They were all useful for their defined purposes, but the authority of each agency was limited to the ordinary world. Where were the interdimensional regulators when you needed them?

In any new technology, regulation lagged technological advances; safety concerns were often discounted—until an accident occurred. But even after an accident, it was never easy to draw a clean dividing line between acceptable risks and irresponsible practices. EPA administrators weren't likely to revoke or suspend a permit unless they had better information, including a direct tie to the Fermilab disaster.

Even the president would hesitate to step in. He had won the last election, but not in the state of Texas. In this case, with both industry and state agencies in alignment, the political fallout of overruling them could be high.

Finding connections is what any investigator does, and Daniel was unquestionably good at it. But if an investigator assumed a connection existed without evidence, the case would be easily picked apart by industry lawyers in court. Fermilab was an aberration, they'd say. They were pushing the envelope, probing for the breaking point. There was no connection. And those lawyers might be right.

The teams of DOE and IAEA accident investigators swarming over Fermilab, along with Jan Spiegel and Jae-ho Park, would need to find the root cause of the accident. As Jan had pointed out, they were still collecting basic data. Any conclusion based on solid science would take time.

With Fermilab in ruins, their ability to retrace their steps was compromised for the foreseeable future. They would be wholly dependent on facilities elsewhere in the world, requiring still more time. But there was another source of information—if Core would cooperate. The alien intelligence certainly knew more than it had shared, especially when it came to quantum discoveries.

Warm water dripped from the end of his nose in a rhythm that helped to concentrate his thoughts and focus toward a purpose.

Daniel was as frustrated with Core as anyone. It was time to challenge the evasiveness that had characterized so many of their conversations. No more *too soon*. Get past *you'll learn*.

Core was right to point out that humans had a long way to go in our understanding of the universe, but if we were treading dangerously close to disaster, a simple warning wasn't too much to ask. Only a sociopath watches a child playing with matches without comment.

No more weasel words. If you're friendly, prove it.

It was, of course, a very human reaction based in frustration and anger. Core was not human in manner or mindset, nor should anyone expect it to be. If Daniel wanted to make headway quickly, the next conversation would need to challenge some of the *rules*. But it was time. Two scientists may have lost their lives.

Daniel resolved to confront the all-powerful alien. How Core would react was impossible to know. But to get to Core, he'd need a facility with the technology to compress space. CERN was probably out of the question; Geneva tended to conform strictly to the rules as defined by IAEA. He could make some calls as he'd promised Jan to gain cooperation from the Chinese. And there was always this rogue lab in Romania. There were possibilities, but all were probably long shots and would take time.

The hot water poured across his shoulders and he wiped water from his face as another thought came in from left field. There was another path.

Aastazin.

He had never met the artificial intelligence, but as far as Daniel knew, he, she or it was still at the Kennedy Space Center in Florida. For that matter, the portal the katanaut team had used to get to Ixtlub should, theoretically, still be operational. Even if the android was the only one who knew how to operate the system, it was a potential path to Core.

Daniel shut off the water and stepped out into the foggy bathroom. He wrapped a towel around his waist and grabbed his phone from the counter. He could have called the White House or the main number of KSC, but there was a better way, faster and more reliable. A former partner and a good friend.

She was still in his list of contacts. Daniel dialed, and Marie Kendrick answered.

20 Void

Nala sat cross-legged next to Thomas, a water bottle in her hand and two more unopened. She gently lifted his head and dribbled a bit of water into his mouth and then carefully lowered his head onto a sheet of bubble wrap that she'd found. She stroked his hair and ran the back of her fingers across the stubble around the edges of his beard. The color had left his skin and his moans were less frequent.

She'd found the first-aid kit, battered but usable. *Thanks, DOE safety guy. I owe you one.* The job of properly dressing the wound had taken time, but she hadn't shrunk from the task, even when an artery had opened up again. At least it showed his body was maintaining blood pressure.

She'd done the best she could with the materials she could find. Thomas lay on pieces of carpeting. He looked comfortable, even though his condition was clearly critical.

Wherever this place was, it was cold and getting colder. With most of her pants used for the initial bandage, all she had left were ripped shorts and bare legs. But the floor felt warmer than the air. Why? The difference in temperature was data... and data could always be leveraged.

Heat is transferred in three ways: radiation, conduction and convection. Radiant heat transfers via photons. We feel the radiant heat of the sun on our skin. Conduction occurs through direct contact. Her legs were warmer where they touched the floor. But more commonly, heat transfers by convection—air movement. Warmer and more energetic molecules of air physically move from one place to another through currents in the air.

Since it was getting colder, that probably meant there was little or no warm air coming in, coupled with radiant cooling, probably radiating out through the dual sizzling walls of death. She could stay warm against the floor, but the lack of fresh air coming in was beyond her control.

Not so good for those of us who like to breathe.

But why was the floor warmer? She had no answer. She leaned forward and studied it closely. A patchwork of colors, mostly gray, black or off-white. A stripe of light blue here, a circle of brown there. A jumble, like layers of shapes laid on top of each other, but flattened into a thin sheet.

She stood up and felt dizzy. The act of standing was extremely disorienting. Up didn't feel like up, and down didn't feel any better. It was an off-balance experience, wobbly and unsteady.

Like being drunk.

Or worse, like being a drunk gymnast doing a balance beam routine. Some of it might be the stale air but she couldn't help but think the floor itself was the primary culprit. Nothing felt right.

Nala picked up a broken length of wood and stepped closer to the vertical wall, still sizzling with tiny sparks, still looking rather deadly. She was thankful the smell of burning meat—Thomas's leg—had dissipated. Bending down, she pushed the stick into the wall. The wood crackled like a campfire, and smoke poured away from its edges, but without any flame. Withdrawing, the end of the stick was cleanly sliced, just like Thomas's leg.

Hell, no. We're not getting out that way.

More information. A boundary she could not cross. Even the floor ended, and whatever was beyond was clearly inhospitable to life, or maybe anything. What were the sparks? Bits of dust vaporizing as they touched a wall of high energy? Air molecules exiting this bubble of reality?

Nala stood again, still dizzy. Keeping the bright light behind her and the *sizzling wall of death* to her right, she proceeded directly into

145

the darkness ahead, kicking debris as she went to clear a path. After thirty paces, she turned around to gauge her position. Debris was spread across a large area and the light remained motionless above it all. The light's position hadn't changed in the slightest. It felt like walking away from the sun hanging in the sky. Another data point to consider.

She kept walking and soon found the edge of the debris field. Beyond it, the floor continued, and without debris covering it, she realized that the floor itself was a secondary source of light—it glowed. She walked on, noting the floor patterns changing as she walked. Above and ahead, there was nothing but a void of darkness. No stars in the *sky*, if it was a sky. No other light at all. Just black.

The walking was easier without debris. Just ahead, she noticed movement on the floor. It looked like running water swirling in a basin. She stopped and bent down. Definitely water; it shimmered and splashed even while remaining strangely flat. Like the fluttering cloth she'd seen before, it looked like a video embedded in the floor. A children's swimming pool as seen from above.

She touched it with the tip of her finger. The watery floor was hard, but her finger came back wet. A circular ripple expanded from where she'd touched. She touched again and produced another ripple. "Okay, this is just too weird," she said aloud.

"Thomas," she yelled. "You've got to see this." Her voice sounded muffled. Thomas was clearly not getting up to run over.

Sigh.

She ran back toward the light, along the same path she'd cleared. When she reached Thomas, she stopped. The dizziness returned, much stronger.

"Okay, running might be a bad idea. Avoid that, if you can, Thomas."

The white bandage on his leg had turned red on the end. Was that a good sign? Blood pumping, tissues around the injury getting what they need?

"Who am I kidding? I'm no doctor."

She bent down next to him and listened to his shallow breathing. Thoughts of their work together entered her mind. They'd been a good team, for several years. She planned, he executed. Together they'd made history, exposing the underlying structure of the universe and even figuring out how to manipulate it. Quantum space was an entirely new branch of physics.

That was all in the past. She looked around the debris field that had once been their laboratory. Smashed chairs, broken electronic components. A family photo that Thomas kept on the workbench. Tears ran down her cheeks and her throat tightened. "I'm really sorry, Thomas. I totally fucked this up. Everything. It's all my fault."

She leaned over and laid her head on his chest. His heart still beat, but it didn't sound very strong. "Can you ever forgive me, my friend?"

She reached across him and picked up his Viking hat. It had been buried under a pile of broken wood and wall insulation. She put the slightly crushed hat on his head and smiled. "You look great, Thomas. If I had my camera..."

She wiped the tears from her cheeks and stood up again. The dizziness returned, stronger. There wasn't much time left.

This is going to end badly.

She walked toward the light—the singularity. Whatever it was, she was determined to meet it head-on. She tripped on some debris, caught her fall, and continued. Woozy now. Her head felt very light, her vision blurred and spinning. Her legs felt wobbly, each step shakier than the last. Her fingers tingled.

The world began to spin. Nala let out her last breath and collapsed to the floor.

21 Florida

Tires squealed as the military Gulfstream G300 touched down on the world's longest runway. The Shuttle Landing Facility at Kennedy Space Center hadn't seen a shuttle for more than a decade, and though the enormous runway more often provided a sundeck for alligators, it still occasionally served as a gateway to and from space. Commercial operators had taken over, launching tourists to twenty-five miles above the atmosphere for a quick look-see and a brief period of weightlessness. For the wealthy, it made a good add-on after taking the kids to Disneyworld.

Daniel had done his fiscal duty, flying commercial to Texas and Chicago. This time, it was worth a phone call to Janine to arrange the military flight. The flight was direct to KSC. No fighting the hordes of tourists at Orlando International, no requests for autographs from the famous scientist, and easier on his frazzled nerves. With Jan joining him, it might even have made financial sense. Janine made it happen; she always did.

Forty minutes later, the pair had their visitor's badges and followed signs guiding them down a long hallway at the Neil Armstrong Operations and Checkout Building. Daniel spotted a familiar face coming from the opposite direction. They both ran the last few steps.

"Marie." Daniel held out both arms and hugged her tight.

"Great to see you again, Daniel," Marie said.

She hadn't changed a bit, even after her well-publicized off-world experience. She still wore the same black glasses she probably didn't need. A clean, fresh look with a wholesome face, short dark hair, with an offset part that pushed most of it to one side. With her impressive list of accomplishments, Daniel had already learned not to judge her by youthful looks. Now, she'd added interstellar katanaut to her resume.

Daniel felt like a proud older brother. "I know you're busy. Thanks for helping us out."

Marie returned a warm smile and held Daniel's arms as she talked. "Zin said he'd be delighted to help, but that's typical Zin."

Daniel hadn't heard the diminutive before, but it made sense. "I'm really looking forward to meeting him. It *is* a him?"

"Oh, yes. He's humanoid by design. Male, but oddly adaptable. Maybe he's got a female voice in there somewhere."

Daniel spent a moment examining his onetime partner. Maybe she *had* changed. Not physically, but she projected a greater maturity that he hadn't sensed before. The baby face had grown up. It shouldn't be surprising; this woman had just spent two days on another planet.

Jan shook Marie's hand. "The very famous katanaut, Ms. Marie Kendrick. I watched you on TV. Intensely exciting."

Marie nodded in acknowledgment. "I was honored to be included on the team and thrilled to stand on another planet."

"But glad to be home?" Jan asked.

"Of course," Marie said.

They caught up as they walked to the O&C clean room. Marie provided a firsthand summary of her adventure to Ixtlub, but a few of her descriptions were cut short. She was withholding, no doubt, but perhaps some of the mission was classified. Daniel didn't press her.

Marie stopped walking and turned to Daniel. "I heard about Nala. So sad." She put a hand on Jan's arm. "I know she was your colleague. Such an incredible talent."

"Thank you," Jan said. "A terrible tragedy, personally, and a great loss for science. It's the main reason we're here. We don't want this to happen again."

Marie nodded. "I hope Zin can help. He said he would try, but it might be complicated." She looked up at Daniel, who remained silent. The only words he had left would wait until he could speak with Core. It seemed a simple task for the android to arrange the connection. He certainly had the technology.

The three continued silently down the corridor until they reached a door with a guard stationed at a desk outside. "Zin should already be here." Marie showed her ID, and the guard checked Daniel and Jan's badges.

As they opened the door, they nearly bumped into a fast-moving figure coming the other way.

"Pardon me, so sorry," Zin said. "I was coming to look for you, Marie, but I see you've found Dr. Rice and Dr. Spiegel."

The spindly android turned to Jan. *"Goede dag Dokter Spiegel, hoe gaat het met u?"* Jan was Dutch, and the android was said to be an accomplished linguist in most if not all Earth languages, but Daniel was still surprised at the impromptu performance.

"Dank u, Aastazin," Jan replied. "But I'm sure we can all speak English."

"Of course," Zin said. "Please call me Zin, everyone does." He extended a metal hand to Daniel. "It's a pleasure to make your acquaintance, Dr. Rice."

"For me, too," Daniel said. He took Zin's slender hand, cold, with fewer digits than normal. His flat eyes jumped around on his face, and his almost normal mouth was turned up into a natural, if overdone, smile. "I've heard much about you, and something about the mission to Ixtlub."

"It went well, I think." Zin looked at Marie. "Though I'm sure Marie has more that she can tell you."

"She just did," Daniel said. "The Dancers sound fascinating."

151

"Yes, they're a delightful species," Zin said. "I do enjoy my visits there. What did you think of the Workers?" Marie looked down at the floor.

"I guess I didn't hear about them." Daniel glanced at Marie. "I gather they're... different?"

"Quite so," said Zin. "Rougher. Most humans might say cruder, but also quite intelligent."

Daniel turned to Marie who still watched the floor. "You seem—"

"Yes, they were fascinating too," she said. "But to be honest, one day with the Workers was enough." Marie had the expression of a mom who had just cleaned up after a sick child, or dog... or both. "Let's just say the experience was a little creepy."

"So, you—" Daniel started, but Marie cut him off again.

"Best not to dig too deep, Daniel." Marie seemed adamant that she wasn't going down that path.

Zin tactfully changed the subject. "Come into the clean room and let's discuss how to best meet your needs."

They entered the cavernous space, their footsteps echoing in the empty chamber. The white oval portal still dominated the center of the room, looking just as futuristic as it had on television. Four chairs on pedestals were arranged between the portal and a large control station.

"So you can take us to Core through the portal?" Daniel asked. A trip had already been implied but not confirmed. Daniel decided to cut through the polite quality that seemed to come naturally to Zin and make this conversation as direct as possible.

"Can I? Yes," Zin answered. "But that's not the real question."

"Is there an issue?" Daniel asked.

Zin motioned to the empty chairs. "Would you like to sit?"

Daniel shook his head no. "What's the issue, Zin?" he repeated.

Zin paused. Whether androids needed time to think before speaking or whether Zin was mimicking human patterns was an open question. "Dr. Rice, as the primary spokesperson for humanity, you more than anyone recognize that there are protocols to follow for any conversation. Your request to meet with Core is impromptu." He held up a hand. "Not out of line, by any means. Just unexpected, which requires some additional analysis."

"This meeting is important. Are we going or not?" *Keep it direct.*

Zin's eyes flitted between the three humans. "Potentially. Please understand that Core has duties—"

"Core is too busy to see us?"

"No, it's not that." Zin lowered his head and lifted his eyes. "It's the concept of eschewal. An uncommon word I believe in English, but it's the closest approximation."

"Eschew? To avoid or bypass?"

"Eschew. To *deliberately* avoid," Zin added. "Eschewal is quite an important concept when it comes to probabilities."

"Explain," Daniel commanded.

"I probably shouldn't… but since you are a rather special person, Dr. Rice." He gave a humanlike shrug. "I'll do the best I can. It probably won't surprise you to learn that Core serves multiple purposes but some of its duties are beyond what most humans can imagine. Stellar stabilization and gravitational leveling for galactic homogeneity, for example. A complex subject. But one of its most critical functions is temporal probability analysis and guidance. It would take some time to cover the details but let me just say that even events as insignificant as your request can figure into the analysis."

The explanation wasn't adequate, but it didn't appear that Zin was going to do more than throw out complex terms. *Get past the gatekeeper.*

"We need to speak with Core. Our request is quite simple," Daniel said.

"But the implications are not. If I say too much I could risk biasing your side of the conversation, should a conversation with Core occur."

The back-and-forth was almost as difficult as speaking with Core. Zin was simply more polite about it. "How can we make it occur?" Daniel asked with determination.

"Sorry, I can see you may be frustrated and I do sympathize. So, let me say this much." Zin looked at Marie and spoke slowly. "It could help if Marie attends with you."

Daniel glanced at Marie, but her surprised expression made it clear she had no prior knowledge of Zin's suggestion. "Marie attending will give us the conversation we need?"

"Yes, I believe it will," Zin said. "Marie has proven to be quite valuable." He turned to Marie who looked a little red-faced. "I hope I'm not embarrassing you."

"No, it's fine," Marie said. "I'm happy to go. Whatever I can do to help."

"Then it's settled," Daniel said. "Marie's coming too." He turned to Zin. "Let's do this."

The android scurried around to the opposite side of the control desk and activated several pieces of unknown equipment. He froze in place and closed his eyes for a moment. He seemed to be thinking.

His eyes opened. "I've just made the arrangements. You'll be using the Antechamber."

"And where, exactly, is this Antechamber?" Jan asked.

"Nearly four thousand light-years away," Zin responded. "Inside Core."

"Inside? Really?" Jan shrugged. "Is that even safe?"

"You can remain right here, if you wish, Dr. Spiegel."

Marie interrupted before Jan could say anything. "Really, Jan, the transfer procedure is safe and I'm sure the Antechamber has been designed for our use."

Zin nodded.

"I think she's challenging us over-forty types," Daniel said to Jan. "Take a deep breath. I'm sure we'll be fine." Zin's eyes flitted laterally between the two men until Jan finally nodded in agreement.

"Then I'll send you on your way," Zin said. "I'll remain here and control your return. Touch the Reset button on the transfer station arm when you're ready, and I'll get the message."

He pointed to the chairs and each of them picked one. They began to buckle the seat harnesses until Zin waved a hand and explained that the straps were purely for show. Katanauts tightly strapped to their seats looked good for the cameras, but as a safety procedure it was unnecessary.

As the hoods descended in unison over their heads, Daniel could feel his body reacting. Higher blood pressure, adrenaline and faster breathing. He couldn't help it. Things were happening fast, and no amount of rational explanation or self-induced tranquility mattered when the clock was counting down to zero. Daniel had spoken with Core many times, but always from a location at Fermilab and using a two-way radio. Though Zin might imagine that a trip across thousands of light-years was routine, for any human it was nothing less than magic.

Daniel peered under the edge of the hood and watched Marie, calm and experienced, reclined in her chair as if she were at the beach. She caught his eye and just smiled. Yes, Marie had definitely changed.

A bright yellow light flashed, and Daniel disappeared from reality.

As the hood retracted, Daniel lifted his head from the chair and stared incredulously at the scene before him. Marie sat next to him. Regardless of how experienced she was with transfers, her expression of amazement made it clear she was just as surprised at their destination.

They were in a bar filled with people sitting and standing all around. The blended noise of many conversations mixed with the clink of glasses and the squeaking sounds of rotating overhead fans. A bartender stood behind a row of beer taps, cleaning a glass. Two men sat on barstools in front of him, pints of beer in their hands. All around, tables were filled with groups of people leaning close to each other and engaged in private conversations.

In the middle of this very ordinary scene, the stark-white transfer chairs perched on pedestals and the oval portal behind them were dramatically out of place. No one in the room seemed to notice that three interdimensional travelers had suddenly intruded into their after-work party.

Daniel hopped down and stepped off the platform to a dusty barroom floor. Marie did the same, her mouth wide open. "Did we take a wrong turn somewhere?" she asked.

The unexpected scene appeared normal, yet something was amiss. "It's fake," Daniel said. "A simulation of some kind." The barroom sounds were accurate, but the motion wasn't complete. Each human figure rocked back and forth, but their general position never changed. The bartender never finished cleaning the glass. The two men never brought the beer to their lips.

Daniel walked over to one of the tables, where several women sat together, each holding a glass of wine. He leaned in close. Their facial features were detailed, their eyes glistened, their mouths moved, and their heads jostled, but the conversation was unintelligible—just white noise. Daniel pushed a finger against one woman's head. He half-expected it to pass through an elaborate projection and was surprised by the feel of something solid. Cool and soft but definitely not a human head. The figure remained in a bouncy kind of motion, unfazed by his touch.

"They're like mannequins," he said. Marie joined him at the table. Jan remained in his transfer chair.

Marie waved a hand up and down between the conversing women. The chatting figures maintained the same repetitive motion. "Very weird. And kind of creepy."

Daniel looked around the room. Hung on the nearest wall were several neon beer signs. The far wall was less distinct, fuzzy, as though the details were unimportant. "I think I know this place." He swiveled around examining the layout. "Yeah, I'm sure of it. This is a bar in Aurora, Illinois, that Nala and I used to frequent. We sat right over there." He pointed to a booth in the corner, where a brown-skinned woman sat alone.

"Oh, no. It can't be." Daniel's nerves prickled at the thought—and the sight—of Nala. He squeezed past tables and humanlike figures with Marie following close behind. They stopped at the edge of the booth.

Her features were less distinct, but the hair, the smile, the arm casually hung over the back of the seat made the source of the forgery clear. It was a mental image of Nala, a view of her that he'd seen many times before at this very bar and stored away somewhere in the recesses of his mind.

Daniel sat next to the figure of Nala and looked deeply into her eyes. They blinked normally, and her lips moved slightly as if she were talking to herself. She was more than a mannequin, but still a distant approximation of a flesh-and-blood human. His heart sank as he wondered about the fate of the real Nala.

"Manipulative SOB," Daniel said under his breath. He tightened his lips in anger, jumped up and started back toward the incongruous transfer chairs at the center of the bar.

Daniel yelled. "Core! Where are you?"

The din of a hundred conversations died down. The clinks of glasses faded away and a deep voice reverberated through the room, seeming to come from everywhere all at once.

"*I am here.*"

Daniel stepped up to the platform where the transfer chairs stood in a row. He waved his arms. "What is all this bullshit?"

"*It disturbs you?*" The voice was unlike their previous radio conversations. The cellolike vibration was still there, but stronger and with a deeper resonance.

Marie stepped onto the transfer platform, staying close to Daniel. The anger couldn't be hidden from his voice, nor did he want to hide it. "You pulled this from my memory."

"*Yes.*" The vibration in Core's voice made it sound more like *yezh.* "*To make you comfortable.*"

Comfortable, my ass.

A blank room would have been comfortable. A seashore would have been comfortable. Daniel pointed to the booth. "That counterfeit sitting over there is a reproduction of a dear friend of mine. A woman killed in pursuit of scientific knowledge. A woman who faced dangers that you could have warned us about." Daniel trembled with anger. He'd never reacted this way to Core and was uncertain what might happen next.

"*You prefer reality.*" It was a statement, not a question, but Daniel answered anyway.

"Yes. Reality. Honesty. Candor. Stop trying to shade things or distort reality for your benefit or because you think we can't handle it. Just give it to us, unvarnished."

"*As you request. Reality.*" Core's voice faded away. As it did, the dark colors of the barroom lightened, becoming brighter and whiter. The people at tables, the booth where Nala sat, the bartender and his customers all softened into shapes of white that glowed like shiny plastic.

A new scene opened up, as if a stage curtain had parted and backstage was suddenly visible. A vast grid of parallel beams curved gently into the distance. The gray beams were both horizontal and vertical, like lines of latitude and longitude on an enormous globe. Between each beam, globs of an oozing white substance hung, forming thin sheets and vertical columns that dripped and flowed in slow motion.

The plasticlike material dripped from a beam overhead, creating dozens of stalactites that gave the appearance of a limestone cavern. Each stalactite thinned to a fine-tipped point as it inched downward. Some of the slow-motion drips had already reached the beam below, creating a thin vertical column with elegant hyperbolic curves between connection points at the top and bottom.

The grid of beams continued indefinitely in each direction, fading into darkness. It was like looking into the reflection of opposing mirrors. The platform that supported the transfer chairs spanned the horizontal distance from one beam to another. As drips continued from above, a solid sheet of white began to form around the platform.

Marie moved closer still to Daniel. She spoke in a whisper. "I'm not sure what I was expecting, but it wasn't this."

"A fixed framework with a moldable interior," Daniel said. "We're literally deep inside Core." There were many photographs of Core's exterior, an enormous sphere capped by a smaller hemisphere. It was essentially a lumpy moon that hovered in 4-D space surrounded by more than fifty orbiting devices that functioned as communication relays. The *hand grenade*, as Nala had christened it.

NASA engineers had calculated its diameter at just under a hundred kilometers. If you dropped Core into Lake Erie, you could step on in Ohio and step off in Ontario without getting wet. No one knew why a single cyborg entity required so much volume, and no one had yet asked.

"The white stuff looks alive."

"It may very well be. Core is cybernetic—part machine, part organic." Daniel began to calm now that Core had acknowledged the deception. He still wasn't happy with the emotional manipulation or the intrusion into his mind.

Jan, still sitting on the transfer chair, spoke up from behind. "If you don't mind, I'd like to get this over with as quickly as we can." He looked pale.

Daniel wasn't ready to let the opportunity pass just because Jan wanted to make a quick retreat now that he was staring into the throat of the beast.

"Core," he shouted. "Show yourself. We didn't come here to speak to a disembodied voice. We could do that by radio."

There was a delay, but the deep vibrating voice eventually responded. *"Your eyes are not capable."*

Daniel stood firm. "The unshaded truth. Remember? Do it. Show yourself."

A large glob of the plastic goo invaded the space and sealed off the view of the framework of beams. They were surrounded now by pure white.

"Could we suffocate in here?" Jan asked.

"Doubtful," Marie answered. "We're clearly in a climate-controlled space with pressure and oxygen set for humans. I can't imagine Zin sending us to our deaths."

Jan eyed the reset button on the seat handle. Daniel couldn't blame him. Having a backup plan was always a good idea. Marie seemed to agree as she repositioned herself closer to the transfer chair.

"Core?" Daniel yelled once more. "We're not simpletons and we're not afraid. Show yourself."

Motion appeared, hovering in midair in front of them. Dark curving lines appeared that stood out against the white background. More lines materialized, hundreds... thousands. They began to twist into geometric shapes of astonishing complexity.

The voice was the same, but it now emanated from the emerging shape that hovered in the air. *"Expect no face, no body."* The curving lines formed a sphere with a smaller hemisphere on top, but the shape continued to morph into greater complexity, like zooming in on a fractal. *"No form that you could perceive."* The lines twisted back on themselves, crossing into a mesh and turning inside out. A glow shone from the interior. *"But I will project my essence into your space."*

The view changed further, the glow breaking apart and forming an array of particles orbiting around a central point. The glow pulsated in a rhythm that cascaded down a line of individual particles like perfectly timed Christmas lights. *"You would call me a quantum computer, and that would be partly correct."*

The moving particles multiplied in number. Their orbital paths increased in complexity. The hovering mass expanded, stretching closer to the platform where they stood. Daniel backed up a few steps as the three-dimensional image engulfed the platform and surrounded them. They were inside, with tiny particles zooming in all directions.

"I am more than you see. I am entangled beyond this single entity. Human limits cannot comprehend all that I am."

The shapes and motion were indescribably complex. Yet the voice had stated there was more, and Daniel believed it. This was an entirely different lesson, unlike any session that had come before. This time, Core wasn't saying *you will learn*. Quite the opposite. *You cannot learn, you are incapable.*

"Don't underestimate us," Daniel said, his emotions now under control. "Our species may be highly dependent upon our eyes, but that single organ produces a visual reality within our brain—a representation of truth like no other."

"*I understand.*" Some of the flying particles sparked in synchronization with the spoken words.

"We have questions," Jan said, several steps behind Daniel as they faced what seemed like the center of particle activity.

"*Jan Spiegel.*" Core's voice reverberated throughout the platform beneath their feet, and Jan jumped at the sound of his name. "*Your questions?*"

Jan looked desperate now that he'd put himself front and center. The Cowardly Lion in front of the Great and Powerful Oz came to mind. Jan swallowed hard. "We have lost two good people... our colleagues. A dimensional mishap. We believe it was due to instabilities from the collapse of quantum space."

Daniel gave a nod of encouragement to Jan. Even though Daniel had taken the lead in past conversations, this time it would be best to have a physicist explain.

Jan continued. "We have measured these instabilities, but we can't control them."

"*Your question?*" Core's voice was sharp.

Jan seemed shaken by the interruption but regained his composure. "Why didn't you warn us? Why not explain the dangers inherent in this technology? Your own agent, Aastazin, used a device to send us here by way of dimensional compression. Your scientists must have faced the same issue and solved it. Why not share this information?"

If Core felt any challenge from Jan's accusation, its tone didn't change. *"Dimensional instabilities are common. You will learn."*

"But two people have died!"

"Over time, you will learn."

They were back to that tired phrase, and Daniel was having none of it. "If you'd warned us, our best scientists might still be alive, and we'd be in a better position to learn." They'd never confronted Core before, but the rules were different this time.

"Daniel Rice. Jan Spiegel. Am I the instructor for your scientists?"

"You could be," Daniel answered. "When lives depend on it."

"Share with others. They will share with you. There are many."

It was a reference to the Dancers, no doubt. But if Marie's experience on their planet was any indication, the relationship was a long way from discussing advanced physics. They'd barely gotten past identifying the difference between sexes.

Jan followed the motion of the flying particles, as if searching for the specific instance of the intelligence they were speaking to. "Explain just one simple concept. Would that break any of your precious rules?"

"Your question?"

"We may have created a singularity, a zero-dimensional point. If I knew how to avoid it, we could protect ourselves but continue to experiment."

"You believe a singularity is simple?"

Jan shrugged. "It's a well-understood concept, mathematically at least. We just don't know how it derives from the collapse of quantum space."

"Is a multivariate universe simple?"

"Hardly."

"Then why should its opposite be simple?"

Jan shook his head. "I... I don't follow..."

"To understand the universe, you must first understand a single point. To understand the point, you must understand both the infinite and the nothing."

Jan seemed to be thinking, but Core's obscurity was on full display once again. "Still not sure I follow."

"Humans still have much to learn. Begin with the density of matter."

"You mean, the ratio of baryonic matter to bosons?"

"Yes."

Jan turned to Daniel. "Well, at least it's confirmation that Nala and I were on the right track. I can work with that."

Jan's work might lead to future insight, but it didn't clear any of the inherent dangers from his path. Daniel jumped in. "We'll do our homework. We'll study these concepts. But lives are at stake. Give us some guidance on how to proceed safely."

"You already have such guidance. Provided by new associates."

New associates? There was only one possible explanation for that bit of obscurity. "Who... the Dancers?"

"As you call them." Core's voice shifted, the source of the vibration moving under the platform toward Marie. The particles flying through the air also shifted, hovering directly over Marie's head. She looked up, mortified. *"Marie Kendrick represented your species and was gifted. Through this gift, she comprehends."*

Marie looked like she'd just been caught sipping a margarita at a business meeting. She shrugged, "Yeah, well...it's kind of a long story."

"Apparently, she does comprehend," Daniel said. "We'll need to discuss this with her when we get back." He sent a piercing stare through Marie.

"Others have learned. Humans have not yet. Nothing is certain. Outcomes follow probabilities. My emissary, Aastazin, selected Marie Kendrick. She is the highest probability for your guidance."

~~~~~~~~~~~~~~~~~~~~~~~

Marie slipped off the transfer chair, happy to be grounded to her home planet once again but still feeling unsettled. The nearly instantaneous transfer across a vast distance of space had no impact physically, but the interruption of consciousness was disorienting. The message from Core made the confusion worse.

I'm a probability.

Core had revealed more than she'd expected. Zin had selected her to join the Ixtlub mission, but not for the reasons she'd thought. It wasn't her qualifications or cheery disposition. We all want to think that good fortune comes our way because of who we are. But there was something else—a calculation of some kind.

She recalled what Ibarra had told her when he assigned her to the team. *Zin says you increase the probabilities of success.* At the time, she had thought he meant the success of the mission. Now she wasn't so sure.

Core had talked about outcomes. A probability for an outcome. Of whose choosing? Zin? Or was it Core? The outcome could mean anything, and Core hadn't elaborated.

The headband? Did they want me to have it?

Daniel looked rankled. She could understand why. Core had implied that she knew something, so Daniel naturally assumed she was holding out. Maybe she was. She hadn't even mentioned the headband to him, but it hadn't seemed relevant until now.

Zin approached. "Everyone alright?" He examined Daniel and Jan for any obvious signs of distress. He'd done the same to the four katanauts when they'd returned from Ixtlub.

"A bit woozy," Daniel said, rubbing his head. "A very strange experience." He looked over to Marie, already standing. "Does it get any better the second time?"

"It's weird, isn't it?" Marie answered. "Like part of your existence disappeared en route and you can't seem to get it back."

"Humans seem to take the transfer somewhat harder than other species," Zin said.

"Maybe we're just natural whiners," Daniel said. "Give us time, we'll get used to it."

"I hope you will. Others have. The Zheraks, an industrious people in the Sigma Aquilae system, reside on one planet and carry out mining operations on another. They travel to work daily, much like humans do, through more than ten million kilometers of compressed space."

"And I thought my commute was bad," Daniel said.

Marie wrapped a hand around Zin's metallic arm. "You've seen a lot of species, Zin. Do we complain too much?"

Zin patted her hand. "I would never say that. I've grown quite fond of humans. I shall miss you desperately when I leave."

"Me too," Marie said. "But let's not say our goodbyes just yet, my shiny copper friend. I might need your help." She looked up at Daniel and winced as if he was going to throw a punch her way. "I think I owe these guys an explanation."

167

23 Eigenstates

Nala inhaled, let the breath out, and inhaled again. Air. Oxygen. Life.

She lifted her head from the hard surface. The surrounding air was cold with a stale smell. She lifted to her knees and sniffed. Stale, lifeless. The dizziness returned.

She dropped to the floor and pushed her nose against it, filling her lungs with fresh air.

Oxygen. In the floor?

It wasn't really a floor, she knew that much. Down was not at her feet, but at some other angle that her inner ear could not quite process. Regardless of direction, the *floor* was a source of fresh air.

She lay on her stomach and pondered this fact, keeping her face close to the glowing surface. Fresh air could mean only that the floor was a flattened version of three-dimensional space. Home, but strangely out of reach.

"Now what?" she said aloud. "I can stay alive as long as I lie here?"

She lay motionless for several minutes, consuming the life-giving air.

Get to Thomas.

She took one last draw into her lungs, pushed up and ran to where Thomas lay. Letting the air out, she pushed her face close to the floor and inhaled.

Fresh air here too. Lying next to Thomas with her stomach on the floor, she remained still and listened. There was no sound of breathing from her friend. Not good. She reached a hand to his face, nothing coming from his nose or mouth. She laid two fingers across his neck but could find no pulse. Concern turned to panic as she repositioned her fingers but still felt nothing.

168

She slammed a fist to the floor. "Damn it! Fuck this shit!" Her throat constricted and tears came once more. Soon her whole body shook with sobs.

"Oh, God," she whispered. "Thomas, I'm so sorry."

She cried for her friend and for herself. "Damn, damn, damn!" She pounded the floor with each word. "Why didn't I think? Just use your fucking brain."

The anger couldn't be kept inside, but it led to no solutions. She'd need to find another path, a more intellectual route to find a way out of her situation. Thomas would have been the first person to point this out.

I can't just lie here.

Nala lifted herself to her knees and took a breath. Bad air, probably low on oxygen. If this was a 4-D bubble, it was sealed from three-dimensional space—like living inside a balloon. The pangs of hunger in her stomach told her she'd been trapped for at least twenty-four hours, enough time to use up the oxygen. At this point, just standing up required survival skills.

She dropped to the floor and sucked good air through the porous boundary once more.

Improvise. Find something.

Flex-tubing. Where had she seen it? Somewhere on one of the debris piles. It was the kind of tube they used to route Ethernet cables in the ceiling. If the tubing was still intact, it could be useful.

She lifted her head and looked around. Piles of debris were everywhere. Lowering herself again, she took a deep breath, then jumped up and began pushing aside debris and turning over planks of wood. Where was it? She swiveled and saw the end of a tube protruding from another pile. Grabbing it, she dropped back to the floor.

Breathe. She examined her find. A corrugated plastic tube, an inch in diameter and six or seven feet long. Dusty, but intact. She held one end up to her lips and blew. Dust came out the other end.

This could work.

She blew a few more times and then held one end to the floor. Lifting to her knees, she twisted the other end around to her mouth and inhaled. Air flowed through the tube; good, clean air. She stood up, keeping one end against the floor. She sucked again and exhaled to the cold surroundings. Workable.

The makeshift device could be improved if she could find the right parts. She wandered through the piles of debris, biting on the tube like a snorkel and pushing the end of the tube on the floor for each breath. Her foot kicked a rectangular piece of plastic, thick and heavy, with a hole in the center; perfect. She slipped the bottom end of the tube through the hole and continued walking, dragging the plastic weight across the floor. Better for the floor end, but her jaw was already aching from biting on the tube, and the additional weight made it worse. A mask would help.

The light hanging in the sky flickered. She swiveled her head just as the light flashed off and then back on again. A chill ran through her body. The plunge into darkness, even for an instant, was disturbing. Up to now, the light had been so steady; why the sudden variation? She waited, but the light continued to shine as if nothing had happened.

"Don't mess with me," she yelled at the light. Trying to find her way around a space with edges capable of slicing off your limbs wouldn't be much fun in the dark. That light had better hold.

Nala returned to Thomas and kneeled. "Good friend. Can I borrow your hat?" The leather Viking hat was crumpled but would make a good mask to complete her air supply system. She picked up a sharp piece of glass and punctured the hat at its top, pushed the flex-tube through and secured it with tape from the first-aid kit. Snug. With a bit

170

more tape, she fashioned a head strap and positioned the mask over her nose and mouth.

She inhaled. Good air with a secure breathing apparatus. *Not bad. At least, I'm mobile again.*

The horns of the Viking hat flared out to each side, looking like tusks coming from her face. "Fucking perfect." Her voice was muffled inside the hat. "Thomas would have loved the warthog look."

The inert body of her friend lay at her feet. "I owe you one, buddy." Of course, there would be no way to repay the debt. Her eyes filled with tears and she wiped them away. *No more, it's time to survive.* She picked up the sweater she'd draped across Thomas and put it on, feeling warmer immediately. She scanned for the water bottles but didn't immediately locate them.

Water was a key requirement for survival, and she'd pulled three bottles from the mini-fridge. They should be right next to Thomas, but they weren't. Perhaps he had moved while she was unconscious, knocking the bottles away. She searched the area, but with so much debris, they couldn't have rolled far. When she came up empty-handed, a feeling of panic arose inside. No one lasts long without water.

Were there more in the mini-fridge? Doubtful. It was a small unit, but it might be worth a second look. She located the smashed refrigerator and pried open its bent door. Inside were three bottles of water, unopened.

"What the hell?" Her heart pounded like she'd seen a ghost. The bottles completely filled the small space. "I took those bottles out, I know I did. I opened one for Thomas and set the other two by his side."

Yet here they were, full of water, unopened. She closed the door and reopened it. It wasn't a mirage; the bottles were still there. She removed one and left the other two inside. Not trusting her senses, she set off down the path she'd cleared through the debris.

The pool I saw earlier had better still be there.

171

It wasn't far, and she found it again without trouble, just beyond the debris field. It was now darker, but still contained rippling water, even if it produced no sound. She removed her mask, bent down and put her lips to the water. She sucked and was surprised to find that her mouth filled. It tasted of chemicals, but it was water.

Bottles that randomly rearrange themselves... but with the pool, at least I won't die of thirst.

Maybe she'd never taken the bottles from the fridge. Maybe it had been a hallucination or false memory. Lack of oxygen? The explanation seemed farfetched, but she couldn't think of anything better. Just as difficult to explain was how a bubbling pool of water was available to her.

You're a scientist. Examine the evidence.

The floor had shapes, air and water. It must be the 3-D world but flattened, as was always the case when any 3-D object was viewed from 4-D space. She was in a 4-D bubble, she theorized, that rested on a 3-D surface just like a soap bubble on the surface of a mirror. It explained the feeling of vertigo every time she stood up. Down was not down. It was *ana* or *kata*. The real *down* was in some other direction.

That explained the floor. But what was beyond the sizzling wall of death? The void? The word was no more than a physicist's placeholder for the concept of nothing. Not nothing—as in empty space—but *really* nothing. As in, not even empty space itself. In the void, not only were there no quarks, no bosons, no particles of any kind, there weren't even any dimensions. Zero dimensions, like a singularity. It made sense. Sort of.

She summarized out loud. "I'm in a 4-D bubble projecting into a dimensionless void that was created by the momentum of a 3-D implosion." It was a working theory.

She looked up at the light hovering at some unknown distance away. She'd originally labeled it a singularity. Was it? Maybe it was more like a knot, tying off 4-D space. Analogies helped. Finding a relation to something known helps to crystalize the unknown.

An inflated balloon, held underwater, would rapidly deflate if its pinched-off nozzle were suddenly opened to the air above the water's surface. If it were a large enough balloon, it might even collapse fast enough to turn the balloon inside out and, with a bit of rubbery momentum, reinflate in the opposite direction above the water. Substitute concepts: the water is our normal 3-D world, the balloon is 4-D space, and the air above the water is the void. The analogy was conceptually neat, but it came with a few huge assumptions—such as whether the void even existed.

How does *nothing* exist? It seemed more of a problem of definitions. True nothingness is not something; it's not anything. It's the absence of everything. But to give it an attribute implies that it's *something*, and something can't be nothing. Circular reasoning always made her head hurt.

But sometimes it helped. With all the science bouncing around in her head, a key property of quantum systems popped into her consciousness.

Eigenstates. Superposition. She'd just been arguing with Jan about it—when? Yesterday?

Orbiting any atom, an electron's position exists as a probability wave, known as superposition, until the moment someone makes a measurement. Only then does the wave collapse to a specific position, an eigenstate. It's one of quantum mechanics' most perplexing but very real effects. Many theorists make sense of it by saying that eigenstates are relative to the observer. Two scientists can find the same electron occupying two different positions simultaneously, yet both measurements are equally valid. Only in the quantum world can something exist in two states without logical contradiction. It's like finding your car parked on the left side of your garage, then closing and reopening the door, and the car is now on the right side.

The water bottles. They're in a state of superposition.

Two eigenstates. Two histories. Two entirely different locations. It was crazy, but it made perfect sense in the quantum world. A quantum bottle of water could be both empty and full, opened and sealed, and these contradictory states were equally valid.

The thought that a macro-sized object might behave like an electron was terrifying. Even if it explained the spooky phenomenon, it meant she couldn't trust her own senses.

She looked down at the pool of water. Still there, at least. Better than the capricious water bottles. She stepped in it, watching the ripples her shoes created. Three-dimensional space, no doubt. Within reach but impossibly distant.

She jumped. Her shoes splashed in the water, but the hard surface resisted penetration. "Okay, only a sliver of me exists within that space," she said with authority. "The bottom of my feet, the tips of my fingers. I can intersect with the three-dimensional world, but just barely." She talked herself into this revelation. It was the only logical explanation that fit the data.

Without overthinking things, she walked on, directly away from the light, her only point of reference. The shapes on the floor changed subtly, with fewer patches. It looked like asphalt, but mixed with dirt. She kept on walking, dragging her breathing hose behind her while scanning in all directions for anything unusual. The light behind never dimmed.

After several minutes, the shapes at her feet changed, with distinct lines, circles, squares and much more detail. There was motion too, all around. A confusing scene, but with nearly recognizable shapes. A doglike shape went by, followed by what looked like a person holding its leash. Both figures were compressed, with a strange mashup of views from multiple directions, but there was no doubt of their reality.

The floor was home. The 3-D world. Theory confirmed.

"Hey," she yelled. The person-shape didn't stop. She ran after it. "Hey, can you hear me? Help!" There was no reaction from either the person or the dog. Nala stopped and watched the shapes as they receded into the distance.

There was more motion to her right. More people, or at least people-like shapes. They were flattened and distorted, and she could see not just their skin and clothes, but also their bones and organs.

"Hey," she yelled again. There was no response and no sound from the moving scene below her.

Like walking on the surface of a television. Or a Picasso painting.

She jumped up into the air, her feet slamming down onto the scene in motion. The misshapen people went about their business, no different than if they were images in a movie.

They can't hear me, but I can drink the water and breathe the air.

She removed her makeshift mask and dropped to the floor. She pressed her lips to its surface and yelled. "Hey, can you hear me? I need help!"

Lying on the surface, she was too close to the images to make them out. She put the mask back on and got on her knees for a better view. Unfortunately, there was still no change. Her voice seemed not to penetrate the barrier, as if a thick sheet of glass separated her from the strange flattened world below.

A one-way path, from them to me.

One of the darker rectangles looked like a counter as seen from the ceiling, with moving people on both sides. At the end of the counter were stacks of food... possibly bagels and muffins. She crawled over and touched the surface. One of the bagel shapes moved, only slightly, but noticeably.

175

She touched again, pinching her fingers over the television-like image. The shape moved further. Pressing harder, she could feel its surface, wiggle it, even lift it slightly like getting a fingernail under a flake of dried-out paint. She used both hands, pushing the shape between her fingers.

Suddenly, it lifted free as if it were a sticker in a children's activity book. She pulled the flat object into her world and held it up. To her surprise and delight, it wasn't flat at all. Between her fingers, she held a normal three-dimensional bagel.

"Holy crap! That's amazing!"

She lifted her mask and bit into it—a bagel as real as any. "Food!"

It was more than a food source, and more than a way to stay alive. She had demonstrated an ability to interact with what was surely the three-dimensional world below her feet.

"I am a goddess!" she yelled. "A four-dimensional goddess, in fact." She pointed to the flattened people-shapes below her. "With my warthog-god face, I stand above all of you who live in the ordinary world. You can't even see me, but I'm right next to you."

Nala pulled off the mask, lowered herself closer to the fresh air and ate the bagel, satisfying the hunger that had been building. She leaned toward one of the people standing behind the counter. "Sorry about the theft. I'll pay for it when I get out of here."

The revelation hit her immediately. "Wait a second. I know where I am." She examined the counter closely, the register where one person stood, multiple stacks of white circles next to her. "I know this place. Corner of Kirk and Butterfield. This is Aurora; my house is just down the street." Nala laughed. Home was much closer than she thought, even if it was on the other side of the mirror.

"Better still," she said with a mischievous smile, "I think I know how to get out of here." She reached to the counter and put one index finger on each end of what looked like a marking pen. With some wiggling and pressure, she managed to lift the flat pen from the *page*. "Behold," she said. "My goddess powers are unlimited!"

Nala uncapped the now-three-dimensional felt-tip marking pen, leaned close to the counter and started writing on the stack of white circles.

~~~~~~~~~~~~~~~~~~~~~~

The man in the business suit stepped to the front of the line. It was only Julia's second day at the coffee shop, but she had the patter down already. "Good morning, what can I get started for you?"

"Grande two-pump mocha with almond milk, no whip."

Julia pulled a paper cup off the stack and reached to the counter. She stopped, looking left and right. "Dang, I had it right here. Now where did that pen go?"

24 Messages

Marie leaned against the wall of an empty conference room at the Kennedy Space Center O&C building. Daniel and Jan stood silently a few feet away. A table with chairs occupied the center, but no one seemed to be interested in sitting. Both men had their eyes fixed on her.

She took a deep breath, looked up at the ceiling and pushed her hair back with both hands. There was so much to explain. Daniel wasn't one of the NASA bosses; he was a lot closer to a friend. Some of the more difficult parts were bound to come out.

"The best way to deal with whatever is bothering you is to share," Daniel said.

Marie snorted a laugh. "You sound like a shrink."

"Core says you *comprehend*. Comprehend what?"

"Yeah. My *gift*, as they say."

"Something the Dancers gave you?"

"Yeah."

"Is it classified?"

Marie shifted on her feet. "No, not classified, just not yet announced. But I can talk about it. The thing is pretty amazing, actually."

Daniel lowered his head and confronted the issue. She knew he would. "You're reluctant to talk about it, Marie. Why?"

Marie stood quietly, twisting a lock of hair behind her neck. "I... think that it gets worse when I talk about it... or even think about it." The statement might not be accurate, but that was the way it felt. The creepy-crawlies waited just under the surface. She quickly banished the thought lest it manifest into something worse.

Daniel nodded. "Kind of a problem for the rest of us who would like to help you out, huh?"

Marie shook her head vigorously. "You can't help me, I already know that."

"How?" Daniel looked serious. He wasn't going to let this drop.

"It's a headband with electronics that nobody understands yet. But when I wear it... I can visualize most of the forces of the natural world with amazing detail... including... my own brain."

"You see your brain working?"

Marie dropped her head. Her feet shuffled uncontrollably. "Yes. Brain activity. Processing of complexity. It's hard to describe."

"Sounds amazing," Daniel said. "But something about it doesn't feel right?"

She shook her head, looked up and clasped both hands under her chin, her eyes staring straight ahead. "I'm sorry, Daniel. Sometimes it... uh... it scares me." She did her best, but it was hard to hide emotions from Daniel. They knew each other too well.

Daniel nodded sympathetically. "Whatever guidance Core thinks you can provide is clearly coming with a personal cost." He moved closer and bent down until she lifted her watery eyes to his. "I think we need a change of scenery. What do you say we get out of here?"

~~~~~~~~~~~~~~~~~~~~~~~~~

The three filled a quiet booth near the back of a restaurant in Cocoa Beach. Jan studied his phone, leaving the conversation to Daniel and Marie, but he looked up from time to time. There was no doubt of his interest.

Marie popped another piece of calamari into her mouth. "Thanks, Daniel, I needed a bit of normalcy." A glass of wine and the casual setting had changed an interrogation into more of a personal support group. Daniel was a master at putting people at ease, and Marie appreciated his efforts. It was time to open up, and she did.

"With the headband activated, forces become colors, information becomes a pattern. It's all really complicated, but somehow simple. No one showed me how, but I can understand what it displays to me." She shook her head in wonder. "I don't know how to describe it. It's really wild."

Daniel sipped on a beer. *"She comprehends.* That's what Core said. It sounds like you do."

Marie put her fork down. "Well, maybe. It depends. When I'm wearing it, everything is crystal clear. Really complex stuff, too. I don't even question how I know it all, I just do. But right now—without the headband—comprehension seems really remote, like I'm forgetting something I should have remembered."

She explained several of the physical data layers as best she could and how she'd been able to interpret the Workers' language and emotion. She even explained the weird ability to glance forward in time. Daniel listened intently, but Jan mostly kept to his phone.

"I could see some beneficial use at Fermilab," Daniel said. "Maybe that's the guidance Core was talking about."

"I'd be happy to help in whatever way I can," Marie said. "Right now the headband is locked away in a NASA examination room. Some of the engineers are looking at it, but I could speak with Ibarra."

"Maybe later," Daniel said. "This thing is alien and it doesn't sound like it's under control just yet." He gazed at her with sympathetic eyes.

His statement was true enough. She still hadn't talked about her collapse next to the tortured Worker, the hallucination and the fear that had come with it. Daniel wasn't pressing the subject, which was fine by Marie. Even with the headband off, the awful feeling was still there.

They talked about alien science for another twenty minutes until Daniel thankfully changed the subject. This was, after all, a support group for distressed ex-katanauts.

"Two off-planet trips within a single week," he said. "You deserve some relaxation time. Are you heading back to Washington anytime soon, or do you have continuing duties here in Florida?"

"Florida for a few more days. When Zin leaves, I'll go home. You know, I think it's fascinating that Core confirmed the rumor that's been circulating around KSC."

"What rumor?"

"That Zin is quantum-entangled with Core."

"You think they communicate with each other that way?"

"I don't know, but Core seemed to know all about me and what happened on Ixtlub, so they must share an intellect in some way."

Jan held up a hand to interrupt their conversation. He stared at his phone, while an agitated finger scrolled its display. "Sorry, but I'm getting some important messages." He touched the screen. "One from Jae-ho Park, another from our head of security. Both say the same thing."

Jan looked up from the phone. "They've found written notes. They're appearing on people's desks at Fermilab, and other places too." Jan's face turned pale and he fumbled the words.

"They... they think the notes are from Nala."

25 Partners

With an unsteady hand, Marie set the glass of wine down, almost spilling it. Nala was alive? Jan seemed convinced of it, and Daniel acted like he believed him. Marie wasn't about to throw cold water on the idea, but it seemed farfetched.

Daniel tapped repeatedly on his phone as he spoke to Jan. "I can get you to Fermilab hours faster than you could get there yourself." Jan was visibly shaken, his eyes glassy and his pale skin devoid of any color.

"Nala is alive," Jan whispered. He looked like he might faint at any minute.

Marie reached for Jan's arm. "Did they say why they think it's Nala?"

"Her handwriting," he said, recovering slightly. "Her choice of words. Dr. Park knows her well. He says the notes are from Nala, no question."

"But how is that even possible?" she asked.

Jan rubbed the side of his face. "The collapse to a singularity. It might have… except…" He seemed to be grasping for an understanding that wasn't quite within reach. "Nala was experimenting. Studying the parameters for quantum space as it collapsed. She'd found instabilities not predicted by theory, and neither of us could figure it out. But… if that light floating in the middle of Fermilab really is a singularity, theoretically there could be something on the other side. An aberration of space, but within the void."

"The void?"

"A placeholder. A fanciful idea, most would say, even among cosmologists who subscribe to the multiverse theory."

"Sorry, multiverse?" Marie questioned.

Jan was succinct in his answer. "If we're part of a multiverse, the void is the stuff in between individual universes. It's basically nothing, not even space in any conventional sense. But, theoretically, it could support ephemeral bubbles."

Daniel finished a phone conversation and hung up. "Come on, Jan. Shuttle Landing Facility. I've got another military jet for us, and it's firing up its engines as we speak."

"You're coming too?" Jan asked.

"Absolutely," Daniel answered. "This time it's personal." He turned to Marie. "It was great to see you again. Sorry to rush off."

There was no way she was going to let them go without her. Marie grabbed one of Daniel's hands, firmly. "Daniel, I have a strong feeling about this. I think I can help. I want to help. Could you use an old partner once again?"

"I'm sure we could," Daniel replied, "but don't you have duties here?"

The plan formed quickly in her mind. She tapped her right temple twice. She could help, she was sure of it. "Go to the plane. I've got two things I need to do, and if it goes well I'll meet you at the FBO. Can you give me ten minutes?"

Daniel nodded in agreement, though he looked a little uncertain. There was no time to explain.

~~~~~~~~~~~~~~~~~~~~~~

The Gulfstream jet was parked at Space Florida, a fixed-base operator, or FBO in aviation terminology. One engine was running with the airstair still deployed. Marie ran, dragging a small roller bag behind. She climbed the stairs just as the first officer arrived to close the door. Inside, Daniel and Jan sat on opposite sides of the aisle. Marie plopped into the seat behind Jan.

Daniel twisted around. "You made it. Last-minute wrangling with the boss?"

"Something like that," she answered. "I'm cleared to stay as long as needed, and I'm authorized to help in any way I can."

"Authorized?" He pointed to the suitcase. Nothing got past Daniel. "You didn't."

"I did," she answered with a confident grin.

"Marie, are you sure you want to put that thing back on your head? It sounds like it produces some nasty side effects. The Dancers didn't do their homework when they altered it for human use."

He was probably right about its flaws. But Daniel had never experienced the headband's power. More importantly, she felt sure she'd been chosen, her importance as a *probability* stated by Zin and now confirmed by Core. It had to mean something.

She had needed only a minute to get Ibarra's permission to take the headband offsite. Before she left his office, he'd stated that in a broad sense her destiny seemed to be intertwined with the alien device. A bit intimidating, coming from her boss, but there was no time to think about the implications. It took only a few minutes more to locate and retrieve the headband from several surprised NASA engineers who didn't put up much resistance. After all, she was the designated *wearer* of the device.

"Daniel, this thing works," Marie argued. "I wouldn't have brought it if I wasn't confident. Jan, you said it yourself—you're dealing with an aberration of space. The void, ephemeral bubbles... or whatever you said."

Jan shook his head. "Marie, I really don't know what we're dealing with. We're going to need a lot more information."

She patted her suitcase. "And that's exactly what I can give you."

It was dark in the Chicago area when they touched down at the DuPage regional airport. A car and driver were waiting for them.

"You've sure got good connections," Jan said.

"I can't complain," Daniel responded. "Those of us lucky enough to be White House staff do pretty well."

Marie rolled her eyes without looking at Daniel. *The rest of us government peons just trudge along without the White House perks.*

The thought was unnecessarily rude, and Marie admonished herself for even thinking it. Yes, Daniel could be full of himself sometimes, and yes, he was a famous science spokesperson now, with special privileges only the president could confer, but he was still her partner and someone to trust.

Marie followed Jan and Daniel into the black town car, and within minutes they arrived at the front door of Fermilab. She recognized the building, the place where she and Daniel had had their first taste of the bizarre world of four-dimensional quantum space. It seemed like a long time ago.

"Bring back memories?" Daniel asked.

"Oh, yeah," Marie said. "That look-inside-your-guts 4-D camera view was so disturbing. Still gives me the creeps."

Most of the lights in the building were off, the workday having ended hours before. The front desk was staffed by a security guard, who said Dr. Park was expecting them. They received temporary badges and rode the elevator up.

At the top-floor hallway, a familiar face peeked out of an office. Jae-ho Park stepped into the hall. "Jan, I thought it might be you. And Dr. Rice and Ms. Kendrick too. So wonderful to see you both again. I only wish the circumstances were better."

The man had aged, his white hair thinning and his eyes sunken. The scientific efforts at Fermilab were well known these days, and probably a lot more stressful for the people who worked here. More hazardous, too. They weren't just scouring the unknown edges of the universe; they were clearly poking around in a field of land mines.

"Is it really Nala? Are you sure?" Daniel asked.

"I am convinced of it," Park said. "Now I must show you. I think you will find the evidence is unambiguous."

Park ushered them into his office, handed a sticky note to Daniel and an empty paper coffee cup to Marie. The writing on the yellow square of paper was bold and black, though one word ran off the edge.

Help me! Singul
Get Jan. Nala

"It was found on my administrative assistant's desk," Park said. "The word *singularity* is cut off, but the remainder appears on the admin's desk as if Nala continued to write even beyond the paper." Park motioned to Marie. "Turn the cup over." Marie did.

The same black writing fit within the paper cup's indented bottom. "Help! Call Fermilab—NP," Marie read.

The handwriting and the pen used to write were the same for both messages. Park reached out and took the cup, turning it over in his hands. "The cup came from a nearby coffee shop. A barista noticed the text even before she filled it with coffee. There were several more found in their garbage."

"And you're confident it's Nala's handwriting?" Daniel asked.

Park nodded. "We use whiteboards frequently in our staff meetings. I've watched her write many times, as has Jan. Her hand is easy to recognize." He picked up another slip of paper, a menu for a Chinese restaurant, from his desk. The Spicy Chicken item had been circled, and next to it was written *Medium hot—Nala.*

"Our admin produced this sample of Nala's handwriting—a group lunch order from last week."

Marie compared both side by side. The handwriting looked the same.

"It's her," Jan said. "I'm sure of it. But with the Diastasi lab gone, we have no hope of accessing wherever she is."

Park nodded. "Yes, with our technology lost, Nala is beyond our reach. But it doesn't mean that hope is lost. We are in touch with colleagues in Geneva, and even though they have suspended their own operations, I believe we may yet get help. This is no longer a disaster investigation, it's a rescue. Please." He motioned for them to follow. "I will show you her most recent communication."

The hallway made a left turn past Park's office, with a break room on one side and Jan's office on the other. A decorative clock hung on the wall next to the break room entrance, and a hand-drawn black line dropped from the clock to the tile floor. The line ended in an arrow. Scrawled in large letters, the message ran across the floor and partially up the side of the doorway.

8 AM — meet me here. Bring food and drink. Vodka would be nice.

Daniel suppressed a smile. "Pure Nala," he said.

Marie had almost forgotten the rumors, but Daniel's face confirmed them—the two had been a couple. Maybe they still were. The words on the floor made it crystal clear—Nala was very much alive.

Park stood next to the writing, without stepping on it. "This message was not here at six p.m. I know, I passed through here at that time. I noticed it later, around eight p.m. She has been here, not here literally, but within range of our dimensions, and only a few hours ago."

"So, we do as she suggests," Daniel said. "We return here at eight tomorrow morning."

"Yes, definitely," Jan said.

"With food," Marie added. "She's probably starved. But... how would she eat?"

"Maybe we leave that for her to figure out," Daniel said. "Let's do exactly as she suggests."

"Even the vodka?" Maybe it was to sterilize a wound. But probably not.

Daniel had a faraway look in his eyes. Recalling a vodka-related memory? "Yes," he said. "Vodka, too."

188

The lower reaches deep underground at the vast Fermilab facility were quiet and dark, the hallway lighting having automatically shifted to a subdued overnight mode. Marie walked alongside Daniel. Park had offered to take them, but Daniel had dissuaded him. Marie was thankful for that. This task would be difficult enough; easier if the people around you were your friends. Daniel was.

In her hand, she carried a leather case the size of a small pizza box. *You can do this*, she reminded herself more than once.

Daniel hadn't spoken since they'd left Wilson Hall and dropped by elevator to the catacombs beneath. So many of the lower hallways looked the same—stark concrete lined with pipes and electrical bundles. She would have never found her way alone, but Daniel had used this facility each time he'd spoken with Core. He probably felt like one of the staff by now.

They stopped at a security desk to sign in, and the guard called upstairs for permission. It seemed like a procedure that had only recently been established. After some back-and-forth on the phone and a double check of their credentials, they were cleared and given instructions not to touch any of the monitoring equipment.

Won't be a problem, Marie thought. *I brought my own.*

"Just up ahead," Daniel said, motioning to a turn in the hallway.

They rounded the corner and stopped. The destruction couldn't have been this large, but it was. The floor of the hall ended abruptly, as if someone had sliced through the metal and concrete with a hot knife. Beyond it was a vast bottomless hole, dark without end. The hole extended above them, with no ceiling in sight. Far out into the darkness floated a small but bright light.

"Oh my God," Marie said. She kept her eyes fixated on the destruction. Wires dangled from above. The crackle of an electrical spark echoed, or perhaps it was just her imagination.

189

"How does anyone survive this?" Daniel whispered, shaking his head.

A spiral of dust revolved around the tiny light. Water dripped somewhere far below, but all else was still. If there was a far side to this cavern, Marie couldn't see it.

They stood in awe of the force that had taken away a large portion of the building. Neither spoke for several minutes, mesmerized by the slowly rotating dust set aglow by the light within it.

Finally, Daniel broke the silence. "She's in there... somewhere."

"I'll know soon enough," Marie said. She unzipped the leather pouch and withdrew the shiny metal band that was inside.

Daniel watched as she prepared. "Is there anything I can do that would help?"

Marie shook her head. The bond with the headband was hers alone. Daniel, along with a lineup of doctors, engineers and psychiatrists, wouldn't make the slightest difference. No one else could help because no one else could grasp the experience, both the fascinating visual show that the device created inside her head and its sometimes-terrifying conclusion.

Daniel stepped back a few feet, and Marie placed the silver band over her forehead. It dropped down to a snug fit, compressing her hair. She closed her eyes and tapped twice.

26 Visualization

She visualized glowing globes in a sea of darkness. Dozens of them, scattered about, some the size of a hot-air balloon, others much larger. Spherical in shape, though the nearest was too large to see the whole. Its surface was a smooth curve that extended far overhead.

They were colorful, varying in shades from navy blue to azure. Two of the spheres were deeper shades of purple. For such large objects, they seemed supremely fragile. Their curving surfaces were a thin film as tenuous as a soap bubble. Gentle fluctuations flowed across the flexible film like wind in a wheat field.

Together the spheres composed a shimmering three-dimensional sculpture, like a collection of enormous but delicate glass balls. What the spheres represented had not yet come to mind.

Marie rotated in twenty-degree increments, a fact confirmed by an unseen readout generated inside her head. She paused at each increment and studied the scene and then moved on until she had completed the full three-hundred-sixty-degree turn.

One of the spherical surfaces—the one nearest—was the deepest purple, a beautiful indigo color. Its surface shimmered like the others, but it also had a number associated with it: 1.324, though it wasn't clear what the number represented. She looked back at the other spheres and realized that they were all associated with a specific number: 0.577, 0.974, 1.629... The numbers weren't displayed anywhere; it was more of a suggestion that came to mind as she looked at each sphere.

She returned her attention to the closest sphere. Its glow was fascinating to watch, a combined effect of billions of tiny points of light covering its surface. Each minute sparkle winked out in a millisecond to be replaced by another equally small and equally temporary speck of light. Somehow, her mind could not only visualize each spark, but also imagine them collectively as a glow across the bubble's surface.

The detail was entrancing, but she had no idea what she was seeing. Daniel was near; she could sense his presence even with her eyes closed. But he remained silent, which was just as well.

She walked forward, sensing the edge of the nearest sphere. Its curving surface soared overhead. It reminded her of standing at the base of the geodesic sphere at Epcot Center. For a moment, she opened her eyes. She stood within a few feet of the edge of broken concrete— the edge of a cliff over a vast spherical hole. The enormous purple soap bubble was somewhat larger than the hole but centered within the same space.

Lifting one hand, she reached out to touch the iridescent purple film. Her hand easily penetrated and produced a slight vacillation that rippled across its surface.

"Very cool."

"What?" came from behind.

"Like a giant bubble. I can reach inside it."

"What's in there?" Daniel asked.

She moved her head through the edge of the bubble, but its interior didn't appear any different. "I don't know. I can see the surface and there's a number associated with it, but nothing else. It sparkles. Really, it's quite beautiful."

She sensed motion, not physical motion and not nearby. She took several steps back from the spherical bubble and looked left to another spherical surface, very far away and much larger. It was the same indigo color as the one nearby, but its surface was different. It warped and bulged. It fluctuated in size and curvature.

"There's something big out there. Moving. Warping."

"What is it?"

"It's another sphere, deep purple in color. But it's too far away. I can't see it in detail, not like the ones nearby. It seems to be deforming; maybe breaking apart, but in slow motion."

"So how many spheres are nearby?"

"Maybe a dozen of the blue ones. They vary in size and a lot of them overlap, so it's hard to count. The one we're standing next to is different. Deep purple. Indigo."

"Are they fourth-dimensional space?" Daniel asked.

"Maybe, but other than the numbers, I'm not getting any identification, at least not in this layer."

"Any holes in any of the spheres? Any connections to 3-D space? I'm just wondering if there's a way in or out."

Marie looked around with her eyes open. The bright light stood out among the glowing spheres. "The light may be associated with this nearest purple sphere, because it seems to be in the center. Other than that, they're just giant balls."

"Can you think of any way to find Nala and Thomas?"

It was a good question. How she flipped between the visual layers was impossible to describe. It was not even clear which choices were available. Her mind controlled the visualizations, but not in any conscious way.

Think about people.

She concentrated. Nothing happened. She knew it wouldn't; the device didn't work that way. It wasn't like flipping to the People Channel. The visualizations arrived as needed.

After a few minutes, she gave up. "I'm sorry, I can't find them." She opened her eyes and turned to Daniel. "I feel like I'm missing something. Like there's something behind a curtain if only I could pull it back."

Daniel stepped closer. "Too bad this thing didn't come with a manual. But you've already provided some clues. It's very likely that you're seeing extradimensional space. If you can give the details to Jan, maybe he can work with it and find an answer."

As Daniel spoke, his words slowed and his voiced deepened. An odd sensation of an image fluttering, like one of those old television sets unable to control its vertical hold. Suddenly, Daniel's face pixelated, converting before her eyes into multicolored dots that vibrated in place. His body followed, becoming a sea of dots that turned him into a wiggling form, no longer human.

A sense of unease escalated into terror as Daniel's face melted before her eyes. She ripped the alien band from her head and dropped it to the floor. Her vision didn't improve. The floor pixelated too, its surface alive with vibrating dots that made the whole room shimmer. The vibration increased in intensity, as if every dot sought out the pattern of its neighbors and chose to synchronize. She felt the vibration enter her body from the floor. Her legs wobbled, her arms shook, her hands trembled. The vibrations continued up each bone, through her nervous system and into her spine. The shaking reached into her head, making her feel like it might explode.

Help me! She yelled, yet nothing came out.

Marie collapsed to the floor. Its surface seethed with vibrating pixels all around. They shaped themselves, becoming millions of individual creatures with legs, eyes at the ends of stalks and antennae. A pixelated army of bugs crawled across the surface toward her, their numbers increasing by the second and their target clear.

She screamed but heard nothing, as if her open mouth was incapable of physical noise. And suddenly, it stopped. The vibration dampened like the surface of a drum no longer struck. The marching insects disappeared as quickly as they had formed.

Her vision returned, even while her heart beat furiously. She lay on a carpeted floor in a darkened hallway. Very quiet. An acrid smell of electricity permeated the air.

Daniel came into view, dropping to his knees, his face inches away. "Marie, can you hear me?"

Her heart pounded, and the fog of terror lingered. Waking from a nightmare was nothing compared with the hallucination. There was no doubt of its fantasy, but that didn't make it any less fearful.

"I... I can."

"You fainted," he said. "Just lie still for a minute."

Marie rolled onto her back and took several deep breaths. Her heart calmed.

A few feet away, the headband lay on the floor. A device with capabilities beyond any human technology. But access came with a price. The hallucination seemed real enough to make her heart race and her adrenaline spike. Luckily, it hadn't lasted long, and the rational world had returned. What she had experienced was all in her head, as the shrinks say. Temporary psychosis.

"Can I get you some water?" Daniel asked.

"No, I'm alright now. Just help me up." She could manage standing, she hoped.

Daniel pulled on one arm and helped her up. The room spun. "Uh... little dizzy."

"Sit down," he said, putting an arm around her. She stumbled to the wall and slid to the floor. Daniel squatted just in front.

After a minute, the spinning room slowed down. "I think I'm okay now. Thanks, Daniel."

He held out a comforting hand and she took it. "Damn, Marie. You had me worried. One minute you were staring at me with a funny look, and the next you just hit the deck."

Of course, there was more that Daniel hadn't seen. "Did I scream?" She'd certainly tried, but like a dream, the mind only imagines what the body is doing.

"No, you just collapsed. Sorry, I didn't catch you in time. It must have hurt falling on that headband."

She felt her head for bumps. "But I threw the headband off well before I dropped."

"No, you didn't." Daniel seemed surprised.

"Didn't what?"

"You didn't throw the headband off," he said. "You just fell. It came off when you hit."

That's weird. I'm sure I threw it down.

Of course, things were going south pretty fast at that point. It might have taken longer to get the headband off than she'd thought. But then... if Daniel was right, had throwing the headband been part of the hallucination? It could explain why the nightmare hadn't stopped until she was on the ground. She was in uncharted territory.

"Sorry, this didn't turn out like I thought it would," Marie said.

"Nonsense," Daniel said. "Your descriptions of the spheres might be helpful. While you were visualizing, I recorded everything on my phone."

Marie snorted. "That'll be embarrassing. Psychic crazy lady thinks she sees purple bubbles floating in the sky."

Daniel grinned. "Yeah, but think how many likes you'll get when you post it."

Marie did her best to smile.

Daniel's grin disappeared. "It was more than just fainting, wasn't it?"

Marie nodded.

"Did it scare you, like you mentioned back in Florida?"

Marie nodded. "Just a hallucination. It wasn't real."

Daniel picked up the empty leather case and handed it to her. "Maybe you should just put that thing away for now. Somebody needs to have a deeper discussion with the Dancers about their technology."

Marie took the case. She understood a little more about herself every day. Today's lesson: finding a path along the narrow dividing line between safety and risk. Daniel had just come down on the side of safety. Something told her she was heading in the opposite direction.

He stood up and reached down for her hand. "Come on, partner. It's late, and we've still got a lot to do before we meet Nala in the morning."

27 Duty

Marie dropped her roller bag by the door and collapsed spread-eagle on the hotel room bed. The clock showed just past one a.m. and they would need to be up early, but sleep would need to wait until emotions were sorted out. It wasn't just the creepy-crawlies. The visualization took a toll, put a noticeable stress on her psyche. In some ways, it was like any mental effort: organizing, writing, designing or just being creative often results in fatigue. The headband was like that too, but amplified.

Psychosis. She'd looked it up on a medical site on their drive to the hotel. *Brief psychotic disorder.* BPD, they called it. A loss of reality on a temporary basis, and more common than most people realized, particularly for women under thirty-five. Treatable, but the web page didn't mention anything about alien headbands.

Be safe, as Daniel advised.

Marie undressed and crawled under the covers. Her mind wandered for another half-hour before she finally drifted off to sleep.

~~~~~~~~~~~~~~~~~~~~~

Daniel closed the door of his hotel room and pulled out his phone. With three text messages and two voicemails, he might be awake a little longer.

At least Marie was safely in her room. She had looked like she could use the rest. It was fascinating to watch the headband in action even if he couldn't see what she saw. Her descriptions showed promise as guidance for Jan, just as Core had predicted. Understanding *where* Nala and Thomas were trapped was the first step to rescue, and Marie's visualization of the extradimensional space that was apparently popping up all around Fermilab would surely be helpful. He was a bit envious of her visual access to an unseen world, though the intensity of the device clearly took a personal toll.

The Dancer technology was impressive. Daniel had always wondered what an atom looked like—not just a computer visualization, but what it really looks like. Could the device do that? Marie hadn't described an atomic layer, but maybe that feature was hidden somewhere in the recesses of the alien device. Of course, a good photoionization microscope can create an image of a single atom, complete with a blurry path for an orbiting electron. But the best anyone had produced was still a computer representation of quantum probability data. There were no actual photographs of atoms and never would be. Even the largest atom, cesium, is six hundred times smaller than the wavelength of visible light, forever invisible to our eyes.

Could Marie visualize the link between quantum-entangled particles? Could she slow time and observe the nearly instantaneous process of radioactive decay? The headband could be an incredibly useful device in a variety of scientific fields. It was a fine gift, even if it produced some disturbing side effects. Maybe they could be controlled.

The physiological impact on Marie was real—she had passed out in front of him. Until they had a better handle on it, NASA should study the headband's capabilities under medical supervision. Marie should set the headband aside; it wasn't worth further risk. He resolved to reinforce his recommendation when they met in the morning.

Daniel pulled up the first text message, a simple note from the night operator at the White House.

Priority message. Please check your voicemail.

The second text was similar, and the third was from Spencer Bradley, the White House science advisor and Daniel's boss. It provided a phone number.

Something was going on. Daniel dialed into voicemail. Message one of two:

"Daniel, Spence here. I've called a few times but I guess your phone was off. We've got a problem developing down in Texas. We're getting credible reports of unusual disturbances just east of Austin. I've got one description from a certified meteorologist of a 'swirling vortex in the sky,' as he called it. The USGS is also reporting ground tremors in the same area, and I really doubt it's from fracking. Something big is happening. I don't have all the details, but based on the location, you and I could both take a guess who might be responsible. Get on-site as soon as you can. I'll text you a contact number for more information. And Daniel, the governor may be deploying the National Guard in the Austin area as we speak—it's that serious."

Holy hell. Not good.

He checked the second voicemail. It was from the EPA district manager, Jeffrey Finch, Daniel's point of contact in Austin. He needed a callback as soon as possible.

Both calls had been placed within the past forty minutes. He'd switched off his phone to be sure there were no interruptions while Marie was using the headband. Bad timing, but at least he wasn't too far behind the curve.

He'd have to leave, and right away. He shoved the thoughts of Nala to the back of his mind, even though it felt wrong.

His next step was a call to Janine's mobile phone. After several rings she answered, groggy, but there. "I always know when it's you, Daniel... the ringtone. Kind of late, isn't it?"

"So sorry, Janine," Daniel said. "It's an emergency and I need to get to Austin. Can you do your magic?"

~~~~~~~~~~~~~~~~~~~~~~~~

The Cessna Citation lifted above the lights of Chicago and turned south. Daniel connected to the plane's Wi-Fi to finish his to-do list. Three a.m. It was going to be a long night.

He had already returned the call to Jeffrey Finch before takeoff. Strangely, the man had answered his mobile phone and offered to meet

Daniel at the airport—even with an estimated five-thirty a.m. arrival time. Working all night wasn't exactly normal government bureaucrat behavior. He hadn't said anything more about the strange goings-on around Austin, but his voice was agitated.

Marie was next on the list, and Jan after that. He composed a short text to each, taking more time and care with the message to Marie.

Sorry, I've been called away to Texas. The power plant issue I told you about has escalated. Wish I could help at Fermilab, but you and Jan have far more to offer. Tell him what you saw, he'll make sense of it. Then put that device back in its case—you've done your job. No more risks. Q: You described a distant bubble—the one you said was bulging. Any idea how far away? As far as Texas? Stay in touch. D.

He attached the recording he'd made of her visualization and sent the message. It was up to her now.

The connection between the distant bubble that Marie had seen and the event in Austin was purely a guess, but hard to ignore. You don't need evidence to identify a suspect in a case. Evidence is uncovered during the investigation.

Whatever was going on, Daniel didn't doubt the reports of ground tremors and swirls in the sky—they had come from trained scientists who, like any police detective, understand the difference between a witness who tells a good story versus one who provides a factual accounting.

Finally, there was Nala. Alive and communicating—all good. Better than good. Fantastic, unexpected and an instant flood of relief. His intuition that she was never dead had served him well.

But communicating from where? A reality beyond our senses, yet a physical place. Daniel was leaving her fate to others, but what else could he do? His note to Marie was only partially accurate. True, Daniel had little to offer, but he wasn't sure if Jan or Park had anything better.

Even if Marie could help pinpoint Nala's location, finding the technology to return her to the three-dimensional world was going to be a tall order.

They'd been in this position before. Just eight months before, three astronauts had been lost in four-dimensional space with no practical way to return home. Daniel hadn't solved it. No one had. Those guys would have been dead if not for the intervention of Core and alien technology.

This time the *alien savior* option didn't seem as likely. Core didn't seem to be the least bit concerned that human scientists were in danger—or dead. It was almost an expected side effect in our efforts to manage the new science and technologies related to quantum space. People die. You will learn, and all that BS.

Still, it could be worth another appeal, especially now that they knew Nala was alive. Maybe Thomas too. Daniel sent one more message to Marie. Maybe the diplomat, Zin, could pave the way.

We're in over our heads.

Being out of control is a humbling experience. But it wasn't just Daniel, or even Fermilab. Maybe it was all of humanity. We'd stumbled into a brand-new science that we barely understood but, instead of carefully studying it, we were dashing as fast as we could toward its promised benefits—and directly into its dangers. Even Nala. She'd probably gone too fast, cutting too many corners. It was just like her.

Nala. Beautifully exotic. Magnetic.

With each passing minute, the jet put more miles between Daniel and Nala. It wasn't the first time he'd left her. Duty called once again, just as it had when he'd declined her invitation to Haiti. Both times, he'd responded by choosing duty over Nala.

She was still alive, but there were no guarantees she'd survive. This was no Haiti, no waving it off with a "we'll get together another time" excuse. This time it was life and death... and yet, he'd still left her.

The guilt felt like a knife twisting in his belly.

28 Huddle

Marie set the bag of groceries on the break room table along with a bottle of vodka and a small bottle of pineapple juice. The juice was intended as nourishment, not a cocktail mixer.

"Should we leave everything wrapped?" she asked Jae-ho Park. There was no telling how Nala would manage to access any of it.

Park pulled several bottles of water out of the kitchen's refrigerator and set them on the same table. "I don't think it matters. If she is dimensionally offset, Nala would see everything all at once. The outside of our bodies and the inside too. It would be the same with the food, the table, the building. Whatever view she has of us may be quite complex."

"Then I guess we just leave it all on the table?" Marie asked.

"I could just as easily have left the water bottles in the refrigerator and she'd still be able to pull them out without even opening the door." Park had a tendency toward fascinating explanations that never answered the question.

"So... table?" Marie asked again.

"It's as good as anywhere," Park said. He glanced at the clock on the break room wall. "It is nearly eight a.m. We will soon see what happens."

They stood around the table and waited. Jan came running down the hall carrying a bundle under his arm, which he dropped on the table. "I thought of a few things she might need... assuming she has some way of taking them."

He unrolled a blanket with a first-aid kit and a flashlight inside. He also set a pair of handheld radios on the table. "Her lab was already supplied with most of this, but I'm guessing it was all vaporized in the explosion."

"Then how was she not vaporized?" Marie asked.

Jan held up both hands. "We're dealing with a situation that none of us understands. This was not predicted by theory. I can't even tell you where she is with any certainty."

"Our best guess," Park said, "is that the hovering light is a singularity, a zero-dimensional point. She may be quite literally inside that point, but only from our three-dimensional perspective."

Marie shook her head. These were top physicists, but they were just guessing. She'd already seen more with the headband than they were able to explain. "Spheres," she said. "I saw multiple iridescent spheres with sparkling surfaces. Some that were very large, and at least one that was very far away. They had numbers associated with them." She was repeating herself; she'd already given Jan a detailed description the night before, but Jan had asked few questions.

Jan and Park didn't speak for a moment of awkward silence. "I'm not making this up," Marie finally said.

"I'm sure you're not, Ms. Kendrick," Park said. "But what does this add to our understanding?"

You're the quantum geniuses, you tell me, Marie could have said. But she didn't. Two people were trapped and needed help. Any squabbles with the physicists would just make the dilemma worse.

She wished Daniel were there. He should have been. Called away, he'd said in his message.

Really? Called away? You couldn't have delayed your Texas thing by a few hours?

Lives were at stake, and one of them was a person Daniel supposedly cared very much about. What was in Texas that could possibly be more important than that? Marie wasn't in any mood to be magnanimous about Daniel's priorities or Park's wandering soliloquies.

205

This rescue team needed a little more focus. There were two people somewhere in that mix of iridescent spheres.

They waited. Marie pulled out a chair and sat, holding the headband in its carrying case on her lap. Daniel's recommendation that she avoid using it was about as useful as him jetting off to Texas in the middle of the night. She'd do what was needed and nothing less.

The clock read ten after eight. Nala was late for her own appointment. Unless, of course, she had already arrived. There was no sign of her presence, but the ghostly idea that she might be standing in the same room but offset in another dimension of space was more than unsettling.

Marie wasn't helpless. She unzipped the case and pulled out the headband. Jan and Park stared at her as she put it over her head.

Park held up a hand. "Ms. Kendrick, an alien device...I'm not sure..."

She gave him her best pissed-off-female look and Park backed away. Jan didn't say a word. She reached up and tapped twice on the side.

The spheres materialized before her but shifted in position—lower. It made sense. She was now high up in Wilson Hall, not below ground at the site of the accident. The bubbles were clearly associated with the underground lab.

"The spheres are still there," she said. "I think we're actually inside the biggest purple one. It's all around us now."

Neither man said anything. Maybe they thought she was conjuring the spirit world and their words would break the spell. As the famous futurist Arthur C. Clarke had once said, any sufficiently advanced technology is indistinguishable from magic. The capabilities of the headband were exactly that.

"There's one sphere that's far away and badly misshapen. Daniel thought it might be 4-D space over Texas, but I can't really tell. It's bigger than it was before. Not sure why." She flipped through several other data layers. "No sign of Nala."

I need that people layer. But it simply wasn't there. The magic had its limits, and if Nala was nearby, Marie had no way to know. She removed the band and returned it to its case. "Sorry, I wish I had more."

As she zipped the headband's case, there was movement on the table. Marie turned quickly. "Did you see that?" She stood upright and stared. A box of crackers trembled and slid, no more than a half inch, but without anyone touching it. "There."

They all gathered around the circular table covered with supplies. The box of crackers wiggled again and then slowly vanished in a wave that started at one end and finished at the other, as if someone had erased it from existence.

Jan dropped to his knees, his eyes level with the table. "Wow. Interdimensional kinesis. Maybe the new-age nutcases weren't so nutty after all."

"It's Nala," Park said. "It must be."

It had better be, Marie thought. *Because this is pretty freaking weird.*

The pineapple juice bottle began to shake. It slid one way and then the other and then disappeared in the same fashion. Three intelligent people with significant training in skeptical analysis had witnessed what anyone would describe as supernatural.

Even the rational explanation was a tough sell: Nala stood among them, but in some other space, unseen. It was an explanation that could make you crazy.

The vodka bottle wobbled and fell over, rolling off the table before anyone could catch it and crashing to the floor. Broken glass and the smell of liquor made the absurdity very real.

Jan pushed the broken glass away with his foot. "That didn't seem intentional. She's struggling."

"Two for three. I'd say she's doing pretty well." Marie picked up a jar of peanut butter and held it in the air. None of them spoke as the jar wiggled and then vanished.

Marie wrapped both arms around her as a chill shivered through her body. "Wow. It felt like someone pulled it right out of my hand."

The blanket shifted slightly and brushed against the radios that stood next to it, causing one radio to fall on its side. "Perhaps we should hold each item up," Park suggested. "It might be easier for her?"

"I'd be careful," Jan said. "Remember the Flatland story."

"Which is?" Marie asked.

Park nodded, apparently comprehending Jan's oblique reference. "A-sphere pulls A-rectangle from the two-dimensional page."

Jan nodded in agreement. "It may not be that simple, but there's the potential for injury, for both you and Nala."

"Sorry, what?" Marie asked again. Why was it so hard to get a simple answer from these guys?

Park spoke while Jan remained deep in thought. "Jan is suggesting that Nala might unintentionally pull on your finger or hand and drag you in."

"You've got to be kidding," Marie said.

Park shook his head, his expression no less serious than if he were delivering a eulogy for an interdimensional death. "Jan might be right. Assuming we are adjacent to space that we can't see, who is to say how much effort it takes to release us from our normal 3-D space, in whole or in part? Nala seems to be pulling small objects out with very little effort. It may not be that hard to pull you in too. We might think the dimensional boundary is impenetrable, but the dividing line between our space and this other space may be nothing of consequence."

The magenta spheres that Marie had visualized were held together by the flimsiest of surfaces, looking very much like giant soap bubbles. *I could put my hand through it.*

Even without the headband, Marie could almost see the dimensional sphere that was unquestionably surrounding them. She lifted the radio into the air and held it by her fingertips.

"Careful," Jan advised. Whatever that meant. There were so many unknowns in this scenario that it was impossible to describe what being careful even looked like. Nala needed that radio, and if no one else was going to do it, Marie would hand it to her.

The radio wiggled. For a moment, Marie thought she felt something brush against her wrist and then the radio disappeared, starting from its base and going all the way to its antenna.

"Yes!" Marie shouted.

Jan switched on the second handheld radio. "There's no guarantee a radio communication is going to work. Part of it depends on how Nala holds it." Marie was familiar with the issue. Antenna gain, or directional control, varied depending on the equipment. NASA high-gain antennae focused the electromagnetic transmissions in a specific direction. It was how a spacecraft orbiting Mars could communicate all the way back to Earth. But radios used for short-distance communication were low-gain, meaning the transmission would broadcast in a disc in all directions perpendicular to the antenna.

"How would she even know which way to point it?" Marie asked.

"She might not," Jan answered. "I'm not sure I would either, but depending on how she holds it—and a dozen other variables—we might receive her transmission."

"But not vice versa. Right?" They'd had the same problem trying to communicate with the missing Soyuz spacecraft. One-way communication only.

"Right," Jan said. "We have no way to point our antenna in her direction. All we can do is wait for her to call."

And so, they waited. But the radio produced nothing, not even static. Jan adjusted the squelch, but the radio remained silent.

"You sure it works?" Marie asked.

Jan nodded. "I tried them out when I picked them up. Fully charged. They work fine."

There was no way to know what problems Nala might be having on the other side of this strange boundary. Their wait ended with a crash that came from somewhere down the hall. When Marie looked up, Jan was already heading out the door.

"Sounds like it came from my office," he said, pulling his key out.

They followed him only a few steps down the hall and around a corner. He slid the key into a door and opened it to reveal a darkened office. Jan flipped the light switch.

A whiteboard had fallen from the wall and was lying on the floor. Jan picked it up and laid it flat on his desk. The whiteboard was partially covered with physics equations and diagrams, but scrawled diagonally in large letters were two words written with a black marking pen.

Sorry, Jan.

As they watched, additional words formed from nowhere, written by an invisible hand. The words ran across the width of the whiteboard, passing over its edge and onto the desk itself as if both were part of the same writing surface. A portion of one word even crossed the top of a white computer mouse in the middle of the desk. It was like a film projection of written words, covering multiple surfaces. They were difficult to piece together, but unmistakably from Nala.

Radio doesn't work … crackers and peanut … good.

Jan grabbed an eraser and wiped the whiteboard clean. He quickly wrote. *Hold the radio parallel to us.*

They waited. The radio in Jan's hand remained silent, but more words were scrawled across the whiteboard, this time even drawing across Jan's hand resting on the desk.

Can't see … you're doing … again.

Jan wiped the board clean again and wrote the same message once more. He looked up at the ceiling, but even Marie recognized that "up" was not the direction where Nala was hidden. Jan couldn't look in her direction any more than he could point to her. No one could.

More writing appeared.

Nope. Too confusing.

"She can't see what you're writing," Park said. "It's the view from four-dimensional space." He leaned close to Marie. "You recall, Ms. Kendrick when you first visited Fermilab, the strange view from the camera? Walls, clothing, skin, bones, all mixed together. Confusing is an understatement. Nala's situation may be even worse."

More words appeared.

Cover it. Black for … white for no. Okay?

Jan grabbed a dark blue blazer that hung on the back of his door and covered the whiteboard as best he could. If he was interpreting Nala's broken words correctly, a dark surface would mean *yes.*

"Now, uncover it so she can write," Marie suggested.

New words appeared as soon as the board was cleared.

You guys learn quickly! ... trained mice. Was radio working?

Jan covered the whiteboard with the jacket for *yes*, and another sentence appeared.

I'm calling. You're ... not hearing me. Write on cracker... easier to pick up.

"She means the cracker box," Marie said. "She had no problem picking that one up. There's another box in the break room." Marie dashed down the hall and returned with the box of crackers. Jan scribbled a note across its surface and handed it back to Marie. He still seemed concerned about holding anything out to Nala.

Marie shook her head and held the box in the air as far from her body as possible. It probably wouldn't be any safer, but it might make it easier for Nala to see it. Within seconds, the box began to wobble in Marie's hand, then disappeared just as the first one had.

Marie smiled. They waited to see what would happen. Writing appeared once more on the whiteboard.

Not bad. Food with a message. ... fortune cookie. As you thought, Jan. Instability ... boson. I totally fucked up. Hang on to your lederhosen ... in the void. Your move.

As they watched, a few more words appeared.

Hurry, would you?

29 Flickers

Nala put the radio down and dipped another cracker into the peanut butter jar. A sweater wrapped around her body, she sat cross-legged on the *floor*, allowing her bare legs to soak up its relative warmth.

She lifted the Viking oxygen mask for a moment, popped the cracker in her mouth and washed it down with pineapple juice. "Just as well that the vodka bottle broke," she said between crunches. "Probably better if I stay sharp."

The bottle had been harder to grasp than the other items. Slippery, with no distinct edges to pinch between fingers. The peanut butter jar was much easier, particularly when someone held it up. Nala wasn't sure who it was, but most likely a woman given the longer hair. Faces were difficult from this fourth-dimensional perspective, though hair was easier. The woman looked a bit like Daniel's old partner. What was her name? But why would she be at Fermilab? More likely it was someone from security.

The other two were easier. Jan and Jae-ho, almost certainly. Even if their faces were jumbled, she could tell just by their motions. People moved a certain way, and after years of working with the same colleague, you got to know them pretty well. Maybe not from another dimension, but the principle was the same.

No sign of Daniel. She wouldn't expect him to be there anyway. She could *wish* he was there. Daniel figured things out, and that kind of help could be pretty handy right now. But Jan was the physicist, and there would be no walking out of bizarroland without a scientific solution. Jan was her best hope, not Daniel.

Finishing the cracker, she licked her lips and made another try with the radio, turning the volume up to maximum and speaking loudly through a gap in the mask. "Calling all scientists. Anyone out there?" She released the transmit button and listened. Nothing, of course. There wouldn't be. Interdimensional conversations were one-way at best. A three-dimensional radio has no mechanism for sending electromagnetic waves into a fourth direction.

She held the button down. "Just kidding. I know you can't talk to me, and I think we've established you can't hear me either… *but* if I'm not mistaken, I think it depends on the position of the radio, or maybe the antenna. Can't remember. But I'll keep talking and twisting the radio around and maybe you'll pick up a few words here and there."

Nala stood up, whatever *up* was. "Thanks for the food. I'm going to grab a few more items if I can and then check out my surroundings. I'll return here at noon, okay? In fact, let me just write that for you." She drew once more on the whiteboard.

She walked a few steps back to the break room, passing directly over—through?—the three-dimensional walls in between. She dropped to her knees for a better look at the table. It was still covered with objects, some recognizable, some not. There was something bulky and gray. She had already tried to pick it up, but it seemed soft—maybe a pillow. It was too difficult to pinch, and she had given up. Nourishment was more important anyway. There was still another bottle, maybe water. No longer a critical need, though with disappearing-reappearing water bottles, you never knew. Other shapes looked like food. Better.

She reached to the floor and pinched a slender yellow shape between her left- and right-hand fingers. It wiggled and bent, but she finally managed to lift it from the *page*. A banana.

"Yum," she said, taking a bite. "Good choice, people of the page world."

She took another bite and picked up the radio again. "Who knows, maybe you can hear me. Probably better for my sanity if I think you might be out there. Hey, the writing sure got your attention, but I had no idea what you were doing in response. Maybe you were writing too, but it just looked like chicken scratches to me."

214

Nala's ability to write in their world made perfect sense; it really wasn't any different from an ordinary pen to paper. A three-dimensional pen intersects a two-dimensional sheet of paper exactly where the pen tip touches the paper. Any flat two-dimensional creatures living in the paper world would never see the pen but would easily detect the ink flowing into their page. From her 4-D perch she was simply intersecting the 3-D world with the tip of the pen, or the tip of her fingers. Same concept.

"I'd love to give you a longer description of where I am. Maybe I'll try to find a clear floor to write on. Anyway, if you can hear me, this might help you come up with a solution."

She looked around in the darkness. The area where she sat was free of debris, but there was no telling if she might encounter the *edge* again. It would be certain death if she did.

"I'm in quantum space, probably propped up by HP bosons, though I couldn't say what the baryon-to-boson ratio might be. My best guess is that the space Thomas and I created was unstable, and it folded back on itself when we forced it to collapse. Along with some 3-D space, we got sucked in."

She glanced to the bright light. "There are two sources of light. One is hanging above me. It's almost like a star, bright and probably far away because walking toward it or away from it doesn't really change its position. It might be the singularity I saw in the lab, but from another viewpoint. Whatever it is, the little shit turned itself off once. It just flickered and was gone. Almost wet my pants. Luckily it turned back on and has been steady ever since. But I'm wary."

She looked down, into the 3-D world. "The other source of light is the real world below me, though down may be a misnomer around here. The real world is dim, but it does glow. That tells me that photons are leaking across the boundary and, of course, any boson leaking into quantum space is normal physics, so that helps to confirm my hypothesis about where I am.

"I can interact with the 3-D world. I can touch things, even pull them out. Well, you've already seen me do that. It probably means that at least a small sliver of me still inhabits the 3-D world. I'd love to find a way to improve upon a sliver, but I haven't thought of anything yet."

She released the transmit key, dipped her head and then pressed the button again. "I fucked up bad... Thomas didn't make it."

She missed her friend and colleague. He would have been highly valuable in getting them out of this mess, particularly with the communications. He was always so good at...

She paused and slapped her forehead. "Dumb shit! What were you thinking? Cables. Fucking wires. That's all you need." The whole world had been wireless for years, but it was still no excuse. After all, they'd communicated with Core through a coaxial cable.

Nala quickly scribbled a note on the whiteboard and then keyed the radio. "Boy, are we dense sometimes. Just hand me a phone. But before you do, make sure it's connected to a computer via USB. Simple, right?"

Once a wired connection was established, there were a number of ways to communicate. They could transfer files, for example. She even recalled a chat app that worked over USB.

Satisfied that better communication was on the way, Nala turned off the radio and put it in the back pocket of her ripped shorts. It was time for some reconnaissance.

She gathered a few items of food and one water bottle and put them in a plastic bag she had found in the debris, tying her supplies through a belt loop. She picked up a metal pole that was now the equivalent of her blind man's cane, a last-chance warning for the edge and the void beyond it.

Wearing a Viking helmet air mask, pushing the pole in front and dragging an air hose behind, she would have been a strange sight if there had been anyone else to see her. With her free hand, she held the

216

radio up to the mask and narrated to friends far away yet uncannily close.

"I'll keep talking just in case you're listening. I doubt it, but you never know. I'm beginning to formulate two theories, both ridiculous, but I'll go out on a limb and describe them since no one's probably listening anyway. The first comes from my encounters with the edge of this space. It's a wall, a defined edge, though you can't really see it until you're close enough to touch it—which you definitely *don't* want to do. But what's beyond? Tricky stuff. You know how some of the multiverse theorists talk about the *void*? A place where nothing exists, not even space itself? Well, what if—"

She was interrupted by a flash of light. It came from the singularity overhead, first plunging her into darkness and then, a split second later, flickering back to life again.

Not again.

She kept her eyes glued to the light. Without it she wouldn't get far. Worse was the nagging question—*why* was it flashing?

Nala continued speaking into the radio. "Okay, so that's pretty fucked up. The light just flashed again. Don't know why. That's twice in the past... oh, twelve hours or so. Maybe it's a clock? It strikes every twelve hours? Weird shit happens around here."

She walked across a broad area, mostly black with white stripes. It could easily be a parking lot back in the real world. "Which brings me to my second theory, which is even crazier than the first. Jan will laugh or call me a physics pussy—which, by the way, Jan, is a form of sexual harassment. We'll deal with that when I get back."

She stood in place, thinking. "Inside this place—this bubble within the void—I think quantum rules apply. Superposition at a macro scale. Yeah, really! Mind-blowing, huh? But here's my example. I'm 100 percent sure that I opened a bottle of water and then found the same bottle of water back in the fridge, unopened. One object, multiple states. Exactly what any self-respecting electron would do. Of course, mixing up the bottles could have been a really hilarious practical joke. I wouldn't put it past Thomas, but he's… he's…"

Nala froze, staring into the blackness. Suddenly, things were not so funny. There was movement ahead, and not from the surface. A person, upright, and not flattened or distorted, walked directly toward her.

She dropped the radio and ran.

30 Apparition

Nala ran straight ahead into the darkness, dropping the rod that would warn her of the edge of the void, and without the slightest fear that such a fate could possibly occur.

She ran into the waiting arms of her friend, Thomas.

The big man, standing upright and apparently very much alive, enveloped the petite woman, his red beard scratching against her forehead. She hardly noticed as the Viking hat was pushed away and fell to the floor. She pressed her ear to his chest, listening to his breath and heartbeat, unable to reconcile what she saw before her with the impossibility that he was alive. She looked down. Both of his legs appeared to be firm and strong.

"I finally found you," he said. "I was looking everywhere."

She pulled away and looked up at his face. "But... you were..."

"Lost? Who, me? No, my pretty princess, it was you who were lost. I, Sir Thomas, did the finding." His demeanor was that of a gallant soldier, or maybe a knight in shining armor. Typical Thomas. This was no illusion.

"Not lost. Thomas, you were dead."

"Dead? You must be confused, m'lady. I've been wandering far afield, searching for you... or an exit." He reached down and picked up the makeshift air mask. "I see you found my Viking helmet. You're supposed to wear it on your head, like so." He put it on his head with the hose dangling behind him like a ponytail.

Nala took a sniff of the air—it felt fresh again. Thomas certainly seemed unconcerned. Her confusion mounted. "There was no oxygen, except along the surface."

"I fixed that problem. Ripped the end of a ventilation duct right out of the 3-D space below us. Plenty of fresh air coming in here now. You feel it?"

She did feel a draft coming from behind him, but maybe that was because her legs were bare. She looked down. Her full-length pants completely covered her legs with only a few small holes near the bottom. Another impossibility.

"What the fuck is going on?" She turned away from him, concerned she might be hallucinating. "I shredded my pants to make a bandage for you. Your leg was cut off, midshin. You bled to death."

She swiveled around to the very solid man. If this was a hallucination, he wasn't cooperating by disappearing when confronted by logic.

"You okay?" he asked. "It's been a tough go, but we're both alive. We'll make it out of here, don't worry."

"This can't be happening, Thomas. You can't be dead and then alive."

"Well, I've never done a zombie voice, but I'll give it a try." He cleared his throat several times. She held a hand over his mouth.

"Stop it. I'm serious. You were dead. Half your leg was gone."

He shook his head. "I may have been unconscious for a while. I'm not sure I can account for all the time. Maybe you found me but left before I woke up?"

She pointed to her covered legs. "I ripped my pants down to shorts and now they're miraculously repaired. This is the same fucking shit with the water bottles." And she stopped talking and put both hands over her mouth.

"What?" he asked.

"Superposition," she answered.

"The quantum wave effect? That kind of superposition?"

She nodded. "You're literally Schrödinger's cat. Both alive and dead while in quantum superposition, with the precise state unknown until there's an outside observer."

"You're serious."

"Yes, very. You're the proof. It fits with my second theory."

"Which is?"

"That we're experiencing quantum effects at a large scale. Quantum weirdness that should be happening only to quarks and electrons is now happening to bottles of water. My pants. And you."

"Unfathomable, m'lady."

She took both of Thomas's hands in hers. "But it can't just be you. It's me too. We're both experiencing multiple, contradictory histories. We're both alive and dead, severely injured and whole, opening water bottles that are then sealed."

"I'm not sure I like the sound of that."

"Thomas, we're in superposition. Our fate is undefined." She looked into his eyes and saw his concern, but there was no point in sugarcoating it. "None of this will settle on a specific outcome until there's an outside observer."

Thomas looked stunned. There were no snappy comebacks, no clever accents. He looked like he'd seen a ghost.

"Nala?" he asked.

"Yeah?"

"You're not making this up, are you?"

"No, superposition is as real as gravity. Electrons, photons, every quantum particle—when nobody's looking, this is how they exist—as a probability wave. But as soon as anyone takes a peek with any kind of measurement, the probability collapses to a specific outcome."

"Yeah, I knew that about subatomic particles. I just didn't think it could apply to people."

"It can't. At least, it shouldn't."

31 Austin

Daniel walked into the small terminal building that provided support for business jets and private pilots. Standing in the middle of the lobby was the man he recognized from his previous trip, the EPA district manager, Jeffrey Finch.

The wiry-haired man stuck out a bony hand. "Thanks for coming down, Dr. Rice. We might need your expertise to figure this one out, and your influence to get it fixed."

"I'll do my best," Daniel replied, hoping he had something to offer. His head was still foggy from limited sleep. The sun crept over the rooftops of the low-slung buildings dotting the edges of the taxiways at the Austin airport. It would soon be a blue-sky spring day in central Texas.

Finch led him to a car, and they were soon on the crowded freeways of the state capital. Most of the traffic was inbound to the city. "Normal commute? Or are these people trying to get away from the anomaly?" Daniel asked.

"Pretty normal actually," Finch responded. "Three million people in the Austin metropolitan area. Fastest-growing city in the country. If anything, the anomaly is drawing people toward it, not away."

Daniel wasn't thinking clearly quite yet and gave Finch a puzzled look.

"You know, the storm chasers," Finch said. "They're coming from all over the state, now that the news broke."

Daniel hadn't thought of that bit of illogic. If it looked dangerous, there were always people who wanted to get as close as possible.

"The FEMA people are dealing with it," Finch said. "They're on-site at the Bastrop facility right now. State emergency management too, plus a whole mess of state police."

"Has FEMA established a perimeter?"

Finch nodded. "But you and I will be going deep inside." He looked over at Daniel. "Hope you're okay with that."

A few minutes later, they were past the last housing development and into the rolling ranchland east of Austin. Through the windshield, Daniel caught a glimpse of the strange phenomenon he'd been called to witness. Just above the trees, a gray swirl loomed. It looked like a dark rain cloud, but with considerably more geometric structure. Circular. Hurricane-like. It popped in and out of view as trees went by, but even at this distance, Daniel could tell the swirling cloud was enormous.

Finch turned off the highway onto a smaller road traveling north. When they got to a clearing, he pulled over on the shoulder. Daniel opened the door and stepped out for a better look.

The dark cloud now filled half the sky, blotting out the rising sun. The slowly rotating swirl was as ominous as any thunderstorm but at the same time oddly different—as if nature were throwing something new at the unsuspecting humans below. He half-expected lightning bolts to strike the ground at any moment, and perhaps they would. Atmospheric motion produced static electricity, and this unnatural swirl was definitely moving.

Rising in the foreground, the four smokestacks of the Bastrop electric generation facility seemed like toys beneath the enormous cloud.

"What do you think?" Finch asked from the other side of the car.

"I had no idea it would be this big," Daniel said. A slight breeze blew in his face, and he detected the scent of flowers even though there were none around. Thunderstorms did that too, with downdrafts that spread out across the land and carried a variety of curious smells with them. "This cloud wasn't here yesterday?"

"Well, it was just starting," Finch answered. "The local police got a few calls yesterday morning. At first, people said it was a UFO, but it kept growing and the calls changed over time. I got down here just at sunset last night. It's doubled in size this morning."

"Any lightning? Hail? Other weather phenomena?" Daniel asked.

"None that I know of, but we have a state meteorologist out here somewhere. We could check with her. They've set up a forward command center at the Bastrop facility. That's where I thought we'd go. You'll have access to anyone you need from there."

"What are we waiting for?" Daniel said with a shrug. "I guess I'm just one of those storm chasers."

Finch nodded. "Just wanted you to see it before we got too close." They climbed back in the car and headed east, toward the ominous apparition in the sky.

32 Interdimensional

Thomas still wore the Viking hat, complete with the trailing hose that Nala had assembled. He said he liked the improvements she'd made.

They'd come to the place where Thomas had rerouted a ventilation duct. Fresh air was still pouring out. How Thomas had managed to bend sheet metal into their space was a mystery, but the man probably had muscles in his fingers that were bigger than Nala's biceps.

She'd had wondered whether they could crawl out through the ventilation, but when they arrived she realized the opening was much too small even for her slim body. Still, it demonstrated that there were ways to break into the 3-D world. They'd have to make any alterations themselves, though. The people below had no visibility and no access to 4-D space. To them, the metal had simply disappeared into thin air.

It was good to have someone to talk to as they walked back to Nala's campsite above Jan's office. "I'm sticking by my theory. I poured water in your mouth. I listened for your pulse. Those aren't false memories, even if you are healthy now."

"Now that you mention it," Thomas said, "I vaguely remember. I was lying on my back and my knee hurt and water dribbled into my mouth." He stopped walking for a minute and lifted up his perfectly healthy leg. "So, tell me again how I could remember having my leg sheared off when it's not?"

"I'm really not sure. Superposition of memories?"

"Which means?" He continued walking.

"If events are probable but not certain, maybe our memories reflect the probability. Maybe we remember every probability. That is, until there's an outside observer."

Thomas nodded, the hose bouncing against his back. "Then... poof, our brains will reset to match the final result? That's going to be

226

weird. Who do you think the outside observer will be? I hope it's Jan. He has a good imagination."

Nala laughed. "I'm really not sure how this works at our level. In ordinary quantum systems, the outside observer isn't a person. It could be a camera or an alpha particle detector—any device capable of measuring a quantum property, like a particle's position or spin."

"A camera determines the fate of a particle? A camera's not even alive."

"Sorry, but it's how things really work. The universe doesn't care whether it makes sense to you." She walked a few more steps, contemplating the weirdness of it all. She patted Thomas on the shoulder. "It's great to have you back, my friend. I'm not sure I could have managed much more of this alone."

The faraway light flashed again, freezing them in their tracks. Nala gave Thomas a glance, glad to see that he hadn't vanished. In fact, nothing about either of them looked any different, and her memory still seemed the same as before. Maybe the flash had nothing to do with probabilities or quantum eigenstates. Maybe it was just a faulty lightbulb.

The universe doesn't have to make sense. They walked on, with Thomas leading the way.

"How come you're not concerned about walking off the edge?" Nala asked. "There is an edge, you know. Bad shit beyond it, too."

"Why would it matter?" Thomas asked. "There's no outside observer yet, so all probabilities are still in play."

"Good point."

"I figure I'm either invincible or dead. It will all sort itself out."

A few minutes later, he stopped. "We're back."

They were. Assorted items of food lay on the floor just where she'd left them, along with several water bottles. For now, the disreputable bottles were behaving themselves.

"Hungry?" she asked.

"Famished." Thomas sat down and opened the second box of crackers. "Peanut butter, too? You've done well, m'lady."

"There's more if you want it." She motioned to the space over the break room. "You might be better at prying the bigger items out than me." Nala sat next to him. Her legs were no longer bare, but the warm floor still felt good.

She had a million thoughts about their predicament, most of it crazy talk, but in the absence of data speculation was all they had. It was time for a brain dump to another physicist. Jan's office looked empty, but there was plenty of blank space on the walls, and she had a marking pen. Until someone offered a phone on a wire, it would have to do.

Nala wrote furiously across the floor, walls and ceiling of Jan Spiegel's office. From this strange perspective, all surfaces tended to blend together. The right angles where walls met were hardly noticeable, as if someone had taken the complexity of a three-dimensional space and compressed it with a waffle iron. A sentence might start on the floor, jump to the desk and finish on the wall. In the 3-D world, it might be hard to read, but Jan would figure it out. At least it was communication.

Nala spoke to herself as she wrote. "Thomas is back. We're in a superposition of paths, each with a nonzero probability of occurring. Eventually, our options will collapse to a single reality. It's a roll of the dice."

She looked up and thought about her next words. She wrote again on the remaining clean surfaces. "Any action you take will produce a random outcome. Do it anyway."

Beneath her knees, there was motion. A figure entered the room. Longer hair and dark, clearly the same woman she'd seen before. The figure walked around the 3-D space, bending down to examine the floor and looking up at the ceiling. Had she seen the writing? A minute later, Jan came in and stood next to the mystery woman.

Nala picked a spot on the wall nearest to the woman and wrote, *Who are you?* The figure moved to the wall, apparently examining the writing. She might have even waved, though it was hard to tell exactly what she was doing. Nala reached down and placed a hand on the thin layer of three-dimensional space and the human shape within it.

~~~~~~~~~~~~~~~~~~~~~~~

"Jan, hurry! Come see this," Marie yelled. "More writing." She squatted closer to the floor. The words were stretched in places and unreadable, but clear in other places: *nonzero probability... a roll of the dice* and more. The floor and walls were covered in writing, and much of it read like a physics paper.

Jan came in and looked around. "Wow, she's been busy." He studied the words. "Instructions—at least, that's what it looks like. Written to me; I see my name up here at the top of the wall."

While Jan pieced together the messages, movement to one side attracted Marie's attention. Black writing appeared on the wall, one letter after another. The phantom handwriting was genuinely eerie, like walking into an episode of *Eyewitness to the Paranormal*. "She's not done yet."

Marie moved closer as words from another dimension formed before her eyes.

Who are you?

"Oh, my God, she sees me," Marie whispered. The creepy feeling of being watched sent a shiver up the back of her neck. She scanned the ceiling and walls, but of course, her eyes were blind to wherever the apparition might be standing. She knew right away it was a terrible comparison. This was not a ghost or any kind of paranormal spirit. It was Nala. Flesh and blood, and she needed help.

Marie picked up a marker from Jan's whiteboard and started writing on the wall. *I'm Marie Kendrick. We've met. Hope you're okay.* It probably wouldn't work; it hadn't before. As Park had explained, the view from 4-D was too complex. But he might be wrong.

Something brushed against her shoulder, a physical touch, very light. Marie jerked her head to the left—the touch hadn't come from Jan, who stood several feet away. That left only one other possibility.

Jan seemed to notice her sudden motion and the I-am-so-weirded-out expression on her face. "You felt her, didn't you?" he asked.

Marie nodded. *It's not a ghost, it's a person*, she reminded herself, but her nerves didn't seem to agree.

She reached upward, opening her hand and spreading fingers. She held her hand in the air for several seconds. The touch returned. A light tap on her index finger, a brush against her palm.

"She's here," Marie said, her voice hushed. "Right now."

"Careful," Jan said. "She might not mean you harm, but…"

A lock of Marie's hair slid across her forehead on its own and a sensation of touch ran up her arm and across the back of her hand. She turned her hand over, palm up. Something touched her hand. It was just a tickle, like the brush of a feather. She watched as a black oval appeared in the center of her palm. She held her arm steady as another oval appeared, and a third. Marie smiled as the figure took shape. This was no ghost. There was a scientist behind that pen.

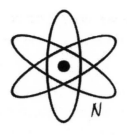

33 Particles

The touch had come from Nala. It must have been her, at least the skin of her hand. Flesh and blood, this was no ghost.

The Dancers might join tentacles as an expression of sexuality, but the human gesture is different. When one hand touches another in a handshake, it provides a connection between two people. It acknowledges, *we are the same, we are familiar.* The touch was certainly from Nala.

It was more than just a touch. Deeper. It felt like an interlacing of two paths. A link between their fates? Marie had been selected by Zin. A probability, a calculation of some sort. Of course, Zin couldn't have foreseen what Marie would do with the headband or that Nala and Thomas would need her help. Could he?

Fate is an imagined property of the universe. The scientist inside her pushed the thought away.

Jan was preoccupied, copying the notes scribbled across the walls onto paper. The words ran around edges, starting on the desk and dropping to the floor. In some cases, relevant sections were missing altogether. The words were mostly Nala's thoughts about physics. One note mentioned Thomas. It brought relief for everyone.

Jan ran his finger along the wall, following a sentence that wrapped around the edge of a bookcase. He lifted his head in thought. "She's right. Why not? She was able to pick up the radio." It wasn't clear what he was talking about, but he ran out of the office and returned a minute later with a phone and a white cord.

He plugged the USB connector into a port on his laptop computer and handed the phone to Marie. "Mind offering this to her? You're better at the handoff stuff than me."

Better didn't figure into it, given that Jan hadn't once tried to hold anything for Nala to pick up. But the phone on a wire made perfect sense. Once a wire was strung between the spaces, there would be some way to communicate that didn't involve radio technology. It was old-school, but certainly better than a pen and paper.

Marie held the phone out, leaving as much slack in the wire as she could. She waited. Was Nala still out there? With so many notes covering the walls, it was impossible to tell how long it had been since she'd written about the phone. Could she even see it?

The phone wiggled, twisting just slightly between Marie's fingers. If Nala could pull the phone into her world, it would represent some much-needed progress. Maybe there was even an app that could make phone calls across the wire? It would be nice to hear her voice.

In quick succession, the phone disappeared, the cable snapped taut and the USB connector slipped out of the laptop port. Marie reached for the dangling wire as it flopped through midair but missed by inches. The wire and the USB connector at its end disappeared like a string of spaghetti being sucked into the mouth of the invisible man.

~~~~~~~~~~~~~~~~~~~~~~~~

Jan's office was now filled with people: two other Fermilab employees and a guy from the Department of Energy. Even a cop, though it wasn't clear why the police were needed. Dr. Park seemed to be managing the chaos as the various experts took photographs of the walls and debated the precise angle of the writing instrument used to produce the scrawl.

Jan himself was searching for a longer USB wire, thinking that the previous failure was only a matter of the distance offset between worlds.

It was all a waste of time as far as Marie was concerned. Did the precise distance really matter? The angle of her pen? Even if they could get a wired connection, it was still just an improvement in communications, not a solution.

None of the experts seemed to have any idea how to reach into whatever strange place had captured Nala and Thomas, much less how to get them out. Marie left the office and walked to the break room around the corner. Jan sat at the food and supplies table, still covered with items that Nala and Thomas might want. Someone had put the blanket on the floor to make room for more food.

Jan raised his head but didn't say anything. He looked tired. The pad of paper he'd used to copy Nala's notes lay on the table in front of him. It now contained additional diagrams, graphs and a few equations that were far beyond anything Marie might grasp.

"Couldn't find a longer cord?" Marie asked.

Jan replied without looking up. "One of the security guys went to an electronics store to buy one. When he gets back, we'll try again."

He tapped his pencil on the pad, and his thoughts became words. "We need to know the spatial relationship relative to the singularity."

Marie had already seen that much. "They're in one of those bubbles I described to you. They must be."

Jan kept tapping on his paper.

"You better start believing me," Marie said. "I'm trying to give you accurate information."

"No, no, it's not that," he said. "I believe you. You're probably seeing the leftovers from experiments of baryon ratios we were running. Four-dimensional space that we didn't clean up properly."

Marie nodded. The leftovers comment made sense. She'd seen quite a few spheres of different sizes and positions, and most of them were nearby.

"So, that's where they are, right? Out in one of these extra dimensions?"

"Probably. But it's different, not like any four-dimensional space we've created before. Nala is trying to tell me, and some of what she says makes sense. They're in a bubble, but it's an aberration caused by the collapse. According to her notes, she seems to think it's a pocket within the void."

"Explain."

"It's a multiverse concept," Jan said. "Used to delineate the difference between *nothing* and *something*. You're an astronomy type, right? It's the same concept as pre–Big Bang. Nothing before the Big Bang, something after."

Marie processed Jan's comments as well as a human mind could, even a mind enhanced with the alien technology. The concept of nothing had always been difficult. For centuries, human mathematics had ignored the number zero precisely because no one could quite conceptualize the purpose of a number that had no value.

The creation dilemma was also well known. Marie even remembered a lecture from college on it. What is nothing, when even empty space is something? Explanations of the Big Bang were sometimes stymied as soon as anyone asked what had existed prior. If cosmologists answered, "we don't know" it felt unsatisfactory, but if they answered with "nothing," then they were stuck trying to define exactly what *nothing* represented and how *something* could spring from it spontaneously.

Marie set her headband case on the counter and reached into the refrigerator for a soda can. She leaned against the counter and refreshed her dry mouth. It had already been a long day. She reached for a pear on the table.

"Hey," Jan said. "That's reserved."

There were several other fruits and snacks still on the table, untouched. "I'm hungry too," Marie said. "We'll get more for them tonight." She was getting a little tired of a brainy physicist who did little more than write equations on a pad of paper. The experts down the hall were still analyzing ink, or handwriting style, or whatever they were doing. And Daniel was gone to Texas.

In the meantime, two people were trapped in hell. The situation demanded action, but she didn't see any evidence it would come from Jan or anyone else.

"You've got this now," Jessica Boyce had told her when Marie had been added to the katanaut team. One step led to another. An alien gift provided the ability to see beyond human limitations, to interpret vast amounts of data, to visualize what others could not.

Whether real or imaginary, fate doesn't shape the events of our lives. It's our resolve, our determination to use whatever abilities we possess that makes a difference.

Time to take control.

Marie grabbed the headband case from the counter and headed down the hallway.

The badge Fermilab had provided cleared her into the underground portion of the facility. She got lost once but backtracked and found the corridor that Daniel had guided her to the night before. The security guard at his post recognized her.

"Back again?" he asked.

"Yeah, just need to check out one more thing." He motioned for her to sign the log. A signature and her status as a colleague of the famous Daniel Rice seemed to be enough. A minute later, she was standing at the edge of the disaster, alone this time.

Nothing had changed. The vast darkened hole in the building's interior felt cold and empty. A slight breeze came down the corridor behind her and blew into the cavernous abyss. Bits of dust still circled the single bright light in the center. It looked like the zone of destruction might remain this way for years.

She watched the dust circling the light. It wasn't *all* dust. There were larger bits too: a few pieces of broken plastic, glints of glass shards, a few splinters of wood. They circled without any evidence of being pulled downward, as if the center of this hollowed-out cavity was a planetary system unto itself.

Why didn't it all just fall into the pit? Where was gravity? It was a question she knew she could easily answer.

Marie withdrew the headband and set the case on the ground. She'd never worn it alone before. If there were *problems*... well, she was on her own. She remembered what Daniel had said. Put it away, send it back to the Dancers for a full reevaluation. Daniel suggested safety.

It'll just be a quick look, she assured herself.

She lowered the band over her hair and tapped twice. The enormous purple sphere popped into view, its filmy surface glistening from the glow of the light in its center.

She kept her eyes open, overlaying the optical world with the mental visualization. It was easy to do and starting to feel almost natural, like getting used to a new pair of glasses.

She flipped to the gravity layer and the building distorted, everything around her stretching downward, validating the body's feeling of being pulled by the earth. But toward the middle of the vast hole, the stretching diminished, flattened. The light, and its disk of rotating debris, didn't stretch downward at all. In the center of the blast zone, it appeared that gravity didn't exist. If anything, there was a slight tug toward the light.

I knew it.

She flipped back to the dimensional layer and the purple sphere. Looking up to the light, she saw a detail she hadn't noticed before. The disk of dust and debris was spiraling into the light. Nothing new there. But the spiral arms of dust seemed to be dipping just below the light, as if something else were causing a detour. It wasn't the light that was sucking the debris in; there was something else. She couldn't quite make out whatever was drawing the dust in, but a different angle of view might help.

With unaided eyes, she looked across the massive hole. On the far side, another corridor ended in much the same way, broken concrete and twisted rebar. The hallway on the other side was lit, the only other light filtering into the scene. Could she get there? It would give a more direct view to wherever the dust was going.

Too bad there was no floor map of the building in the headband's list of capabilities. She would need to figure how to get there the old-fashioned way—ask for directions.

"I wonder," she said innocently to the guard. "Could I take a look from the other side?"

"Sure," he said. "Two flights up, then straight down the hallway to the far end. There's another stairwell that will get you back down to this level."

"Thanks, I won't be long," Marie said and started back to the stairs.

"But be careful, ma'am," he yelled after her. "Don't go near the edge." The guard made a note in his logbook.

It didn't take long. Up two flights, down a parallel hallway and then back down. As she approached, the chasm didn't look much different from the other side.

She put the headband on once more and looked up into the darkness of the hole. It all became clear.

From this new perspective, the gravity visualization clearly displayed a funnel shape just below the singularity. Streams of dust entered its opening like water going down a drain. The perimeter of the funnel was tilted slightly, like a basketball hoop pulled down by a player hanging on its edge. It explained why the shape was almost invisible from the other side.

She watched the dust and debris draining slowly into the funnel in a whirlpool-like flow. There was no question—this was a passageway. A hole to something not *below* but *ana* or *kata*.

Exactly where the flow of dust ended up was impossible to tell.

~~~~~~~~~~~~~~~~~~~~~~~~

Don't be ridiculous, she thought as she scrambled back up the stairwell. *You wouldn't just pull off a manhole cover and jump into a sewer, would you?*

Of course, this was anything but an access point to a sewer. This was an interdimensional passageway, hovering in a no-gravity zone in the middle of a half-destroyed building—probably leading to certain death. At least there were ladders to climb into a sewer.

Exaggerations, she told herself. *You're trying to talk yourself out of it.*

The headband didn't lie. The drain *was* a passageway. It had an entrance and an exit. She couldn't describe how she knew, but there was no doubt in her mind that it provided clear passage, large enough for a person to fit through. There weren't any *rotating blades of death* within its depths, no vacuum of space on the other side. The air flowed into it smoothly with normal atmospheric pressure. The headband told her so.

But there was one slight problem. The passage was a one-way trip. Down only. The air, the particles—nothing was coming back up. It wasn't physically possible, a fact the headband had confirmed.

Marie reached her decision by the time she'd climbed the stairs to the ground level of Wilson Hall. She pulled out her phone and dialed Daniel.

239

34 Bluebonnets

Jeffrey Finch parked next to one of the four primary combustion buildings at the Bastrop power plant. Daniel stepped out of the car and craned his neck. A five-hundred-foot smokestack adjacent to the building reached to the sky, the swirling mass of the clouds not much farther above the blue-and-orange cap at its top. Gusty wind swirled through the parking lot.

"Intimidating, isn't it?" Finch said, his voice loud over the wind.

Daniel shielded his eyes with one hand. "The center of the cloud is offset from the power plant. Could be an atmospheric effect, similar to a low-pressure system. The maximum point of vorticity in the upper atmosphere always lags behind the surface low."

Finch laughed under his breath. "That's quite a different reaction than I've seen from everyone else who stands under this monster." He motioned toward the door in the side of the building.

Daniel shrugged. "It's fluid dynamics. The atmosphere is complicated, that's all I'm saying. And, yeah, it's intimidating, too."

They entered a hallway and descended a flight of stairs to a large basement room filled with people and the cacophony of simultaneous conversations. Some wore uniform shirts with FEMA written on the back. Almost everyone had a phone to their ear. In one corner, two state troopers in tan uniforms sat at a table, holding their cowboy-style hats in their hands. Davis Garrity, the businessman who had started the whole affair, sat across from the troopers. He looked pale.

A gray-haired man wearing a blue FEMA vest over his white shirt yelled across the chatter. "Listen up, everyone! We're pulling the plug here and falling back to the Highway 71 command center. You've got sixty minutes to finish up whatever you're doing and get your field personnel back in time to evac."

Finch introduced Daniel to the on-site federal coordinator, Gonzalo Ayala. Ayala carried the no-nonsense look of a military field commander. "Dr. Rice," he said in a deep baritone. "Your reputation is well known. I imagine you could shed some light on this problem?"

"I'll try. Or connect you to people who can."

Ayala held a firm expression in his substantial lower jaw, speckled with gray whiskers. "Good. First question—are we dealing with the Chicago scenario? The Fermilab-style disaster?"

Daniel took a deep breath. "Not precisely, no, but the fundamentals are probably the same. Four-dimensional space affecting a boundary of 3-D space."

"An odd way to think about it," Ayala said. "But I'll take it. Second question—how bad could this get?"

"That's a question I can't answer," Daniel said. "Unfortunately, I don't think the physicists could either. By the looks of things outside, it's already affecting a one-to-two-mile radius, and Mr. Finch tells me it's growing. So, what happens next? A lot depends on what the people who are controlling this do. Is the power plant shut down?"

"Oh, yeah. First thing we did. Nothing's been coming out of those stacks for more than twelve hours." He motioned to the corner where the state troopers were giving Garrity the third degree. "Mr. Garrity is cooperating, but he doesn't seem to know much. Apparently, there's a Romanian firm that's involved."

Garrity was in deep conversation with the state troopers. One of the officers examined a short piece of PVC pipe.

"I'm aware of the Romanians," Daniel said. "Any contact with them?"

"None yet. But with the plant shut down, do we even need them? We've got a couple of scientists out here that think the cloud might just go away on its own now that it's not being fed from the smokestacks."

Daniel paused in thought for a minute. "No… I wouldn't count on that. Picture a giant invisible water tank out there. Just because you stop filling it doesn't make the tank go away. These dimensional expansions can be locked in place or collapsed at will. But it's the physicists at the accelerator facility who control it, not anything you do at the power plant."

Ayala nodded. "So, this Romanian connection is important."

"Yeah, I'd say so. Do we know how to reach them?"

"Yup. Got the contact information from Garrity." He reached into his pocket and pulled out a worn business card. "Institut—". He handed the paper to Daniel. "Here, you can read it."

Daniel studied the card.

Pavel Iliescu
Institutul de Fizică Aplicată Belciugatele
DN3 44 Belciugatele 917010, Romania
+40 761 904 791
p.iliescu@ifab.ro

"I'll call him," Daniel said. "They'll need to be very careful with their next step. Playing around with large volumes of quantum space isn't a good idea for beginners, so we need to find out how much expertise the Romanians have."

Finch interrupted, "I can suspend the permit, if that helps."

A monster storm was brewing outside, linked to a vast unseen dumping ground somewhere out in extra dimensions of space, and it was all the result of an EPA permit issued without consulting the scientists who might have advised on the dangers. Daniel tried to keep the scorn out of his voice. "Yeah, suspending the permit would be a great idea." It wasn't Finch's fault; he was just doing his job.

Ayala pointed to the business card. "Dr. Rice, if you can find out what the Romanians are doing, then I can stay focused on evacuation."

"I'll get on it. How far out are you evacuating?" Daniel asked.

Another FEMA person ran over and handed Ayala a note. He looked at it and then responded to Daniel. "We just issued a mandatory order for Bastrop County. Eighty thousand people. That's going to be challenging enough. Rural. A lot of them are already saying it's fake news."

"A rumor is going around that the government created the cloud and is forcing people out to confiscate their property," Finch added.

"Gotta love Texas," Ayala said. "But we'll get everyone out. Unfortunately, I'm a lot less confident about the next level."

Daniel had a good idea what he was going to say next. "Austin?"

"Yup. If this thing keeps growing, or you tell me it's a nuclear bomb waiting to go off, then I've got to evacuate several million people in Travis County. Nobody's ever done that before, not with hurricanes or tornadoes or any other disaster. Dr. Rice, I need to know what the hell is going to happen here."

~~~~~~~~~~~~~~~~~~~~~~~~

Daniel ambled through an open pasture of bluebonnets, the Texas state flower. The field's proximity to the parking lot meant that the seeds had surely been scattered as part of a beautification project by the power company. It didn't matter whether they were natural or planted, the flowers were just as pretty.

Daniel held his phone to his ear. The reception was better outside, and a call to Romania was easier outside the noisy command center.

The cloud loomed above, a giant eddy in the sky. It twisted with the slow-motion speed of any normal cloud, but in the distinctly curved path of a vortex. Daniel multitasked, listening to the conversation on the phone and keeping an eye on the brewing storm.

The Romanian physicists were surprised to hear they might be the source of panic half a world away. They were following a plan established weeks ago, they said, increasing the volume of the bubble of quantum space in well-defined steps to provide additional space as requested by their American client.

For the time being, Daniel persuaded them to stop expanding, though he hesitated to recommend they collapse the four-dimensional structure. Where would it go? How would its contents of noxious gases be dispersed? These were questions only a small subset of quantum physicists could answer. Jan Spiegel was Daniel's second call.

"We're in contact with Nala and Thomas," Jan said when he picked up. "Nala is writing on the whiteboard, walls, floor, everything. She even drew on Marie's hand. We tried radio communication. That didn't work, so now we're attempting a wired connection."

Daniel could imagine how writing from an invisible pen wielded by an unseen hand might shake things up at Fermilab. "How about the food she asked for?"

"Success. She's able to pull it out of 3-D space," Jan answered.

"Remarkable," Daniel said. He was relieved, but the image of Nala lost in an infinite maze with no exits was still distressing. "Any ideas how to get them out?"

"We're working on it, with input from Nala herself, I might add."

Jan outlined a few options. There had been no damage to the accelerator, so Fermilab facilities engineers were drawing up an emergency plan to reconstruct what had been lost in the disaster. It would take a few weeks, but they'd regain a limited ability to expand quantum space. One idea was to create a larger overarching bubble that would act as a container to the various 4-D remnants that Marie had identified, including the space where Nala and Thomas were trapped. It would provide the precision they would need to collapse the space when the time came.

Partners at CERN were also busy experimenting with techniques for bringing living things back from 4-D space. Collapsing the space would hardly be a solution if it shredded every cell in their bodies. The plan would require more research, but the situation wasn't hopeless. In the meantime, they had already found ways to keep Nala and Thomas alive.

"It's going to be complicated from here," Jan said. "I'm not sure when we'll have the answer."

Jan was up to his neck in the rescue effort, but Daniel couldn't avoid the dangerous-looking cloud circling above his head. A call between physicists was essential if they were going to prevent an even greater catastrophe. "Jan, I need your help. The situation here in Austin has a lot of similarities."

Jan's voice was strained. "Things are pretty crazy here, Daniel."

"I understand, but you're the right person. I just need you to make one call to a physics lab in Romania. Explain to them what you know but they don't. You help them, and maybe they'll have resources they can offer you."

The last point seemed to resonate, and Jan agreed. Daniel gave him the contact information. One step complete.

Daniel pocketed his phone and stared up into the sky. The cloud was a natural phenomenon in that it was made of condensed water vapor. But it came with an unnatural structure... and a human origin. This cloud hadn't arisen from a natural process any more than global warming had. Humans had done this, not only through their natural curiosity, their creativity and ambition, but also through their neglect. Would we ever learn? Or would advances in technology forever come with an illustration of how deadly the world can be? Core had said we would learn in time. Daniel was not so sure.

He headed back inside and passed state troopers, who accompanied Davis Garrity down the hallway.

Garrity flagged Daniel down. "Dr. Rice, they said you would call Romania. Did you get the problem fixed? I know it's something small. They probably just have some knob at the wrong setting."

Ignorance is bliss.

"Yes, Mr. Garrity, I did call. But you should know it's going to take more than a few adjustments. This is a serious business with a lot of unknowns."

One of the troopers put a hand on Garrity's elbow. It was clear they would be leaving the building regardless of what hallway conversation their suspect was interested in having. "Uh, yeah," Garrity said, noticing the tug. "They want a deposition. I'll be at the state courthouse today but available if you need me. I want to make sure we do everything possible to get this little problem cleared up so ElecTrek can get back to normal operations."

"I wouldn't count on normal operations anytime soon," Daniel said, as the trooper guided Garrity down the hallway.

Normal? If we get to sunset without an apocalypse it'll be a good day.

His phone vibrated in his pocket, and Daniel ducked into a side room off the hallway. The call was from Marie, and she sounded more agitated than Daniel had ever heard her.

"Daniel, I know you just talked to Jan, and that you're putting all your faith in him," Marie said. "But in my view, none of these so-called geniuses has any idea how to fix this. They're arguing the minutiae. They're absorbed in their theories and their math, but they're running blind. They can't see what I see. They just wave me off as a nutcase with a toy crown."

Even over the phone, it was clear that she was upset. "You explained what you saw to Jan?"

Marie nearly exploded. "Don't you do it too, Daniel. Of course I explained it! Why does everyone think I'm so incompetent?"

Daniel waited without response. This was unlike the Marie he knew.

"Sorry," she said eventually. "I know you don't mean to be condescending, but sometimes you are anyway. I'm calling you to coordinate, assuming you ever get back to Fermilab. Look, Jan doesn't have the answer. Park doesn't either. But I do. I've seen it."

She was angry, upset and probably on the verge of doing something irrational. His assessment was, of course, condescending. An *emotional woman* about to do something rash. But she was in possession of powerful alien technology, and he wasn't sure how far she could go with it. "What are you proposing?"

"I'm tired of sitting around listening to them. I've told Jan. I can solve this. Me, alone. I'm going in."

"In? Where?"

"There's an opening. I can see it with the headband. It might be dangerous... well... it's *going* to be dangerous. But once I'm in, the headband will tell me everything we need to know. Of *that*, I'm sure."

"Don't." He couldn't articulate why, and any justification would likely be thrown out anyway as yet more condescension from the male who knew everything the female couldn't possibly fathom.

Her response was just as simple. "Bye, Daniel. Watch for messages." The phone connection ended.

35 Resolve

Marie ran down the empty corridor and skidded to a stop at the edge of the yawning cavity. Her chest heaved with deep breaths as she studied the scene once more. The bright light in its center beckoned.

She turned the headband over in her hand and examined the electronic components along its sides. An amazing device that could provide such a wealth of information. She had no doubt there was more information waiting to be discovered on the other side, but it was impossible to guess how she would use it.

She looked past the crumbled edge of the corridor into the zone of destruction and began to wonder if she was doing the right thing. Jan had said it was a terrible idea. She dropped to her knees, feeling vulnerable.

Do you have any idea what you're doing?

With the headband off, everything seemed so confusing. The images it created in her head, the ideas that appeared from nowhere. The horrifying hallucinations. How and why any of this had occurred was still a mystery, magnified once the headband was off and her mental abilities reverted to those of any mortal.

There was a dumpster behind the building. She could throw it in and no one would ever know. She could tell people that she'd lost it. Daniel would come back to Fermilab and figure out this mess. He'd find a way; he had last time.

The guard will be here soon.

Jan had rejected her proposal. She had told him she was tired of waiting and would go ahead anyway. As she'd left his office, he'd called for security.

Now, at the edge of the precipice, nothing felt right. She wasn't herself and probably hadn't been since the first day she'd worn the headband. It was affecting her, altering her personality, changing her thought processes. She'd never in her life been so rude to people, lashing out at Stephanie at the end of the mission, at Daniel on the phone, and yelling at Jan just now.

The creepy-crawlies hadn't surfaced for a while, but she knew they were still there. She could feel them hiding just beneath the surface, ready to spring when she least suspected it. They'd come again. Of course they would.

Footsteps echoed in the corridor far behind her.

The power she could summon from the headband was breathtaking, but the courage to use the alien device was becoming harder to find. She'd have to reach deep. There was danger, both physical and mental. But two people were trapped. They needed help, and all that she'd seen in the past twenty-four hours had led to one inescapable conclusion: Marie was the only person who could save them.

I volunteered. I'm the highest probability.

The footsteps were getting closer. "Ms. Kendrick!" a voice yelled. "Wait."

She stood up, put the band over her head and backed up a few steps.

"No, don't!" the security guard yelled.

Marie took three long strides, and with every bit of energy her body could muster, she leaped into the void.

36 Rabbit Hole

The fall should have killed her. Her body should have been found among the tangle of twisted rebar and broken concrete at the bottom of the vast hole. But gravity no longer functioned as expected here. Space warped into a direction other than *down*. It wasn't surprising. In fact, it was completely expected—she'd already visualized the lines of gravitation, and they pointed in an altogether different direction.

She passed through darkness and landed with a jolt. Unable to stay on her feet, she tumbled. Pain shot up her arm as she hit something hard. Her knee scraped against a sharp point. She came to rest among piles of broken wood, bent metal and shredded carpet, the debris only dimly illuminated.

She lifted herself onto her elbows, allowing her eyes to become accustomed to the dim light and taking stock of what hurt. Her shoulder ached, but not enough to worry about. The sharp sting in her knee demanded greater attention. She reached down and felt blood just below the hemline of her skirt.

Pants. From now on, always wear pants.

It was a scrape, deep, but she'd live. She sat up and looked around.

Where am I?

The headband would tell her everything she'd need to know. She reached up to tap it and was surprised to feel only hair. The familiar ring was gone, and panic quickly followed.

It must have fallen off in the leap. There was so much debris around, it could be anywhere. Without it, she'd be lost.

Marie stood up—*really* stood up, for the first time in her life. It was as if she'd been lying down forever, unaware of the more vertical position that was available. Up wasn't up. It was something else, not describable but felt in the inner ear. Her balance was tenuous, like being on ice skates for the first time.

She took a step. Not easy in the darkness, but at least she didn't fall. Another step, easier. And another. A slight dizziness filled her head, and she began to regret her decision to make the leap. If standing and walking were this hard, what chance did she have of helping anyone else? The headband was the only reason to be here, and it was lost.

This was a one-way trip with only one destination. She'd assured herself of that before she'd made the leap. Wherever she was, the headband had to be here too.

Marie walked, tentatively at first but with increasing confidence. The material was scattered everywhere, requiring that she step over boards and twisted metal. The balance required to stand on one foot, even for just a second, took some concentration.

Just as she was stepping over a large plank of wood, she noticed a body. A person, lying perfectly still among the debris.

Oh God, I'm too late.

The light was better as she approached. It was a man lying on his back. Red hair and a red beard. Part of his leg was missing, the stump wrapped in a bloody bandage. Thomas, no doubt, though why Nala had failed to mention his grave injury was a shocking oversight.

Marie bent down and felt for a pulse in his wrist. Nothing. The body was cold; another discontinuity from Nala's notes. She'd just told them that Thomas was with her.

Marie took a deep breath and shouted. "Nala!" Her voice sounded dampened, like she was deep inside a clothes closet.

From the periphery of her vision, there was a flash of light, startlingly bright. With the flash, everything went black.

~~~~~~~~~~~~~~~~~~~~~~~~

Marie awoke. Her body was tilted at an odd angle, her feet above her head. The heap of carpeting she lay on was twisted and torn, but soft.

She shifted her weight, lowering her feet to the surface and standing up, not sure why it seemed easier. Her balance was still off, but those first steps now seemed like a faraway dream. She reflexively touched her knee, half expecting to feel a painful scrape, but there was none. No blood either.

Very odd. Surreal, like a dream.

Her shoulder didn't hurt, though it was hard to remember why she'd thought it would. She lifted the alien band from her head and examined it for damage. It looked intact, though there was something not right about it—a vague feeling that she shouldn't be holding it at all. She finally remembered.

The headband was lost.

She had lost it and panicked. Yet now it was back in her hands.

The body.

She hopped over some debris to where she'd seen the red-haired man lying on the floor and scanned the area. No man, no sign of blood, just the dark floor covered with debris. Had he really been there? The image of the injured man was now as fuzzy as a childhood memory, that mental image of the essence of the event but with none of the detail.

The confusion was disturbing, and in another time and place she might have allowed it to overwhelm her, forcing her to seek the safety of reality. Those days were over.

I have a mission. People need me.

She tapped twice on the side of the headband, and it lit up the darkened space as if someone had powered up a searchlight.

"Oh, wow," she whispered.

She twisted her head in all directions, absorbing the nearly magical scene it displayed. A purple glow came from everywhere, creating an elegant spherical dome that intersected the flat floor just as a soap bubble rests on a surface. The glow from its edge pulsed, first from the left and then from the right, as if the bubble had a life of its own. Its surface was translucent, and additional blue bubbles hovered beyond. It was the same collection of spheres she'd seen before, but she was now on the inside.

The floor provided its own magic, very different from the bubbles. Its position was not *below* her, but somehow next to her, above her, and even within her simultaneously. The limits of human eyes could detect only a *surface*, but the headband expanded the view to the full complexity of the 3-D world. It was almost like one of those pop-up paper cutouts that when unfolded turned flat paper into the Eiffel Tower or a three-dimensional garden of flowers. The view below was both complex and beautiful.

But she sensed yet another layer, beyond the colorful bubbles and pop-up paper cutouts. It showed yet greater complexity. The layer represented time, and she flipped to it.

The visualization was still of her surroundings, but with the movement of objects and people in a jumbled blur. The motion overwhelmed the detail, making it impossible to see a specific person or object, but each became a set of related images. It was like a photograph of a busy street scene where the photographer had left the shutter open for several minutes, causing the motion of every car and pedestrian to become a blur in the final image.

The layer was a portrayal of time, that much was clear. But unlike a timeline of what *had* happened in the past or *would* happen in the future, the blurs showed a set of probabilities of what *might* happen. Each portion of the blur was a conceivable position without giving away the actual result.

Like rolling dice, she thought. A shiver ran down her neck. They were words that Nala had written on the wall. Words that had suddenly become visual. Marie could see the options playing out right before her eyes, each outcome, each position of the rolling die equally valid.

As she watched, one of the blurs began to throb in a pulsating rhythm. Fear and nausea surfaced quickly, and she realized the pixels and insects would be next.

"Oh, no," Marie yelled. "No, no, no! Not going there."

Marie pulled the headband off, but the awful feeling didn't subside. She squeezed the metal band hard enough to put deep creases in the palms of her hands. The band was surely off her head because both hands were in pain. Still, the pulsating scene began to separate into pixels.

"Stop it!" she yelled and fell to her knees, her heart racing. "Go away, go away, go away." Tears filled her eyes, and she squeezed the headband ever tighter.

Concentrate on reality.

She thought of home, of ordinary things. Her kitchen, the coffeepot by the stove, the magnets on her refrigerator, the view outside to the garden. She closed her eyes. "I'm home. Not lost. Home. My home."

Her breaths came in uncontrolled bursts of air, and her chant continued until the feeling finally disappeared. Her heart calmed, and her breathing shallowed, finally finishing with a deep inhale and a long exhale.

Marie opened her eyes. She kneeled on a darkened floor with debris all around. No pixels, no insects. Of course, they'd never been there, it was all in her mind. Concentrating had helped. Even the chanting had helped, banishing the frightening feeling of being out of control and allowing the more reliable conscious mind to take over.

Marie put a hand on her forehead. *You can do this.*

Her determination had renewed, just as it had when she'd made the leap into the pit. She rose to her feet and walked with purpose, pushing debris out of the way as she went.

"Nala!" she called. She repeated it several more times as she walked, eventually leaving the debris field altogether.

Far in the distance, two figures emerged from the darkness.

37 Probabilities

The two women almost bowled each other over in an enthusiastic collision in the most improbable of settings.

Nala embraced Marie, grasping both of her arms. "I thought I recognized you. You're Daniel's partner!" A broad smile and an expression of pure joy spread across her face. They'd only met once via videoconferencing. Nala was darker and more beautiful in person, though she looked like she could use a shower and a cup of tea.

"Marie Kendrick, at your service. We finally meet. Odd circumstances, but it's the best I can offer." Nala turned Marie's hand over and touched the atomic drawing still visible on her palm.

"It turned out better than I thought," Nala said.

"I knew it was you drawing on my hand," Marie said, "but to tell you the truth, it was still pretty weird." Marie reached out to Thomas and hugged the big man. "You gave me a scare when I first arrived."

"Uh-oh," Thomas said. "What did I do this time? Hopefully no zombies involved."

Marie laughed. "It was just a dream, I see that now."

"I wasn't, like… dead, was I?"

His guess was uncannily accurate. "Um…"

"Dang," he said. "That's twice now. My odds seem to be getting worse."

"Don't say that," Nala admonished. "It's one possible state out of many. Thomas, we're going to get out of here. Marie has arrived to show us the way home." Nala locked eyes with Marie. "You *are* going to get us out, right? Jan and Jae-ho, they have a plan? They got you in here somehow, so there must be an exit, right?"

A tough question to answer. *Well, you see, this crown on my head gives me superpowers, and I thought I'd just pop in to your interdimensional bubble and have a look around.*

It didn't sound very credible. Childish, even. Jan's more scientific plan was sounding a lot better, even if it might take weeks to carry out.

Thomas must have noticed her hesitation. "Of course she has a plan. She's a princess." He pointed to the headband. "Just watch any Disney movie. They always have a plan."

"Um... yeah," Marie said. "The band is more advanced than it looks, but it's not perfect. It collects information from the physical world and projects a visualization into my brain. It gives me a lot of leverage, but it can't just bring us back home."

"Well," Nala said. "I wasn't expecting ruby slippers, but I was hoping for something more along the lines of science, not magic."

"Oh, it's definitely not magic," Marie said. "It's technology. Alien."

"Alien?" Thomas asked.

They both looked skeptical. Anyone would be. "I'll show you. Let's try this. Rub your hands together. Get some friction going." They both did, but their skeptical looks didn't change. "Okay, now turn around. Both of you." She tapped the headband as they turned. "Make sure I can't see your hands but pick a number between one and ten and hold up that many fingers."

She flipped to an electromagnetic layer and dialed into the infrared portion of the spectrum. The view was better than any night-vision goggles, with easily recognizable heat signatures for both their bodies and their hidden but warm hands.

"Nala, seven. Thomas, four. Am I right?"

They looked at each other. "Do it again," Thomas said. He shuffled closer to Nala to ensure their hands were hidden from view.

257

"Nala, six. Thomas, two. I could do this all day."

They slowly turned. "You're seeing heat?" Nala asked.

"Any electromagnetic radiation, any force, plus dimensional space and a whole lot more. I can even predict what you're going to say next."

Marie flipped to the most unusual of data layers, a kind of temporal view of outcomes based on available input. The layer came up, but it didn't provide the same visualization that she had demonstrated to the higher-ups at Kennedy Space Center. The outcomes, spoken words or otherwise, had popped up immediately when she'd performed this trick before, but that layer had been replaced with something very different.

"What am I going to say next?" asked Thomas, in a taunting tone, but lighthearted.

A hundred versions of Thomas stood before her, each image of the man standing behind the one in front. The column receded into the distance, getting more blurred and eventually disappearing into the darkness. Each face carried a slightly different expression, some exuberant, some tired. A few seemed utterly defeated. There were a few alarming gaps in the lineup where Thomas didn't appear at all.

"Wait a second, this is not right," Marie said.

"Nope. I was going to say, 'rubber baby buggy bumpers' three times fast." It was the Thomas at the front who spoke, but the mouths moved on several of his duplicates.

"No, I mean something's wrong. I'm not getting the same image I was in Florida. There's a whole bunch of you, different versions. Maybe they're images of you at different times, but I'm not sure. It kind of feels like the rolling-dice layer I saw earlier."

"Rolling dice?" Nala asked. "You mean you're seeing the probability of outcomes?"

258

"Maybe," Marie said. "But the rolling dice layer was fuzzy moving images. Blurry, like I couldn't make out anything specific. This one is blurry too, but I can see duplicate versions of Thomas all in a line." She turned to Nala. A hundred images of the woman receded into the distance. "You too."

Nala and Thomas exchanged a glance, nodding their heads in unison. "Superposition," they said together.

"Huh?"

"You just stepped into the quantum world," Nala said. "Just like a quark or an electron, every possible outcome occurs and doesn't occur. In physics, we call each possibility an eigenstate, and unfortunately we won't know which state becomes reality until there's an external observer."

Thomas pointed to Marie. "Maybe she's the external observer?"

Nala shook her head. "Nope. She's in this quagmire too. She saw you dead, just like I did. She may have changed, too." Nala turned to Marie. "After you found your way in here, did you see the light flash?"

"Yeah, I did. I must have fainted because I woke up and the *body* wasn't there."

"You probably didn't faint. It was some other physical change. Anything could have happened."

Marie thought about the dreamy recollection. "I had lost the headband. I was in a panic. But after the light flashed, I was wearing it."

"Bingo," Thomas said.

"You're just as affected as we are," Nala explained. "The crown is on your head and it's lost—all at the same time. Its state hasn't yet been determined."

The memory of the lost headband was vague, but it hadn't faded away completely. She had a sinking feeling that Nala might be right. Its permanence was questionable.

259

"So, I might lose it again?"

Nala nodded.

"Hoo boy." Marie felt the knot in her stomach. "If that happens, we may never get out of here."

38 Ratios

"He says I shouldn't have jumped," Marie said, translating what she visualized from the pad of paper lying on Jan's desk. The man himself sat patiently in his office chair back in the 3-D world, no different from if Marie was in the room with him. Of course, he couldn't see her.

"He's right, you know," Nala said. She put a hand on Marie's shoulder. "Thanks for wanting to help us, but you've put yourself in the same danger."

Marie removed the headband, automatically deactivating it. Best to use it in spurts to avoid, or at least delay, the psychosis that always seemed to be lurking around the corner. "A decision I can live with," she said. "I'm still confident I can help from the inside. Just look at what we're able to do now."

Communication was vastly easier with the headband. Without it, the confusing view below their feet was impossible to interpret as writing. There were just too many other objects—the ceiling, the desk, the floor, the fourteen floors below Jan's office, the various layers of rock beneath the building... it went on and on. The result was nothing more than a mishmash of shapes.

But with the headband, it all became clear. She could isolate a specific plane and viewing angle of the three-dimensional space. Jan's desk was a good choice, allowing her to focus on a single sheet of paper. The headband also made seeing the objects in the break room easier. The blanket was a blanket, not an obscure whitish-gray mass. No wonder Nala had struggled to pick it up.

But there was one activity that was far more entertaining *without* the headband. Marie watched in fascination as Thomas carefully pinched a round red oval and then lifted a whole apple from the scene below. "That is so cool," she said as he handed it to her.

"Jan's back," Nala said. "He's carrying something but I can't tell what it is."

Marie reactivated the 3-D layer and got a fix on the man she'd argued with in person no more than an hour before. In his hand was a USB cable, much longer than the first cord, which lay unused next to Nala.

"You still have the phone, right?" Marie asked.

Nala rummaged through her bag of essentials and pulled it out. "Right here."

Marie bent down and focused on the white wire that Jan held in the air. "And look at that, this time he's actually holding it up."

"Wait a second, Jan wasn't pulling that chickenshit 'A-square being ripped out of the page' crap, was he?"

Marie nodded.

Nala shook her head. "So *that's* why you were holding everything. Jan, Jan, Jan... we've got some serious talking to do when I get back. Prick."

Marie reached out, pinching the floor where the wire dangled. "Is this how you do it?"

"Being a dimensional goddess is a learned skill," Nala said. "But you're doing well."

Marie felt the wire touch her fingers and with a hard pinch managed to stop it from wiggling. She pulled and magically drew the phone-connector end of the cable through the floor.

"You got it!" Nala patted her shoulder. "Promotion to goddess first class. Don't pull too hard, though, that was my mistake."

"Jan's holding the other end this time," Marie said. "That was our mistake." The longer cord helped too, easily providing enough length to reach between the phone and the computer on Jan's desk. A few minutes later, Nala had located a chat app on the phone and pressed a button to connect. She waited.

Initializing USB port...

... connected to Spiegel244.

Spiegel244: We did it!

A big smile spread across Nala's face as she typed back.

MyPhone: Works like a charm.

Spiegel244: Outstanding! Is it really you?

MyPhone: No, it's the office cleaning lady.

Spiegel244: It's you.

MyPhone: And you were a prick to Marie. But let's talk bosons.

With instant two-way communication, Jan and Nala were soon in sync on theory and evidence, along with a few snide remarks passing between them. Mostly baryons, bosons and density ratios. Marie didn't pretend to understand it all and eventually switched her attention to Thomas, who munched on a pear he'd lifted from the page world.

"You should have been here earlier," he said. "We stopped by the bank over at Aurora Commons. I could reach right into the vault."

"Get out of here."

"Really. Stacks of brand-new hundred-dollar bills. It would have been simple to lift a few bundles. So tempting. But... all I did was draw a mustache on Ben Franklin. They'll wonder how *that* happened."

Marie smiled. "I'm glad you didn't take anything. You're going to make it home, Thomas. You don't want to be a criminal when you get there."

She thought about what he'd said, and an idea formed. "How far is Aurora from here?"

"Well, in the real world, a couple of miles, but inside this bubble, distance is compressed. Getting to Aurora takes only a minute or two."

"How far does it go? The bubble, I mean."

Thomas swallowed a bite of pear and wiped his mouth. "Nala and I have been pretty far, probably half a mile."

"And what's beyond?"

"The void. At least that's what Nala says. You can't go there. Nothing can."

"I doubt I'd want to. But I was wondering how far this bubble stretches." Marie stood up. "I'll see if I can get some better numbers for us." She reached to the headband but hesitated. "Um… Thomas. If you ever see me kind of zoning out, do me a favor and take the headband off, would you?"

"Sure," he said. "Does it need a reboot sometimes?"

"It… takes over my brain. It's not a good thing, either."

He didn't ask for any more information, and she didn't feel like explaining. There was something personally invasive about the creepy-crawlies, like a personal hygiene problem that's best left vague.

Marie tapped on the side of the headband and popped back into its strangely beautiful but overwhelming visualization. She ignored the complexity of the 3-D floor and the fuzzy multiple images of Thomas and focused on the multicolored bubbles all around. The ones nearby looked just as they had before, but the lone bubble in the distance had changed substantially. It was larger now and bulging dramatically on one side. She thought of Daniel in Texas.

Is it possible? Can I see that far?

"What's the compression ratio for these four-dimensional spaces? You know, weird-world distances compared to real world."

Nala had finished her communication with Jan and spoke as if she was on autopilot. "Compression varies. Anywhere from negligible to 99 percent, depending on the expansion size."

She appeared to be reciting from memory, but a faraway look made it clear she was pondering something far more important.

"What?" Marie asked. "You and Jan figured something out, didn't you?"

Nala brushed her hair back with one hand, staring at nothing. "Yeah, I think so. Jan was right, density is the key." She shook her head. "I understand it, but I need to let this settle in before I really believe it."

Marie had watched part of their conversation, but that didn't mean the language of physics made sense. Clearly, the exchange meant something more to Nala. "You found a way out?"

"No, at least not directly. But I think I know how we got here." Thomas stopped eating and eyed Nala with interest.

She explained. "Before the big implosion, Thomas and I were testing various volumes of four-dimensional spatial expansion, and we began seeing an instability that affected 3-D space. Waves were literally passing through our lab, and I had no idea why. But now I do."

She turned to Thomas. "It's the density—technically the baryon-to-boson ratio, but it's the same thing. Greater mass in a smaller volume leads to unstable four-dimensional space, which then causes an interaction with neighboring three-dimensional space. We created a very unstable chunk of real estate and it collapsed, taking us with it. Sorry, Thomas, my fault."

Thomas didn't seem too concerned, or else he was a very forgiving type of person.

"Jan and I had talked about this before," Nala continued, "but it was not much more than a guess. He's got the data now. In fact, he found the inflection point—the exact density where instability starts to occur."

"Well, good for him," Thomas said.

Nala looked perplexed. "At first, I didn't want to believe him, but he's calculated it to six-digit accuracy. This is weird shit—creepy-god kind of weird. According to Jan, our tests started going haywire precisely when mass density reached nine point four seven times ten to the minus twenty-seven kilograms per cubic meter."

Thomas perked up. "Wait a second, that's the value for critical density, isn't it?"

Nala nodded. "It's a hell of a coincidence. Either that or we've just confirmed one of the most mind-boggling parameters in our very strange universe."

39 Evacuation

Daniel pressed to one side of the hallway as several FEMA team members passed by carrying electronic equipment and a disassembled antenna. Sometime in the next thirty minutes, the entire crew, Jeffrey Finch and Daniel included, would be falling back about ten miles to a safer location.

The number of FEMA and Texas state emergency personnel had grown even since Daniel had arrived, and their efforts to evacuate the area were aided by announcements from the governor, the mayor of Austin and the sheriff of Bastrop County. Still, there were holdouts even near the power plant. Reports of people pointing rifles out their windows kept emergency personnel at bay. The local authorities took those cases, attempting to identify relatives who might talk the obstinate cranks to safety.

Daniel ducked into an empty room just off the hallway and checked for any new messages from Jan, Park, or anyone from Romania. He couldn't help but wonder about Marie's fate. Her last words had made it clear that she was impatient. But an impulsive attempt to vault into the extradimensional prison that had trapped Nala and Thomas was lunacy.

There might be more going on than just frustration. Was her grasp on reality becoming tenuous? Perhaps it was spurred by the alien-induced psychosis, as she herself had suggested. Or was she just being irrational?

Daniel switched to a self-critique, his usual approach when an initial assessment didn't feel right. He wasn't at Fermilab, didn't have all the information and was in no position to judge. Marie's action might have been impulsive, but if a man had done the same, he'd probably be deemed heroic. Certainly not irrational.

He took a deep breath and tried to recharacterize the Marie he knew in a new light. She was gone, that much was clear. A call to Jan had confirmed it. A security guard had seen her jump but never heard the thump of a body hitting concrete. They'd sent a rescue team member to the bottom of the pit but found nothing. Under normal circumstances, someone disappearing into thin air would be cause for alarm, but in this case, it was probably a good thing.

If she made it to the other side of the singularity, would Marie be able to help? She'd seemed to think so, but simply assuming she could see more on the inside wasn't the best of plans. Not that Daniel had anything better. He should. It was what the *famous Daniel Rice* was known for—seeing the detail that no one else did and finding the solutions. He'd need to focus, but being pulled in two directions wasn't helping.

His phone rang. A call from the one person who might resolve this crisis. "Jan, any news?"

"Yes, I just heard from them," Jan said. His voice was more upbeat than the previous call. "It's hard to believe, but Marie is inside. There's a path of some kind, and it goes all the way through. Marie found it with that headband."

"An opening between 3-D and 4-D space?" Daniel asked. It was exactly what they'd needed—what Daniel had asked about when Marie had first visualized the glowing spheres.

"Not an opening in any conventional sense," Jan said. "Don't expect to be able to throw in a rope and pull them out. It's an area where 3-D space has collapsed to a point, but it's also a gravity well, so objects are apparently able to pass through to the other side."

"A one-way trip, then," Daniel said. It wasn't a question, but Jan's confirmation would help him picture the problem.

"One-way," Jan said. "I'm afraid so. It does give us another path to provide supplies, but whatever we throw in will never come out again."

Daniel's anxiety level was going nowhere but up. Nala and Thomas trapped, and now Marie too.

Jan explained how communications had improved. Daniel listened, but Jan's voice began to fade into the background as his attention focused on the small office where he stood. It was shaking. The walls were moving.

Are we having an earthquake?

"Hold on, Jan," he said. "Something's up."

The floor rolled as if someone had picked up one end of the carpet and shaken it. The wave passed through the room, through Daniel and through the wall behind him. A smaller wave followed it, and another, slowly dampening until the strange effect was no longer noticeable. He'd been in an earthquake before. This was something very different.

He heard a voice from the hallway. "Fall back. Everyone out. Now!"

40 Density

Marie plopped on the floor, sitting between Nala and Thomas. Nala was onto something, but it was impossible to decipher the advanced physics gobbledygook. "Sorry, I really don't follow any of this. Critical density? You talk about it like it's some mystical number."

"Mystical. Not a bad description," Thomas said.

Nala seemed as confused as anyone. "Most people have never heard of it. I'll explain, but you might want to take that crown off first." She gestured with both hands like her head was going to explode. "Crazy stuff."

The exploding head metaphor was a terribly overused joke. Marie took the headband off anyway.

"The universe is expanding, right?" Nala said. Marie nodded. Edwin Hubble had discovered this in the 1920s. "And gravity tries to halt that expansion by pulling things together. More mass, more gravity. *Critical density* is a number with deep meaning. It tells you the precise amount of mass that is needed to exactly cancel expansion. It's what makes our universe flat."

Marie had read about the flat universe, but it was one of those social media memes that seemed unimportant. "Makes the universe sound a bit boring. You know, flat instead of exotic."

"It's anything but boring," Nala said. "It's fundamental. What existed before the Big Bang?"

Changing the subject seemed to be common for physicists, but Marie understood why they did it. When the topic was complex, an analogy often helped. She pondered the question. "Jan brought this up too. Nobody knows what came before the Big Bang. That's the edge of scientific knowledge."

"Not true," Nala answered. "Astrophysicists are pretty sure, but they haven't explained it very well to everyone else. The data comes from two satellites, one in 2000 and another in 2013. Being from NASA, you've probably heard of them—WMAP and Planck?"

"Rings a bell, but I'm in human spaceflight. Those missions were probably research," Marie answered.

"Okay. But you probably know what those missions produced—almost everyone does. They mapped the cosmic microwave background radiation, the leftovers from the Big Bang."

"Ah, yes, now I remember. A spotty orange-and-blue map of the whole night sky."

"Right. The map itself is fairly well known, but most people never heard what happened *after* that map circulated on the internet. The scientists used the data to make precise calculations of two numbers: *critical* density—the tipping point for expansion versus gravity—and the *actual* density of the universe."

Nala paused, either in thought or maybe just for dramatic effect. "They're the same number. Critical density and actual density are *exactly* the same, to the degree that we can measure them. There's absolutely no reason that they should be the same, they just are."

"Is that bad?" Marie asked, still not sure of the deep meaning that Nala apparently saw.

"It's not good or bad. It's flat. It's like sitting down at a restaurant, picking from the menu blindfolded and then finding out at the end of the meal that the bill is exactly the amount of money you happen to have in your wallet, to the penny. A flat universe happens to have exactly the right amount of mass to perfectly balance out its expansion. What's more, Jan says we just confirmed it from an entirely different angle. Expanded four-dimensional space becomes unstable at exactly the same density."

"Which means?"

"Think about it. All the expansion energy in the universe is completely canceled by all the mass energy. The pluses and the minuses perfectly balance to zero. Taken as a whole, the universe is literally *nothing*. And that tells you where it came from."

"Nothing?" Marie asked, finally beginning to see Nala's point.

Nala nodded. "Our universe and everything in it sprang from nothing. Prior to the Big Bang, there was nothing. No mass, no energy, no space. Nothing. The *void*, as they call it. It's hard to wrap your head around that idea, but it's reality and we just helped to prove it. There's no reason that 4-D space should obey this same rule, but it does."

Something from nothing. It had come up in Core's answer to one of Jan's questions. Marie hadn't realized it at the time, but Core might have been pointing the way. There was something else in the back of her mind. She couldn't put a finger on it, but Nala's explanation was almost like an extension of the visualizations.

"I don't think any of this is a coincidence," Nala said. "It's—"

The light from the singularity flashed off and then back on again, freezing her in midsentence. Nala looked at Thomas, who hadn't disappeared. Thomas looked at Marie, with the headband still in her hand. And Marie hoped for an explanation from either one of them. "Is this flashing, like, a regular occurrence?"

"It's becoming more frequent," Nala said. "Anyone have any fuzzy thoughts that feel like a dream?"

No one said anything. Nala patted herself down like she was checking for wounds. "It could be something small, maybe something we wouldn't even notice."

"I'm alive this time," Thomas said. "Two out of four. Not bad."

Nala leaned across and gave him a hug. "We're in this together, big guy."

"This is ridiculous," Marie said. "We've got to get out of here while we're all still whole." Marie thought more about Nala's explanation. "There was something you said... the visualizations are so similar. I should know what it is, but I can't quite place it."

"Something I said?" Nala questioned. "About a flat universe? Or critical density?"

Marie tried to piece it together. Critical density. A single number that measured the stability of space. She'd seen this concept before. Colors. Ratios. All floating in a grand visualization of space.

"What was the number for critical density again?" Marie asked.

Nala picked up one of the cracker boxes and wrote on it: 9.47×10^{-27} kg / m^3. "Nine point four seven times ten to the minus twenty-seven kilograms per cubic meter," she recited.

Marie nodded. "And the actual density is the same number, right?"

"Right," Nala said. "The ratio is exactly 1.0, which tells you the universe is flat, or that 4-D space is stable."

The headband had been talking to her; she just hadn't realized what it was saying until now. "That's it!" she yelled.

Nala and Thomas were startled by her shout. They both stared silently as she stood up, placed the headband over her hair and tapped twice. Multiple spheres popped into view, hovering all around. Their colors told a story, one that she now recognized and finally understood.

The spheres glowed in various shades of color. Most were shades of blue, with numbers like 0.912, 0.974 and 0.877. In every case, the value—a density ratio—was less than one. Stable space. They were four-dimensional bubbles, probably created by Nala and Thomas during their experiments, and they weren't going anywhere.

Yet two spheres were very different, colored in shades of deep purple. The first purple sphere surrounded them. She'd seen it both

273

from the outside and now from the inside. Its number, provided by the visualization, was 1.324, *larger* than one. Unstable space, the result of a cataclysmic explosion that had destroyed much of Fermilab.

The other sphere was far beyond their position, also deep purple, but larger, bulging and distorted. Its number was 1.629, the highest ratio of any.

"You okay?" asked Nala.

"No… yes… well, I'm okay, but I'm worried that Daniel and a whole bunch of people in Texas are in big trouble."

"You want to explain?" Nala might still be skeptical of the headband, but Marie hadn't done a good job of explaining how she knew these things. She wasn't entirely sure herself.

"I can see space in a very different way," Marie said. Nala and Thomas both listened intently. "There are dozens of spheres—bubbles—all around us, and I'm pretty sure you created them. They're colored. Most are blue, but two are purple. They all have numbers associated with them, and I never knew what the numbers meant until now. They're ratios. I don't know why I didn't understand it before, but once you explained it… well, it's obvious now." She shrugged. "Just by looking, I can tell when four-dimensional space is unstable."

"Holy shit," Thomas said.

"Holy *fucking* shit," Nala said.

"I like her version better," said Thomas, pointing at Nala. "Sounds more important."

"So, what's this about Daniel?" Nala asked.

"He's in Texas, called away on an assignment." Marie explained the details of the situation, as best she knew them.

Nala picked up on one point. "So, these guys down in Texas are filling quantum space they created with smoke?"

274

"Yeah—well, gases, soot, whatever comes out of a power plant."

"That's it, then," Nala said with authority. "It's the density. They're pouring a shitload of stuff into an unnaturally confined space, and the mass-to-volume ratio has skyrocketed. Their little gimmick to get rid of pollution is probably unstable as hell."

"Then, the explosion that destroyed Fermilab..."

"Yeah," Nala agreed. "They're walking into the same disaster we did, and just as blind. But this one could be bigger. Maybe a *lot* bigger."

"We need to warn him," Marie said. "Jan could get a message to him."

"Shouldn't we have heard a big boom by now?" Thomas asked. "If the ratio is even higher than ours, doesn't that mean this Texas bubble is even more unstable?"

Marie thought about the question and compared it with what she'd visualized. The answer wasn't clear, but perhaps there were clues. "It's bulging, not spherical like all the others. Maybe the distortion is relieving some of the pressure?"

Nala shrugged. "I suppose it's possible. Density is all about mass in a given volume, but I have no idea why one bubble would be more elastic than another. Hell, this is all new. There's a ton of stuff we just don't know." She turned to Thomas. "If we ever get out of here, I've got a long list of tests you and I are going to make."

Thomas held up a finger. "With better safety protocols."

"Yeah, you're right," Nala said with a tight smile. "I've learned my lesson. Promise."

Thomas held out a bent pinky finger. "Pinky swear."

Nala hooked her finger into his. "Really, I absolutely, positively promise."

275

Nala picked up the phone and started to type another message to Jan, but Marie grabbed her hand. "Wait." She paused in thought.

"I was just going to tell him to warn Daniel about this."

"Yeah, wait," Marie said again. "I might have an idea."

Thomas perked up. "Ideas are good, especially around here."

Marie tossed the components of a plan around in her mind like pieces in a jigsaw puzzle thrown onto a table. Whether they would all fit into a whole picture was another matter. An enormous bubble of 4-D space, hanging over a power plant in Texas. Growing bigger by the minute. The weird property of spatial compression. A ratio of instability, mass versus volume.

Definitely a jumble, but one by one, the pieces began to fall into place. There were complications, not the least of which was the degree to which this fabulously dangerous headband was scrambling her brain. Was she even capable of solving this problem?

The puzzle pieces weren't well defined, and neither was the final picture they might represent. But it was better than standing around waiting for the light to flash again. She'd come here to use her unique ability to rescue people. It was time for action.

"I have a plan," she said, still holding Nala's hand. "Tell them to make the bubble bigger. Make it as big as they can."

"Bigger?" Thomas asked. "You sure? Wouldn't that make the explosion worse?"

Nala smiled. "Ah, yes. Clever girl. I think I see your point." Nala returned her attention to the phone and tapped out a message.

41 Non Sequitur

Finch drove, Daniel rode shotgun and two FEMA employees hitched a ride in the backseat—a man and a woman, both young, both frazzled, but in an excited kind of way.

"Did you see that? Some kind of crazy shit," the young woman said, waving her arms. She had brown bangs that almost completely covered her eyes.

"Never seen anything like it," said the young man, a grin breaking across his stubbled face. "But I could *easily* do that again."

"Whoa, I don't know. I was just standing out in the parking lot, recalibrating my Lidar, when the asphalt literally rolled under my feet." She reached a hand out to Daniel. "Hi, I'm Audrey. This is Parker."

"That's what was so freaking weird," Parker continued. "It was suddenly like, surf's up. And it wasn't just the parking lot. The whole place was jiggling. That building where they burn the coal is seven freaking stories tall. Even the stacks looked like... what are those long red candy things called?"

"Twizzlers?" Audrey asked.

"Yeah, like a Twizzler getting shook. Wacked out."

"Everybody on your team okay?" Daniel asked. The evacuation had turned out to be far more rapid than anyone had anticipated, but at least all the buildings had still been in place as multiple vehicles had roared out of the parking area.

"Yeah, probably," Audrey said. "Most of the rest of them were in the van. We couldn't fit. Hey, thanks for the lift."

"No problem," said Finch. He was doing sixty in a thirty-five, but the only other cars on the road were in a single-file line, ahead and behind. The fallback position was about eight miles away and located on the primary route back to Austin. Easy access, in case they needed to retreat even further.

"Dude, you're that famous scientist guy," Parker said, pointing to Daniel.

Daniel nodded. "You've seen me on TV?"

"Seriously? Nobody watches TV. I saw you on *Jacked Up*."

"Sorry?" Daniel asked. The program name didn't ring a bell.

Audrey and Parker exchanged a knowing glance: *The old guy who has no clue.*

"It's pretty cool," Audrey said. "Quick clips. Twenty seconds each. You should check it out. You're on it all the time."

Besides press conferences, Daniel had been involved in several science-based programs. Even if the next generation was getting their information chopped into bite-sized pieces on a show named after cocaine addiction, as long as it included science, the state of the world couldn't be too bad.

They arrived at the fallback command center, which turned out to be a restaurant that had probably been closed for at least a year. A variety of police and government vehicles filled the parking lot, and dozens of tripods with cameras and various electronics had been set up in a patio area that looked as though it had once been an outdoor barbeque pit but now sprouted weeds between paving stones.

Gonzalo Ayala stood on the patio, staring off into the distance. Several others encircled the busy man, including FEMA, state troopers and other officials. Several reporters and photographers clustered on one side of the patio, setting up cameras and preparing for their live broadcasts.

Daniel gazed southeast, the same direction everyone else was looking. The swirling cloud that hung over the power plant was still visible in the distance. It had grown since he'd first seen it, and the air beneath shimmered like heat waves over hot pavement.

"Dr. Rice," a voice behind him called. It was Ayala, with his entourage following. "Best estimate. Are we far enough away?"

Daniel had little information other than what his eyes could tell him, but he wasn't likely to get much more within the next few seconds. Time-constrained decisions weren't like science; someone had to make a choice based only on *best available* information, however poor.

"Those waves under the cloud appear to be the same physical wave that we all just experienced. Based on that, it looks like 3-D space is being impacted out to two or three miles. I'd use the waves as an indicator. Unless they spread, we're probably okay."

"Then we'll stay," Ayala said. "Evacuation is complete to this distance, about eight miles, though there's still a lot of livestock inside that circle. Austin is still the main concern."

"How far is Austin?"

"Eastern suburbs, about fifteen miles from the plant. Downtown, more like twenty. If it gets any worse, we'll push back to twenty miles and evac the eastern side of the city. One step at a time, though."

There was no way to know if twenty miles or even a hundred miles was perfectly safe. More information would help. Given all the tripods and electronics around the patio, some of that information was probably right here. Daniel gave Ayala a summary of the calls he'd made to Romania and Fermilab, including the plan to freeze the 4-D space as-is and avoid any spatial collapse. For the time being, it was all he had to offer.

For most people, unfamiliar electronics are something to avoid, like finding fried yak on a dinner menu. For Daniel, it was just the opposite; a complex-looking device with protruding lenses, tubes and dozens of cables perched on top of a tripod was an intellectual magnet.

Audrey, the young woman who had joined them in the car, was connecting cables on just such an instrument. Her colleague, Parker, lifted a high-powered telescope onto a heavy-duty tripod and screwed a camera onto its visual back. At least the telescope was recognizable.

"Is this your Lidar?" Daniel asked. He could only guess what the device might be used for, but she had mentioned it in the car.

Audrey nodded and connected a cable to a box that looked like a cross between a television studio camera and a gun sight. It sat atop three sturdy legs at eye level.

"Is it the same as Doppler radar?" Daniel's best guess.

"Same idea," she answered. "But Lidar works with a laser, not a radar beam. I'm taking cross-sections through the cloud every five minutes... well, as soon as I get it set up again."

Daniel wasn't familiar with the equipment, but any data was better than none. "What can you measure?"

"We're doing real-time processing of twelve parameters. Wind, aerosols, cloud base, droplet size, molecular composition and a few others." She pointed to a cable that ran across the ground to a NOAA van parked nearby. "We have a mobile analytics station for whatever parameter we need to study. Of course, it's not a vertical profile like it was at our forward location, but it should still give a good view of what's going on up there. You need something in particular?"

"For starters, how high is the cloud?"

"Base is thirteen hundred meters. Top varies, but generally around three thousand. Kind of compressed compared with most cumulonimbus clouds." Audrey seemed to know her stuff.

"Can you measure vorticity?"

"You bet. But vorticity is a measure of synoptic scales... low-pressure systems and hurricanes. This cloud is more of a mesoscale event, so we're using an angular momentum circulation measure—same thing we do for tornadoes. I can get that data if you want it."

Pouring through reams of cloud cross-sections probably wasn't the best use of his time, but it was great to have a sharp meteorologist who seemed to be ready to answer whatever questions might come up. "No need. But one thing I'm curious about: is the rotation increasing?"

"Just like an ice skater pulling in her arms," she said. "This baby is spinning up, at least the central core."

"Good to know. Thanks."

"Science rules," Audrey said.

"Damn straight," said Parker, who was set up only a few feet away, adjusting the camera-telescope combination.

"Mind if I take a look?"

"Go for it," Parker said. "I'm spotting the power plant."

The SLR camera on the back end of the scope put a highly magnified image onto the camera's display. The scope was trained on the center of the power plant, two of the four smokestacks visible. They wobbled just like Twizzlers.

Five questions in two minutes, and his understanding of an otherwise unknown phenomenon had just gone from *severely limited* to *not bad*. Science did, in fact, rule.

Daniel's phone rang. "Excuse me."

It was Jan, probably the busiest man in Illinois right now. "Daniel," he said breathlessly. "Listen carefully. We need a big change. I've been in communication with Nala and Marie. They have a plan. I agree with their assessment, but we're going to need the help of the Romanians to pull this off."

Even over the phone, Jan's concern was obvious. But so was his passion. "How can I help?" Daniel asked.

"The stability of dimensional space is a direct consequence of the ratio of mass to volume. Call the Romanians. Tell them to ramp up their neutrino oscillation. Make the space bigger. Double its size."

The four-dimensional space hovering over this part of Texas was certainly the underlying reason for the ominous cloud that threatened to do what had already happened at Fermilab. Yet Jan wanted to double its size. It wasn't the most obvious path to success. Daniel's understanding of the situation had just reset back to *severely limited*.

"I have to get back to Nala," Jan said. "Call them. And hurry."

Daniel tried to piece together any scenario where this crazy idea might make sense, but he couldn't think of any. It was a very foreign feeling for a man who usually not only had the answers but also assumed control of the solution. Double the size of the four-dimensional space? The evacuation perimeter eight miles out might suddenly seem entirely too close.

But there were times when decisions had to be made with the best available information. Jan and Nala were the experts, and they had clearly come up with a plan. After a minute of thought, Daniel dialed the contact in Romania.

42 Intersection

Marie and Nala kneeled side by side above the pancaked view of Jan's office. The compressed figure of the three-dimensional man walked in and out, looking like he might be talking on his phone.

Nala finished typing a note and offered the phone to Marie. "Anything else before we go?" Nala asked.

Marie took the phone. "Yeah, just one more message to pass along to Daniel." She finished typing and handed the phone back to Nala. The two exchanged a long look and Nala reached out, hugging Marie tightly around the neck.

Nala spoke into Marie's ear. "This is a brilliant idea. I can see why Daniel loved you so much as a partner."

Marie pushed back, still holding Nala by the shoulders. "Any idea is only as good as its chance of success. Realistically, what are the odds that we can pull this off?"

Nala shrugged and started counting on her fingers. "Let's see. Death by asphyxiation... death at the edge of the void... then there's death from dimensional misalignment of every cell in our bodies... and, of course, death by a massive explosion. I'd say our chances are one in five."

Both women laughed. "You know, I think I can live with that," Marie said.

Thomas returned from the break room. He held out three paper masks, the kind commonly worn by doctors during surgery and by the Japanese to avoid germs. Marie had remembered seeing a stack of the masks at the Fermilab security desk and had texted Jan to provide them.

Thomas looked very confused. "I managed to peel them off the break room table, but somebody needs to tell me what the heck we're doing."

Marie grabbed his hand and pulled herself up from the floor. "Come on, we've got to hurry. I'll tell you on the way."

Except for the masks, one bottle of water and the headband, they left everything else at the makeshift campsite over Jan's office. If the plan worked, they wouldn't need supplies. And if it didn't work, there were at least four ways they were going to die. One way or another, their dimensional imprisonment was coming to an end.

They moved directly away from the singularity, away from its flashes of probability and eigenstates, away from the debris field and away from the one-way portal that had dropped Marie into this impossibly strange bubble of existence. She wouldn't miss any of it.

Had it been a colossal mistake to leap down the rabbit hole? Probably. Words echoed from what now seemed like the distant past. *You're in over your head, Kendrick.* Tim's assessment, just before their mission to Ixtlub. Tim was a jerk, but his call had been spot-on, both then and now. She was unquestionably in over her head. But Tim had vastly underestimated her resolve.

There was a way out of this place. It might offer no better than a one-in-five chance of success, but at least it was a path. The three raced forward into the darkness.

"Don't mind me," Thomas said between breaths as they ran. "Go ahead and make your clever plans without explaining. I'm just the lab assistant. Probably just here for comic relief."

Marie took two strides for each one of Thomas's. "Sorry, Thomas. It's all happening really fast. It's the critical density that Nala and Jan figured out. We can change it, or at least Daniel can. If they make the bubble over Texas bigger, the density goes down, the ratio goes below one point zero and the bubble stabilizes. At least that's the theory."

"Okay, that part makes sense," Thomas said.

Marie stopped running. "Hold up a second, let me check status." She tapped the headband and tuned in to the colored spaces all around. Most of the smaller blue bubbles were already behind them. The purple bubble that surrounded them extended for another kilometer, maybe more. The larger bubble, the one she was sure was over Texas, had grown larger still. "It's started!" she yelled. "It's growing again. Daniel got the message!"

"How's the ratio?" Nala asked. She leaned her hands on her knees, panting from the run. The only person who didn't seem to be affected was Thomas, who looked like he was out for a Sunday stroll.

Marie examined the unseen numbers that displayed only within her mind. "Uh... down a little, 1.508."

"But still well above 1.0," Nala said. "Still dangerous. Is the edge getting closer?"

"Yeah, definitely."

They started to run again. Thomas continued to ask questions. "You're trying to make a stable 4-D space over Texas, right?" Marie nodded. "Great for the people of Texas, but how does that help us?"

"There's a chance that the bubble will grow large enough to intersect this one." It was the same technique that Zin had used to get them to Ixtlub. A small bubble on the departure side, a larger bubble at the arrival point, intersecting to provide a continuous 4-D path from one point to another. It was the germ of an idea that had flashed into Marie's head. Two bubbles, and the larger one would be their savior.

"A bubble merge? All the way from Texas?"

"Think about it," Nala said, providing the expert validation for Marie's plan. "It's four-dimensional quantum space. When it expands, a direction in 3-D space must compress, right?"

"Right," said Thomas. "We've established that relationship a million times."

Nala waved one arm as she talked, her run reducing to a jog. "From our point of view inside 4-D space, the distance from here to Texas could become negligible—just a hop, skip and a jump. We've got two bubbles of 4-D space with the 3-D distance between them getting smaller by the minute. Merging should be no problem at all."

"I like it," Thomas said. "We just jog from Chicago to Texas."

Marie examined the two bubbles in her mind. Though there was no specific data on their widths, she was confident the visualization represented each to scale. If they were currently in a sphere a kilometer wide, then the other bubble was probably ten times that size.

"Once they merge, it should be about six kilometers to the center," Marie said. "At least from our perspective on the inside."

"At a jog, we could cover six kilometers in thirty minutes," said Thomas, clearly happy that he was contributing to the calculations.

Marie slowed to a walk, breathing heavily. "Another check," she said. "It's easier if I'm not running." The distant bubble was not so distant anymore. A curving purple surface intersected the floor not far in front. "We're really close. The bubbles could merge any minute. Ratio is down to 1.471. Still pretty high."

"Going in the right direction," Nala said, "but the whole thing might still collapse. Who knows where that would throw us?"

One of the four ways to die. There was no avoiding it. They had to cross the boundary into the larger bubble. Marie looked around, comparing the view her eyes provided against the one inside her brain. "We're close to the edge. Might be safer to wait here for a minute until the bubbles join up."

Thomas croaked in a classic voiceover of a movie trailer. "Welcome to... *the void*. Your worst nightmare."

His repertoire was impressive, but his scary voice wasn't what was bothering Marie at just this moment. What caused her heart to pump faster were the contortions on his face. His forehead began to pixelate, and it quickly spread to his nose, mouth and chin.

Crap! Not a good time.

Marie would need to wear the headband continuously, or none of this was going to work. She forced herself to concentrate on what she knew was real.

"Grrrrr," she yelled through gritted teeth. She kept her eyes open and grabbed Thomas's arm. His face was *not* melting into colored dots. His skin was *normal*. She touched his cheek. Her fingers felt skin with whiskers, not the vibration of a thousand tiny insects that overwhelmed her vision. "Damnit! Stop!"

She felt a wave of dizziness coming over her while the insectlike dots rotated in place, as if the hive was deciding whether to pour out and devour her or resume the shape of a man. She squeezed Thomas's arm. "Slap me!" she yelled. And Thomas did.

The buzzing bees slowed their motion and faded away into the normal skin of the man standing in front of her. She buried her face in his chest. "Thanks, I needed that."

Her cheek stung where he'd slapped, but the terror was over. Not the most pleasant of solutions, and probably not a permanent answer either. She could feel the creepy-crawlies lying in wait for another opportunity for permanent psychosis. They didn't belong to the headband; they weren't even external. These little buggers were buried deep inside her own mind.

"You okay?" asked Thomas with watery eyes. "I'm really sorry. Did I hurt you?" Nala looked on from behind the large man with an expression of deep concern on her face.

"Whatever just happened to you, Marie, it's not good," Nala said.

Marie sheepishly pointed to the headband. "It does things to me. I'm okay now."

"Can you turn it off?" Nala asked.

Marie shook her head. "Not if we want to get out of here. This is going to get really crazy, really fast. I'm going to need that visualization, or our chance of success drops to one in a thousand."

She looked up, noticing a change in the bubbles. Their edges were no longer spherical, but in the shape of a lopsided dumbbell. Like two soap bubbles, one large and one small, they had joined.

A distinct odor filled the air, a foul smell like burning tar, fortified by an acidic taste on the tongue.

"What's that smell?" asked Thomas.

"We're there," Marie answered. "The bubbles have joined. Unfortunately, we're going to have to suffer through whatever pollutants they've been pumping into this space. But..." Marie held out the paper masks. "These might help." They each donned a mask over their nose and mouth.

"Better," said Nala. "But I can feel it stinging my eyes already. This could get ugly."

"Can't be helped. Let's get going," Marie said.

They resumed their run, with the headband providing guidance to their destination. It wasn't far; they'd be there in a few minutes.

"This stuff is nasty," Thomas said, coughing under his mask. "Tell me again why we're running toward this stuff instead of away from it?"

Breathing was twice as hard and harder still when trying to talk. "We've got to get to the center of this bubble," Marie yelled.

"But if this new, even bigger bubble might still collapse, isn't the center the worst place to be?"

Marie nodded. "Yeah, probably true. But it's also our best chance."

"Best chance to get blown up again?" he yelled.

"It's why Daniel went to Texas. There's a power plant down there with some kind of special cap at the top of the smokestacks. They've been sending pollution into 4-D space through it. I'm guessing the cap is big. Maybe as big as a tunnel."

"So, you think—"

"Yeah," Marie yelled. "It's our way out of here."

43 Rupture

Audrey, the meteorologist operating the Lidar instrument, waved her hand at the group of FEMA managers huddled to one side. "Um, Jesse, Gonzalo, anybody? I'm getting something weird here."

Daniel perked up. The combination of a smart scientist operating high-tech equipment and calling attention to *weird* results was a detail not to be ignored.

One of the FEMA managers broke away from the group and hurried over. Audrey pointed to a monitor attached to one side of the instrument. "Pressure wave. Large-scale, spreading out from just below the cloud in all directions. It's big, and it's coming right at us."

"Is this the same thing we experienced at the plant?" the manager asked.

She looked nervous but meticulously kept on message. "No. It's natural, but there's no telling what caused it. We only have about thirty seconds before it hits. I think we should we take shelter."

"Thanks." He turned and shouted to the crowd of scientists and reporters. "Everyone in the building. Now!"

Daniel approached Audrey as her hands flew around the tripod, quickly disconnecting the equipment. "How bad?"

"It might die out before it gets here, but you never know."

Daniel nodded. "Good plan, let's get inside."

She pulled the instrument off its tripod base, and they headed through the single door into the old restaurant. The building was brick, but it had large picture windows facing the oncoming pressure wave.

"Stay away from windows," the FEMA manager shouted to the group gathering inside.

Seconds later, a blast of air twisted tree branches and stirred up dust. It shook the windows like a sonic boom, but the glass held. The sudden storm was over as quickly as it had come.

"Yow," Audrey said to Daniel. "A gust front. This thing must be generating downdrafts."

Ayala poked his head out the door. "All clear. Meteorologist? Where are you?" He caught Audrey's eye among the crowd of people. "Keep monitoring and give us regular readings on this." She picked up her Lidar unit and pushed out through the door. Daniel followed.

A few minutes later, she had the event analyzed. Ayala and several other FEMA officials gathered around as she explained. "It was a pressure wave—compressed air responding to something going on under the cloud. The data shows it's happening repeatedly. The air is being pushed and pulled, a lot like waves on a beach. That was a big one, but there are a lot of smaller waves around the plant. Just like at the beach, most waves don't go past the wet sand, but a few of the big ones make it all the way up to where you put out your towel."

"Cause?" Ayala asked. His furrowed brow and military stance were intimidating, but the young woman handled herself well.

"Sorry, no direct data on a cause, but I can tell you I'm picking up higher-than-normal concentrations of carbon dioxide, carbon monoxide and sulfur dioxide."

"Power plant emissions," Daniel said.

"Finch!" called Ayala. Jeffrey Finch, sitting in a patio chair raised his hand. "I thought the plant was shut down."

Finch stood up. "It is. There's nothing coming out of those stacks."

"Backwash," said Daniel. All eyes turned to him. "The plant may be shut down, but for weeks they've been pouring effluents into hidden space. It may be leaking out."

"Another one!" Audrey yelled. "Bigger. Forty seconds until impact."

Daniel looked toward the power plant. Even with unaided eyes, he could tell this wave was a major step up. Trees around the plant were uprooted, branches ripped away. A portion of the roof of one of the buildings shredded, with material flying into the sky as if a tornado had just blasted through. The line of destruction advanced across the ranchland of Texas, tearing apart a house and fences.

But worst of all, the swirling cloud itself had transformed, with a dark slash opening up on one side. From deep within its interior, a cloud of brown smoke poured out of the slash and down upon the land.

The group needed no command—they ran for the shelter of the building. Daniel helped Audrey remove the instrument and lent a hand to Parker, who carried the telescope inside. Seconds later the blast hit, this time exploding the large picture window and spraying the room with glass. Everyone ducked down and held up arms to protect themselves. A tree branch skidded across the patio outside, taking out several camera tripods.

As before, once the pressure wave had passed, things in the immediate area calmed. "Injuries?" Ayala called out. Several people shouted that they were okay. Though broken glass was everywhere, there had been sufficient warning to keep their distance.

"Jesse, find something to put over that window," Ayala yelled. "Okay, folks, I still need monitoring. Give me your best call on what we can expect next."

They dashed back outside. Daniel messaged Jan. *All hell is breaking loose here. You sure about that expansion?*

He got an immediate response. *Yes. It would be worse if we'd done nothing. Stick with it. Interior density should be dropping.*

Audrey slapped her equipment together and had everything plugged in faster than a marine reassembles his rifle. A minute later, she called out, "A receding phase. It's sucking air back in."

Daniel looked over Parker's shoulder. He had repositioned the telescope on the gash in the cloud, which was indeed sucking material in like a giant vacuum cleaner. The telescopic view showed broken wood, tree branches, even farming equipment in a gravity-defying blast into the sky. As it rose, the dust and debris began to swirl like an upside-down drain.

"Check it out," Parker said, pointing to what looked like a chicken coop, complete with chickens, flying through the air.

Over time, the pull of debris ended, and the gash even closed somewhat. It left a sky filled with drifting dust, leaves, hay and whatever other materials were light enough to drift on air currents.

The pressure waves continued to pulsate, pushing outward and then back in. Now that the pattern had been identified, it could be seen with the naked eye without the need of Lidar or a telescope. Trees bent one way and then another; dust blew in, swirled and then switched directions.

A tone from Daniel's phone told him another message had arrived, from Jan again. This one was puzzling.

Passing this along, from Marie. She says—meet us at the stacks.

44 Passageway

Smoke, particulates, carbon dioxide and a potpourri of poisonous combustion gases filled the darkened space. Even with the medical mask, Marie could visualize each molecule that entered her lungs and automatically compare the ratio of toxins with the nitrogen, oxygen and argon normally sucked in with each breath. Unfortunately, the headband couldn't tell her when the toxicity might become lethal.

Their run had reduced to a fast walk, with pauses for bouts of coughing. They rubbed irritated, watery eyes and struggled to breathe through the simple masks. Nala seemed to be taking it the hardest. Thomas sailed right through as if nothing at all were wrong, but he kept looking behind as the singularity, their primary source of light, disappeared below a horizon. Nala said it proved they were following a curved path, parallel to the three-dimensional surface of the earth. But it also meant that the dim glow from the surface was their only source of light. It would last only while there was still daylight back in the 3-D world.

Marie didn't relish the idea of finding their way in pitch blackness with only the headband's visualization to guide them. If the singularity flashed again, at least they wouldn't see it. There was some comfort in not knowing. The dice were still tumbling, and she could still lose the headband at any time.

The psychosis was ever-present. She could suppress it, force the pixilating view of the world back into some deep, dark corner of her mind, but she couldn't make it go away. Worse, it felt permanent, as if it had always been there but was now awake. Removing the headband wouldn't help any more than removing her clothes. Those things were external. The psychosis felt internal, like a dental cavity, or a tumor.

"Still on track?" Nala asked in between coughs. Only her eyes were visible. In addition to the mask, she had pulled her long black hair around her face and wrapped her sweater on top.

Marie flipped to a layer that provided the layout, not just of the bubble of four-dimensional space that surrounded them but of the neighboring three-dimensional space as well. Not far ahead, the dimensions intersected—their destination.

"We're getting close," Marie answered. She pulled her blouse up and stretched it over the mask to add another layer of filtering. It exposed her bare belly, but the air was getting warmer.

"So, this is Texas?" Thomas asked, pointing to the patchwork of browns and greens beneath their feet.

"Must be," Marie answered. The headband wasn't exactly a GPS unit. Nala explained that a larger 4-D bubble would mean a larger compression of three-dimensional length, making anything on the surface unidentifiable. It made sense. If this was Texas, they had covered more than a thousand miles in less than twenty minutes.

"Look," said Thomas, pointing. "An exit point?"

From behind clouds of smoke, a slash of bright light appeared like a sunbeam around the edges of fog. It had an irregular shape, as if someone had taken a knife to cloth. To the eye it looked like a promising way out, but the headband told another story.

"Not our exit," Marie said. "It's an opening, but there's no connection to the ground."

"You sure?" Thomas asked. "It's huge. We'd could easily get through."

"I think you'd find yourself falling. The visualization is telling me there's no 3-D ground out there. Plus, I'm seeing incredible turbulence on the other side. Even if we had parachutes, I'm not sure we'd survive."

"Where, then?" Thomas asked.

"Ahead," Marie answered. "Follow me."

They alternated between walking and jogging, with the slash appearing larger and rising higher in their view. The smell of combustion diminished, and the air became fresher, but it was also filled with dust and bits of floating debris. There were even leaves and small pieces of hay and grass floating by.

Thomas stopped and held out a hand for them to stop too. "Wait a second, did you hear that?"

They listened. There was something out there, maybe a faint rustling sound. "Wind?" Marie asked.

"No, not that. I thought I heard a rooster crowing."

Nala held her sweater and hair over her nose with one hand, her eyes rolling. "Good imagination, funny man."

"No joke. That's what it sounded like."

They continued walking until a distant but distinct crowing interrupted the silence.

"There you go," he said.

"Holy shit," Nala said. "There's a farm in here? I am so ready to get out of this hellhole."

Marie could sympathize. She'd been *inside* for only a few hours. Nala and Thomas had been trapped for days, and they were entirely dependent on Marie's guidance to get them out.

They were very close. The farm smells and sounds confirmed the reality of the gash and of the three-dimensional world just beyond. The visualization showed not one but four separate intersections between the dimensions ahead. Marie focused on the nearest one.

It was a circular cross section with a solid connection to 3-D on the other side. If Daniel's description was accurate, it was the tip of a smokestack that had been capped by a device that made a right-angled turn into the 4-D bubble. A passageway out, or at least she hoped.

A welcome breeze blew in their faces, coming out of the darkness ahead. It cleared out the remainder of the smoke, though the smell of soot and tar remained. A soft glow of light from its center illuminated the outline of a large circular shape just ahead.

It was a low wall that rose hip-high, dirty white in color and somewhat shiny, like it was made of plastic. It formed a circle about fifteen feet in diameter. They stopped at its edge and peered inside. A breeze arose from its interior depths.

"Jesus," Nala said.

"That's a long way down," Thomas said.

The view was still the same flattened version of the 3-D world, but the shape of a deep cylindrical shaft was unmistakable, the illusion reinforced both by the air blowing into their faces and by the rim that extended into their space. It was like looking into an enormous well with no clear view of the bottom.

"It's the top of a smokestack," Marie said. "It must be."

"It's open, too," Nala said. "This isn't just a boundary between dimensions, it's a hole. That's 3-D air coming out." She pulled the mask from her face and took a deep breath. "Clean, too."

They followed Nala's lead and removed their masks. They had arrived, though the next step didn't look like it would be easy.

Within the dark depths of the stack, one thin shaft of light entered from the side. With eyes alone, the distance into the flattened 3-D world was almost impossible to tell, but the headband estimated twenty feet to the source of light and more than five hundred feet to a solid surface at the base of the smokestack.

Most likely concrete at the bottom. You wouldn't want to fall.

Yet this was the way out, their portal back home. It was true there were three more just like it, but each certainly had its own concrete pad of death waiting at the bottom.

"Sorry, this is all I have," Marie lamented. "I thought there'd be some way to climb through, but assuming gravity applies, I'm afraid that jumping in is going to get us killed."

"Yeah," Nala said. "Gravity still applies." She studied the vertical shaft. "There must be some way to get down. Can I borrow that headband of yours?"

Marie just smiled. "You know you can't."

Nala smiled back. "I know. But you're making me really curious. Tell us all you see down there, every detail."

Marie had gotten so used to seeing an enhanced reality that she had almost forgotten to provide the description to everyone else. Three heads were better than one, and even if they couldn't see what she saw, they might think of something she hadn't.

She flipped through several layers of data, describing the distances, the diameter, the constituents of the rising air, even the spectrum of the light coming in from one side, which Nala said matched sunlight.

"So how is sunlight getting into a smokestack?" Marie asked.

"It's a door," Thomas said.

"How do you know?" Marie asked. As soon as he said it, she thought he might be right. The headband could examine the composition of materials, and where the light entered, the curved wall of the smokestack changed from concrete to metal. There was some additional metal too, protruding out into the smokestack from where the light shone in.

"When I was a kid, my dad and I used to build whole cities out of Legos," Thomas said. "Houses, offices, bridges, the works. I remember making a cheese factory once."

Nala smirked. "A factory where they make cheese?"

"Hey, go with it. I was twelve. It's not relevant to the story anyway. What's important is that we made the factory look just like a real one that I saw in a magazine. And the real factory had a smokestack, so we made an exact replica in Legos."

"Fascinating, but where is this going?" Nala asked.

"The smokestack in the magazine had a door, so we put one in. I don't know, maybe all smokestacks have doors at the top. I think they use them for inspection or sampling or something like that."

Marie examined the spot where the light came in. Two thin lines of light, both vertical and parallel to each other. "It does look like a door. And I think there's some kind of structure in front of it." She stood up straight. "We should test this. Throw in the water bottle and let's see what it hits."

"Wait a second," said Thomas, "I've got something better." He reached into his pocket and pulled out a coin. "Just like a big wishing well. Maybe we'll hear it hit."

"Will sound travel from 3-D to 4-D?" Marie said.

"Normally, no," Nala said. "But if this is a hole, all bets are off."

"Shh," Thomas said. "Listen for a minute." He tossed the coin into the hole, aiming directly at the source of light. It dropped right through what would have been the 3-D surface and continued down into the real world. There was a slight ring as it hit something metal. Marie held up a hand and they waited, listening for the final ring as the coin hit concrete far below. Whether her hearing was normal or enhanced by the headband was hard to tell, but Nala and Thomas seemed to hear the ring as well.

"Solid evidence," Nala said. "This is a hole, and that's the three-dimensional world."

"And that's a long way down," Thomas said.

"But best of all, there's a metal platform in front of that door," Marie said. "I can barely make it out. It's not very big, but it's horizontal, possibly with a railing."

Thomas had a wide grin on his face. "Swan dive, I'm going in!"

"Wait a second," Nala said, putting an arm in front of him just in case he really was about to jump. "You're going to hit a small metal balcony that Marie can just barely see even with her alien vision?"

"Any better ideas?"

"How far down, Marie?" Nala asked.

"About twenty feet. Maybe less."

Nala stood in deep thought. "We could tie all our clothes together, make a rope and climb down."

Thomas laughed. "Your dainty sweater is going to hold me?" He waved his hands over his substantial bulk like a model showing off a new outfit. "Besides, you'd see me naked. Nope. I'll jump."

"Wait, wait, wait," Nala said, still holding an arm out. She was half his size and her thin arm could hardly hold the big man back if he was ready to go. "What else you got in that headband?"

Marie shook her head. "This is it. This is our only way out of here. I think Thomas is right. We're going to have to jump."

"Wait," Nala said again, more forcefully and holding her hand up like a traffic cop. "Here's the deal. I've been thinking about this for a while now, and I don't even know how this could work. We're standing in an extension of four-dimensional space, but we're each a set of three-dimensional atoms. Gravity still pulls us toward 3-D because that's where the mass of the earth is located, but how does our body suddenly flatten out right at Kata Zero?"

"True," said Thomas. He probably saw the blank expression on Marie's face and stepped in to explain. "Kata Zero is where all three-dimensional space exists. It's like a page, a flat piece of paper, and we're like paper-thin cutouts from that page. Right now, only the bottoms of our feet are touching it."

Nala looked grim. "To rejoin the 3-D world, every bit of our body, every atom has to return to the plane of Kata Zero."

"The coin made it," Marie said.

"The coin isn't alive," Nala said. "We struggled at Fermilab to get the alignment right. Electronics were no problem, but the tolerance wasn't good enough for anything alive. Cell walls break open. Blood vessels rupture. People coming back from 4-D die."

Marie was certainly not going to question Nala's mastery of quantum physics, but there was something she was missing. Marie couldn't put her finger on it, but the headband seemed to be treating this as a fortuitous intersection between dimensions, not the pit of doom.

"It's not the same as your lab," Marie said. "I remember, I was with Daniel at Fermilab for Dr. Park's demonstration. You displaced the contents of a test box and then returned it to its original position. But this is different; it's a hole, a tunnel between dimensions. The coin just proved that. It didn't need a neutrino beam or an advanced physics lab. It just fell into 3-D. Gravity did it."

Nala shrugged. "Okay, I grant you that this is different. We never created an open passageway at Fermilab. But if we jump, I really don't know how every one of our atoms is going to manage to hit the 3-D page at the same time. We're really in uncharted territory."

Marie flipped to a data layer of forces. Gravity loomed large, bending space downward. There was no question if they jumped, they would plunge through the hole. The headband even calculated the velocity of any falling object and retrieved the exact momentum of the coin when it had hit the metal grating.

Momentum. A simple Newtonian force. Mass times velocity.

Marie leaned over the edge and looked down. A person falling five hundred feet would produce the same momentum of a car hitting a wall at sixty miles per hour. The human body plus gravity could create a *lot* of momentum.

Marie turned to Nala. "If we jump, how fast do you figure we'll be going when we hit 3-D?"

"I don't know, ten meters a second."

"All parts of us?"

"Sure."

"Every atom?"

"Of course."

"And what's on the other side of this plane of Kata Zero?"

Nala furrowed her eyebrows. "Nothing, assuming they created the 4-D bubble in only one direction, not two."

"Is that the way it's usually done?"

Nala slowly nodded. She seemed to be listening.

Marie wasn't sure if this was coming from the headband or her own brain. It was hard to tell the difference anymore. Maybe she'd already crossed the line into crazy and the idea was entirely psychotic. "So, if there's nothing beyond it, then we just splat against the plane of Kata Zero. Every atom. We jump off this wall, and just like the coin, our momentum carries us into 3-D."

Nala scratched the back of her head. "I don't know, it's not that simple. You're betting your life on it."

On impulse, Marie pushed herself to the top of the plastic rim, first on her knees and then standing erect. She teetered on the edge of the five-hundred-foot abyss.

Nala ran over. "Jesus, this is fucking crazy. You're guessing. Let's try the clothes rope and lower ourselves down."

Marie stared into the distant darkness below. Her heart pounded. "Won't work. There's no momentum in it." She glanced at Thomas and smiled. "Besides, you'd see me naked."

Marie held both arms out like a platform diver. "Ladies and gentlemen, this is it. This is all I've got. I came here to find a way out, and I have done exactly that. Here it is, this hole at the top of a smokestack. There's nothing else, so it's time to take that one-in-five chance to survive."

Marie looked down at Thomas and Nala standing respectfully on each side. Her feet wobbled on the narrow rim; her toes stuck out well beyond its edge. "Just so you know, that's not the headband talking, that's me. And, yes, I might very well be fucking crazy."

Thomas took off his Viking hat and covered his heart. Nala bit her lip and acknowledged the decision with a dip of her head.

You're in way over your head.

Marie pushed off and plunged into the shaft.

45 Kata Zero

There was a clang of metal and pain in her head. Marie lifted herself up, winced and fell back to her side. Sharp edges of a metal grating pressed into her right arm. She touched her free hand to the pain in her face and withdrew, revealing blood-covered fingers.

The pain centered around her nose and cheek. There was also something wrong with her eyes. She blinked, and the inside of an enormous circular chimney came into focus. The curving wall of gray concrete was streaked with black soot, to be expected for the inside of a smokestack.

But the waves were unexpected.

She watched, oddly entranced by the wavy movement of what should be a solid structure. It wasn't her eyes, she quickly decided. The metal grating where she lay also pulsated along with the concrete walls. The waves even passed through her body, making the pain in her head throb with each crest and trough and verifying that the undulating scene was not just another hallucination.

Rolling onto her back, Marie searched for the smokestack's rim with Nala and Thomas peering over its edge. Instead, twenty feet above, dirty white plastic sealed the top of the huge cylinder. There was no sign of the bubble of extradimensional space above it. No sign of Thomas or Nala, either. She hadn't really expected to see them. Three-dimensional eyes wouldn't be able to see around a four-dimensional corner. The peculiar world of quantum space was once again sealed off.

Back in the page, as Thomas had described. *Kata Zero*.

She reached up, grabbed the railing and pulled herself up to a seated position. The platform was no more than a ledge, perched on a curving vertical wall. The railing extended on three sides, bent in one place. Probably where she'd hit. Her head ached.

Holding tightly to the railing to steady herself in the unnatural waves, she peeked over the edge. The huge structure dropped into darkness far below. Air rushed upward, bringing with it greasy smells of the power facility somewhere in the depths.

Marie carefully stood up without releasing her grip on the rail. She looked up to the white cap overhead and called out. "Nala! Thomas!"

It wasn't a cap, it just looked that way with three-dimensional eyes. Somewhere *up there*, around the 4-D corner, they waited, perhaps even able to hear her through the interdimensional hole.

"They'll need room," she said to herself and pushed herself as far against the wall as she could. It was remarkable that she'd managed to land on such a small platform. Maybe it was the headband.

The headband.

She reached up, but even before she touched her head she knew the headband was gone. She looked down into the depths below. The headband was most likely at the bottom, probably destroyed forever.

There was a blur and a scream, and a large man slammed into the metal deck, hitting on his feet and bouncing into the wall just inches from Marie. Thomas dropped to his knees and rubbed a hand on the back of his head where he'd hit.

"Thomas!" Marie shouted and hugged him. "Are you okay?"

"Didn't quite stick the landing," he grunted, rising back to his feet. He looked at her face. "You're bleeding."

"Yeah, I know."

Thomas looked around, observing the pulsating interior of the smokestack. "Damn. It's that wavy thing."

"I have no idea what's going on," Marie said.

"I do," Thomas said. "And it's not good. This place is about to turn into rubble." He looked up, unshaken by the view of the solid cap just above. "Nala!" he yelled. "Quick. Jump!"

They waited. "Hurry!" he yelled again. "You can do it." He held out both arms and as they watched, another blur dropped from above. She was off target and Thomas leaned far over the railing to catch her. Nala's leg hit him first, twisting her fall. He managed to get both arms around her torso but momentum carried her through his grip. His body bent over the railing, and one hand caught her forearm, stopping the plunge.

"Got you," he grunted. Nala dangled in midair with Thomas bent in half across the railing. His large hand squeezed her thin arm.

She looked up with desperation on her face and nothing but darkness below her. "Don't let go," she cried.

"Don't wiggle," he said through gritted teeth.

Marie put all her weight against Thomas's back and gripped the rail on either side of him. She had no way to reach Nala, but she could keep Thomas from slipping over the side. The waves passing through the structure were only making matters worse.

Thomas grunted and heaved himself upward, dragging Nala up with him. With one more mighty pull, the big man stood up straight and threw the much smaller woman over the railing and onto the metal platform. All three of them fell backward against the wall and slumped to the deck, Thomas heaving with each breath.

Nala wrapped herself around his neck, hugging him tight. "Damn, I'm glad you're here," she said. When she released him, tears were streaming down her face.

Thomas gently lifted her arm, bright red where he had gripped her. "I didn't break anything, did I?"

306

Nala shook her head and hugged him again. "It'll bruise. I can live with it. You saved my life." She reached over and touched Marie's chin. "You're bleeding."

Marie felt again. "Yeah, I know. Does it look bad?"

"Coming from your nose," she said. "Does it hurt?"

"Yeah, my nose and cheek."

"Good."

"Good?"

"Yeah, it means you're bleeding because you hit something in the fall, not because your cell walls ruptured."

"Then we made it back to 3-D okay?"

Nala smiled. "I think we did." She looked up at the solid cap and shook her head with amazement.

"We're not out of here yet," Thomas said, motioning to the waving surfaces all around them. "You know what this means."

Nala nodded. "Yeah, I noticed. Bad shit. How do we get out?"

Marie stood up. Behind them was a door with light coming in around its edges. There was no doorknob, but Marie pulled on a metal handle welded to its surface. The door wiggled but didn't open. "Locked, probably from the outside," she said.

"Stand back," Thomas said. The two women squeezed to one side of the platform and Thomas backed up to the railing. He threw his weight into the door with a loud bang. The metal bent, but the door remained in its frame.

"One more try," he said, rubbing his shoulder. He backed up again and slammed into the door, further bowing it outward, but leaving it intact. The gap on one side was larger now, and daylight streamed in. A dead bolt was visible between the door and its frame.

307

"Hmm," Thomas said, inspecting the bent door and frame. He took off his Viking hat and pushed one of the horns into the gap, twisting hard to one side. The door frame bowed outward, increasing the gap. With a loud crack, the horn broke in half and Thomas lurched forward.

"One down, one to go," he said, sticking the other horn into the gap. He twisted again, putting his weight into it. The frame warped further, popping the dead bolt from the frame slot. The door burst open, swinging outward, with Thomas and the Viking hat following into the glare of day.

Nala grabbed the belt on his pants and Marie grabbed one arm, barely preventing him from sailing out into open air. He grabbed the door frame and pulled himself back in. Five hundred feet below, his Viking hat smacked the ground.

There was no corresponding balcony on the outside, nothing but a sheer drop. A gust of wind blew in through the open doorway.

"Holy shit, that was close," Nala said, peering outside. Marie peeked over her shoulder, thankful for the fresh air.

The countryside of Texas spread out before them. Trees, pastures, farmhouses. It would have been a lovely scene except for the wavering. Everything moved with ripples that spread in every direction. It was like looking into a pond disturbed by a thrown rock.

Far below, industrial buildings and a parking lot wavered too. The branches of nearby trees bent violently in the wind, with dust and debris blowing across the pavement.

It was a long drop, and there didn't seem to be any way down. "Jesus. Can we get a fucking break, here?" Nala asked.

Thomas grabbed the door frame, hooked his left foot on its edge and swung out into the air with his right leg and arm.

Nala yelled, "Wait! What are you—"

He reached into a recessed space, barely noticeable on the smokestack wall, and grabbed a bar inside. His foot found a step just below in another recess. The bars he'd found were embedded directly in the concrete structure, and they continued one after the other, hundreds of steps all the way to the ground five hundred feet below.

"Come on," he said. "A ladder."

The whole structure wobbled, more like a strand of spaghetti than a concrete building, but Thomas managed several more steps down the outside. He seemed unconcerned. "I'll go down ahead of you. Don't worry. If you slip, I'll catch you."

Nala looked at Marie, incredulous.

"Well, he caught you once before," Marie said.

"Let's get out of here," Nala said. She reached out and grabbed the first rung of the ladder, carefully placing one foot below it and then a second. "Kind of scary getting to the first one," she yelled back to Marie over the wind. "But it's sturdy once you're on."

The workers who used this ladder probably wore a climbing harness and hooked carabiners into each bar on their way up and down. No such luck for the three of them. Marie reached out, taking care not to look down. A gust of wind blew the door, and it clanged against the frame just as she retracted back inside.

And, of course, the whole world is blowing up around us.

Nala was already ten feet below and descending. Marie held on tight to the door frame and reached a shaky hand outside, feeling for the recessed space. Another gust knocked her off-balance, and she desperately grabbed for the rung, barely holding on.

"You can do it," Thomas called up from below.

She'd have to; climbing down the outside of a shaking industrial smokestack seemed to be the only option. She closed her eyes and swung a leg out, scraping across the surface to find the recess. Her foot found the solid bar, and she shifted her weight from the relative safety of the interior platform to the insanity of hanging on to the outside of a five-hundred-foot tower.

With both hands and feet now on the ladder, she looked up. Just above was the lower edge of a blue-and-orange cap with bold lettering across its surface: *Garrity Enterprises*.

Thank you, Mr. Garrity, Marie thought. The man who'd created this industrial device had certainly never expected it to act as an escape route, but here it was, functioning as a tunnel from four-dimensional space.

A huge swirl of clouds filled the sky above the smokestack. A slash split the swirl near its center, with smoke and debris spilling out. It was almost certainly the same jagged hole they'd seen from the inside, but without the headband, she had no way to validate her suspicion. Whatever it was, it didn't look good.

Her motivation to get to the ground was strong, but the shaking tower and gusts of wind were stronger, and she was completely exposed. She lowered her foot to the unseen rung below, trusting there was one.

The wind suddenly changed directions, blowing across the wall of the stack and upward to the cloud. Its intensity increased to a gale and it carried leaves and twigs. Below her, an entire tree branch slammed into the side of the tower, sending a vibration up its length.

One step at a time. She lowered herself down one more rung. And again. *I just jumped into the throat of this monster. I can climb down its outside too.*

Somewhere at the bottom, a car horn honked. She squeezed the rung tighter and dared to look down. In the parking lot was a lone white van. Two people stood outside, waving their arms. It was the most welcoming sight she'd ever seen, even if they were still hundreds of feet below. Nearby, a portion of the roof of one of the buildings ripped off and blew past the stack. She had to will her foot down to the next rung.

The rest was like a slow-motion nightmare that never seemed to end, with the waves and shaking growing stronger as she descended. With shouts of support from below, the final rung came, and Marie stepped onto solid ground. Thomas and Nala were there, and behind them stood Daniel.

Daniel wrapped his arms around Marie. "Message received, I'm meeting you at the stacks," he said. The tower groaned, and Daniel took her by the arm. "Let's get out of here."

They ran to the van and piled in through an open side door. The other man, whom Daniel identified as Parker, hit the gas and the van squealed out of the parking lot. Crammed into the back of a van full of electronics equipment, with the asphalt bucking up and down, Marie thought real-world space had never looked so good.

A whole tree was uprooted on one side, and Parker zipped around as it crashed onto the road. "Welcome to Texas!" he yelled to his backseat passengers. "Sorry about the weather."

Daniel handed several tissues to Marie, and she dabbed at the blood that had now run down her neck. "I think they have a medical person at the command center," Daniel said. "From there we can get an ambulance."

"I'll be alright," Marie said, even though her nose still shrieked in pain. "It could have been a lot worse."

"Any one of us could have vanished," Nala said without a hint of exaggeration. "The dice fell into place as soon as we jumped."

"Our external observer," Marie said, pointing at Daniel.

"I'm still here," Thomas said, checking his body with his hands.

"Thankful for that," Nala said, grabbing him around his neck and hugging him.

311

"Uh-oh," said Parker, looking in his rearview mirror.

They turned around, peering out the back windows of the van. In the distance, the smokestack they'd just climbed down leaned first one way and then the other and sheared off at its base, collapsing onto the neighboring building in a massive cloud of dust. The deep rumble caught up to them like thunder after a lightning strike.

As they watched, a second smokestack collapsed, taking out several electrical towers as it went down.

"We'll be alright if we can get out of this zone of turbulence," Daniel said.

"Working on it," Parker said, and he pressed the accelerator pedal down further. The wind still whipped trees around, but the waves dampened as they drove. A minute later, they skidded into a dirt parking area. Dozens of people watched the unfolding spectacle from a nearby patio.

"Medical assistance!" Daniel yelled as they stepped out of the van. A woman came running carrying a first-aid kit. Marie sat on a picnic table as the woman donned rubber gloves, checked Marie's face and wiped away blood.

Daniel sat next to her. "We have a telescope set up here. After your message, we kept an eye on the stacks. Still, it was crazy to see the three of you climbing down."

With her face mostly cleaned of blood, Marie turned to Daniel. "Thanks for paying attention, partner. That was close."

While the medical tech hovered over Marie, Daniel held out a hand and she took it. "I felt bad leaving you alone at Fermilab. And worse when you decided to go rogue. Looks like you got pretty banged up in there."

Marie laughed. "Stories to tell."

"I'd love to hear them. Buy you a beer?" he asked.

312

"She's got a broken nose," the medical tech said. "She's going to the hospital, not a bar."

"Another time," Marie said, smiling through cotton swabs taped over each nostril. "You've got my number. Don't be a stranger."

From the other side of the patio, a young woman yelled out, "Something's happening out there! This one's off the charts!"

The slash in the swirling cloud opened to a yawning chasm that stretched across the sky and swept everything around it into its dark depths. Trees were uprooted, an entire side of one building exploded outward, and debris rose only to disappear into the chasm as if it were an enormous sewer drain in the sky.

The power plant and the entire area surrounding it vibrated. Clouds of dust rose, and with a roar that was easily heard from their remote position, the buildings and the land exploded upward in a cataclysmic eruption. The cloud of dirt, rocks, buildings, and four smokestacks roiled into the air and drained away into the giant hole in the sky.

A blast of wind hit them, blowing people and equipment around. Marie shielded her eyes.

When she looked up, it was over. A few streams of brown dust and debris flowed upward, leaving behind a massive crater where the power plant had once stood.

46   External Observer

Marie relaxed in the comfortable patio chair and took another sip of coffee. "Haiti sounds lovely. I never knew."

Nala, her newest friend, sat across the table and finished the last bite of her onion-and-pepper omelet. Warm morning sunshine peeked above a line of small trees that kept the city sounds of Austin at bay.

They enjoyed a quiet table on the outdoor patio of the hotel restaurant—their rooms paid courtesy of ElecTrek Inc. A comfortable night's sleep with excellent medication had helped Marie to forget about the broken nose, though it still felt like she had a cold, and the semihard bandage the hospital had applied itched a little.

The drawbacks of stepping into the role of interdimensional rescuer.

A hot shower had transformed Nala into the beautiful woman that Marie knew had been hiding under the scruffy appearance the day before. She would become a fast friend—Marie was certain.

"Of course, there's poverty in many parts of the island," Nala explained, "particularly Port-au-Prince. It's what most people think of whenever I mention Haiti. But, if you get a chance, go to Île à Vache or any place along the south Caribbean coast. It's really beautiful."

They'd invited Thomas and Daniel to join them, but Thomas was already on a flight back to Chicago. Apparently, he had a girlfriend who was out of her mind, first with grief and then with joy that Thomas was alive. Nala said she hadn't even known he had a girlfriend. For such a gregarious guy, he kept his personal life remarkably private.

Daniel indicated that he would join them—once he'd finished making a few phone calls. Typical of Daniel. Nala just rolled her eyes, and their conversation pushed on to travel, foreign cultures and languages, along with their shared interest in science. Nala turned out to be fascinated by just about everything.

"Did you see the morning news shows?" Nala asked. Marie shook her head. "There's a new 'star' hanging over the crater out there. Of course, it's not a star—it's a quantum singularity just like we had in the lab. I wouldn't be surprised if this one hung around for a while. It's the sealed end to a big chunk of inside-out 4-D space. At least, that's my working theory."

"And it will just hang there?" Marie asked.

Nala nodded. "Probably become a tourist attraction. But they should put up a sign that reminds everyone how it got there. 'Don't get cocky,' or something like that."

"Yeah, people should keep their distance. The Fermilab version produced its own gravitational field."

"The headband showed you, right? That's why you jumped in?"

"Right. The former headband," Marie said. An amazing device, but she wouldn't miss it. "It went up with the power plant, probably pulverized to dust and blasted into that inside-out space."

Nala set down her coffee cup. "Good riddance?" She asked it as a question, and Marie had to think before she answered.

"We should learn from our mistakes. I was trying to prove something to myself. Dumb, really. I shouldn't have assumed the device would work as advertised. But now that it's gone, I kind of wish it hadn't been destroyed. I'm sure some smart engineers could have figured out how it works and then created something better, more attuned to the human brain and without the side effects."

"They still can," Nala answered. "I'm sure the Dancers can make another one, and maybe even send it with some instructions this time."

Marie smiled. "Put a label on the side: 'Warning: continuous use may result in intense hallucinations and a desire to leap into singularities.'"

Nala laughed. "Sounds like half the pharmaceuticals on the market these days."

Marie stared at the table, not focusing on anything in particular. "You know, somebody has to take the risks or science doesn't advance. My parents were both scientists, my mom works with stem cells and my dad is in genetics. They named me after Marie Curie. I'm sure you know, she didn't recognize the damage she was doing to herself by handling radium until it was too late. Even after learning that she was dying, she told people, 'There is nothing to fear in life, only more to understand.'"

"Brave words," Nala said.

"A brave person," Marie said. "I could never live up to the name."

Nala reached out and took her hand. "Nonsense. Thomas and I wouldn't be here if you hadn't done what you did. It doesn't get any braver than that."

Marie looked up and locked onto Nala's eyes. "Thanks. It was mostly because of that... that..."

"Fucking headband?" Nala answered for her.

"Yeah. That fucking headband," Marie said.

Nala patted her hand. "Fantastic job expanding your vocabulary. I'm proud of you."

It was a good wrap-up for the alien device, a subject that Marie was ready to move away from. "So, what's next for you?"

Nala rubbed her arm, a bruise showing just below her wrist where Thomas had grabbed her. "Well, Fermilab has some rebuilding to do before we can get back to any lab work. But I'm going to submit a proposal that we study the baryon-to-boson ratio—carefully, of course.

316

What we've found so far is that when we exceed critical density, things get unstable. We'll need to learn why. It seems to suggest that quantum space, just like the whole universe, is flat. You really *can* produce something from nothing. I can't wait to dig deeper into it."

Nala looked up, noticing something behind Marie. Marie twisted around to see Daniel walking toward their table. He was dressed more casually than she'd seen him before, with a V-neck pullover and jeans.

He made brief eye contact with Marie but walked straight to Nala. He pulled out a chair and sat for a moment without saying a word.

"Before anything else," he said, leaning close to Nala, "I owe you an apology." Nala sat perfectly still in her chair, her body language not giving away anything more than polite interest in what Daniel had to say.

"I've neglected you, terribly," he continued. "It's the job, of course, but that's not an excuse. It never was. I want to tell you that I'm sorry."

Nala didn't respond immediately, but she wasn't crossing her arms and looking the other way either. She seemed to be studying his face, looking for sincerity.

The silence was awkward, and being a third wheel is never fun. Marie stood up. "I think I'll just take a break."

Nala looked up, her expression much softer than the glare she was giving Daniel. "Don't be long, dear friend."

Marie left the two alone on the patio and found a quiet place to sit in the hotel lobby. She had her own catching up to do. Marie pulled out her phone and dialed Stephanie Perrin.

"Where are you?" Stephanie screamed into the phone as she answered. Stephanie had returned to Paris to tell her story of their mission to Ixtlub to a waiting French audience. The phone connection to France was good.

317

"Austin, Texas. I'm okay. Well, I have a broken nose, but otherwise okay."

"Everybody is talking about you. They said the headband made you crazy and you tried to kill yourself. But then I saw the news—one reporter called you a heroine for saving those scientists at Fermilab. *Putain de bordel!* Marie, what's going on?"

A heroine. That was overstating. But as Marie recounted the events of the past twenty-four hours, she could see how it might make a good news story. There would be parts left out, of course. All the fear, the self-doubts and the hallucinations. Stephanie knew all about those parts.

"Marie," Stephanie said. "Tell me the truth. Are you really okay? Don't lie to me. If you need help, I will bust into Ibarra's office with the cameras rolling and scream bloody murder until he recognizes his duty to take care of his own employee. ESA would be all over this. NASA should be too."

"It's gone," Marie said. "The headband was destroyed."

"I don't care about the headband," Stephanie said. "What about you?"

"Yeah, I won't lie. It's done some damage. I can still feel it."

"The hallucination you told me about?"

"I can keep it in check."

"But it's still there?"

Marie hesitated. "Yeah, Steph, it's still there. I think it always was. Maybe it's been with me since I was born and was just exposed by all this mental stimulus. You know, like a genetic disease that only comes out later in life. I read that forms of psychosis are common in women our age, more than men. Maybe it was just my time."

"Get help, Marie. Professional help."

"Yeah, I will," Marie responded, and meant it.

"And if Ibarra gives you any shit, tell me. This is a big deal, and I've been worried sick about you ever since you told me about the side effects."

"Thanks, Steph… it's really good to know I have friends."

"Forever," Stephanie said. "Friends forever."

Two new friends, three if you counted an alien jellyfish living more than three hundred light-years away. It was both surprising and comforting to find out that people cared. When the world goes crazy, a friend can be the difference between a crushing defeat and *I might just make it.*

They arranged to talk again the following week, and Marie returned to breakfast on the patio. Daniel and Nala were absorbed in a conversation. Nala was even laughing—a good sign. As Marie approached, they noticed and stopped talking, another good sign.

Daniel deftly switched away from their private topic. "How's the nose?"

Marie returned to her chair opposite Nala. "It's not bad. A little hard to breathe, but they told me swelling would be normal. It doesn't hurt anymore. You know… drugs."

Marie allowed her eyes to silently flash *the Daniel question* to Nala. Nala responded with a small shrug and a twist of the eyebrows.

Answer received—no headband required. Daniel still had potential, but repentance was in order. Marie smiled. He deserved whatever Nala dished out and would probably be the first to admit it. They did make a nice couple. Marie made a mental note to wish them the best, assuming the two of them left the restaurant together.

"I woke up this morning stumped," Daniel said. He clearly hadn't noticed the eye-to-eye messaging going on right in front of him.

"Why?" Marie asked.

He looked confused. "Well, you didn't mention the headband yesterday, and in all the rush of getting you to the hospital, I admit I didn't think to ask. But I woke up this morning baffled. I thought the whole idea of the rescue was to take the headband in with you."

Marie scrunched up one eye, equally confused. "What are you talking about? Of course that was the plan. I knew the headband would show me things I couldn't see from the outside."

Daniel held a finger in the air like an exclamation point. "Then you didn't take it off. It must have fallen when you leaped."

"Yeah, it did. All three of us jumped to a balcony inside the smokestack. The headband probably fell to the bottom when I hit. Of course, it's gone now, blasted somewhere up there."

"No, no, no," Daniel said. "I wasn't talking about jumping into the smokestack. I mean the first time you leaped, back at Fermilab. It must have fallen off there."

"Okay, Daniel, now *you're* not making any sense," Nala said. "Marie had the headband inside the 4-D bubble. That's how we got out."

Daniel gave a quizzical look to both of them, still clearly confused. "Hang on, let's reset. I talked to Jan just a few minutes ago. He said he has the headband in his office. He was holding it while we talked. He wants to know what he should do with it."

Marie leaned forward, "Jan has the headband? How is that possible? We were standing at the top of the smokestack right here in Austin, a thousand miles from Fermilab. It was on my head when I jumped. The headband fell into the smokestack; it couldn't be anywhere else."

"She did," Nala confirmed. "I saw her. How could Jan have it now?"

Daniel looked at Nala and then Marie, holding one hand to his mouth and tapping a finger on his lip. "Jan said that security picked the headband up off the floor at Fermilab. The security guy said he saw you set it on the floor just before you leaped, as if at the last minute you decided you didn't want it."

"Well, that's ridiculous," Marie said, waving it off with a flip of her hand. "I had the headband on when I landed—" Marie covered her mouth. "Oh shit."

Nala sat bolt upright in her chair. "Double shit. You *didn't* have it when you landed, did you? When we hooked up, you told me you thought you'd lost the headband but decided that was part of the hallucination."

Marie ran through her memories of that first leap into the singularity. The sound of steps behind her. The guard calling out. Her determination to jump, backing up and then leaping into the pit. But there was something else. A hesitation, a last-minute thought. Could she really have set the headband down?

Impossible. She had worn it inside the 4-D space. She'd visualized inside. The headband had guided them to the smokestacks.

"No. Of course I had the headband," she said, staring off into the distance. "At first, yes, I did lose it... that's when Thomas was dead. But then, there was a flash from the light. I blacked out, and when I woke up, the band was on my head."

Nala shook her head continuously, a strange look falling across her face. "Superposition. Multiple eigenstates, each existing only as a probability." She looked at Marie. "You had the headband and you didn't. It was inside the bubble and it wasn't."

Marie tried to absorb what Nala was telling her. Superposition was being blamed for Thomas being dead and then alive, but this seemed like an even greater paradox. "If I didn't have it, how did we get to the smokestacks?"

"Don't expect sensible cause and effect," Nala said. "This is quantum physics. If you try to match it to our day-to-day world, you'll only get more confused. Yes, you had the headband, and no, you didn't. All at the same time. But as soon as we jumped into the smokestack, we left the quantum effect, an external observer came into the picture and the dice stopped rolling."

Marie's heart quickened. She worried about what this detour into the bizarre meant to her state of mental health if Nala was right.

The words were senseless, but Nala spoke with the seriousness of a scientist. "The external observation ended the superposition. The random probabilities settled on a single result, and as it turned out, you *didn't* have the headband after all. From an external perspective, you never did. You set it on the floor. Security picked it up and gave it to Jan."

"But our memories." Marie flinched at the confusion of thoughts. If she wandered far enough down this mental trap, the hallucinations would no doubt return. "You have the memories, too."

"I do," Nala said. "And those memories are accurate, but that doesn't make them real. I know it sounds strange, but I think Jan has confirmed the final state. You left the headband outside."

"So how do you account for the memories?" Daniel asked. "It sounds like you both remember the same thing."

Nala thought for a minute and laughed. "It's definitely confusing. If an electron could think, this is probably how it would feel too. Marie and I have been in quantum superposition, but now we've settled back into reality. What's left in our heads is... well, a phantom memory, a leftover, an unused probability from the multiverse."

"You think we really live in a multiverse?" Daniel asked. "Every outcome exists?"

Nala shrugged. "Marie visualized it. A hundred different versions of each of us. Not an infinite number of probabilities, maybe not even *every* probability, but a big number."

Her statement hit home. Marie gazed off into nothing. The events of the past several weeks now made complete sense. "I was a probability," Marie said slowly. "Zin said so. Core said so."

Daniel echoed the statement Core had made during their visit. "Nothing is certain. Outcomes follow probabilities."

An intensity flooded Marie's thoughts, and she turned to Daniel. "Did Core know? Is that why Zin chose me? Was this whole thing a manipulation from the start?"

Daniel shook his head. "Unknown, but highly doubtful. It's hard to imagine a mechanism for peering into the future, even if you are a quantum computer."

"Don't expect the quantum world to make sense," Nala repeated. "An artificial intelligence based on quantum computing may be wholly different from anything we can imagine. Who knows what Core can do?"

Nala had an impish smile on her face. "But I do know one thing."

"What's that?" Daniel and Marie asked together.

Nala reached for Daniel's hand and interlaced her fingers with his. Her brown fingers complemented his pink. She reached out with her other hand and took Marie's.

"Outcomes really do follow probabilities." She turned to Daniel. "What happens tomorrow between you and me? Will we be together or not?"

Without waiting for an answer from Daniel, she turned to Marie. "What will you do next at NASA? Will you wear the headband again now that you know it hasn't been destroyed? Will you visit Haiti after our chat? None of these outcomes, the important stuff and the trivial, has been determined. But there are plenty of probabilities, and some outcomes are more likely than others."

Nala gripped their hands tightly. "If you ask me, that's the multiverse in a nutshell. We live it every day. Today is the result of yesterday's probabilities, and tomorrow will materialize from today's."

"Sounds more like philosophy than science," Daniel said.

Nala smiled. "Yeah, it does, doesn't it? And here I thought I was strictly a scientist." She lifted Daniel's hand and kissed it and then did the same to Marie's. "The quantum world will do that to you."

Afterword

I hope you enjoyed the story. I had a lot of fun writing it. Like most people I relish a good adventure, but I could spend days contemplating the unanswered questions of our fascinating world. If this story spurred deep thoughts about the structure of the universe or why it works the way it does, then I've been successful.

I also had fun writing this story because I've developed an affection for the three scientists that held hands in the final chapter. I would love to join them in their conversation out on the hotel patio in Austin. It makes me think of *Stranger than Fiction*, the movie with Will Ferrell and Emma Thompson in which an author meets her character. That would be fun.

Just as I did after the first book (*Quantum Space*) I thought I'd write one more chapter. I'll step out of the story and talk about the science and the science fiction by diving into three scientific topics: critical density, nothingness and quantum superposition. Don't roll your eyes; I'll be nice.

Critical Density

While drifting effortlessly in her float pod, Nala contemplates the density of space in Chapter 6, Bosons. Later, in Chapter 38 and 40, she explains that the universe is *flat* because its density exactly matches *critical density*, measured to be 9.47×10^{-27} kg/m^3.

First, let me say that every bit of this is real science, as accurately as I could write it. Second, it absolutely blows my mind that our universe is flat, and it doubly blows my mind that so few people realize how mind-blowing this bizarre coincidence is!

Allow me to expound. In 1915, Albert Einstein published his Theory of General Relativity, which is all about gravity and the shape of space. Space, Einstein said, is curved wherever there is mass. The curvature is what we experience as gravity. But curved into what?

Einstein's explanation required extra dimensions of space that we cannot see.

Fast-forward a hundred years and dozens of confirmations of Einstein's theory. As it turns out, space really is curved into an extra dimension and remarkably this curvature is measurable with highly accurate lasers. How?

Space can have positive or negative curvature, or it can have no curvature at all (flat). Like this:

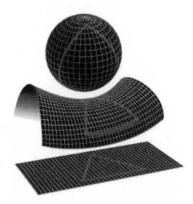

You probably learned in high school geometry that the sum of the angles inside any triangle always equals 180 degrees. Right? But when space is positively curved (the top image), the sum of those angles is slightly more than 180. And when space is curved negatively, the sum is slightly less than 180. Only when space is flat do the angles inside a triangle sum to 180.

For our routine life on Earth, the curvature of space is negligible, and sure enough, any triangle you measure will sum to 180 degrees. But shine three lasers between Earth, Venus and Mars to precisely measure the triangle formed by the planets. You won't get exactly 180 degrees; the sum of the angles will be a little larger as a result of the positive curvature of space around the sun. (Full disclosure: No one has ever performed this specific experiment, but NASA's Gravity Probe B in 2004 and the LAGEOS satellite in 1976 both did something similar to measure the warping of space around the Earth. Answer: space is indeed curved.)

What if you wanted to measure the curvature of the whole universe? Is the universe itself curved? If so, does it curve like a sphere or a Pringles potato chip?

Astronomers have been eager to find out ever since Einstein explained how space curved. They got their chance in 2001 when NASA launched the Wilkinson Microwave Anisotropy Probe (WMAP). The probe took pictures in every direction, measuring the 2.7 Kelvin cosmic microwave background (CMB) radiation, the residual radiation left over from the Big Bang. The results looked like this (which Nala explains in Chapter 40 Density):

With WMAP's sensitive instruments and some clever thinking, mission scientists measured overall curvature. What did they find? The universe is flat. Not everywhere—there are local positive curvatures and local negative curvatures—but as a whole it all balances out to perfectly flat. An enormous triangle spread across the whole universe would have angles that add to exactly 180 degrees. That's important. But before I cover why, let's talk about density.

Measuring triangles with lasers or estimating curvature from the CMB radiation map is what scientists call the *geometric approach* but there's another way to measure the shape of the universe, called the *accounting approach*.

In Chapter 40, Nala takes a stab at explaining it:

"The universe is expanding, right?" she says. "And gravity tries to halt that expansion by pulling things together. More mass, more gravity. *Critical density* is a number with deep meaning. It tells you the precise amount of mass that is needed to exactly cancel expansion."

In this story, these two forces are represented as the interaction between quarks and the HP boson. In our real world, quarks are well established as the foundation for matter, and matter is what causes gravity. But in the real-world HP bosons don't exist. Oh well, the story *is* science fiction.

If HP bosons are just a figment of my imagination, what really causes the universe to expand? The answer: unknown. Astronomers call it *dark energy*, but that term is really just a placeholder. Another way of saying, *we don't really know*. Seems like we need some aliens to come along and explain it to us.

But even if scientists haven't discovered the force itself, they can measure how fast the universe is expanding. It's called the Hubble constant (*H*) and WMAP provided the most accurate measure anyone has ever had. Along with Newton's gravitational constant (*G*), physicists derived this very simple equation for critical density, ρ_c.

$$\rho_c = \frac{3H^2}{8\pi G}$$

Critical density is the balance between *H* and *G*, between the expansive force and the gravitational force (which derives from mass). Critical density is the bullseye on a target, a *what-if* calculation of the relationship between these two opposing forces.

To find out whether we've hit the bulls-eye, we need to know the *actual density* of the universe. Can we measure it? Get a really big scale and pile every quark, every atom, every star, planet, nebula—

every shred of mass in the entire universe—on one side. Place the mysterious expansive force on the other side of the scale.

What happens? Well, your eyes should pop out of your head when you find that the scale *exactly* balances. Critical density equals actual density. The amount of mass needed to exactly cancel the expansive force is precisely how much mass there is in our universe. The WMAP mission (and the European Space Agency Planck mission in 2013) both performed something like this humongous scale by accurately measuring real-world values for H and G and plugging them into the equation above.

To the accuracy humans can measure, we live in a universe of critical density, otherwise known as a flat universe. What does this mean? It means the entire universe sums to this digit: 0.

The universe is zero, nothing, nada, zilch. Everything we see around us—the stars, galaxies, everything that floats out there in empty space—is simply a local perturbation of energy and mass. The universe can be thought of as a wave where every trough balances every crest. Taken together the sum is nothing. This tells us with some certainty that the universe sprang from nothing. Exactly *how* this springing-thing happened is not yet clear, but scientists have confirmed just in the past ten years that *nothingness* was the original state.

The universe is not just a random pile of *stuff*—the result of a cataclysmic explosion. We shouldn't think of the Big Bang as just a larger version of a supernova, it was a very different kind of event. The Big Bang was literally *something from nothing*.

This newfound knowledge should be disturbing or enlightening or emotional in some way to every person on the planet. We know where we came from. We know what existed prior to the Big Bang—nothing.

Nothingness

So, what is nothing? In this book, I called it *the void* though physicists and cosmologists use other words depending on the topic. For example, in brane theory they call it the *bulk*. Sometimes you'll see references to *hyperspace*. In mathematical descriptions it's called Hilbert space. In my opinion, none of these terms are as compelling or as conjuring as *the void*.

The void is not a place. It's not space of any kind. It has no dimensions, no contents, no volume, nowhere to put anything of substance. It also has no attributes (length, density, position, etc.) except for the sole attribute that it represents the absence of everything.

Light cannot propagate across the void because there is no "across". Quarks, leptons and bosons cannot exist within the void because there is no "within". In Chapter 20 Void, Nala pushes a stick beyond the vertical edge of her prison. The stick disappears into nothingness, crackling and sizzling as it goes. (Just a guess on my part. What exactly is the sound of a trillion quarks simultaneously being eliminated from existence?)

The void is unquestionably crazy stuff. Instead of describing the void, it's easier to describe space. The void would then be anything else. But a word of warning—it gets crazy from here. My advice, take two aspirin before you continue reading.

The multiverse. Multiple universes.

If you enjoy science fiction, you've probably come across a story or two that incorporated the idea of multiple universes, or parallel universes. This is the notion that the universe we see (about 14 billion light-years of space containing billions of galaxies) is *not* all there is. In fact, there may be many universes like our own, possibly an infinite number of them.

Complete fantasy, right? Certainly unscientific.

I don't think so. Not every idea related to multiple universes is scientifically testable, but some are. And even if only one idea is testable, it makes the question of multiple universes a valid scientific endeavor. Others agree because quite a few physicists, astronomers and cosmologists are actively working in this field.

Take Max Tegmark, for example. He's a professor of physics at the Massachusetts Institute of Technology—not exactly a hotbed of crackpots. Tegmark has examined each of the current multiverse ideas in detail and has identified four levels of multiverses.

In a Level I multiverse, we live in a sea of never-ending infinite space. Within that space, we can see only a "small" sphere with a diameter of 13.8 billion light-years (that's how long it's been since the Big Bang, thus we have no ability to see objects that might be farther away). But this visible sphere is merely a *pocket universe*—a bubble within the never-ending sea. The bubble came into existence from a Big Bang and a period of inflation (the few microseconds after the Big Bang during which space inflated faster than the speed of light). If this model represents the true nature of our universe, there could be many other pocket universes out there, far beyond our limited view, each of them also a result of local inflation within the infinite sea.

A Level II multiverse is much the same except that each pocket universe has different versions of the fundamental forces, different elementary particles, etc. For example, the force of gravity might be stronger in one pocket universe than another.

A Level III multiverse is derived from quantum superposition, and I'll talk about that in the next section. A Level IV multiverse is purely mathematical, and I'll leave that one to the deep-thinking mathematicians like Tegmark.

Each multiverse concept has one thing in common: every universe was created from nothing, springing from a fluctuation in a quantum field that caused a single point of nothingness to blossom.

Something from nothing, many times over. That's the gist of the multiverse concept. It represents a chain of events that may have been going on forever and will continue forever more. No beginning and no end. Infinite in both space and time with every instance derived from exactly nothing.

Are these multiverse ideas testable? Or is it all just metaphysical nonsense?

First, inflation is testable. The cosmic microwave background measured by the WMAP and Planck missions confirmed that the inflation theory is accurate and the best explanation anyone has given for the parameters of the universe we measure today. Every multiverse theory is based on inflation. Check.

The shape of the universe is also testable. As I described above, these same space missions confirmed that the universe is flat, not spherical or open in shape. Mathematically, a flat plane has no end; it goes on forever. Infinite space certainly supports the Level I or II multiverse idea. Check.

It's a start, and I think there is more evidence too. To find it, let's dive into the insanity of superposition.

Quantum Superposition

Starting in Chapter 30, the story moves into the very real but very weird quantum world of superposition. Nala and Thomas (and later Marie) become probabilities with outcomes that are not determined until there is an outside observer.

Can this really happen? To people, who knows? But it happens all the time to quantum particles. The mental gymnastics are easier if you stop thinking of them as particles. Call them a quantum probability wavefunction instead.

The conundrum is best represented by the famous double-slit experiment, the scenario in which a gun shoots a stream of particles toward a barrier containing two slits. (If you're not familiar, this is a good video: https://www.youtube.com/watch?v=M4_0oblwQ_U or read my blog post here: http://douglasphillipsbooks.com/blog/the-double-slit-experiment).

Blast a stream of particles through two slits, and two bands of particles will come out the other side, right? Wrong. Quantum-sized particles like electrons produce a very different result. Instead of two bands, we see multiple bands just like the interference pattern that waves of water produce. Does that mean quantum particles are really waves?

Modern thinking is that quantum particles are a mathematical probability that is wavelike. The particle isn't really smeared across space, but its true location might be at point A or it might be at point B. That's superposition in a nutshell. It's a roll of the dice. The chance you'll find the particle at A or B is determined by a mathematical probability called the wavefunction. As Core said in Chapter 22, *outcomes follow probabilities*.

Superposition ties very well with the idea of a multiverse driven by events, which Max Tegmark identifies as Level III. In this kind of multiverse, events that we perceive to be random such as whether a leaf falling from a tree lands in my yard or my neighbor's are comparable to the choices we each make every day, such as whether to stop the car when a traffic signal turns yellow. Every random event and every choice we make results in a separate branch—a new path to follow in a never-ending complexity of differing outcomes. (Side note: check out Season 3 Episode 4, Remedial Chaos Theory of the television show, *Community*, if you want to experience the full comedic impact of a Level III multiverse. It's a classic.)

In a universe like this, the sheer number of random branches is staggering with downstream effects that go on forever. A woman barely catches a train home and finds her boyfriend in bed with another woman or she misses the train and never learns of the affair (*Sliding Doors*, 1998). You recognize the idea; it's been in sci-fi for a long while.

We perceive our universe as the *chosen path* with randomness that has settled on a specific outcome. But in the multiverse explanation, *every outcome* has occurred, each equally valid and equally real. The other versions of ourselves that follow those other paths are just as sure their outcome was the real one, with no opportunity for us to compare notes.

Is this possible? Does it make any sense? A significant number of physicist and cosmologists not only believe it's possible, they say it's a rigorous mathematical explanation for the superposition of quantum particles and thus a reasonable explanation for our reality.

But science doesn't establish reality by taking a poll. Science requires evidence. Is there any?

Maybe. I'll throw out two more bits of multiverse evidence for your perusal. First is the CMB radiation, measured by WMAP and in greater detail by Planck. Colors in the CMB image above show slight temperature variations away from the average of 2.7 K. The deviations are tiny, only 0.000018 K (or 18 µK), telling us that the CMB is exceedingly smooth. But one spot near the lower right stands out:

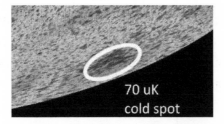

It's called the *cold spot*, because the temperature there is 70 µK below the rest of the map—significant enough that scientists have ruled out random variation. Both WMAP and Planck independently confirmed this cold spot, so it's not a measurement error either. Something about our universe is different in this direction.

At first, astronomers thought it was a relatively empty area containing fewer galaxies than normal but a study in 2017 demonstrated that this interpretation was false. The mysterious spot is still being studied, but one explanation is remarkable: the cold spot may be a cosmic bruise, a place where our bubble universe collided with another bubble during cosmic inflation. It's potential evidence that our universe is not the only one.

Cosmic bruises aside, perhaps the most compelling evidence is all around us. The parameters of our universe appear to be fine-tuned to produce stars, galaxies and especially life. For example, if the *down* quark were just a little bit heavier, hydrogen wouldn't be the most common element. Helium—an inert gas—would take its place, making the formation of complex molecules far more difficult and making good old H_2O very rare. Likewise, if gravity were a little stronger, stars would exhaust their fuel more rapidly and planets like Earth wouldn't have billions of years to evolve life.

There are dozens more parameters that if adjusted just a little result in a radically different universe, most variations far more hostile to life than our own. We haven't done enough exploring to know whether our universe is teeming with life, but with so many deadly permutations, isn't it odd that we're here at all?

Some people see divine intent in a universe that is exquisitely fine-tuned for life but there is another explanation that doesn't require invoking the supernatural. Our universe is one of many universes, each with different parameters.

Our universe happens to have the right mix of matter and forces to be transparent yet organized, to allow stars to burn steadily for ten billion years and to make it easy for hydrogen, carbon, oxygen, nitrogen and phosphorus to form self-replicating molecules and evolve into higher life forms. We were lucky. Perhaps a thousand other universes weren't so lucky.

In the 19th and early 20th centuries, science fiction writers imagined the moon, Mars and Venus to be populated with creatures much like us—a humorous idea today. We've learned in the past twenty years of examining exoplanets that most are inhospitable, and that Earth is one gem among a thousand duds. As we search the cosmos, I think we'll discover life here and there, but we may eventually learn that intelligent life is exceedingly rare, perhaps only a few civilizations per galaxy.

It's not a stretch to imagine the same scenario played out across many universes. Some have life, many don't. If true, it would explain the fine-tuning of the parameters in our universe. We really are just lucky.

~~~~~~~~~~~~~~~~~~~~~~~~

If you'd like more details plus a lot of pictures and diagrams related to the story, please go to my web page: http://douglasphillipsbooks.com. While you're there, add your name to my email list and I'll keep you informed about additional books in the series and other events.

I hoped you enjoyed this second book in the series. But wait... there's more! *Quantum Time* is the next book and the final story in the Quantum series. We've had our fun with space; let's switch to the very rich and fascinating topic of time. Details below.

And finally, books live or die on reviews. If you enjoyed this story, please consider writing a short review. It takes only a minute, and your review helps future readers as well as the author. For more information on how to leave a review, go to http://douglasphillipsbooks.com/contact.

Thanks for reading!

Douglas Phillips

Acknowledgments

Thanks to all the authors at Critique Circle, but especially Kathryn Hoff, Travis Leavitt and Zoe Carmina. Once again, you've shown me that a critique from someone who's down in the trenches writing their own book is more valuable than a pot of gold. You helped me shape the plot and characters and warned me when I strayed too far from realism or wandered into a long soliloquy of dense physics.

Thanks to my editor, Eliza Dee, who can see a plot hole a mile away and always has good advice for written words that are tight and clean. Much appreciation also to Gabe Waggoner and Christine Lane, who provided significant corrections and helped me across the finish line.

Thanks also to Rena Hoberman for the fantastic cover. We tried a few options this time, and I love the simplicity of the final result. Your covers will also appear on the audiobook productions of the Quantum Series, a testament to their design.

I tried something new with this book: an army of beta readers— seventy-six to be exact! I was initially worried I had gone too far, but happily surprised at the feedback that I received from so many people. A special thanks to Attila, Bill, Brad, Chandler, Gary, Gert-Jan, Guy, James, Jeff B, Jeff C, Kim, Lili, Michael, Nancy, Paul, Rob, Bob, Steve H, and Steve R. I studied every comment and found your feedback incredibly helpful in shaping the final version. Thank you!

Many thanks to my friends and family for your time and your advice, not only on this book but also in your enthusiastic support of my writing in general. Phil, you know you're my best cheerleader.

And to my wife, Marlene, thank you for your love, your support and your patience as I spend countless hours in front of the computer. Hopefully, our on-site reconnaissance trips will expand beyond Fermilab for future books. Haiti, perhaps?

Quantum Time

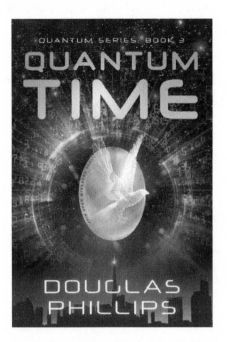

Book Three in the Quantum Series

By Douglas Phillips

Everyone knew time travel was impossible. Then reality intruded.

A dying man stumbles into a police station and collapses. In his fist is a mysterious coin with strange markings. He tells the police he's from the future, and when they uncover the coin's hidden message they're inclined to believe him.

Daniel Rice never asked for fame but his key role in Earth's first contact with an alien civilization thrust him into a social arena where any crackpot might take aim. When the FBI arrives at his door and predictions of the future start coming true, Daniel is dragged into a mission to save the world from nuclear holocaust. To succeed, he'll need to exploit cobbled-together alien technology to peer into a world thirty years beyond his own.

The third book of the Quantum series goes far beyond extra dimensions of space to expose the curious paradoxes of time in a wild ride along the edges of scientific knowledge.

Book three in the series, *Quantum Time*, is available now at Amazon for Kindle and in paperback https://www.amazon.com/dp/B07L5967VP.

To whet your appetite, here's the first chapter!

1   Traveler

A yell shattered the quiet lobby. Almost a scream, though when men scream it comes out kind of wonky.

Sergeant Jamie Copley glanced up from her work, scowling. The double-pane door at the police station's entrance was slightly ajar, allowing the heat and humidity of central Florida to seep in, along with whatever commotion was going on in the parking lot.

Another scream, almost animal-like.

"Not again," she griped. The station had been calm for a Tuesday morning, and Jamie liked it that way. One drug dealer booked— that was it. Officer Doherty had already taken the scumbag to a cell down the hall, along with the guy's street stink, leaving the lobby tranquil once more. A young couple sat in one corner, waiting to provide a statement on a stolen car case. Another guy, who said he needed to speak with Chief Jones about something or other, paced.

Doherty leaned against the counter of the reception desk, entering an arrest record on his tablet. He seemed unconcerned about the yelling.

"Can you get that?" Jamie asked him. The door sometimes didn't shut properly, and arguments seemed to break out at least once a week between lowlifes in the parking lot. Just the sight of Doherty in uniform would shut them up fast.

"Yeah, no problem." Doherty set his tablet on her desk and headed across the lobby.

As he reached for the handle, the door burst open and crashed against the wall. A huge man lurched through, knocking Doherty to the floor. The man's face was scarlet, his eyes ablaze. He beat a fist against the side of his bald head. Like a savage dog, he bared his teeth.

Doherty scrambled away on all fours as the big man threw his head back and screamed once more. The young couple in the corner flattened against the wall. Jamie leaped from the chair, nerves tingling and heart pounding. She reached for the service pistol on her hip.

Assess the situation, her training echoed.

Weapon? One hand carried a motorcycle helmet, and the other continued to pound rhythmically against his head. But the oversized belt covered with electrical wires wasn't there to hold up his pants.

"Bomb!" she yelled. "Take cover!"

Jamie dropped behind the desk. Down the hallway, doors slammed. The front door crashed against the wall again, hopefully someone getting away.

So much for the light day.

Rising, Jamie peered over the desk and leveled her weapon at the intruder. He swayed in the center of the lobby, eyes glazed. The couple still cowered in the corner, but pacing guy was gone. Crouching behind a large chair, Doherty aimed his gun.

There was no control unit that Jamie could see, but some bombs detonate on a preset timer. The man took one stumbling step, almost tripping. His face contorted in a grimace and blood dripped from one ear, streaming down his neck in a red ribbon. This guy was in pain, not rage.

"Drop!" Doherty yelled. "On the floor, now!"

The intruder collapsed, whether from pain or following orders, Jamie didn't care. He was down, with no visible weapon or detonator. No reason for either of them to pull the trigger just yet. If it was a bomb, a bullet might even set it off. Hopefully, Doherty was thinking the same.

Jamie rose higher, keeping both hands on her weapon, pointed at the man's head. She motioned to the frightened couple. "Come over here. Get behind me." They hurried across the lobby and squatted behind the desk, the young woman sobbing quietly.

With the civilians as safe as she could manage, Jamie's focus returned to the intruder. He lay on his side, his body heaving with each breath. A red smear across the tiles marked where he'd hit the floor. The leather belt around his waist was at least ten inches wide with what looked like an elongated D-cell battery on one side. Wires crisscrossed its surface, connecting a variety of electronics components. The man's shirt had lifted above the belt with skin showing. Thank God, no sign of explosives.

Eyes still glued to the figure on the floor, she yelled over her shoulder. "All station personnel. Situation is under control. Suspect is down with injuries."

Doherty spoke into the radio attached to his left shoulder. "Orlando Southeast precinct, one at gunpoint, two officers on the scene. Signal thirty, forty-four."

The radio screeched, "Copy, Southeast, two units en route."

Jamie holstered her gun and pulled out handcuffs. "I've got him. Cover me."

Doherty nodded, keeping his weapon pointed while Jamie rounded the desk and bent over the crumpled body. The man offered no resistance as she cuffed his hands behind his back. She donned latex gloves, put a finger to his neck and located a pulse. She lifted eyelids and checked inside his mouth.

She squatted close to his face. "Can you hear me?"

The man murmured.

"What's on the belt? Anything dangerous?"

His voice was weak and slurred. Each of his heavy breaths pushed out one word at a time. "Nothing... not... bomb."

"That's good. Very good," Jamie said. She turned to Doherty, whose expression had relaxed a bit even if the grip on his gun was still viselike. "Ambulance on the way?"

Doherty nodded.

Jamie patted the man's shoulder with a gloved hand. "We've got help coming, sir. But before they get here, I need to take this belt off."

The man mumbled something, but the words were slurred. Up close, the belt didn't look threatening—more like a utility belt that a carpenter might wear. Electronics components with connecting wires were stapled into the leather like a homemade array of superhero gadgets. The mega-battery, if that was what it was, fit into a sleeve on one side that might have otherwise held a hammer. Still no sign of any explosive material. False alarm, but she'd made the right call and would do it again.

She flipped two snaps and the belt loosened. With a few tugs, it released from the man's hips. A workman's tool belt—enhanced— though what the wires and electronics components might do was anyone's guess. She laid it flat on the tile floor. There would be time later to figure out what this guy was up to.

A quick scan didn't find any external wounds, but the internal injuries were probably serious, most likely head trauma. Blood still leaked from one ear—and now from his nose too.

The man croaked, not much louder than a whisper. "Help."

She bent down. "Yes, sir, medical help is on the way. Hang in there. Just a few more minutes." A faraway siren could be heard through the still-open front door.

"No… this," the man said. He wiggled one hand bound by the cuffs, loosening his clenched fist. A glint of silver shone between his chubby fingers. "I come… from… the future."

"Huh?" Either she'd hadn't heard him right or this guy was a serious wack job. Doherty moved closer, his weapon still pointed.

She held up a hand. "Wait, he's holding something."

He opened the hand further to reveal a large silver coin. Bigger than a silver dollar and thicker, with markings on its face that wiggled.

"Give… this," the man grunted.

Jamie leaned in closer. "You want me to give the coin to someone?"

The man nodded. "Daniel."

"Daniel? Daniel who?"

"Rice," the man wheezed. "Give… to Daniel Rice."

****

The EMTs, the bomb squad and the frightened couple were gone now, returning the lobby to calm. One of the detectives had taken the belt to a back room for examination. The bomb guys had declared it harmless.

The intruder had had no wallet, no phone on him. One of the police techs was running a face and fingerprint match. No results yet. But the guy had left a calling card, of sorts.

Jamie, Doherty, and two other patrol officers stood in a semicircle around Chief Jones, who held the oversized coin in a gloved hand, twisting it beneath overhead lights.

Both sides of the silver coin shimmered with a rainbow of colors when tilted, like the surface of a DVD. Closer examination revealed animated holographic images. On one side, a three-dimensional golden eagle popped out, its wings flapping as the coin was tilted one way and then the other. On the back, an imposing building was fronted by columns that extended beyond the coin's surface.

It seemed far too complex to be money, but Jamie had never traveled the world. Maybe this was money in some faraway place. Or maybe it was a commemorative coin of some kind.

"And you say this guy wanted you to take it?" Chief Jones asked, still studying the details on its surface.

"Yes, sir," Jamie answered. "He said I should give it to Daniel Rice." She looked down, combing fingers through her hair. "Those were his last words."

They'd received a call from the EMTs—dead on arrival at East Orlando Hospital, brain hemorrhage. Jamie hated when people died, even the perps.

Jones' brow twisted. "Did he mean the scientist? *That* Daniel Rice?"

Jamie shrugged. "I'm not sure, sir. But the scientist Daniel Rice is on TV all the time. It's probably who he meant."

Jones turned the coin on its edge. "Did he say anything about the writing?" He held out the coin for her examination. Given the coin's thickness, the bold capital letters stamped around its circumference were easy to read:

SPIN UPON MIRRORED GLASS

"No, sir," Jamie answered. "The man didn't explain the writing or anything else. He just asked me to take it."

The chief looked her squarely in the eyes. "Did you try spinning it? Did anyone?" Jones looked at each officer in the circle.

Jamie shuffled her feet. They'd all been curious as soon as they'd read the words but had played things by the book. "None of the detectives were in the office, so we bagged the coin and put it in the evidence room along with the belt and the helmet." She paused and lifted her eyebrows hopefully. "But, Chief... there's a small mirror in the bathroom that's only attached by a few screws."

Jones rubbed a hand on his chin for a moment and then spoke. "Yeah, I guess we'll need to know what we're dealing with before I take this any higher up the chain of command." He glanced around the empty lobby. "Okay, Sergeant, go get the mirror. The man who thinks he's from the future certainly has some interesting toys. Let's see what it does."

She hurried down the hall and returned carrying a rectangular mirror, which she laid on the front desk. Jones touched the edge of the coin to the mirror and cocked his wrist.

Backing away, Jamie asked, "You don't think it will explode or anything, do you?"

Jones shook his head. "We got an all clear from the bomb squad, but hell, who knows. The world is full of strange things these days." He lifted the coin from the mirror. "You want to leave?"

Jamie's curiosity was piqued. After the excitement of the morning, she couldn't miss the grand finale. How bad could it be? It was just a coin. A smile spread across her lips. "No way, Chief, I have to see this."

"Here we go, then." Jones returned the coin to the center of the mirror's surface, pinching it between his thumb and index finger. With a quick snap, he started it spinning.

It spun like any other coin but made a low hum. A vibration, almost like the sound of a helicopter's rotor beating the air. After a few seconds, rather than slowing down and falling over, the coin's spin intensified. It rotated ever faster, becoming a blur. The vibrational hum increased too, its pitch getting higher as the coin sped up. Maybe this coin-helicopter-thing was going to lift off the mirror and fly through the station lobby.

Jamie took a step back, as did everyone else. The sound became shrill, piercing the air with an almost inaudible pitch, and then faded away altogether. Maybe a dog could still hear it.

The spinning coin emitted a sharp click, and a vertical cone of white light flashed from its base toward the ceiling. The onlookers flinched in unison.

Images appeared around the perimeter of the light cone, human faces, each twisting as if the perspective was spinning along with the coin. A rainbow of colors reflected across the faces, cycling from red to yellow, green, blue and finally to violet. It was a bizarre mashup of light, form, and color, startling in its seemingly impossible origin but strangely beautiful too, like a modern art exhibit.

The rotating faces stabilized like an old flickering film projection that eventually locks into synchronization. The multitude of perspectives and colors came together within the center of the cone, forming a single face with natural skin color. It was a man's face, and fully three-dimensional.

As Jamie stared in awe, the eyes of the floating head blinked, looked left and then right. The lips of the apparition lifted on one side, forming a wry smile.

"Holy cow," Jamie whispered. "Maybe this guy really did come from the future."

****

Order Quantum Time from Amazon today!

https://www.amazon.com/dp/B07L5967VP

47152447R00210

Made in the USA
Middletown, DE
04 June 2019